Henry F. Keenan

The Iron Game

A Tale of the War

Henry F. Keenan

The Iron Game
A Tale of the War

ISBN/EAN: 9783337242893

Printed in Europe, USA, Canada, Australia, Japan

Cover: Foto ©Andreas Hilbeck / pixelio.de

More available books at **www.hansebooks.com**

The Iron Game

A TALE OF THE WAR

BY

HENRY F. KEENAN

AUTHOR OF THE ALIENS, TRAJAN, ETC.

"Heavy and solemn the cloudy column
Over the green fields marching came,
Measureless spread like a table dread
For the cold grim dice of the iron game."

NEW YORK
D. APPLETON AND COMPANY
1891

TO

BERNARD JOHN McGRANN

WHOSE LIFE AND CONDUCT EMBODY AND ILLUSTRATE

THE MANLINESS, MODESTY, AND WORTH

THAT FANCY DELIGHTS TO EMBALM IN FICTION

THIS BOOK IS INSCRIBED

BY ONE AMONG THE MANY WITNESSES OF HIS NOBLE CAREER

HENRY F. KEENAN

New York, *25th March*, *1891*.

CONTENTS.

BOOK I.

THE CARIBEES.

CHAPTER   PAGE

I.—THE BOY IN BLUE 5

II.—FLAG AND FAITH 11

III.—MALBROOK S'EN VA-T-EN GUERRE 19

IV.—GUELPH AND GHIBELLINE 30

V.—A NAPOLEONIC EPIGRAM 40

VI.—ON THE POTOMAC 47

VII.—THE STEP THAT COSTS 55

VIII.—AN ARMY WITH BANNERS 65

IX.—"THE ASSYRIAN CAME DOWN LIKE THE WOLF ON THE
FOLD" 72

X.—BLOOD AND IRON 85

XI.—THE LEGIONS OF VARUS 99

BOOK II.

THE HOSTAGES.

XII.—THE AFTERMATH 108

XIII.—A COMEDY OF TERRORS 124

XIV.—UNDER TWO FLAGS 136

XV.—ROSEDALE 144

XVI.—A MASQUE IN ARCADY 159

XVII.—TREASON AND STRATAGEMS 177

XVIII.—A CAMPAIGN OF PLOTS 187

XIX.—"HE EITHER FEARS HIS FATE TOO MUCH" . . . 199

XX.—A CATASTROPHE 219

XXI.—THE STORY OF THE NIGHT 231

CHAPTER   PAGE

XXII.—A Carpet-Knight 239

XXIII.—All's fair in Love and War 263

BOOK III.

THE DESERTERS.

XXIV.—Between the Lines 275

XXV.—Phantasmagoria 287

XXVI.—In the Union Lines 301

XXVII.—"The Absent are always in the Wrong" . . 317

XXVIII.—The World went very ill then . . . 331

XXIX.—A Woman's Reason 339

XXX.—A Game of Chance 350

XXXI.—Two Blades of the Same Steel . . . 364

XXXII.—The Lost Caribees 382

XXXIII.—Father Abraham's Joke 395

BOOK I.

THE CARIBEES.

CHAPTER I.

THE BOY IN BLUE.

WHEN expulsion from college, in his junior years, was visited upon Jack Sprague, he straightway became the hero of Acredale. And, though the grave faculty had felt constrained to vindicate college authority, it was well known that they sympathized with the infraction of decorum that obliged them to put this mark of disgrace upon one of the most promising of their students.

All his young life Jack had dreamed of West Point and the years of training that were to fit him for the glories of war. He knew the battles of the Revolution as other boys knew the child-lore of the nursery. He had the campaigns of Marlborough, the strategy of Turenne, the inspirations of the great Frederick, and the prodigies of Napoleon, as readily on the end of his tongue as his comrades had the struggles of the Giant Killer or the tactics of Robinson Crusoe. When, inspired by the promise of West Point, he had mastered the repugnant rubrics of the village academy, the statesman of his district conferred the promised nomination upon his school rival, Wesley Boone, Jack passionately refused to pursue the arid paths of learning, and declared his purpose of becoming a pirate, a scout, or some other equally fascinating child of nature delightful to the boyish mind.

When Jack Sprague entered Warchester College, he carried with him the light baggage of learning picked up at the Acredale Academy. At his entrance to the sequestered quadrangles of Dessau Hall, Jack's frame of mind was very much like the passionate discontent of the younger son of a feudal lord whose discrepant birthright doomed him to the gown instead of the sword.

Long before the senior year he had allured a chosen band about him who shared his eager aspiration for war, and when the other fellows dawdled in society or wrangled in debate, these young Alexanders set their tents in the college campus and fought the campaigns of Frederick or Napoleon over again. Jack did not give much heed to the menacing signs of civil war that came day by day from the tempestuous spirits North and South. A Democrat, as his fathers had been before him, he saw no probability of the pomp and circumstance of glorious war in the noisy wrangling of politicians. The defeat of Douglas, the Navarre of the young Democracy of the North, amazed him; but all thought of Lincoln asserting the national authority, and reviving the splendor of Jackson and Madison, was looked upon as the step between the sublime and the ridiculous that reasoning men refuse to consider.

When, however, the stupefying news came that a national garrison had been fired upon by the South Carolinians, in Charleston Harbor, the college boys took sides strongly. There were many in the classes from Maryland and Virginia. These were as ardent in admiration of their Southern compatriots as the Northern boys were for the insulted Union. Months passed, and, although the forces of war were arraying themselves behind the thin veil of compromise and negotiation, the public mind only languidly convinced itself that actual war would come.

The college was divided into hostile camps. The "Secessionists," led by Vincent Atterbury, Jack's old-time chief crony, went so far as to hoist the flag of the Montgomery (Jeff Davis's) government on the campus pole, one morning in April. A fierce fight followed, in which Jack's ardent partisans made painful havoc with the limbs of the enemy—Atterbury, their leader, being carted from the campus, under the horrified eyes of the faculty, dying, as it was thought. Then followed expulsion. When the solemn words were spoken in chapel, the culprit bore up with great serenity. But when he announced that he had enlisted in the army, then such an uproar, such an outburst, that the session was at an end. Even the grave president looked sympathetic. The like of it was never seen in a sober college since Antony with Cleopatra invaded the Academy at Alexandria. The boys flung themselves upon the abashed Jack. They hugged him, raised him on their shoulders, carried him out on the campus, and, forming a ring round him, swore, in the classic form dear to collegians, that they would follow him; that they would be his soldiers, and fight for the *patria* in danger.

"I have nothing to offer you, boys. I'm only sergeant; but if you will join now, I'm authorized to swear you in provisionally," Jack said, shrewdly, seizing the flood at high tide.

So soon as the names could be written the whole senior class (forty-three) were enrolled. Jack refused the prayerful urgings of the juniors, who pleaded tearfully to join him. But the president coming out confirmed Jack's decision until the juniors could get the written consent of their parents.

The recitations were sadly disjointed that day, and the excited professors were glad when rest came. The humanities had received disjointed exposition during that session. Jack had been summoned to the president's sanctuary, where he had been received with a parental tenderness that brought the tears to his big brown eyes.

"Ah, ha! soldiers mustn't know tears. You must be made of sterner stuff now, sergeant," the doctor cried, cheerily, as the culprit stood confusedly before him. "O Jack, Jack, why did you put this hard task upon me? Why make me drive from Dessau the brightest fellow in the classes? What will your mother say? I would as soon have lost my own child as be forced to put this mark on you? But you know I am bound by the laws of the college. You know I have time and again overlooked your wild pranks. We have already suffered a good deal from the press for wink-

ing at the sympathy the college has shown in this political
quarrel."

"Yes, professor, I haven't a word to say. You did your
duty. Now I want you to bear witness how I do mine. I
do not complain that I am condemned rather through the
form than the fact. I was carried out of my senses by the
sight of that rebel flag."

The Warchester press, known for many years as the
most sprightly and enterprising of the country, was too
much taken up with the direful news from Baltimore to
even make a note of Jack Sprague's expulsion, and the soldier boy was spared that mortification. Nor did he meet
the tearful lament and heart-broken remonstrance at home,
to which he had looked forward with lively dread. His
friends in the village of Acredale were so astonished by his
blue regimentals that he reached the homestead door un-
questioned. His mother, at the dining-room window, caught
sight of the uniform, and did not recognize her son until she
was almost smothered in his hearty embrace.

"Why, John! What does this mean? What—what
have you on?"

"Mother, I am twenty-two years old. A man who won't
fight for his country isn't a good son. He has no right
to stay in a country that he isn't willing to fight for!" and
with this specious dictum he drew himself up and met the
astonished eyes of his sister Olympia, who had been apprised
of his coming. But the maternal fears clouded patriotic
conceptions where her darling was involved, and his mother
sobbed :

"O Jack, Jack! what shall we do? How can we live
without you? And oh, my son, you are too young to go
to the war. You will break down. You can't manage a—
a musket, and the—the—heavy load the soldiers carry.
My son, don't break your mother's heart. Don't go—don't,
Jack, Jack! What shall I do?—O Polly, what shall
we do?"

"What shall we do? Why, we'll just show Jack that
all of war isn't in soldiering ; that the women who stay at

home help the heroes, though they may not take part in the battle. As to you and me, mamma, we shall be the proudest women in Acredale, for our Jack's the first—" she was going to say " boy," but, catching the coming protest in the warrior's glowing eye, substituted "man" with timely magnanimity—"the first man that volunteered from Acredale. And how shamed you would have been—we would have been—if Jack hadn't kept up the tradition of the family! He comes naturally by his sense of duty. Your father's father was the first to join Gates at Saratoga. My father's father was the right hand of Warren at Bunker Hill! If ever blood ran like water in our Jack's veins, I should put on—trousers and go to the war myself. I'm not sure that I sha'n't as it is," and, affecting Spartan fortitude, Olympia pretended to be deeply absorbed in adjusting a disarranged furbelow in her attire to conceal the quavering in her voice and the dewy something in her dark eyes. The mother, disconcerted by this defection where she had counted on the blindest adhesion, sank back in the cane rocker, helpless, speechless.

"Yes, mother, Polly is right. How could you ever lift up your head if it were said that son of John Sprague's—Governor, Senator, minister abroad—was the last to fly to his country's call? Why, Jackson would turn in his grave if a son of John Sprague were not the first to take up arms when the Union that he loved, as he loved his life, was in peril!"

Mrs. Sprague listened with woe-begone perplexity to these sounding periods, conscious only that her darling, her adored scapegrace, had suddenly turned serious, and was using the weapons she had so often employed to justify his conduct. For it was using one of the standing arms in the maternal arsenal, to remind the wild and headstrong lad that his father had been Jackson's confidant, that he had been Governor of Imperia, that he had enforced the demands of the United States upon European statesmen, that after a life spent in the public service he had died, reverenced by his party and by his neighbors. Jack, as an infant, had been fondled by Webster, by Clay, and, one never-to-be-forgotten day, Jackson, the Scipio of the republic, had placed his brawny hand upon the infant's head and declared that he would be "worthy of Jack Sprague, who was man enough to make two Kentuckians."

"But you—you ought to be a colonel. Your father was a major-general in the Mexican War at twenty-five. A Sprague can't be a private soldier!" she cried, seizing on this as the only tenable ground where she could begin the contest against the two children confederated against her.

"I don't want to owe everything to my father. This is a republic, mamma, and a man is, or ought to be, what he makes himself. I saw in a paper, the other day, that the Government has more brigadiers and colonels and—and—officers than it knows what to do with. I saw it stated that a stone thrown from Willard's Hotel in Washington hit a dozen brigadiers. I want to earn a commission before I assume it. I'll be an officer soon enough, no fear. I could have had a lieutenant's commission if I had gone in Blandon's regiment. But I hate Blandon! He is one of those canting sneaks father detested, and I won't serve under such cattle."

Mrs. Sprague, like millions of mothers in those days, was cruelly divided in mind. When the neighbors felicitated her on the valor and patriotism of Mr. Jack she was elated and fitfully reconciled. When, in the long watches of the night, she reflected on the hardships, temptations, the dreadful companions her darling must be thrown with, country, lineage, everything faded into the dreadful reality that her darling was in peril, body and soul. He was so like his father—gay, impressionable, easily influenced—he would be saint or sinner, just as his surroundings incited him. This was the woe that ate the mother's heart; this was the sorrow that clouded millions of homes when mothers saw their boys pranked out in the trappings of war.

Our jaunty Jack enjoyed the worship that came to him. He was the first boy in blue that appeared in the sandy streets of Acredale. Never had the rascal been so petted, so fêted, so adored. He might have been a pasha, had he been

a Turk. The promising down on his upper lip—the object
of his own secret solicitude and Olympia's gibes during the
junior year—was quite worn away by the kissing he under-
went among the impulsive Jeannettes of the village, who
had a vague notion that soldiers, like sailors, were indurated
for battle by adosculation. Jack may have believed this
himself, for he took no pains to disabuse the maidens as to
the inefficacy of the rite, and bore with galliard fortitude the
wear and tear of the nascent mustache, without which, to his
mind, a soldier would figure very much as a monk without a
shaven crown or a mandarin without a queue. And though
presently big Tom Tooker, chief of the rival faction in Acredale, gave his name to the recruiting officer in Warchester,
and a score more of Jack's rivals and cronies, he was the
soldier of the village. For hadn't he given up the glory of
graduation and the delights of "commencement" to take up
his musket for the Union? And then the fife was heard in
the village street—delicious airs from Arcady—and a great
flag was flung out from the post-office, and Master Jack was
installed recruiting sergeant for Colonel Ulrich Oswald's
regiment, that was to be raised in Warchester County. For
Colonel Oswald, having failed in a third nomination for
Congress, had gallantly proffered his services to the Governor of the State, and, in consideration of his influence with
his German compatriots, had been granted a commission,
though with reluctance, as he had supported the Democratic
party and was not yet trusted in the Republican councils.

CHAPTER II.

FLAG AND FAITH.

If Acredale had not been for a century the ancestral seat
of the Spragues, and in its widest sense typical of the suburban Northern town, there would be merely an objective

and extrinsic interest in portraying its sequestered life, its monotonous activities. But Acredale was not only a very complete reflex of Northern local sentiment; its war epoch represented the normal conduct of every hamlet in the land during the conflict with the South. Now that the war is becoming a memory, even to those who were actors in it, the facts distorted and the incidents warped to serve partisan ends or personal pique, the photograph of the time may have its value.

Made up of thriving farmers and semi-retired city men, Acredale mingled the simple conditions of a country village and the easy refinement of city life. The houses were large, the grounds ornate and ample, the society decorously convivial. People could be fine—at least they were thought very fine—without going to the British Isles to recast their home manners or take hints for the fashioning of their grounds and mansions. There was what would be called to-day the English air about the place and some of the people; but it was an inheritance, not an imitation. Save in the bustling business segment, abutting the four corners, where the old United States road bore off westward to Bucephalo and the lakes, the few score houses were set far back from the highway in a wilderness of shrubbery, secluded by hedges and shaded by an almost primeval growth of elms or maples. The whole hamlet might be mistaken for a lordly park or an old-fashioned German Spa. Family marketing was mostly done in Warchester; hence the village shops were like Arabian bazaars, few but all-supplying. The most pregnant evidence of the approach of modern ways that tinged the primitive color of the village life, was the then new railway skirting furtively through the meadows on the northern limits, as if decently ashamed of intruding upon such idyllic tranquillity. The little Gothic station, cunningly hidden behind a clustering grove of oaks at a respectful distance from the Corners, like the lodge of a great estate, reconciled those who had at first fought the iron mischief-maker.

The public edifices of the town—the Episcopal church,

the free academy, the bank, the young ladies' seminary—
were very unlike such institutions in the bustling, treeless
towns of to-day.   Corinthian columns and Greek friezes
adorned these architectural evidences of Acredale's affluence
and taste.   The village had grown up on private grounds,
conceded to the public year by year as the children and de-
pendents of the founders increased.   The Spragues were the
founders, and they had never been anxious to alienate their
patrimony.   Acredale is not now the sylvan sanctuary of
rural simplicity it was thirty years ago—before the war.   The
febrile tentacles of Warchester had not yet reached out to
make its vernal recesses the court quarter for the "new rich."
In Jack Sprague's young warrior days the village was three
miles from the most suburban limits of the city.   There was
not even a horse-car, or, as fashionable Warchesterians have
it, a "tram," to remind the tranquil villagers that life had
any need more pressing than a jaunt to the post twice a day.
Some "city folks" did hold villas on the outskirts, but they
used them only for short seasons in the late summer, when
the air at the lake began to grow too sharp for outdoor
pleasures.
    Society in the place was patriarchal as an English shire
town.   The large Sprague mansion, about which the village
clustered at a respectful distance, was the "Castle" of local
phrase.   Much of the glory of early days had departed, however, when the Senator—Jack's papa—died.   The widow
found herself unable to maintain the affluent state her lord
had loved.   His legal practice, rather than the wide acres of
his domain, had supported a hospitality famous from Bucephalo to Washington.   But with prudent management the
family had abundance, and, as Jack often said, he was a fortune in himself.   When the time came he would revive the
splendors his father loved to associate with the home of his
ancestors.
    "But where are we to get this splendor now, Jack?" Olym-
pia inquired, as the youth was dilating to his mother on the
wonders to come.   "Private soldiers get just thirteen dollars
a month; and if you continue smoking—as I am informed

all men do in the army—I expect to have to stint my pin-
money expenses to eke out your tobacco bills."

"Oh, I'll bring home glory. Napoleon said that every
soldier carried a marshal's *bâton* in his knapsack."

"I'm afraid you won't have room for it if you carry all
the things that I know of intended for you in this and other
families."

"Yes; but, Polly, you know, or perhaps you don't know,
a *bâton* is like a college love—no matter how full your heart
is, you can always find room for another !"

"John," Mistress Sprague reproves mildly; "how can
you ? I don't like to hear my son talk like that even in jest.
Don't get the idea that it is soldierly to treat sacred things
with levity. Love is a very sacred thing; it ought to be
part of a man's religion; it was of your father's."

"Then Jack must be a high priest, for there are a dozen
girls here and in the city who believe themselves enshrined
in that elastic heart."

"Olympia, you are a baleful influence on your brother.
If anything could reconcile me to his going it is the thought
that he will escape the extraordinary speech and manners
you have brought back from New York. Do the Misses
Pomfret graduate all their young ladies with such a tone
and laxity of speech as you have lately shown? Strangers
would naturally think that you had no training at home."

"Don't fear, mamma; strangers are not favored with my
lighter vein; I assume that for you and Jack, to keep your
minds from graver things. I preserve the senatorial suavity
of speech and the Sprague austerity of manner 'before folks,'
as Aunt Merry would say. Which reminds me, Jack, Kitty
Moore declares that you are responsible for Barney's enlist-
ing. The family look to you to bring him home safe—a
colonel at least."

"Well, by George, I like that! Why, the beggar was
bent on going long ago. He was the first to ask me to run
away and enlist. The other day he wanted me to have him
sworn in, and I told him to wait until—until I got a commission." Jack was going to say until he was older, but he

suddenly recollected that Barney was his own age, and that, in view of his mother's argument, struck him as unfortunate. He saw Olympia smiling mischievously and turned the subject abruptly. "I suppose you know, Polly, that Vincent is going home to join the rebels?"

"Is he?" She had turned swiftly to gather a ball of worsted, and when it was secured began to rummage in her work-basket for something that seemed from her intentness to be vitally necessary to her at the moment.

"Yes, he wrote to President Grandison that he should go as soon as his passports and remittances came. He's promised a captain's commission. I'm very, very sorry. Vint is the noblest of fellows. I hate to think of him in the rebel army."

"That's the reason you half killed him the other day, I suppose," Olympia said, sweetly, still investigating the contents of the basket.

"What, John, you've not been in a broil—fighting?" and Mistress Sprague could not, even in imagination, go further in such an odious direction, and let her eyes finish the interrogatory.

Jack, a good deal subdued by what Olympia had left unsaid, rather than what she had said, blurted out: "It was a campus shindy : Vint led the rebel side and they got licked, that's all."

"Oh, was that all?" Olympia had ended her search in the basket and fastened a glance of satiric good humor upon the culprit, which did not tend to relieve the awkwardness of the moment. Jack blushed under the glance and began to hum an air from Figaro, as if the conversation had ebbed into an impass from which it could only be rescued by a lively air.

Mrs. Sprague looked at the uneasy warrior, then at her daughter, darting the crochet-needles placidly through the wool.

"Well," she said, "never mind what's past; we must have Vincent out here for a visit before he goes. I must send Mrs. Atterbury a number of things. I hope she won't think that we intend to let the war make any difference in our feeling toward the family."

Jack was very glad to set out at once for his quondam foe, and in ten minutes was driving down the road to Warchester. Vincent's bruises were nearly healed, and he saluted Jack as a "chum" rather than as the agent of his late discomfiture.

"I'm mighty glad you've come to-day. I didn't know whether you meant to break off or not. I don't cherish any rancor. I don't see any use in carrying the war into friendships. We made the best fight we could. We did better than your side. You had the most men and the biggest fellows. We showed good pluck, if we did get licked. If you hadn't come to-day I should have been gone without seeing you, for I began to think that you were as narrow as these prating abolitionists. My commission is ready for me now at Richmond, and I'm just aching to get my regimentals on. I'm to be with Johnston in the Shenandoah, you know, and—"

"You mustn't tell me your army plans, Vint. I'm a soldier," and Jack drew himself up with martial pomposity, "and—and—perhaps I ought to arrest you now as an enemy, you know. I will look in the articles of war and find out my duty in such cases." Jack waved his arm reassuringly, as if to bid the rebel take heart for the moment—he would not hurry in the matter. Vincent eyed his comrade with such a woe-begone mingling of alarm and comic indignation that Jack forgot his possible part as agent of his country's laws, and said, soothingly: "Never mind, Vint, I'm not really a full soldier in the technical sense until the regiment is mustered in at Washington. After that, of course, you know very well it would be treason to give aid or comfort to the country's enemies."

Vincent didn't leave next day, nor for a good many days. He seemed to get a good deal of "aid and comfort" from those who should have been his enemies. Mistress Sprague found that he was not in a fit state to travel; that he needed nursing to prepare him for his journey, and that no place was so fit as the great guest-chamber in the baronial Sprague mansion, near his friend Jack. Strange to say, Vincent's eagerness to get to Richmond and his shoulder-straps were forgotten in the agreeable pastimes of the big house, where he spent hours enlightening Olympia on the wonders the Southern soldiers were to perform and the glory that he (Vincent) was to win. He went of a morning to the post-office, where Jack was installed recruiting-agent for Acredale township, and made very merry over the homespun stuff enrolled in defense of the Union.

"Our strapping cavaliers will make short work of your gawky bumpkins," he remarked to Jack as the recruits loitered about the wide, shaded streets, waiting to be forwarded to the rendezvous.

"Don't be too sure of that. These young, boyish-looking fellows are just the sort of men that met the British at Bunker Hill. They laughed too, when they saw them; but they didn't laugh after they met them, nor will your cavaliers," Jack cried, loftily.

"But there's not a full-grown man among all these I've seen. How do you suppose they are to endure march and battle? None of them can ride. All our young men ride, and cavalry is the main thing in modern armies."

In the Sprague parlors conversation of this risky sort was eschewed. Mistress Sprague was anxious that the son of her oldest friend should return to his mother with only the memory of amiable hospitality in his heart to show that, although war raged between the people, families were still friends. Vincent's mother had been one of Mistress Sprague's bridesmaids, and it was her wish that the children might grow up in the old kindly ties. So Vincent was made much of. There were companies every night, and drives and boating in the afternoons, and such merry-making as it was thought a lad of his years would enjoy. He was a very entertaining guest; that all Acredale had known in the old vacations when, with his sister, the pretty Rosa, he spent a summer with the Spragues.

But, now that there was to be a separation involving the

2

unknown in its vaguest form, the lad was treated with a tenderness that made the swift days very sweet to the young rebel. It was from Olympia that he met the only distinct formality in the manners of his hosts. He had known and adored her in a boyish way for years, and now, as he contemplated going, he thought that she ought to exhibit something of the old-time warmth. In other days she had ridden, walked, and flirted to his heart's desire. Now she avoided him when Jack was not at hand, and when she talked it was in a flippant vein that drove him wild with baffled hope. The day before he was to bid the kind house adieu he had his wish. She was riding with him over the shaded roadway that curves in bewildering beauty toward the lake. She seemed in a gentler mood than he had lately seen her. They rode slowly side by side, but Vincent had a dismal awkwardness of speech in whimsical contrast to his habitual fluency.

"There's only one thing hateful to me in this war," he said, caressing the arching neck of his horse, "and that is, the better we do our duty as soldiers the more sorrow we must bring upon our own friends."

"That's a rather solemn view to take of what Jack regards as the path of glory."

"Oh, you know what I mean : under the flag there can or ought to be no friendships—the bullet sent from the musket, the sword drawn in fight, must be aimed blindly. It might be my fate, for example, to meet Jack, to—to—"

"Yes," Olympia laughed demurely, ignoring the sentimental aspect of Vincent's remark. "Yes, that might paralyze the arm of valor; but, then, you and Jack have met before, when duty demanded one thing and affection another: I don't see that the dilemma softened the blows, or that either of you are any the worse for them."

Vincent was the real Southerner of his epoch—impulsive, sentimental, ardent in all that he espoused, without the slightest notion of humor, though imaginative as a dreamer; love, war, and his State, Virginia, were passions that he thought it a duty to uphold at any and all times. He

colored under the girl's satiric sally. If she had been a man
he would have bid her to battle on the spot. Her sly fun
and gentle malice he resented as insulting, coarse, and un-
womanly. He flashed a look of piteous, surprised reproach
at her as she flecked the flies from the neck of her horse.
He rode along moodily—too angry, too wretched to trust
himself to speak, for he felt sure he must say something bitter. But, as she gave no sign of resuming the discourse, he
was forced to take up the burden again. Venturing nearer
her side, he said in a conciliating, argumentative tone, as if
he had not heard the foregoing speech :

"Do you know, it seems to me, Olympia, that you of the
North do not seem to realize the seriousness of the war, the
determination of our side to make the South free? Here
you go about the common business of life, parties, balls, dress,
and all the follies of peace, as if war could not affect you at
all. Your newspapers are full of coarse jokes at the expense
of your own soldiers, your own President. There seems no
devotion to your own cause, such as we feel in the South.
I believe that if put to a vote more than half the North
would side with us to-day."

CHAPTER III.

MALBROOK S'EN VA-T-EN GUERRE.

OLYMPIA had been jogging along, apparently oblivious
to everything but the blazing vision of sun and cloud above
the lake, purpling shapes of mirage, reflecting the smooth
surface of the glowing water. But as the young man's voice
—fallen into a melodious murmur—ceased, she took up the
theme with unexpected earnestness.

"That's the error the South has made from the first. You
know my father was a public man. I have been educated
more at our dinner-table and in his talks with guests than at

school. That is, the things that have taken strongest hold
of my mind young girls rarely hear or understand. Now I
think I can tell you something that may be of value to you
in official places where you are going. The North is not
only in earnest—it is religiously in earnest. If you know
Puritan history you know what that means. For example :
If Jack had hesitated a moment or made delay to get rank
in the army, I should have abhorred him. So would our
mother, though she seems to be dismayed at his serving as a
common soldier. I adore Jack ; I think him the finest, the
most perfect nature—after my father's—that lives. But I
give him up gladly, because to keep him would be to degrade
him. We know that he may fall; that he may come back
to us a cripple, or worse. But, as you see, we make no sign.
Not a line of routine has been changed in the house. Jack
will march away and never see a tear in my eye or feel my
pulse tremble. It is not in our Northern blood to give much
expression to sentiment; but we feel none the less deeply—
much more deeply, I think, than you exuberant Southerners;
you are impulsive, mercurial, and fickle."

"Oh, don't say that; I can't bear to hear you say it; we
have deep feelings, we are constant, true as steel, chivalrous—"

"Yes, you are delightful people; but you are always living in the past. Shall I say it ? You are womanlike; you
can't reason. What you want at the moment is right, and
only that; with us nothing is real until we have tried and
proved it. If you count on Northern apathy you will soon
see your mistake. When Beauregard fired on Fort Sumter
the North was of one mind, and will stay so until all is again
as it was."

"Pray don't let us talk on this subject. I'm free to own
that it does not interest me. Then," he added adroitly, "you
are readier in argument than I, because you were brought
up in it. But what I want to say is, that it seems base for
me to turn upon the goodness I have met in this house, and
—and—"

"But you need not turn. In battle do your duty like

a man. If it should fall to you to do a kindness to the
wounded, do it in memory of the friends you have here.
War is less savage now than it was when your ancestors and
mine tortured each other in the name of God and the king."

"All murder is done for love of one sort or another: war
is love of country; revenge is love of some one else—men
rarely kill from hate," Vincent stammered, his heart beating
at the nearness of what he was dying to say.

"In that case I hope I shall be hated. I shall shun people
who love me," and with that she struck the horse a lively
tap and soon was far ahead of her tongue-tied wooer. Was
this a challenge? Vincent asked himself, as he sped after
her. When he reached her side the tender words were
chilled on his lips, for Olympia had in her laughing eye the,
to him, odious expression he saw there when she made the
irritating speech about himself and Jack a few minutes before. Fearing a teasing retort, he bridled the tender outburst
and rode along pensively, revolving pretexts for another
day's stay in Acredale. But when they reached home he
found an imperative mandate to set out at once, as his lingering in the North was subjecting himself and kinsmen
to doubt among the zealous partisans of the Davis party.
Olympia was alone in the library when he ran down to tell
Jack that he must start at once. He took it as an omen, and
said, confusedly:

"It is decided; I must go in the morning."

As this had been the plan all along, she looked up at him
in surprise, not knowing, of course, that he had been thinking of putting off the fixed time.

"Yes, everything has been made ready; Jack will take
you to Warchester, and we shall drive over to see you *en
route*."

"It is fortunate the letter from my mother came to-
night." He stood quite, over her chair, his eyes glittering
strangely, his manner excited.

"Do you know what they think at home? They say that
I—I am not true to my cause; that my heart is with the
North—that I want to stay here."

"They won't think that when they hear you, as we have, breathing fury and wrath against the Lincolnites," Olympia briskly replied, as if to proffer her services as witness to his misguided loyalty to the South.

"Ah, don't be so ungenerous, now—at this time. I never talk like that now—here—never before you." He hesitated, and his voice dropped. "Why will you put a fellow in a ridiculous light? Your sneers almost make me ashamed of my honest pride in my State—my enthusiasm for our sacred cause."

"Deep feeling isn't so easily shaken; true love should brave all things—even sneers and blows."

"If I should tell you that I loved somebody, I am sure you would make me seem ridiculous or ignorant of my own mind."

"Then pray be wise and don't tell me. It's bad enough to be in love, without being photographed in the agony."

He looked at her in angry perplexity. Could she ever be serious? Was all the tenderness of the past only heedless coquetry? Had she danced with him, drove with him, sailed with him, walked in the moonlight and made much of him in mere wanton mischief? What right had she to be so pretty and so—without heart or sensibility? A Southern girl with the word love on a young man's lips would have become a Circe of seductive wooing until the tale were told, even though she could not give her heart in return.

"I—I am going to-morrow, you know, and—" Then he almost laughed himself, for the droll inconsequence of this intelligence, after what had passed, touched even his small sense of humor. "O Olympia, I mean that I shall be far away; that I shall not see you after to-morrow. Won't you say something to encourage me—to give me heart for the future?"

"Let me see," and she leaned on her elbow musingly, as if construing his words literally, and quite unaware of the tender intent of his prayer. "It ought to be a line to go on your sword—there's where you have the advantage of poor Jack, he has only a musket. But, no, you being a South-

erner, have a coat of arms, and the line must go on that.
I used to know plenty of stirring phrases suitable to young
men setting out for the wars. Perhaps you know them, too;
they are to be found in the copy-books. 'The pen is mightier
than the sword' wouldn't do, would it? Pens are only fit for
poets and men of peace ? We should have something brief
and epigrammatic. 'That hour is regal when the sentinel
mounts on guard.' There is sublimity in that, but you won't
go on guard, being an officer.

> 'No blood-stained woes in mankind's story
> Should daunt the heart that's set on glory.'

That's too trivial—the sort of doggerel for newspaper poets'
corners rather than a warrior's shield.

> 'Think on the perils that environ
> The man that meddles with cold iron!'

"That's too much like a caution, and a soldier's motto
should urge to daring. So we'll none of that. What do
you say to the distich in honor of your great ancestor, Poca-
hontas's husband, John Smith:

> 'I never yet knew a warrior but thee,
> From wine, tobacco, debt, and vice so free.'

"Perhaps, however, that might be regarded as vaunting
over your comrades, who, I've no doubt, relax the tedium
of war in temperate indulgence of some of these vices. 'Put
up thy sword; states may be saved without it,' would sound
out of keeping for a warrior whose States drew the sword
when the olive-branch was offered them. You see, I can
not select any text quite suitable to your case ?"

"O Olympia, I did not believe you could be so heartless!
Be serious."

"Well, Mr. Soldier, if you insist, I know nothing better
for a warrior to bear in mind in war than these simple lines:

> 'The bravest are the tenderest,
> The loving are the daring.'"

"You are right, Olympia—those are noble lines. It gives me courage; the loving are the daring! I love you; I dare to tell you that I love you! Ah, Olympia, I love you so well that I have been traitor to my fatherland! I have loitered here in the hope that you would give me some sign—some word to take with me in the dark path Fate has set for me to follow."

He came back to her side now, passion and zeal in his shining eyes, ardent, elate, expectant. But she put the hand behind her that he reached out to seize as he fell upon one knee by her chair. Her voice softened and a warm light shone in her eye when she spoke:

"I beg you to get up; we cold-blooded people up here don't understand that old-fashioned way." As he started back with something like a groan she gave him a quick glance that electrified him. He seized her hand before she could snatch it away, and pressed it to his lips.

"Pray, be serious. You are too young to talk of love."

"I am twenty-two; my father was married at nineteen."

"No, dear Vincent, don't talk of this now. You don't know your own mind yet. I am sure that when you go home and think over the matter you will see that it would be impossible. But, even if you were sure of yourself, I never could think of it. You are going to take up arms against all I hold dear—sacred. If I were your affianced, with the love for you that you deserve, I would break the pledge when you joined in arms against my family and country."

"You have known for years, Olympia, that I loved you; that I was only waiting to finish college to tell you of my love. Why didn't you tell me—"

"Tell you what?"

"I say, Polly," Jack cried, bursting in, radiant and eager. "I have the last man of the one hundred—" Observing Vincent he stopped. It seemed to him a sort of treason to talk of his regiment before the man who was so soon to be in the ranks against them. "Oh, I can't tell our secrets before the enemy," he ended, jocosely. The word went to Vincent's heart like the prod of sharp steel. He gave Olympia one pathetic glance, and, without a word, hastened from the room. In spite of a great many adroit efforts, Vincent could get no further speech with Olympia alone that night. Early in the morning he was driven, with Mrs. Sprague and Jack to the station. Olympia sent down excuses and adieus, alleging some not incredible ailing of the sort that is always gallantly at the disposal of damsels not minded to do things people expect.

Presently, when the lorn lover had been gone three days, a letter came from Washington to Olympia, and, though it was handed to her by her mother, the maiden made no proffer to confide its contents to the naturally curious parent. But we, who can look over the reader's shoulder, need not be kept in the dark.

"Dear Olympia" (the letter said), "it was hard to leave without a last word. All the way here I have been thinking of our little talk—if that can be called a talk where one side has lost his senses and the other is trifling or mystifying. I told you that I loved you. I thrill even yet with the joy of that. You are so wayward and capricious, so coy, that I began to fear that I never could get your ear long enough to tell you what I felt you must have long known. You didn't say that you loved me; but, dear Olympia, neither did you say that you did not. The rose has fallen on the hem of your robe. When its fragrance steals into your senses, you will stoop and put the blossom in your bosom. It is the war that divides us, you say. It will soon pass. And who knows what may happen to make you glad that, since there must be strife, I am one of the enemy rather than a stranger? I feel that we shall be brought together in danger, when it may be my happiness to serve you or yours. But, even if I am not so favored, I shall still ask your love. You know our Southern ways. Whom I love my mother loves. But my mother and sister Rosa have loved you long and dearly. They have known you as long as I have, and when you consent to come to us you will take no stranger's place in the heart and home of the family. Remember the motto you gave me. You are a woman, therefore tender; I am daring, Heaven knows, in aspiring to such a reward as your love. But I dare to love you; if you cast that love from you, love will lose its tenderness, bravery its daring. One of the high mountains of hope whereon I sun my fainting soul is the knowledge that you love no one else. I won't say that you should in love hold to the rule 'first come first served,' but I do say, 'first dare, first win.' And when you reflect on what you said about the accident of war separating us, just put Jack in my place. What would you think of a Southern girl who should refuse him because he fought on the side of his family and his State? What is the old line? 'I could not love thee, dear, so much, loved I not honor more.' I'm sure I couldn't ask your love if there were not honor in my own. The war will be over and forgotten in six months, but you and I are young; we have long years before us. The right will win in the contest, and, right or wrong, I am yours, and only yours, while there are life in my body and hope in my soul.   VINCENT."

In a little glow of what was plainly not displeasure, the young woman "filed" this "writ of pre-emption," as Jack afterward called it, in careful hiding, and resumed meditation of the writer. It could not now be answered, for letters be tween the lines were subject to censorship, and Olympia perhaps shrank from adding to her lover's misery by exposing his rejection to the unfeeling eyes of the postal agents. There was pity in the resolve as well as prudence. Had Vincent been able to read the workings of the lady's mind, he would have donned his rebel gray with more buoyant joy that day in Richmond. Another ally of the absent came in the course of the day. Miss Boone, the daughter of the opulent contractor and chief local magnate, called to plan work for the soldiers. Vincent's name being mentioned, Miss Boone said, in the apparent effusion of girlish inti macy:

"I like Mr. Atterbury very much. He is a charming

fellow. But, for your family's sake, I am glad he is away from this house." At Olympia's surprised start she nodded as if to emphasize this, continuing: "Yes, and for good reasons. You know our house is the high court of abolitionism? Well, papa's cronies have made Mr. Atterbury's visit cause of suspicion."

"Suspicion? What do you mean?"

Miss Boone was paling and blushing painfully. "Dear Olympia, I hate to say it: but you should know it. You will hear it elsewhere. Cruel things like this always come out. You know that feeling has been very bitter here since the dreadful attack on the Massachusetts soldiers in Baltimore? Radicals make no distinction between Democrats and rebels, and—I'm to say it—but Mr. Atterbury is charged with being a spy here—and—and your family, being Democrats, are thought to sympathize with the rebels. Of course, your friends know better. I and many more know that the Atterburys and Spragues have been intimate for thirty years. But in war-time people seem to lose their senses and change their opinions like lake breezes; prejudices grow like gourds, and the people who do least and talk loudest make public sentiment."

"What an outrageous state of things!" Olympia cried, hotly. "Our family sympathize with traitors indeed! Why, it was my father who, in the Senate, upheld Jackson when he stamped out South Carolina in its rebellion. Oh! it is monstrous, such a calumny. Why, just think of it! The only man in the family is a private soldier, when he might have been high in rank, with such influences as we could bring to bear. O Kate! it almost makes one pray for a defeat to punish such ingrates!"

"Yes; but for Heaven's sake don't let any one hear you say such a thing—for your brother's sake! He is already the victim of the feeling I have spoken about. He was to have had the captaincy of the first one hundred men he raised. But the Governor has been made to change the usual rule, and the colonel is to appoint the officers."

"And Jack isn't to have a commission?"

"No, not now; only men of the war party are to be made officers."

"Good heavens! Nobody could be more eager for the war than Jack. It is his passion. His delight in it shocks my mother, who hates war. What stronger evidence of sympathy for the cause could he show than joining the army before finishing college?"

"But he is a Democrat—and—and—only Republicans are to be trusted—at first." Miss Boone blushed as she stammered this, for it was her own father, in his function as chairman of the war committee, who had insisted upon this discrimination. Worse still—but this Kate did not mention—it was Boone's own work that kept Jack from his expected epaulets. There had long been a feud between Boone and the late Senator Sprague, and Olympia conjectured most of what the daughter reserved.

"Your brother has done wonders, everybody says; he has the finest fellows in the township, and he ought to be colonel, at least," Miss Boone said, rising to go.

"Oh, I have no fear that he will not win his way," Olympia replied, cheerfully. "The brave in battle are captains, no matter what rank they hold."

The odious partisanship and ready calumny of her own compatriots gave a strange bent to her mind in dealing with another problem. Vincent, too, had suffered from the wretched tattle of his family's enemies. After all, might he not be right? Might the war not be a mere game of havoc played by the base and unscrupulous? Country, right or wrong, had been her family watchword since her ancestor flew to fight the British invaders. It was Jack's watchword, too, and his conduct in battle should put these wretches to shame. She thought more kindly of the rebel in this vengeful mood, and straightway ran up-stairs, where, sitting by the open window and lulled by the piping of the robins, she took the letter from its pretty covert, read it again with heightened color, and, smiling rosily at the face she saw in the mirror, raised it to her lips and sighed softly.

When a whole people have but one thought in mind

that thought becomes mania. Acredale had but this one thought, "Beat rebellion and punish rebels." "On to Richmond!" was the cry, and forming ranks to go there the business that everybody took in hand. These had been great days to Jack. He began to feel something of the burden that a feudal chief must have borne at the summoning of the clans. So soon as it spread in the country-side that "young Sprague had 'listed," all the "ageable" sons of the soil were fired with a burning zeal to take up arms and bear him company. Boys from sixteen to twenty these were for the most part, and there was bitter grumbling when Jack firmly refused to take the names of any under twenty. Some he solaced with a gun, a pistol, or such object as he knew was dear to the country boy's heart. They returned to the relieved hearthstone loud in Jack's praise, having his promise to enlist them when they were twenty, if the war lasted so long; and if the wise smiled at this, wasn't it well known that the great army now gathering was to set out at latest by the 4th of July? And didn't everybody know that it was going to march direct to Richmond? There were trying scenes too, in the *rôle* Jack had assumed so gayly. He began to see that war had ministers of pain and sorrow hardly less cruel than those dealing death and wounds. Tearful parents came to him day by day to beg his help in restoring sons who had fled to the wars. Others came to warn him that if their boys applied to him he must refuse them, as they were under age.

In this list the Perley sisters, Dick's three maiden aunts, came on a respectful embassy to implore Jack to discourage their nephew, who had quite deserted school and gave all his time to drilling with the "college squad." Jack pledged himself that he would hand Dick over to the justice of the peace, to be detained at the house of refuge, if he didn't give up his evil designs. But, when that young aspirant appeared, so soon as his aunts had gone, and reminded Jack of years of intimate companionship in dare-deviltry, the elder saw that his own safety would be in flight, and that night, his company was removed to Warchester. There in the great camp, surrounded by sentinels, his Acredale cronies were shut out, and Jack began in earnest his soldier life.

CHAPTER IV.

GUELPH AND GHIBELLINE.

The shifting of Jack's company to the regimental camp in Warchester left a broad gap in the lines of the social life of Acredale. Jack's going alone, to say nothing of the others, would have eclipsed the gayety of many home groups besides his own, in which the Sprague primacy in a social sense was acknowledged. Since the influx of the new-made rich, under the stimulus of the war and Acredale's advantages as a resort, there were a good many who disputed the Sprague leadership—tacitly conceded rather than asserted. Chief of the dissidents was Elisha Boone, who, by virtue of longer tenure, vast wealth, and political precedence, divided not unequally the homage paid the patrician family. Boone was fond of speaking of himself as a "self-made man," and the satirical were not slow to add that he had no other worship than his "creator." This was a gibe made rather for the antithesis than its accuracy, for even Boone's enemies owned that he was a good neighbor, and, where his prejudices were not in question, a man with few distinctly repellent traits. He delighted in showing his affluence—not always in good taste. He filled his fine house with bizarre crowds, and made no stint to his friends who needed his purse or his influence. He had in the early days when he came to Acredale aspired to political leadership in the Democratic party.

But Senator Sprague was too firmly enshrined in the loyalty of the district to be overcome by the parvenu's manoeuvres or his money. His ambition in time turned to rancor as he marked the patrician's disdainful disregard of his

(Boone's) efforts to supplant him. Hatred of the Spragues became something like a passion in Boone. Sarcasms and disparagement leveled at his social and political pretensions he attributed to the Senator and his family. All sorts of slurs and gossip were reported to him by busybodies, until it became a settled purpose with Boone to make the Sprague family feel heavy heart-burnings for the sum of the affronts he had endured. It was to them he attributed the whispered gibes about his illiteracy; his shady business methods; the awful story of his handiwork in the ruin of Richard Perley, the spendthrift brother of the Misses Perley. Once, too, when he had so well manipulated the district delegates that he was sure of nomination in the convention, Senator Sprague had hurried home from Washington and defeated him just as the prize was in his grasp. The Senator made a speech to the delegates, in which he pointedly declared that it was men of honor and brains, not men of money, that should be chosen to make the laws.

"The time will come, Senator, that you'll be sorry for this hour's work," Boone said, joining Sprague at the door as he was leaving the hall.

"How's that?" the other asked, with just the shade of superciliousness in the tone admired in the Senate for suavity. "I hope I am always sorry when I do wrong, in speech or act; I teach my children to be."

"Well, if you think it right to run the party for a few lordly idlers too proud to mix with the people—men who think they are better born and better bred than the rest of us—I don't want to have anything more to do with it. I will go elsewhere."

"That's your privilege, sir. The Whigs have plenty of room for self-made men. Though I do think you are taking too personal a view of to-day's contest, your defeat was purely a matter of duty. Moore, whom we have chosen, was a poor Irish settler here before you came. He was promised the nomination two years ago." With a lofty bow the Senator turned and stalked in another direction as if he did not care for the other's further company. Even this small and wholly unintended affront worked in the poor, misjudging victim of morbid self-esteem, as a cinder in the eye will torture and blind the sufferer to all the landscape. Boone mingled no more with the Democrats. He threw himself with the fervor of the convert into the radical wing of the Whigs, and was brought into close relation with some of the most admired of the band of great men who created the young Republican party. If Douglas, Dickinson, Cass, Van Buren, Seymour, or any eminent Democrat passing through Warchester stopped to break bread with their colleague Sprague in his Acredale retreat, straightway the splendid Sumner, the Ciceronian Phillips, or the Walpole-Seward, or some other of the shining galaxy of agitators, whose light so shone before men that the whole land was presently brought out of darkness, met at Boone's table to maintain the balance in distinction.

It was Boone's liberal purse that paid the expenses of the memorable campaign in the Warchester district, wherein the Democrats were first shaken in their hold. It was his money that finally secured the seat in Congress for Oswald, who was his tenant and debtor. It was therefore no surprise when Oswald—who had been greatly aided in business affairs by Senator Sprague—passed over the prior claims of his old patron's son, and gave the cadetship to Wesley Boone, the son of his new liege. It was looked upon as another step in the ladder of gratitude when Wesley carried off the captaincy in the Acredale company, though everybody knew that young Boone was not in any way so well fitted for the "straps" as Jack. When one day an item appeared in the local paper to the effect that President Lincoln had shown the "sagacity for which he was so well known, in honoring our distinguished townsman, Elisha Boone, Esq., with the appointment of ambassador to Russia," everybody thought the statement only natural. There were many congratulations. But when, having declined this splendid proffer, the authorities pressed the place of "Assistant Secretary of the Treasury" upon their townsman, the whole village awoke to the fact that all its greatness had not gone when Senator Sprague was gathered to his fathers.

The event was potent as the cross Constantine saw, or dreamed he saw, in the sky, in the conversion of party workers to the new Administration. Everybody looked forward to an eminent future for the potent partisan and millionaire, the first of that—now not uncommon—hierarchy that replace the feudal barons in modern social forces. Had he listened to the eager urging of Kate, his daughter and prime minister, Boone would have accepted the foreign mission ; but he stubbornly refused to listen to her in this.

Kate Boone was like her father only in strong will, vehement purpose, and a certain humorous independence that made her a great delight among even the anti-Boone partisans in both Acredale and Warchester. Since the death of her mother, Kate had been head of her father's household —an imperious, capricious, kind-hearted tyrant, who ruled mostly by jokes and persuasions of the gentler sort. It was her father's one lament that Kate was not " the boy of the family, for she had more of the stuff that makes the man in her little finger than Wes had in his whole body." She kept him in a perpetual unrest of delight and dismay. She espoused none of his piques or prejudices; she was as apt to bring people he disliked to his dinner-table as those he liked. She was forever making him forgive wrongs, or what he fancied to be wrongs, and causing him seem at fault in all his squabbles, so that he was often heard to say, when things went as he didn't want them:

"I don't know whether I am to blame or the other fellow until Kate hears the story."

His illiteracy and lack of polish were the secret grief of the rich man's life. Kate was quick in detecting this. Much of it she saw was due to the shyness that unschooled men feel in the presence of college men, or those who have been trained. On returning from her seminary life, the young girl set about remedying the single break in her father's perfections. She was far too clever to let him know her ambitious purpose. With a patience almost maternal and an

3

exquisite adroitness, she interested him in her own reading, which was comprehensive, if not very well ordered. But she won the main point. During the long winter evenings her father found no pleasure like that Kate had always ready for him in the cheery library. He was soon amazed at his keen interest in the world of mind unrolled to his understanding; more than all, he retained with the receptivity of a boy all that was read to him. Kate made believe that she needed his help in reviewing her own studies, and so carried him through all she had gone over in the seminary classes. Boone began presently to see that education is not the result of mere attendance in schools and the parroting of the classics in a few semesters in college. Without suspecting it, his varied business enterprises and his wide experience of men had grounded him as well in the ordinary forms of knowledge as nine in ten college men attain.

"Education, after all, papa, is like a trade. A man may be able to handle all the tools and not know their names. Now, you are a well-informed man, but, because you didn't know logic, grammar, scientific terms, and the like, you thought yourself ignorant."

In the new confidence in himself he was surprised at his own ability in launching a subject in the presence of his eminent friends when especially Kate was on hand to support the conversation. She got him not only to buy fine pictures, as most rich men do, but she made him see wherein their value lay, so that when artists and amateurs came to admire his treasures, he could talk to them without gross solecisms.

"I'm not a liberal education to you, papa, as Steele said of the Duchess of Devonshire. That implies too much, but I am an index. You can find out what you need to know by keeping track of my ignorance."

Elisha Boone's domestic circle was a termagancy—as Kate often told his guests—tempered by wit and good-humor. He was prouder of his daughter than of his self-made rank or his revered million. In moments of expansive good-nature he invited business or political associates to

"Acre Villa," as his place was called, to enjoy the surprise
Kate's graces wrought in the guests. But these were not
always times of delight to the doting parent. Kate was a
shrewd judge of the amenities; and if the personages who
came, at the father's bidding, gave the least sign of a not
unnatural surprise to find a girl so well bred and self-contained in the daughter of such a man as Boone, she became
very frigid and left the father to do the honors of the evening visit. No entreaty could move her to reappear on the
scene. In time, the prodigal papa was careful to submit a
list of the names of his proposed guests, as chamberlains
give royalty a descriptive list of those to be bidden to
court.

Kate was on terms that, if not cordial, were not constrained, with the Spragues. She had gone to the same
seminary with Olympia, had danced with Jack, and, in the
cadetship affair, had plainly given her opinion that her
brother Wesley, having no taste or fitness for military life,
Jack, who had, should have the prize. But two motives entered into the father's determination: one was to annoy and
humiliate the Spragues; the other, the sleepless craving of the
parvenu to get for his son what had not been his, in spite of
all the adulation paid him—the conceded equality of social
condition. The army was then, as I believe it is considered
now, the surest sign of higher caste in a democracy. Wesley, by the mere right to epaulets, would be of the acknowledged gentility. Nobody could sneer at him; no doors could
be opened grudgingly when he called. He would, in virtue
of his West Point insignia, be a knighted member of the
blood royal of the republic. Some of this mysterious unc-
tion would distill itself into the unconsecrated ichor of the
rest of the family, and Kate, as well as himself, would be
part of the patrician caste. The daughter looked upon all
this good-humoredly; she shared none of her father's morbid delusions on the subject. She rallied the cadet a good
deal on his mission. When Wesley, after the June exami-
nations, which he passed by the narrowest squeeze—'twas
said by outside influence—came home to display his cadet

buttons and his neat gray uniform in Acredale, Kate ban-
tered the complacent young warrior jocosely.

"We shall all have to live up to your shoulder-straps
and brass buttons after this, Wesley," she cried, as the
proud young dandy strutted over the arabesques of the library, where the delighted papa marched him, the better to
survey the boy's splendor. "And think of the fate that
awaits you if, in the esteem of Acredale, you should turn out
less than a Napoleon."

"Be serious, Kate, and don't tease the boy. Wesley knows
what's expected of him; he has an opportunity to show what
is in his stock. Thank God, men in the North can now
come to their own without going down on their knees to the
South!"

Wesley grinned. He was no match for his sister in the
humorous bouts waged over his head against his father's
prejudices and cherished social schemes. During the vacation she put a heavy penalty of raillery upon his swelling
pride and vanity, sarcasm that tried the paternal patience as
well as his own. Wesley, however, had a large fund of the
philosophy that comes from a high estimate of one's self.
He was well favored in looks and build, though somewhat effeminate, with his small hands and carefully shod feet. He
would have been called a "dude" had the word been known
in its present significance; as it was, he was regarded as a coxcomb by the derisive group hostile to the father's social pretensions. He was the first of the golden youth of his set to
adopt the then reviving mode of parting the hair on the
middle of the head. In the teeth of the village derision, he
persisted in this with a tenacity that Kate declared gave
promise of a "Wellington." For many who had at first
adopted the foreign freak had been ridiculed out of it, discouraged by the obstinate refusal of the generality to follow
the lead. In those sturdily primitive days the rich youth of
the land had not so universally gone abroad as they do now,
and "the proper thing" among the "well born" was not so
distinctly laid down in the code of the *élite*. The accent and
manners that now mark "good form" seemed queer, not to

say *bouffe*, to even the first circles of home society, and the
first disciples of "Anglomania" had a very hard time polish-
ing the raw material. The home life of the Boones was .
something better and sincerer than the impression made
upon their neighbors by the father's invincible push and
high-handed ways. His daughter and son had been born to
him in middle age. They had the reverence for the parent
marked in the conduct of children who associate gray hairs
with the venerable. With all her strong sense and self-
assertion, Kate was proud of the fact that she was her father's
daughter. It was a distinction to bear his name. His solid-
ity, his masterful will, his well-defined, if narrow, convictions, were to her the sanctities one is apt to associate with
lineage or magistracy. Wesley, though less impressionable
than his sister, shared these secret devotions to the parent's
parts, and bowed before his father's behests, in the filial reverence of the sons of the patriarchs. When Elisha Boone
denounced the outbreak of John Brown at Harper's Ferry
as more criminal than Aaron Burr's treason, his children
made his prepossessions their own; when, three years later,
the father proudly eulogized the uprising he had so luridly
condemned, his children saw no tergiversation in the swift
conversion. When to this full measure of lay perfection
the complexion of Levite godliness was superadded by election to the deaconate in the Baptist Church, it will readily
be seen that two young people, in whom the hard worldliness
of wealth and easy conditions had not bred home agnosti-
cism, were material for all the credulities of parent worship.
Kate, a year older than Wesley, soon encountered the influences which gave the first shock to her faith and gradually
tinctured her sentiments with a clearer insight into her
father's character. Oddly enough, it was through the rival
house this came. Olympia, a sort of ablegate in the social
hierarchy of the village, had been thrown much with Kate,
and was greatly amused with her point of view in many of
the snarls arising in a provincial society. The intimacy had
been begun in the New York school, where both had been
in the same classes, and, though the families saw nothing of

each other, the girls did. Kate was soon led to see that the
Spragues had none of the patrician pretension her father attributed to them. Jack, too, had made much of her, and
seemed to delight in her sharp retorts to the inanities of would-
be wits. The episode in Elisha Boone's life, that all his success, wealth, and after exemplary conduct had not condoned
in the village mind, was his handiwork in the ruin of Richard
Perley. I set this down with something of the delight Car-
lyle expresses when in the rubbish of history he found, among
the shams called kings and nobles, anything like a man.

It is worth the noting, this trait of Acredale, at a time when
riches and success are looked upon as condoning every breach
of the decalogue. Just how the intimacy between the two
men came about was not known. It, however, was known
that when Boone first came to Acredale he had been helped
in his affairs by Dick Perley's lavish means. In a few years
Boone was the patron and Perley the client. As Boone grew
rich Perley grew poor, until finally all was gone. Then the
fairest lands of the Perley inheritance passed to Boone. It
was the fireside history of the whole Caribee Valley that the
rich contractor had encouraged the ruined gentleman in the
excesses that ended the profligate's career; that the two men
had staked large sums at play in Bucephalo, and that ina-
bility to meet his losses to Boone had caused Dick Perley's
flight. He had been seen by one of the village people a year
or two before the war in Richmond, and had been heard of
in California later, but no word had ever reached his family,
not even when his wife died, two years after his exile. There
were those who said that Boone was in correspondence with
his victim, and it was known that drafts, made by Dick Perley, had been paid by Boone at the bank in Warchester. Between Boone and the Perley ladies, whose house was separated from "Acre Villa" by a wide lawn and hedge, there
had always been the tacit enmity that wrong on one side
and meek unreproach on the other breeds. The rancor that
manifested itself in Boone's treatment of the Misses Perley
was not imitated by them. They never alluded to their affluent neighbor, never suffered gossip concerning the Boones in

what Olympia humorously called the "Orphic adytum," the
"tabby-shop," as Wesley named the Perley parlors. Young
Dick, however, had none of the scruples that kept his aunts
silent. One dreadful day, when he had been nagged to fisti-
cuffs with Wesley, whose dudish dignity exacted a certain
restraint with the hot-headed youngster, Elisha Boone, behind the thick hedge, heard on the highway outside his
grounds this outrageous anathema :

"You're no more than a thief, Wes Boone ; your father
stole all he's got. Some day I'll make him give it back, or
send him to jail, where he ought to be now."

Schoolboy though the railer was, Boone staggered
against the hedge, the words brought a dreadful flush and
then a livid pallor to the miserable parent's cheek. He
dared not trust himself to speak then. Nor was the antipathy the outbreak caused mitigated by the savage thrash-
ing that Wesley, throwing aside his dignity, proceeded to
administer to the unbridled accuser. After that, by the
father's sternest command, neither of his children was to
return the courteous salutation the Perley ladies had never
ceased to bestow in meeting the Boones walking or in company. Now, Dick was the kind of boy that those who know
boy nature would call adorable. To the Philistine, without
humor or sympathy, I'm afraid he was a very bad boy. He
was until late in his teens painfully shy with grown people
and strangers ; even under the eyes of his aunts and with
youths of his own age, diffident to awkwardness. He had
the face of a well-fed cherub and the gentle, dreamy, and
wistful eye of a girl in love. With his elders he had the
halting, confused speech of a new boy in a big school. But
in the woods or on the playground he was the merriest,
most daring, and winningly obstreperous lad that ever filled
three maiden aunts with terror and delight.

CHAPTER V.

A NAPOLEONIC EPIGRAM.

FOR weeks the regiment expected every day the order to march. The guns had been distributed and all their fascinating secrets mastered. In evolution and manual the men regarded themselves as quite equal to the regulars. The strict orders forbidding absence overnight were hardly needed, as no one ventured far, fearing that the regiment would be whirled away to Washington during the night. Had the men been older or more experienced in war, the weeks of waiting would have been delightful rather than dreary. The regiment was the object of universal interest in the town. Base-ball and the alluring outdoor pastimes that now divert the dawdlers of cities were unknown. Hence the camp-ground of the Caribees was the matinée, ball-match, tennis, boating, all in one of the idle afternoon world of Warchester. At parade and battalion drill the scene was like the race-ground on gala days.

All the fine equipages of the town drew up in the roads and lanes flanking the camp, where with leveled glasses the mothers, sisters, and sweethearts watched the columns as they skirmished, formed squares, or " passed the defile," quite sure that the rebels would fly in confusion before such surprising manoeuvres. This daily audience stimulated such a fierce rivalry among the companies that the men turned out at all hours of the day to drill and practice in squads, rather than loiter about the camp. One day great news aroused the camp : the Governor was to review the regiment and send it to the front. All Warchester poured out to the Holly Hills, and when at five o'clock the companies filed out on the shining green there was such a cheer that the men felt repaid for the tiresome wait of months. The civic commander-in-chief watched the movements with affable scrutiny, surrounded by a profusely uniformed staff, to whom he expressed the most politic approval. He was heard to remark that no such soldiers had been seen on this continent since Scott had marched to Lundy's Lane.

There was a throb of passionate joy in the ranks when this eulogium reached the men, for the words were hardly spoken when they were known in every company by that mysterious telegraphy which makes the human body a conductor swift as an electric wire among large masses of men. Nor were the words less relished that the eulogist was as ignorant of military excellence as a Malay of the uses of a patent mower. The men, it was easy to see, were much more efficient in movement than the officers in handling them. Colonel Oswald had wasted weeks in the study of the occult evolutions of the battalion ; they were still a maddening mystery to him that fatal day. For six weeks his dreams had been haunted by airy battalions filing over impossible defiles. The commands he gave that day would have thrown the companies into hopeless confusion had the junior officers not boldly substituted the right ones for the colonel's blunders. This, however, passed unnoted, for the crowds, and even the men, were not the sharp critics they afterward became when mistakes by an incompetent officer were saluted by shouts of ridicule, and the men contemptuously disregarded them. When Colonel Oswald ordered them to " present arms " from a " place rest " there was more perplexity than merriment, and the admiring crowd saw nothing peculiar in one company snatching up bayonets to present while others remained perfectly still.

Jack, to whom the manual was a very sacred thing, broke into fierce ridicule of the commander, declaring that he was better fitted for sutler than colonel. When the savage speech was reported to headquarters that young fellow's prospects for the straps—never the best—were by no means improved. The review brought bitter disappointment to the regiment. The inspector-general, who was present, informed the colonel that no more than a thousand men could be accepted in one body; that five hundred of the Caribees would have to be divided among other troops in the State. The order aroused wild excitement. Half the men looked upon the edict as a

scheme to give the politicians more places for their feudatories. Indeed, though that was not the origin of the order,
that was the use made of it. Some of the junior officers, who
disliked Oswald and distrusted his capacity to command,
drew out very willingly, and of course carried many of their
men with them.

But in the end the matter had to be decided by lot. Now
this chance threw Wesley Boone out, and there was great
rejoicing in the Acredale group, who hoped that this stroke
of luck would make place for their favorite, Jack Sprague.
But, to everybody's astonishment, a day or two after the
event, Wesley resumed his place in Company K, and gave
out that it was by order of the Governor. Jack was urged
by the major of the regiment, who had gone with the five
hundred, to cast his fortunes with the new body, promising
a speedy lieutenancy. But Jack would not desert the Caribees. All of Company K, and many in the others, had enlisted on his word, and he could not in honor leave them.
The opposition journals had from the first denounced the
division of the Caribees as a trick of the partisans, and, sure
enough, the men were given to understand that there would
be no move to Washington until after the election, then
pending. This was a municipal contest, and the Administration party made good use of the incipient soldiery to obtain a majority in the town.

Promotion was quite openly held out as a reward for
those who could influence most votes for the Administration
candidates. At night the various companies were sent into
the city to take part in the political propaganda; to march
in processions or occupy conspicuous places at the party
meetings. The private soldiers were almost to a man Democrats, but the chance to escape the long and irksome evenings
of the camp and join the frolic and adventure of the street
made most of them willing enough to play the part of claque
or figurantes. Jack, of course, refused to take part in these
scenic rallies, making known his sentiments in vehement
disdain. He detested Oswald, who had quit his party, not
on a question of principle, but merely for place, and Jack

did not spare him in his satirical allusions to the new uses invented for the military.

A still more trying injustice befell the luckless Jack. For a long time he had, as senior, acted as orderly sergeant of Company K. This officer is virtually the executive functionary in the company. It is his place to form the men in rank, make out details, and prepare everything for the captain. The orderly sergeant is to the company what the adjutant is to the regiment. He carries a musket and marches with the ranks, but in responsibility is not inferior to an officer. One evening when it was known that orders had come for the regiment to march, Jack, having formed the company for parade, received a paper from the captain's orderly to read. He opened it without suspicion, and, among other changes in the corps, read, "Thomas Trask to be first sergeant of Company K, and he will be obeyed and respected accordingly." Jack read the monstrous wrong without a tremor. The men flung down their arms and broke into a fierce clamor of rage and grief. Many of them were Jack's classmates. These swarmed about him. One, assuming the part of spokesman, cried out:

"It's an infamous outrage. They cheated you out of your captaincy; they have put every slight they could upon you. But we have some rights. We won't stand this. There are thirty of your classmates who will do whatever you say to show these people that they can't act like this."

There were mutiny and desperation in the air. It needed but a spark to destroy the usefulness of the company. But, as is often the case with impetuous, hot-headed spirits, Jack cooled as his friends grew hot. He was the more patient that the injustice was his injury alone. He remained in his place at the right of the company, and confronted the rebellious group with amazing self-control. Then loud above the murmuring his voice rang out:

"Company, attention! fall in, fall in! Any man out of the ranks will be sent to the guard-house. Right dress, steady on the left."

Many a time afterward these angry mutineers heard that

sonorous, clear, boyish treble in stern and determined command; but they never heard it signalize a more heroic temper than at that moment, when, himself deeply wronged, he forced them to go back in the ranks to receive the interloper. They "dressed up" sullenly as Jack called the roll for the last time, and received Trask, the new orderly, at a "present," which, though not in the tactics, Jack exacted as a penitence for the momentary revolt. Poor Trask looked very unhappy indeed as his displaced rival stepped back to the rear and left the new orderly to march the company out from the narrow way to take its place in the parade. It was easy to see that he would have been very glad to postpone or evade his new honors, on any pretext, for the time. He was so confused that Jack, from the flank, was obliged to repeat the few commands needed to get the company to the field.

Fortunately for the efficiency of the raw army, as this public discontent reached its most acute stage orders came to march the troops to Washington. The Caribees were the first body of soldiers sent from Warchester, and there was a memorable scene when the jaunty ranks filed through the streets to the station. By the time the men reached the train they discovered that they could never make war laden down as they were by knapsacks filled with the preposterous impedimenta feminine foresight had provided.

The men's backs bulged out with such a pack of supplies that when the regiment halted each man was forced to kneel and let a comrade take off or put on his knapsack. And then the march through the streets—every man known to scores in the throng! The brisk, high-stepping drum corps rat-a-tatting at intervals; then tempests of cheers, flashing banners and patriotic symbols at every window; tears, laughter, humorous cries, jokes, sobbing outbreaks. The whole city was in march as the Caribees reached the thronged main thoroughfare. Ready hands relieved the soldiers of their burden as the line filed in sight of the Governor, who had come to speed the parting braves.

Lads and lasses made merry with the elated warriors.

The muskets were turned into bouquet-holders, and the first move toward real war took on the air of a floral *fête*. There were popping corks and sounds of convivial revelry that made the scene anything but warlike. Jack, in a cluster of his town cronies, caught sight of his mother at one of the windows of the Parthenon Hotel. He wafted her a joyous kiss, pretending not to see the tears falling down her cheeks. Olympia was not apparently very deeply affected. She made her way through the crowd to her brother's side, and with an air of the liveliest interest demanded:

"Jack, what have you in your knapsack ? Let me see."

"O Polly, it's such a job to close it! What do you want ? It is harder to manage than a Saratoga trunk. I can't really stuff another pin or needle in, so pray keep what you have for my furlough."

"No, I am not going to put anything in." She bent over while Barney Moore, one of Jack's Acredale comrades, gallantly loosed the straps. She searched carefully through the divers articles, taking everything out, Jack looking on ruefully while his companions gathered about in vague curiosity. When she had removed and restored everything she arose, saying: "I feel easier now. I merely looked to see if that marshal's *báton* I have heard so much about was there. I shall feel easy in my mind now, because a *báton* in your baggage would have made you too adventurous."

There was a great shout of laughter as the fun of the incident flashed upon the listeners, many of whom had heard the ingenuous Jack often in other days sighing for war, and the chance that Napoleon said every man had of finding a marshal's *báton* in his knapsack. Jack bore the banter very equably, knowing that Olympia was rather striving to keep his spirits up and divert him from the tears in his mother's eyes than indulge her own humor. Indeed, most of the gayety at this moment was contributed by those whose hearts were heaviest. The consecrated priesthood of patriotism must see no weakness in those left behind. The only son, now brought face to face with the meaning and consequence of his rashly seized chance for glory, must not be reminded that perhaps a grave lay beyond the thin veil of the near future; must not be reminded that heavy hearts and dim eyes were left behind, feeding day by day, hour by hour, on terror and dread, unsupported by the changing scenes, the wild excitement, and the joyous vicissitudes of the soldier's life. It was a cruel comedy acted every day between 1861 and 1865. They laughed who were not gay, and they seemed indifferent who were fainting with despair. The courage of battle is mere brutish insensibility compared with the abnegation of the million mothers who gave their boys to the bestial maw of war.

The harrowing ceremonial of parting is ended. The train moves slowly out of the station, and a murmur of sobs and cheers echoes until it is far beyond the easternmost limits of the city. After a journey of two days and a night the train reached Philadelphia. Jack was all eyes and ears for the spectacle the country presented. In every station through which the regiment passed crowds welcomed the blue-coats. Women fed them, or those who seemed in need, thinking, perhaps, of their own distant darlings receiving like tenderness from the stranger.

In Philadelphia the regiment marched across the city to resume its journey. It was a cold spring night, and the regimental quartermaster and commissary had made no provision for the men. Indeed, as the observant Jack afterward learned, it was part of the plan of the groups that first began to create great fortunes during the war to make the soldiers pay for their rations *en route* to the seat of war, or depend upon the charity of citizens along the railway lines. The Government paid for the supplies just the same, while the money went into the pockets of contractors and quartermasters. After a weary tramp through what seemed to the soldiers the biggest city in the world, the regiment, with blistered feet, hungry and cross, were halted before a long, low wooden building, through whose rough glass windows cheerful lights could be seen. A rumor spread that they were to have a hot supper, and, sure enough, they were marched in, dividing on each side of four long tables that stretched into spectral distance, in the feeble glimmer of the oil-lamps hanging from the ceiling. Most of the men in Jack's company, at least, were gently nurtured, but the steaming oysters, cold beef, and generous " chunks " of bread, filled their eyes with a magnificence and their stomachs with a gentle repletion no banquet before or after ever equaled. The feast was set in the same place during four years, by the Sanitary Society, I think, but the memory of that homely board, plenteously spread, is in the mind of many a veteran who faced warward during the conflict.

CHAPTER VI.

ON THE POTOMAC.

THE next morning, when the men debarked to march through Baltimore, every one was on the *qui vive* to fasten in his memory the scene of the shameful attack upon the soldiers of Massachusetts on the 19th of April. But, as the line marched proudly down Pratt Street, there were no signs of the hostile spirit that made Baltimore a center of doubt and suspicion in the North for many a day afterward. It was, however, when the train dashed out from among the hills to the northwest of the sheet of water behind the capitol that the Caribees glued their eyes to the panes in awe not unmingled with delight. No American will ever look upon that imperial dome again with the sensations that filled the breasts of those who first saw its rounded outlines in the war epoch. What the ark of the covenant was to the armies that marched in the wilderness, or the cross of St. Peter to the pilgrims approaching Rome, that the great dome, towering cloudward in the perpetual blue, was to the wondering eye of the soldier as his glance first fell upon it; that it was for months—yes, ever after—on the plains of Arlington and in the deadly exhalations of the Chickahominy. Every one

looked anxiously to see signs of war—indeed, since leaving
Baltimore, there was a delicious feeling of suspense—as the
train shot over embankments or skirted the deep pine woods.
Perhaps an adventurous rebel vanguard might attack them.
Perhaps they might have the glory of fighting their way to
the beleaguered capital. Perhaps Father Abraham might
come out and smile benignantly at them for a brave deed
well done. Faces flushed and eyes sparkled in the delightful anticipation; and some of the ardent spirits, more eager
than the others, loaded their muskets to be ready ! But, beyond the Federal picket-post at the stations, no sign of war
was seen, nor much sign of hostilities, such as the vivid
fancies of the raw young warriors conjured.

But now the train was at rest, and the officers—who had
not been seen during the journey—turned out in resplendent
plumery. The station—in those days a tumble-down bar-
rack—was already crowded with soldiery. The Caribees
were aligned along the track, the officers so bewildered by
the confusion that it was by a miracle some of the groups of
moving men were not run over by the backing engines.
After an interminable delay, the band set up "We're coming
down to Washington to fight for Abraham's daughter!" and
with exuberant joy a thousand pairs of legs kept brisk step
and elastic movement to the inspiriting strain. Now the
longing eyes see the circumstance and even some of the pomp
of war. The regiment debouches into Pennsylvania Avenue,
under the very shadow of the Capitol, which looks sadly
shabby and disproportioned to the eyes that had an hour or
two before opened in such admiration at the first view. But
there is no time for architectural criticism. They are moving down the avenue toward the White House, toward the
home of that patient, kindly, sorely-tried ruler—the Democ-
ritus of his grisly epoch. The Caribees excite none of the
sensation here they have been accustomed to. The streets
are not crowded, and the few civilians passing hardly turn
their heads. Mounted orderlies dash hurriedly, with hideous
clatter of sabre and equipments, across the line of march,
through the very regiment's ranks, answering with a dis-

dainful oath or mocking gibe when an outraged shoulder-strap raised a remonstrating voice. At Fourteenth Street the Caribees were halted until the colonel could take his bearings from headquarters, just around the corner. The wide sidewalks were dense with bestarred and epauleted personages in various keys of discussion. Jack and his crony, Barney Moore, studied the scene in wonder. Their company was halted exactly at the corner of Fourteenth Street and Pennsylvania Avenue, and the two were standing at Willard's corner.

"I wonder if the President just stands and throws the stars down from that balcony?" Jack said, as the crowd of brigadiers thickened before the hotel door. "What on earth are they all doing here?"

"Oh, they come to make requisition on General Bacchus; he's the commissary-general of the brigadiers—don't you know?" Barney said, innocently.

"General Bacchus? Barney, you're crazy—there's no such officer in the army—I know all the names—you mean General Banks, don't you?"

"Oh, no, I'm not mistaken—General Bacchus has been selected to deal out the *esprit de corps!*"

"*L'esprit de corps?* Barney, you're certainly tipsy. I'm ashamed of you!"

"Yes, the spirit of that corps, as you can tell from the whiffs that come this way, is the whisky-bottle. Bacchus presides over that spirit. One would think you'd never read an eclogue of Virgil—you're duller than a doctor of divinity's after-dinner speech! A tutor's joke is the utmost wit you ought to bear."

"And so you call that a joke?"

"Well, it isn't a cough, a song. an oath, or—or anything old Oswald would say, so it must be a joke."

"Well, in that sense it may pass, like a tipsy soldier without the countersign."

"Oh, come now, Jack, these stars are really dazzling you!"

"Not but I'll make you see some that will dazzle you, if you don't treat your superior more respectfully."

4

"Oh, the punch you think of giving me wouldn't solve
this star problem; it requires to be made in the old—the
milky way."

But Barney's astral jokes were brought to a period by
the sharp note of the bugle, as Colonel Oswald, very important under the eye of so many big-wigs, magnificently
ordered the march. The regiment passed up the steep hill,
out Fourteenth Street—then a red clay thoroughfare of sticky
mire with only here and there a negro's shanty where the
palaces of the rich rise to-day. The men learned something
of their future enemy, Virginia mud, as they climbed the
red gorge and debouched on Meridian Hill, where, presently, an aide-de-camp marked the ground assigned the regiment, and the real life of the soldier began. How tame to
tell, but how "imperial the hour" when these one thousand
lads first went on guard! Yes, the fact was now before
them. They were no longer segregated atoms. inert, inef-
fective, eccentric. They were part of that mighty bulwark
of blood and iron that stood between law and rebellion,
between the nation's heart and the assassin dagger of dis-
union.

How proud and glad and manly they felt, these bright-
eyed boys—for boys they mostly were; not a hundred in the
regiment had seen their five-and-twentieth year. One razor
would have been ample for the beards of the whole battalion. And oh, the nameless, the intoxicating sense of soli-
darity as they swept the vast reach of hillsides, and saw the
white tents in brooding immensity on either hand! Yes,
yonder, far across the wondrous belt of water, touching loyalty and rebellion in its mighty rush seaward, they could distinguish the cities of canvas on the distant Virginia shore.

"It makes a fellow feel as Godfrey's hosts felt when they
came in sight of the Bosporus, and the hordes of the Sara-
cens on the plains of the Hellespont," Jack said, exultingly,
as Barney stood on a pile of camp equipages above him, surveying the quickening spectacle.

"I don't know how Godfrey's fellows felt, Jack, but it *do*
make a man feel kinder able to do something with so many

near by to lend a hand. But, stars and garters ! what a head
it must take to manage all these ! Fair and square, now,
Jack, you feel the fires of military genius in your big head
—do you think that you could disentangle this enormous
coil—put each corps, division, and regiment, in its proper
place—at a day's notice ? "

"Oh, I couldn't perhaps do it just to-day; but give me
time ! "

" Yes, I'll give you to the age of Methuselah, and then if
you can manage it I shall not lose faith in you."

" Come, men, the tents must be up before dark. Sergeant
Sprague, your squad has five tents for its detail. You'll find
axes and tools at the quartermaster's wagon on the hill yonder ! " It was the captain who spoke, and, an instant later,
the plot of ground, perhaps an acre and a half in area, was
a scene of rollicking labor. Each company had a street, the
tents—calculated to hold four each, but the number varied,
going up often as high as six—faced each other, leaving room
enough for the company to march in column or in line between the white walls. As the regiment would be presuma-
bly some time on the ground, the canvas tents rested on the
top of a palisade of logs cut in the neighboring woods.
These were five feet or more in length, and when driven
into the ground a foot, and banked by the sticky clay, served
excellently as walls upon which to rest the A tents. Two
berths, sometimes four, were fastened laterally on these
walls, frames running up to the center of the A held the
guns, while lines stretched across from above served as
wardrobes for such garments as could be hung up.

All this manoeuvring for space in such close quarters was
great fun for lads accustomed to roomy houses, and careless,
almost to slovenliness, in the matter of keeping things in
place. Absurd as these details may seem, they were all
parts, and very important parts, in the life and training of
that mighty host that carried the destiny of the country in
its discipline during four years. There was rigid inspection
of quarters every Sunday morning, and during the week the
non-commissioned officers were expected to see that cleanli-

ness was not intermitted. The company "street" was "policed" every morning after breakfast, swept and garnished, that is, with the care of a Dutch housewife. Order is the first law of the soldier as well as of Heaven, and many a careless lad brought from his four years' drill method and painstaking that made him of more value to himself and his neighbors.

Personal traits, too, could be divined in these toy-like interiors. The regulations prescribed the arrangement of the "bunks," blankets folded, knapsacks laid at the head of the bed, accoutrements burnished until, at first sight, the four guns in the rack seemed to be a mirror for the orderly spirit of this thrifty grot. The shining plates, cups, and spoons, would have done no discredit to the most energetic housewife, as they hung from pegs either above the bunks or along the wall. If running water were not accessible, every tent had a tin basin for the morning ablution, each soldier taking turn good-humoredly. The household duties were scrupulously observed, each man assuming his *rôle* in the complicated *ménage*.

It was fully a week before the Caribees were installed ready for Sunday inspection, as no exigency was permitted to interfere with morning and afternoon drill, guard-mount, and parade. Battalion and brigade drill, too, were new diversions for the Caribees, as now, camped near other troops, these more complicated movements were part of the regiment's allotted duty. After they were sufficiently trained in this they were to take part in a grand review by the general-in-chief, when the President, the Secretary of War, and all the great folks in Washington rode out to witness the spectacle.

There was no time for dullness. Every hour had its duty, and these soon became second nature to the zealous young warriors. Such rivalry to best master the manual, to hold the most soldierly stature in the ranks, to detect the drill-sergeant when, to test their attention, he gave a false command! And then the coronal joy of a reward of merit for efficiency and alertness on guard! The rapture the bit

of paper brought, and the exultation with which the hero
thus signalized went off to town for the day, wandered
through the waste of streets, stood before Willard's and admired in awe and wonder the indolent groups from whose
shoulders gleamed one and sometimes two stars! One day
Jack and Barney, walking in Fifteenth Street, saw a stout
man, with no insignia to indicate rank or station, coming
out of the headquarters hurriedly. He walked to the edge
of the pavement, and, looking up and down, seemed disconcerted. Noticing the two lads, he came to where Jack was
standing in a preoccupied way, and the two saluted decorously. He returned the salute and asked:

"Sergeant, are you on duty?"

"No, sir; I'm on leave for the day."

"Ah, good; my orderly was here a moment ago, but I
don't see him anywhere. Would you mind taking this telegram to the War Department, through the park yonder?"

He gave Jack an envelope and hurried back into the
building as the two lads started with alacrity across the
street.

"I've seen that chap before, somewhere," Barney said,
panting with the rapid pace.

"He's a staff officer, I suppose, not very high rank, for
he only had a blouse on. General officers always wear
double-button frocks even if they don't carry the insignia."

The War Department was easy of access, an old building
not unlike Jack's own home in Acredale. He asked the sentry at the door where his envelope was to be delivered. The
man looked at it, pointed to a closed door, and Jack, receiving no response to his knock, entered. Three men were in
the room. One was seated at a vast desk with papers, maps,
dispatches, and books piled in disheartening confusion, within reach of his hand. Behind him a young captain in uniform sat writing. But the figure that fixed Jack's reveren-
tial attention was half sprawling, half lying over the heaped-
up impediments of the big desk. The young soldier caught
sight of the serious, sad face, the wistful humorous eyes, and
he knew, with a thrill through all his body and an adoring

throb in his breast, that it was the President—hapless heritor of generations of disjointed time. All thought of his errand, all thought of place and person, faded as he realized this presence. How long he would have remained in this mute adoration there is no telling. The restless, keen eyes looked up sharply and a dissonant, imperious, repellent voice jerked out:

"Well, my man, what is it?"

Without a word Jack handed him the envelope, and with a sort of reverence to the tall figure whose face was turned kindly toward him he backed to the door.

"O Barney, I've seen the President!"

"Seen the President! No? Oh! Why could not I have gone in with you? It's always my luck."

"No; it was my luck. But take heart. He will come out pretty soon, and we'll loaf about here. Perhaps we can see him as he goes back to the White House yonder."

But though they waited far into the afternoon, forgetting their dinner in the impulse of homage, they did not catch sight of the well-known figure, for the President's way to the Secretary's room was a private one, and when he went away the boys of course could not see him. But Jack's good fortune was the talk of the regiment for many a day, and for months when the fellows of the Caribee got leave they lingered expectantly about the modest headquarters, hoping that a missing orderly might bring them Jack Sprague's proud distinction of seeing the President face to face. On the grand review, a few days later, Jack and his crony were reminded of the encounter at headquarters, for the man who had given the envelope to carry to the war office was riding a splendid horse next to the President. Two stars glittered on his shoulder now, and as he answered the cheers that saluted the group, the young men saw that it was General McDowell, the commander of the forces. The President rode along the lines, with a kindly wistfulness in the honest eyes that studied with no superficial glance the long line of shouting soldiery. He was not an imposing figure in the sense of cavalier bravery, but no man that watched as he moved in the glittering group, conspicuous by his somber black and high hat, ever forgot the melancholy, rapt regard he gave the ranks, as at an easy canter he passed the fronts of the squares or sat solemnly at the march past that concluded the review.

CHAPTER VII.

THE STEP THAT COSTS.

WHAT between the doings of the camp and the daily visit to Washington, "soldiering" grew into an enchanting existence for the young warriors of the Caribee. Their quarters were on the high plateaus north and west of the city—which were in those days shaded slopes, that made suburban Washington a vale of Tempe. In the streets they saw bedizened officers, from commanders of armies down to presidential orderlies. In the Senate and House they heard the voices of men afterward potent in public councils.

What an exuberant, vagrant life it was! The blood warms and the nerves tingle after the tensions and heats of a quarter of a century as those days of sublime vagabondage come back. The melodious morning calls that waked the sleepy, lusty young bodies ; the echoing bugle and the abrupt drum ! And then the roll-call, in the misty morning when the sun, blear and very red, rose as if blushing, or apoplectic after the night's carouse ! It was an army of poets—of Homers—that began the never monotonous routine of these memorable days, for the incense of national sympathy came faint but intoxicating to the soldier's nostrils in the visits of great statesmen, the picnics of civilians, the copious descriptive letters of correspondents and the daily scrawls from far-away valleys, where fond eyes watched the sun rise, noted the stars, to mark the special duties their darlings were doing in the watches of the night. And then the mad music of cheers when the news came that the young

McClellan in West Virginia had scattered the adventurous
columns of Lee, capturing guns, men, and arms, and forever
saving the great Kanawha country to the Union! And in
Kentucky the rebels had been outmanœuvred; while in Missouri the glorious Lyon and the crafty Blair had, one in the
Cabinet, the other in the camp, routed the secret, black, and
Janus-like rabble of treason and anarchy.

To feel that he was part of all this; that, at rest in the
iron ring girdling the capital, he was might in leash; that
to-morrow he would be vengeance let loose—this was the
sustaining, exulting thought that made the volunteer the
best of soldiers. His heart was all in the glorious ardor
for action. Night and morning he looked proudly at the
sacred ensign waving lightly in the summer breeze, and he
remembered that the eyes of Washington had rested on the
same standard at Valley Forge; that the sullen battalions
of Cornwallis had saluted it at Yorktown.

It was a beautiful ardor that filled the young hosts that
waited in leash on the green hills of the Potomac those
months of turmoil, when Scott and McDowell were straining the crude machinery of war to get ready for the vital
lunge. Jack and his Acredale squad, as the college fellows
were called, lived in a perpetual dream, from which the
hard realities of drill, now six hours a day, could not waken
them. In days of release they scoured the Maryland hills,
secretly hoping that an adventurous rebel picket might appear and give them occasion to return to camp decked with
preluding laurels. Mile after mile of the charming woodland country they scoured, their hearts beating at the appearance of any animate thing that for a brief, intoxicating moment they could conjure into a rebel advance post.
But, beyond wan and reticent yokels, engaged in the primitive husbandry of this slave section, they never encountered
any one that could be counted overt enemies of the cause.
Money was plenty among these excursive groups, and they
were welcomed in Company K with effusive outbreaks by
their less restive comrades.

As July wore on, the signs of movement grew. Regi-

ments were moved away mysteriously, and soon the Caribees were almost alone on Meridian Hill. Jack was filled
with dire fears that the commanding officer, having discovered the incompetency of Oswald, feared to take the Caribees
to the front. Something of the rumor spread through the
regiment, and if, as reputed, "Old Sauerkraut" (this was the
name he got behind his back) had spies in all the companies,
the adage about listeners was abundantly confirmed. In the
secrecy of Jack's tent, however, the subject was freely discussed. Nick Marsh, the poet of the class, as became the
mystic tendencies of his tribe, was for poisoning the detested
Pomeranian—Oswald was a compatriot of Bismarck, often
boasting, as the then slowly emerging statesman became
more widely known, that he lived in his near neighborhood.
Marsh's suggestion fell upon fruitful perceptions. Bernard
Moore—Barney, for short—was to be a physician, and had
already passed an apprenticeship in a pharmacy, coincident
with his college term in Jack's class.

"By the powers of mud and blood, Nick, dear, I have
it!"

"Have what, Barney, me b'y ?" Nick asked, mimicking
Barney's quaintly displaced vowels.

"Why, the way to get rid of Old Schnapps and Blitzen—
more power to me!"

"All the power you want, if you'll only do that; and
your voice will be as sweet as 'the harp that once in Tara's
halls—'"

"Never moind the harp—Sassenach—here's what we
can do. Tim Hussey is Oswald's orderly; he and I are good
friends. I know a preparation that will turn the sauerkraut
and sausages, that Oswald eats so much of, into degluted fire
and brimstone, warranted to keep him on the broad of his
back for ten days or a fortnight. Will ye all swear secrecy ?"

"We will! We will!"

"On what ?"

"On the double crown on your head," Jack answered,
solemnly, "which you have often told us was considered a
sign that an angel had touched you—I'm sure nothing could

be more solemn than that. It isn't every fellow that can get an angel to touch the top of his head."

"No; most fellows can consider themselves lucky if an angel touches their lips—or heart," Barney cried, naïvely.

"Well, never mind that sort of angel now, Barney," Nick said, pettishly; "I notice that you always bring up with something about the girls, no matter what the subject we set off on. It's the jalap—isn't that what it's called ?—we want to hear about."

"There isn't enough poetry or sentiment in the two o' ye to fill a wind-blown buttercup. No wonder ye don't care to talk of the gurls—they'll have none of ye."

"We'll be satisfied if they'll have you, Barney. I'm sure that's magnanimous. But if your jalap takes as much time in working Old Schnapps as you take in explaining it, the war will be over, and we shall have seen none of it."

"It's too great a conception to be hastily set forth. Give me time. I'll lay a guinea that Oswald goes to the hospital before this day week. Let us see. This is the 14th; before the 20th—" and Barney gave the barrel of his gun, near him, a furtive wipe with his coat-sleeve.

"Barney, if you'll do that, I'll gather every four-leaved clover between here and Richmond to give you; and, what's more, if I die I'll leave you my bones to operate."

"Ah, Nick, dear, I'd rather have your little finger living than all the possessions of your father's bank. If you were dead—" And honest Barney seized the poet's hand sentimentally.

"Come, come, fellows, what sort of soldiering do you call this ? You remind me of two school-girls," Jack remonstrated, as in duty bound to keep up the warrior spirit.

"Yer acquaintances among females being chiefly of the silly sort, it's no wonder we remind you of the only things you can look back on without blushing," Barney retorted; and a neighbor poking his head in the door to learn the cause of the hilarity, the conspirators sallied out for a jaunt until parade-time. Now, what means Barney employed, or whether he had any handiwork in what befell, it does not fall to me to say, but this is what happened: A market hawker came into camp the next morning and went straight to the big marquee tent where Colonel Oswald stood, in all the bravery of a new broadcloth uniform with spreading eagles on the shoulders. The savory fumes of hot sauerkraut aroused the warrior from his reveries, and he asked, in vociferous delight:

"*Was haben sie? Kohlen, nicht wahr—sauerkraut—das is aber schon?*"

"Yes, mein golonel, I hof cabbage und sauerkraut und"—looking about circumspectly—"*etwas schnapps aus Antwerpen gebracht?*"

The "golonel's" eyes glistened and he made a motion for the vender to go to the rear of the marquee. Passing through from the front, he met him at the rear, and the bargain was hastily concluded, Marsh secreting three portly bottles in his chest, and turning the edibles over to Hussey to store in the larder. There had been a good deal of uneasiness in camp over rumors of cholera, yellow fever, and other dismal epidemics. When, therefore, the evening after the colonel's purchase the regimental surgeon was summoned in alarm, it was instantly believed in the regiment that "Old Sauerkraut" was stricken with cholera. He at first suffered hideous pains in the stomachic regions. This was followed by a raging thirst, and, unknown to the physician, the three bottles of schnapps were quite emptied. On the fourth day the poor man, very woe-begone, but now suffering no pain, was carried to the hospital, and the next day, as the campaign was about to begin, he was sent North, to leave room near the field for those who should be wounded in the coming engagement.

Company K was drilling on the wide plateau between the camp and the highway when the ambulance bearing the afflicted officer came slowly over the road worn through the greensward. Hussey sat solemnly on the seat with the driver, and as the vehicle reached the company, standing at rest, Barney Moore in the rear rank spoke up:

"Tim, is the poor colonel no better?"

"Divil a betther; it's worse he's intirely. God be good till 'im!"

Neither Jack nor Nick Marsh dared trust himself to meet the other's eyes as the helpless chief disappeared down the hillside, while Barney entered into an exhaustive treatise on the symptoms of cholera and the liability of the most robust to meet sudden disaster in this malarious upland, circumvallated by ages of decaying matter in the damp swamps on every hand. But when, an hour later, Company K's whole street was aroused by peal on peal of Abderian laughter, Jack and Nick were found helpless in their bunks, and Barney was engaged in presenting a potion to settle their collapsed nerves!

"Well, haven't I won the guinea, now? It cost me just twice that. If ye's have a spark of honor ye'll pay your just dues, so ye will," Barney said, in the evening, returning from parade, where Lieutenant-Colonel Grandison officiated as commander, to the unconcealed delight of all but the Oswald parasites among the officers.

"Don't say a word, Barney—to whom the medicos of mythology and all the wizards of antique story are clowns and mountebanks—you shall have the guinea or its equivalent."

"Twenty-one shillings gold, bear in mind. Yer father's a banker, ye ought to know that!"

"I do. You shall have the twenty-one shillings in the shinplasters of the republic."

The colonel had been routed none too soon. The very next morning, when the Caribees "fell in" for roll-call, the orderly received a paper from the commander's orderly which read, "Tents to be struck at twelve o'clock and the men ready to march, with ten days' rations."

At last! All the future, glowing with heroism, exciting with the march, the attack, the battle—ah! what after? With something of joy and regret the comely tents, that had given them home and harbor, were taken down, folded in precise line, and carried away for storage—for in the field the ranks were to bivouac in the open air. Such gay-

ety ; such jokes ; such bravado ; and augury of the to be !
And the rumors ! Telephones, had they been invented;
stenographers, had they been present in legion, could not
have kept track of the momentous tales that were instantly
bruited about. General Scott was going to lead the army in
person. His charger had been seen before the headquarters.
The rebels were going to be swooped up by another such
famous dash as the flank march from Vera Cruz to the plateau of Mexico ! Then came a numbing fear that Beauregard's bragging host had fled, and that the movement would
turn out a tedious stern chase to Richmond. In the agony
of all this Jack, returning from a "detail" to the quartermaster's tent, heard his name shouted where his tent had been.
He hurried to the spot and Nick saluted him with the cry—

"Here, Jack, are two recruits who declare they must enter
Company K."

His gun was on his arm and his knapsack on his back,
but only the realization that a score of eyes were upon him
saved Jack from dropping limply on the ground, as, looking
in the group, he saw Dick Perley and Tom Twigg grinning
ingratiatingly at him.

"Where—how in the name of all that's sacred did you
get here ?" he gasped.

"Why, we enlisted for drummers in the Caribees, but the
recruiting officer told us as we were eighteen we could carry
muskets if we wanted to. We do want to, and we're going
to come into Company K."

They looked him confidently in the face as Dick repeated
this evidently long-practiced explanation. It would not do
to take them to task before the company. Jack waited until
the rest were scattered, and then, leading the boys aside, said,
sternly:

"Don't you know you can be put in prison for this ?
You have run away from your parents and guardians. No
one had a lawful right to enlist you. I shall send for
the provost marshal and have you put in prison until
your parents can come and get your enlistment an-
nulled."

Appalled by Jack's stern manner as much as by his words, the two lads began to whimper and expostulate tearfully. They had trusted to his ancient friendship. They could have gone into any other regiment, but they had enlisted to be with him. Whatever happened, they were soldiers, and, if Tom Twigg wasn't eighteen until September, it was perfectly lawful for him to enlist as a drummer. Perley was eighteen in April last, and he was a soldier in spite of all that Jack could do. Jack was deeply perplexed. What could be done? If he attempted to put the machinery of reclamation in order, the boys would be subjected to all sorts of vicissitudes, prisons, everything distressing and demoralizing to tender youth.

"Do they know at home what you have done?" Jack asked, doubtingly.

"Yes," Dick said, noting with boyish quickness the inde-cision in Jack's troubled face. "I sent a letter to Aunt Pliny, from New York, telling her we were soldiers, and that we were happy and well."

"You impudent young scamp—to write that to your best friend! Don't you know it will kill her?"

Dick had no answer for this, and looked perplexedly at Tom, who was lost in admiration of a neighboring group engaged in athletic exercises. He felt rather than heard the question put by the Mentor, and observing Dick's discomfiture, stammered:

"It didn't kill your mother when you went for a soldier, I guess."

The astute young rascal had hit upon the weak place, and Jack stood in anxious doubt wondering what to do. An aide that he recognized from division headquarters rode past at the moment and Jack turned to watch him. He leaped from his horse at the colonel's tent. Jack again looked at the boys. They were lost in delight at the scene and oblivious of the debate going on in their guardian's mind.

"Stay here till I come back," he said, authoritatively, and strode off to Grandison's tent. As he reached it the major, McGoyle, was entering, and Jack waited until that officer should come out. He came presently, and Colonel Grandison with him. Jack saluted, and stated his dilemma to the commander, who listened with amused interest.

"I don't see that anything can be done now, Jack. I'm just about leaving the regiment. I have been assigned to General Tyler's staff during the campaign. McGoyle takes command of the regiment. He will need orderlies, and the boys can serve with him until we can get time to look into the business. I will settle the matter with him, and if you will write a telegram to the lad's family I will have it sent as I go to headquarters."

Jack's relief and gratitude were best seen in the brightening eye and the more buoyant movement that succeeded the heaviness and agitation of his first impression. The boys' coming would weigh upon him every minute until he was in some sort relieved of even passive complicity. He would feel that the kind-hearted " Pearls," as the aunts were often called, would look upon him as having led the truants into the army. But Grandison's interposition had shifted from him a weighty anxiety. The boys would not be left friendless and irresponsible in the turbulent streets of Washington. Nor would they, as orderlies, be in continuous or inextricable danger in battle—for whereas the soldier in the line must keep in ranks even when not in actual battle, with the enemy's missiles as destructive as in the charge or combat, the orderlies may take advantage of the inequalities of ground and natural objects. Jack explained something of this to the young Marlboroughs, and was fairly irritated at the crest-fallen look that came into their eager, shining faces when they comprehended that they were not to be with their hero.

"But you couldn't be in the company in any event. You look more like rebels than soldiers, with your gray jackets and trousers"—for the boys still wore their Acredale uniform, an imitation of the West Point cadet's costume. "We shall be on the march in a few minutes, and there is only one of two things to be done. Remain here in the 'unassigned' camp, where you may be transferred into any regiment in the service that needs recruits; or go, as Colonel Grandison has very kindly consented to have you, as orderlies or clerks."

The very possibility of being sent into some unknown regiment was a terror so great that the other alternative became less odious to the boys, and they trotted after Jack, as he stalked moody and distracted to Major Mike McGoyle's tent, now the only habitable spot left where a few hours before a symmetrical little city had stood.

"And so ye want to be solgers, me foine b'yes? Well, well, 'tis fitter for yer mothers' knees ye are, with yer rosy cheeks and curling locks. It's a poor place here for yer bright oies and soft hands, me lads; but I'm not the wan to throw the dish after th' milk when it's spilt!"

He stroked the bared heads of the blushing lads, and, turning to their unhappy sponsor, he added with official brevity: "I will put Twiggs's son at me papers in the adjutant's office. Young Pearley can remain with your company until I make out a detail for him."

It was impossible for Jack to sustain the *rôle* of frowning displeasure as Dick skipped back with him to the company. He remembered his own delight three months before, even with the haunting thoughts of his mother's reproaches to dampen his ardor, and he was soon dazzling the neophyte with the wonders that were just about to begin.

It was the afternoon of the 16th of July, and the hillsides, which the day before were covered with tents as far as the eye could see on every hand, were now blue with masses of men, while other masses had been passing on the red highways since early morning, taking the direction of the Potomac bridges.

CHAPTER VIII.

AN ARMY WITH BANNERS.

IT has always seemed to me that the life, the routine, the many small haps in the daily function of a soldier, which in sum made up to him all that there was in the *devoir* of death, ought to be read with interest by the millions whose kin were part of the civil war, as well as by those who knew of it only as we know Napoleon's wars or Washington's. For my part, I would find a livelier pleasure in the diary of a common soldier, in any of the great wars, than I do in the confusing pamphlets, bound in volumes called history. I like to read of war as our Uncle Toby related it. I like to know what two observing eyes saw and the feelings that sometimes made the timidest heroes—sometimes cravens.

For a month—yes, months—the burden of the press, the prayers of the North, had been, " On to Richmond! " Jack, through Colonel Grandison, knew that General McDowell and the commander-in-chief, the venerable soldier Scott, had pleaded and protested against a move until the new levies under the three-months' call could be drilled and disciplined. But on the Fourth of July Congress had assembled, and the raw statesmen—with an eye to future elections—took up the public clamor. They gave the Cabinet, the President, no peace until General Scott and McDowell had given way and promised the pending movement.

" Our soldiers are so green that I shall move with fear," McDowell said to the President.

" Well, they " (meaning the rebels) " are green too, and one greenness will offset the other," Lincoln responded with kindly malice. It was useless to argue further ; useless to point out that the rebels were not so " green," for the young men of the semi-aristocratic society of the South were trained to arms, whereas it was a mark of lawlessness and vulgarity to carry arms in the Puritan ranks of the North. Something of the unreadiness of the army, every reflecting soldier in the ranks comprehended, when he saw within the precincts of his own brigades the hap-hazard conduct of the quartermaster's and staff departments. Some regiments had raw flour dealt them for rations and no bake-ovens to turn it into bread ; some regiments had abundance of bread, but no coffee or meat rations. As to vegetables—beans, or anything of the sort—if the pockets of the soldiers had not been well supplied from home, the army that set out for Manassas would have been eaten with scurvy and the skin diseases that come from unseasoned food.

Now, at the very moment the legions were stripped for the march, many of them were without proper ammunition. Various arms were in use, and the same cartridge did not fit them all. Eager groups could be seen all through the brigades filing down the leaden end of the cartridge to make their weapons effective, until a proper supply could be obtained. This was promised at Fairfax Station, or Centreville, where the army's supplies were to be sent. So, in spite of the high hopes and feverish unrest for the forward movement, there was a good deal of sober foreboding among the men, who held to the American right to criticise as the Briton maintains his right to grumble. For the soldier in camp or on the march is as garrulous as a tea gossip, and no problem in war or statecraft is too complex or sacred for him to attempt the solution. Of the thirty thousand men leaving the banks of the Potomac that 16th of July there were, at a low estimate, ten thousand who believed themselves as fitted to command as the chieftains who led them.

By two o'clock the Caribees were in the line that had been passing city-ward since daylight. The sun had baked the sticky clay into brick-like hardness, and the hours of trampling, the tread of heavy teams, and the still heavier artillery, had filled the air with an opaque atmosphere of reddish powder, through which the masses passed in almost spectral vagueness. The city crowds, usually alert, when great masses of men moved, were discouraged by heat and dust, and the streets were quite given over to the military. Eager as Jack and his friends were to note the impression the march made upon the civilians, most of whom were thought to be secretly in sympathy with the rebellion, it was impossible to even catch sight of any but soldiers. Pennsylvania Avenue, when they reached it, was a billowy channel of impalpable powder. But at the Long Bridge the breeze from the wide channel of the river cleared the clouds of dust, and the men, catching glimpses of each other, broke into jocose banter. On the bridge they looked eagerly down the river, where the low roofs of Alexandria were visible, and upward on the Virginia shore where the gleaming walls of Arlington recalled to Jack far different times and scenes.

"Now we're in Jeff Davis's land," Barney called out from one of the rear files, as the company reached midway in the bridge.

"Not by a long shot," Nick Marsh cried. "Davis's land begins and ends within cannon-shot of himself. He is like the Duke of Saxe-Meiningen—he has to beg his neighbor's permission to hold battalion drill."

"He isn't so polite as the duke; he takes it without asking," Barney retorts.

"But now we are on the 'sacred soil,'" Jack cries. as the company debouched from the bridge up the steep, narrow road that seemed to be taking them to Arlington. In spite of the burning heat and the exhaustion of the three hours' march, the scene was, or rather the imagination of the men, invested each step with a sort of awe. They were at last in the enemy's territory. It had been held by the Union forces, only by dint of large numbers and strong fortifications. There wasn't a man in the company that didn't resent the fact, constantly obtruding itself on the ranks as they marched eagerly onward by every knoll, every bush in the landscape, that Union soldiers had been there before them! that their devouring eyes were not the first to mark these historic spots.

Tired as they were and burdensome as the heavy knapsacks and still heavier ammunition had become, they heard an aide give the order to bivouac with chagrin! They so longed to put undebatable ground behind them and really be where the distant coppice might be a curtain to the ene-

my! The Caribees marked with indignant surprise that,
when they had turned into a field about seven o'clock, the
long line following them pushed onward until far into the
night, and they envied the contiguity this would give the
lucky laggards to first see and engage the enemy! But they
turned-to very merrily, in this first night of real soldiering.
They were " in the field." All the parade part of military
life was now relaxed. The hot little dress coats were left
behind; there was no display. Even guard-mount was re-
duced to the simplest possible form.

With one impulse all the men—that is, all who had been
alert enough to provide pen and paper—bestowed themselves
about the candles allotted each group, and began letters
" home," dated magniloquently " Headquarters in the Field.
Tyler's Division, Sherman's Brigade, 16th July, 1861." The
imperial impulse manifested itself in these curt epistles. I
can't resist giving Jack's:

" DEAR MOTHER: How I wish you and Polly could see us
now! We are really on the march at last. The battle can't
be far off. We are not many miles from the enemy, and, if
he stands, what glorious news you will hear very soon! I
wish you could have seen us to-day. Colonel Sherman, who
is the sternest-looking man I ever saw, a regular army officer, once a professor, told the major—you know McGoyle is
commanding us now—he is a brick—Sherman told him that
the Caribees did as good marching as the regulars, who came
behind us. Dear old Mick, with his brogue and his blarney,
has won every heart in the regiment, and you may be sure
we shall see the whites of the enemy's eyes under him, which
we never should have done under that odious Hessian, Oswald—in hospital now, thank Heaven—though some time,
when I tell you the story, you will see that in this, as in
most other things, Heaven helps those who help themselves.
Taps will sound in five minutes, and I can only add that I
am in good health, glorious spirits, and unshaken confidence
that we shall return to Acredale before your longing to see
your son overcomes your love of glory. We shall return

victors, if not heroes—at least I know that you and Polly will believe this of your affectionate and dutiful son

"JACK."

Barney read one or two phrases of his composition to the indulgent ear of Jack and the poet, over which they laughed a good deal. "We are," he said, "before the enemy. I feel as our great ancestor, Baron Moore, felt at Fontenoy when the Sassenachs were over against the French lines—as if all the blood in Munster was in my veins and I wanted to spill it on the villains ferninst us."

The poet declined to quote from his epistle, and the three friends sat in the dim light until midnight, wondering over what the morrow had in store. Dick Perley listened in awe to Jack's wonderful ratiocinations on what was to come—secretly believing him much more learned in war than this General McDowell who was commanding the army. The first bugle sounded at three in the morning in the Caribees' camp, and when the coffee had been hastily dispatched, the men began to understand the cause of their being shunted into the field so early the evening before while the rear of the column marched ahead of them. The Caribees passed a mile or more of encampments, the men not yet aroused, and when at daylight the whole body was in motion they were in advance, with nothing before them but a few hundred cavalry.

A delirious expectation, a rapturous sense of holding the post of danger, kept every sense in such a thrill of anticipation that the hours passed like minutes. The dusty roads, the intolerable thirst, and the nauseous, tepid water, the blistered feet, the abraded hips, where the cartridge-box began to wear the flesh—all these woes of the march were ignored in the one impulse to see the ground ahead, to note the first sight of the enemy. It was not until four o'clock in the afternoon that the column was halted, and two companies, K and H, were marched out of the column and formed in platoons across the line of march, that the regiment learned with mortification that hitherto the route had been inside

the Union lines! They soon saw the difference in the tactics
of the march. The company was spread out in groups of
four; these again were separated by a few yards, and in this
order, sweeping like a drag-net, they advanced over the dry
fields, through the clustering pines or into cultivated acres,
and through great farm-yards.

Back of them the long column came, slowly winding
over the sandy highway which curved through the undulating land. Here and there the skirmishers—for that was
the office the two companies were now filling—came upon
signs of picket-posts; and once, as Jack hurried beyond his
group to the thicket, near a wretched cabin, a horse and rider
were visible tearing through the foliage of a winding lane.
He drew up his musket in prompt recognition of his duty,
but he saw with mortification that the horse and rider continued unharmed. Other shots from the skirmish-line followed, but Jack's rebel was the only enemy seen, when, in
the early dusk, an orderly from the main column brought
the command to set pickets and bivouac for the night. Jack
would have written with better grounds for his solemnity
if he had waited until this evening; but now there was no
chance.

The companies were the extreme advance of the army;
nothing between them and the enemy but detached pickets
of cavalry, at long distances apart, to fly back with the report of the least signs made by the rebels. These meager
groups were forbidden fires, or any evidence of their presence that might guide hostile movement, and the infantry
outposts felt that they were really the guardians of the sleeping thousands a mile or so behind them. No one minded
the cold water and hard bread which for the first time
formed the company's fare that night. Like the cavalry,
fire was forbidden them. They formed little groups in the
rear of the outer line of pickets, discussing with animation
—even levity—the likelihood of an engagement the next
day. It was the general opinion that if Beauregard meant
to fight he would have made a stand at some of the excellent points of vantage that had been encountered in the

day's march. Jack smiled wisely over these amateur guesses, and quite abashed the rest when he said:

"Beauregard is no fool. His army is massed near the point that he is guarding—Manassas Junction. You seem to think that war is a game of chance, armies fighting just where they happen to meet each other. Not at all. Our business is to march to Richmond; Beauregard's business is to prevent us. To do this he must, first of all, keep his lines of supply safe. An army without that is like a ship at sea without food—the more of a crew, the worse the situation. Of course, Beauregard had his skirmishers spread out in front of us, but, as there is no use in killing until some end is to be gained, they have got out of our way. If the spies that are in our ranks should send information that promised to give the rebels a chance to get at a big body of our men, before the whole army came up, you'd see a change of things very quick. We've got fifty thousand men, or thereabout" (Jack was wrong; there were but thirty thousand). "Now, these men are stretched back of us to Washington, fifteen miles or more, because the artillery must be guarded, and infantry only can do that. Now, suppose Beauregard finds that there is a gap somewhere between the forces stretching back, and he happens to have ten or fifteen thousand men handy? Why, he just swoops down upon us, and, if we can't defend ourselves until the rest of the army comes up, he has won what is called a tactical victory, and endangered our strategy."

"Goodness, Jack, you ought to have been commander-in-chief! You talk war like a book!" Barney cried, in mock admiration.

The war-talk went on late into the night, for the company, detached from camp, was not obliged to follow the signals of the bugles that came in melodious echoes over the fragrant fields. It was a thrilling sight as the lone watchers peered backward. The June fields for miles were dotted with blazing spires, as if the earth had opened to pour out columns of flame, guiding the wanderers on their trying way. The sleep of the night was desultory and fitful, excitement stimulating everybody to wakefulness.

CHAPTER IX.

"THE ASSYRIAN CAME DOWN LIKE THE WOLF ON THE FOLD."

THE next morning the march was resumed by daylight, the two companies remaining on the skirmish-line. The country gradually became more rugged as the route brought them near Centreville. There were no hills—a bare but not bleak champaign, mostly without houses or farms, as the North knows them. Sluggish brooks became more frequent, but none that were not easily fordable. There were no landmarks to hold the mind to the scene, nor, in case of battle, give the strategists points of vantage for the iron game. About noon, the detached groups stalking a little negligently now over the tedious plains, were startled by the unexpected.

On the green slope of a hill, a mile or more ahead, a score of little puffs of white smoke were seen, then a sharp report, and, in some places near by, the ground was broken as if by a thrust of a spear, and little scraps of clay scattered over the greensward. Then the bugle sounded a halt. A few minutes later the horsemen spread in a chain across the line of march, rode swiftly to a common center, formed in a solid group, turned to the rear and rode back of the skirmishers to the main body. Company K watched them as they galloped back, and as they reached the group at the head of the long line, a half-mile or so distant, a body of men hastened forward laden with stretchers and hospital appliances. Ah! at last! It is now real war. The bugle sounds Forward! and with an elastic spring the groups of four push dauntlessly ahead. Their eyes are fixed on the brow of the hill, separated from them by a narrow depression.

The whole line—perhaps three miles wide—but, of course, not at all regular, conforming largely to the difficulties encountered, moves down the sloping bank on a run. Before they reach the bottom they are an excellent target, and for the first time that most blood-curdling of sounds—the half-singing, half-hissing z-z-z-ip of the minie-ball—numbs the ardor of the bravest. It is such a malignant, direct, devilish admonition of murder; it comes so unexpectedly, no matter how well you are prepared, that Achilles himself would feel a spasm of fear. And when it strikes it does its work with such a venomous, exultant splutter, that there seems something animate, demoniac in it. The volley, as I said, came as the men were hurried down the hill by their own momentum and by the sharp fall in the ground. The balls passed too high or too low, but they impressed the fact on enthusiasts, who had longed for battle, that one might die for one's country and not die gloriously. It seemed such an ignoble, such a dastardly, outrageous thing, that death could come to them from unseen hands, for as yet they had not seen a soul. But now they are at the foot of the hill—though it is not correct to so call it, for it was a long, winding valley, through which ran a dancing streamlet, very welcome to the thirsty warriors when they had succeeded in breaking through the vicious natural *chevaux de frise* of blackberry-briers and nettles. But now there wasn't much time to slake thirst. The bullets had begun to come regularly; and suddenly, as Jack conducted his squad across the stream, he was startled by the exclamation, uttered rather in reverence, it seemed to him, than surprise or pain:

"My God, I'm hit!"

Yes, a fair-haired lad—one of his class—tottered a second in a limp, helpless way, and fell headlong, pitching into the little stream. Jack ran and lifted him out; but even before the hospital corps came the boy was dead. The bullet had gone quite through his heart.

However, now the first numbing terror of the bullet was changed to a sort of revengeful delight. Relinquishing any return fire for a moment, the company, with a great shout, that sounded all along its front, dashed up the hill, through the scrub-oak at the brow, and then they could see the enemy slowly retiring, a chain of them a mile or more wide. While one of the rebel ranks fired the other knelt, or lay flat upon the ground loading, where there were no natural obstacles to take shelter behind. A vengeful shout ran along the Union lines.

"Capture them—don't fire!" and with one impulse the groups fled forward so swiftly that the enemy, believing the rush only momentary, delayed too long, and in two minutes the Union line was pell-mell among them.

"Surrender!" Jack shouted to the squad just ahead of him—"surrender, or we'll blow your heads off!" and along the line for some distance to his left and right he could hear his own exultant demand echoed. There was nothing to do for the rebels, who had neglected to keep their enemies at the proper distance, but throw up their hands. Jack's squad sent back twenty-three prisoners to Major Mike, who took them in proud triumph to General Tyler, riding with the head of the column, now that the tenacity of the rebel skirmishers made it seem probable that there would be serious work. But though the firing kept up as the Union forces advanced, no obstacle more serious than the thin lines of the skirmishers revealed itself.

At dusk the bugles, moving with the captains in the rear, sounded the rally, and then the scattered groups came together in company. They were to bivouac on the spot to await their regiment when it arrived. Meanwhile, to the bitter discontent of the Caribee companies, their post of honor was taken by new troops, and they knew that next day they would march in line. They had so enjoyed the glory of the first volleys, the first deaths, and the first prissoners, that, not remembering military procedure, they resented the change as an aspersion upon their valor.

When the regiment came up, however, they forgot their mortification in the eager questioning and envious jocularities of the rest. Companies K and H were so beset that they forgot to boil their coffee, and would have gone thirsty to their dewy beds, if the other companies' cooks had not shared their rations with the gossiping heroes. As darkness fell, the sky was reddened for miles with pillars of fire, and for a time the Caribees thought it was the enemy. But Tom Twigg, who had been with the major at headquarters, explained to Jack that the army was divided into three bodies of about ten thousand men each, and that Tyler's column,

of which the Caribees were the advance, were the extreme
northern body; that they were now at Vienna, far north of
Manassas, where Schenck had been beset a month before in
his never-enough-ridiculed reconnaissance by train; that in
the morning they were to push on to Fairfax Court-House
and thence to Centreville, where the army was to come together for the blow at the rebels. Jack and his friends were
a good deal chagrined to learn that they were not as near
the enemy as the column to the south of them, whose fires
had been mistaken for Beauregard's. Though the levée
came to an end at " taps," no one felt sleepy, and the excitement banished the pains of fatigue. Major Mike, saunter-
ing through the dark lines near midnight, heard the tale
still going on in drowsy monotone, but, good-naturedly, made
no sign.

Though not given the skirmish-line next day—the 17th—
Jack was delighted to find that the Caribees led all the rest.
With them rode the commander of the brigade, Colonel
Sherman, whom the soldiers thought a very crabbed and
" grumpy" sort of a fellow. His red hair bristled straight
up and out when he took his slouch hat off, as he did very
often, for the heat was intolerable. His eyes had a merry
twinkle, however, that won the hearts of the lads as he rode
by, scrupulously striking into the fields to save the panting
and heavily laden line every extra step he could. Often, in
after-days—when Sherman had become the Turenne of the
armies—Jack, who was often heard to brag of his gift of
detecting greatness, used to turn very red in the face when
he was reminded of a saying of his on that hot July day:

" That chap is too lean and hungry to have much stomach
for a fight ; he looks better fitted for wielding the ferule than
the sword. Schoolmaster is written in every line of his face
and stamped in his pedagogue manner."

The march that day was south by a little west, and about
nine o'clock a cool morning breeze lifted the clouds of dust
far enough above the horizon to reveal the distant blue of the
mountains. The whole line seemed to come to a pause in
the enchanting, mirage-like spectacle. "The Shenandoah,"

Jack said, mopping the dust, or rather the thin coating of
mud, from his face and brow, for the perspiration, oozing at
every pore, naturally covered the exposed skin with an unpre-
meditated cosmetic.   The march to Fairfax Court-House, for
which judicial temple the curious soldier looked in vain, was
but eight miles from the point of departure in the morning, but it was two o'clock in the afternoon when the Caribees passed the hamlet, turning sharply to the right.   They
marched up the deep cut of projected railway, where, for a
time, they were shaded from the sun by the high banks.
But, emerging presently on the Warrenton pike, they saw
evidences that other columns—whether friends or foes they
couldn't tell—had recently preceded them.   Scores of the
raw and overworked were breaking down now every hour.

The dust and heat were insupportable.   Whenever the
march came near water, all thought of discipline was forgotten, and the panting, miner-like hosts broke for the inviting stream.   The officers were powerless to enforce discipline ; when these breaks happened the column was forced
to come to a halt until every man had filled his canteen—
and here is one, among the many trivial causes, that brought
about the reverses of McDowell's masterly campaign.   A
march that ought to have been made in twenty-four hours,
or thirty at the utmost, took more than three days !   One of
those days saved to the army would have enabled McDowell
to finish Beauregard before the ten thousand re-enforcements
from the Shenandoah came upon his flank at Bull Run.   But
we shall see that in proper time, for there is nothing more
dramatically timely, or untimely, than this incident in the
history of battles, unless it be Blücher's miraculous appearance at Waterloo, when Napoleon supposed that Grouchy
was pummeling him twenty miles away.

There was no provost guard to spur on the stragglers; and
when, late in the afternoon, the way-worn columns spread
themselves on the western slope of the hamlet of Centreville,
at least a third of each regiment was far in the rear.   Nearly
every man had, in the heat and burden of the march, thrown
away the provisions in his haversack, and that night ten

thousand men lay down supperless on the grateful greensward, happy to rest and sleep. Mother Earth must have
ministered to the weary flesh, for at sunrise, when the music
of the bugles aroused them, they started up with the alert
vivacity of old campaigners. Provisions, that should have
been with the column the night before, arrived in the morning. While the reinvigorated ranks were at coffee, there
was a great clatter in the rear, and presently a *cortége* of
mounted officers appeared, General McDowell among them.
Dick Perley, who was at the brigade headquarters, with
Grandison, came to the Caribees presently with great news.

The battle was to begin that very day. General Tyler
was to go forward to a river called Bull Run, where Beauregard was waiting. The whole army was to spread out like
a fan and fight him. He had seen the map on the table, and
the place couldn't be more than four miles away. Yes, they
all looked eagerly to the westward now. The mountains in
the distance rolled themselves down into lower and lower
ridges, and just about four miles ahead could be seen a range
that seemed to melt into a wide plateau fringed deeply with
scrub-oak and clusters of pine. Jack had provided himself
with a field-glass. Standing in the middle of the Warrenton pike, a fine highway, that ran downward as solid as a
Roman causeway, for four or five miles, he could see the
break made by the Bull Run River, and—yes, by the glaive
of battle!—he could see the glistening of bayonets now and
then, where the screen of woods grew thinner.

The general, too, was examining the distant lines, and
Jack took it as a good omen that Sherman grew jocose and
appeared to be making merry with Tyler, whose face looked
troubled, now that the decisive moment seemed at hand.
But the day passed, and there was no advance. It was not
until late in the evening that the cause became known. The
army had been waiting for supplies, ammunition, and what
not, that should have been on the field the day before. The
Caribees were made frantic, too, by what seemed a battle
going on to the south of them, a few miles to the left. The
camp that night was a grand debating society, every man

propounding a theory of strategy that would have edified General McDowell, no doubt, if he could have been given a *précis* of the whole. How such things become known it is difficult to guess, but every man in the columns knew that the general had planned to put forward his thirty thousand men in the form of a half-moon, covering about ten miles from tip to tip. The right or northward horn was to be considerably thicker and of more body than the left or southern. When the time came this right was to curve in like a hook and cut the ground out from the left wing of the rebel army.

This is the homely way these unscientific strategists made the movement known to each other, and it very aptly describes the formulated plan of battle, save that, of course, there were gaps between the forces here and there along this human crescent. Long before daylight Sherman's brigade, with a battery of guns and a squadron of cavalry, set out due south, leaving the broad Warrenton pike far to their right hand. Such a country as the march led into, no one had ever seen in the North outside of mountain regions—deep gullies; wastes of gnarled and aggressive oaks, that tore clothes and flesh in the passage; sudden hillocks rising conical and inconsequent every few rods; deep chasms conducting driblets of water; morasses covered with dark and stagnant pools, where the pioneers fairly picked their steps among squirming reptiles. A stream, sometimes large as a river, crawling languidly through deep fissures in the red shale, protected the left flank of the column. The cavalry was forced to hold the narrow wood-road, as the bush was hardly passable for men.

"Hi, Jack!" Barney cries, catching his breath at the edge of a muddy stream, "what sort of a place must the rebels be in if they let us promenade through such a jungle as this unopposed?"

"I have been thinking of that," Jack replies. And so had every man in the expedition—for to think was one of the drawbacks as well as one of the excellences of the soldier in the civil war. But presently, after five hours of laborious work, a halt is called. The men dive into their haversacks, and even the brackish water in the nearest sedge pond has a flavor of nectar and the invigoration of a tonic. On they tear again, the whole body pushing on in skirmish-like dispersion. Suddenly the land changes. They are climbing a rolling table-land, cleared in some places as though the axe of the settler had been at work. The march is now easier and the picket-lines are strengthened. Then a sharp volley comes, as if from the tree-tops.

The march is instantly halted. The mass, moving in a column, is deployed—that is, stretched out to cover a mile or more as it moves forward ; the cavalry divides and rides far to right and left, to see that no ambush is set to enable the rebels to sneak in behind the vast human broom, as it sweeps through the solemn aisles of the pines, now rising in vernal columns thicker and thicker. The firing is going on now in scattering volleys, and soon the wounded—a dozen or more—are carried back through the silent ranks. Joking has now ceased. Lips are compressed ; eyes glitter, and the men avoid meeting each other's gaze. It is the moment of all moments, the most trying to the soldier, when he is expecting every instant a hurricane of bullets, and yet sees no one to avenge his anguish on or forestall in the deadly work. But they have been moving forward all the time, the hurtling bullets sweeping through the leafy covering, now and then thumping into the soft pine with a vicious joyousness, as if to say to each man, "The next is for you, see how well our work is done." For these hideous missiles have a language of their own, as every man that stood fire can tell. The skirmishers are now all drawn in. The solid line must do the work at hand. No one but the commander and his confidants knew the work intended, save that to kill and be killed was the business to be done. The panting lines are on high cleared ground now, and they can see absolutely nothing but the irregular depressions that mark the channel of the Bull Run, as it rushes down to the Rappahannock. The line is moving along steadily. Looking to left and right, Jack can see the colors of three regiments, and his eye rests with pleasure on the bright, shining folds of the Caribees' dark-blue State flag spread to the breeze beside the stars of the Union. Are they to cross the river? Evidently, for the command is still "Forward, bear center, bear right." Then, square in front, where the thick, broad leaves of the oak glitter in the sun, there is seen a cylinder of steamlike smoke, with fiery gleams at the end, a crackling explosion of a hogshead of fire-crackers, then a rushing, screaming sound in their very faces, then a few rods behind a ringing, vicious explosion. They are in the very teeth of a masked battery. The Union skirmishers have been withdrawn too soon. The main line will be torn to pieces, for retreat is as fatal as advance.

"Lie down, men!" The command rings out and is echoed along the column. The guns have the range, and the enemy knows the ground. The Caribees are directly in the sweep of the artillery, and the command comes to them by company to crawl backward, exposing themselves as little as may be. Presently two brass guns are brought up behind the Caribees. The gunners have noted the point of the enemy's fire. The men point the big muzzles with intrepid equanimity, firing over the prostrate blue coats. For twenty minutes, perhaps half an hour, this is kept up; then there is silence on the hill beyond. The column rises to its feet, and at the command, "Forward!" they start with a rush and a cheer. Five hundred yards onward, and a solid mass of gray coats confront them. A volley is fired and returned; the exulting Caribees, with two lines behind them, give a loud cheer and, in an instant, the gray mass has disappeared, as if the earth had opened. The skirmish-line, advancing now, picks up a half-dozen or more wounded rebels, besides two or three who had become confused in the hasty retreat and run toward the "Yankees" instead of their own line. Jack's comrade held this conversation with one of the prisoners:

"I say, reb, what place is this?"

"Mitchell's Ford."

"Much of your army here?"

" 'Nuff to lick you uns out of your boots, I reckon."

" What did they run across the ford for, then ? "

" Oh, you'll see soon enough—when our folks get ready."

" Who's in command here ? "

" General Bonham, of South Carolina."

" How many men, about ? "

" Well, there's right smart on to a million, I reckon.
They had to cut the trees down, yonder, to get room for
'em."

The man's eyes twinkled as he gave this precise approxi-
mation ; but Barney, who had brought the humorist in,
whispered to the captain to let him have a moment's speech
with the man before he was sent away. The captain nodded,
and Barney said innocently :

" Had anything to eat to-day ? "

" Not a mouthful. The trains were all taken up with
soldiers coming from Richmond."

" Have a bit of beef—and here's a cracker or two. You
can have some coffee if the guards will let you make it."

" Old Longstreet himself would envy me now," the rebel
cried, his mouth stuffed with the cold meat and hard-tack,
almost as fresh and crisp as soda-crackers, for the contractors
had not yet learned the trick of making them out of sawdust, white sand, and other inexpensive substitutes for flour.

" Longstreet ? " Barney said, carelessly.

" Yes, that's the commander of the right wing, just below,
at Blackburn's Ford."

" Blackburn's Ford ? "

" Yes, that's a mile down, and really behind you uns, for
the run makes a big elbow to the east. I tell you what it
is, Yank, you'll see snakes right soon, for our folks are behind you."

Sure enough, a crackling to the left confirmed this, and
the captain, who had listened to Barney's adroit cross-ques-
tioning, sent the man with a note to Colonel Sherman, a
few rods in the rear. Ten minutes later the column fell into
ranks again and moved off swiftly southeastward. A march
of a mile or so brought them to a bold ridge cutting down

6

almost aslant to the clear water of the run. The skirmishers, for some reason, had not pushed ahead to explore the
ground, and the regiments, marching in close masses, came
out in a rather disorderly multitude on the ridged crest. A
hundred yards nearly below the water-course was fringed
with thick copses of oak, and the gently ascending slopes on
the western bank were completely hidden from the Union
lines. A few gaunt, almost limbless trees rose up spectrally
on the ridge, offering the compact masses neither shelter
from the sun nor security from the enemy—if there were an
enemy near.

Dick came up to Jack out of breath with great news, just
as the Caribees were aligning themselves to move forward.

"General Tyler just told Richardson"—a brigade commander—"that the rebels had retreated from Manassas, and
he (Tyler) is going to have the glory of occupying the works;
that McDowell thought the army would have to fight a big
battle to get—"

"Glory!" the group shouted, near enough to hear; and
the delightful story ran up and down the lines by a tele-
phone process that was much swifter than Edison's electric
invention. A roar of gratulatory triumph broke—a roar so
loud and inspiring that for a moment the densely packed
masses did not distinguish an ear-splitting outburst just in
front of them. But on the instant piercing shrieks among
the huddled cheerers—cries of death and agony—changed
the pæans of triumph into wails of anguish and mortal pain.
A panic—instant, unreasoning, irresistible—fell upon the
mass, a breath before so confident. A third of the regiment
seemed to wither away. The colors fell in the struggling
group in the center. Hoarse shouts, indistinguishable and
ominous, could be vaguely heard from the staff and line.

Direr still, hideous clamor of masked cannon, right in
their very faces, added the horror of surprise to the disorder
of attack, and the thick blue lines broke in irrestrainable
confusion. The terror of the unknown seized officers and
men alike. In five minutes the crest was cleared, and the
ignoble vanity, ignorance, and self-sufficiency of one man

had undone in an hour the splendid work of the commander-in-chief. A *mêlée* of miserable, disgraceful disorder ensued. The rebel sharpshooters, hurrying to the flank, poured in hurtling, murderous volleys, filling the minds of the panic-stricken mob with the idea, the most awful that can enter a soldier's mind, that his line is surrounded. Hundreds threw away guns and everything that could impede flight. Other hundreds fired wildly wherever they saw moving men, and thus aided the rebels in killing their own comrades, for it was into the supporting Union forces they directed their random shots. The fire grew every instant more bewildering. Shots came in volleys from every direction, and the helpless hordes darted wildly together—sometimes toward, instead of from the enemy. Had the rebels been as numerous as they were crafty, the brigade could have been seized *en masse*. But now Sherman is at hand with fresh regiments, others are at his heels, and the contest takes on some of the order of intelligent action. The rebels, too, are re-enforced, but the dispositions made by the Union chiefs bring the combat to equal terms. The clamor of cannon and musketry continues an hour, though the lines are now among the friendly undergrowth, and the losses are not serious. But the Caribees, with the regiment supporting them, have been blotted from the scene as a factor. For hours the scattering groups fled—fled in ever-increasing panic, and it was long after dark before the remnants of the regiment came into camp at Centreville.

Poor Jack! He gave no heed to supper that dreadful night. He threw himself on the ground, too exhausted to think and too disheartened to talk. He couldn't understand the shameful panic. The Caribees were not cowards ; every man in the regiment had longed for the battle. When under fire at Mitchell's Ford, an hour earlier than the disaster at Blackburn, all had stood firmly in place, fought with coolness, and gave no sign of fear. The volume of fire when they broke was not much greater than the Mitchell's Ford volleys. During the night Grandison came to camp and assembled the officers. He expressed his sorrow at the sudden shadow that had fallen on the fair fame of the regiment, but since the panic had not been followed, as such outbreaks often are, by the total destruction of the men, there would be abundant chance to redeem the disgrace of the day. He had himself begged the division commander to give the men another trial, and he had staked his commission on their doing such duty as would remove the tarnish of the afternoon from their banners.

The officers had been dispirited. Major Mike had raged over the field, through the woods, a very angry man indeed, belaboring the fleeing men with his sword and imploring those he couldn't reach to "come to me here. Dress on me. There's no call to be afeard. We've more men than they have, and we'll soon wallop them."

But the resounding blows on the backs of those near the officer did not give the encouraging emphasis to his appeal that captivates men whose reasoning faculties are almost gone for the moment. Before daylight on the next morning—Saturday, the 20th—the companies were called together and little addresses were made to the men by the officers. The substance of Colonel Grandison's words was imparted, and the hope expressed that when, in the course of that or the next day the regiment was again under fire, they would show that the panic of yesterday had not been cowardice. The men said nothing, and every one was glad that the light was so dim that the officers could not look in their faces, though, as a matter of fact, the shoulder-straps had shown as little fortitude as the muskets in the dispersion. All that day the forces rested, the Caribees providing themselves with new arms and equipments, or the two or three hundred who had flung their own away. During the afternoon an incident happened in the division that lessened the mortification of the Caribees. A splendid regiment and a battery of bronze guns came into the highway from the extreme of the line that was expected to take part in the battle which all knew would be opened the next morning. Every one was surprised to see the men moving without muskets and the colors wrapped in their cases.

"Where you bound for?" some one at the roadside yelled curiously.

"Our time is out; we're going home."

Then a derisive howl followed the line as it passed through the masses of the army, and remarks of an acrid nature were made that were not gratifying to the departing patriots:

"Don't you want a guard to protect you?"

"Does your mamma know you're out alone?"

"Wait till to-morrow and we'll send Beauregard's forces to see you safe home."

The men and officers looked very conscious and uncomfortable under the gamut of jeers, for word went along the line, and all along the route to the rear they passed through this clamor of contemptuous outcry.

"Well, I thought we had reached the eminent deadly pinnacle of disgrace," Barney said, with a sigh, as a group of Company K watched the considerable number taken out of McDowell's small army, "but this sight makes me feel like the man on trial for murder who escapes with a verdict of manslaughter."

CHAPTER X.

BLOOD AND IRON.

LATE at night Dick came down to Jack's bivouac with a strange tale. McDowell had come to Tyler's quarters storming with rage. He had accused that officer of disobeying orders in forcing a fight on the fords of Bull Run where he had been told to merely reconnoitre.

The staff believed that Tyler would be cashiered, for he had not only wrecked the general's plan of battle, but he had given the rebels the secret of the movement and demoralized one wing of the army by putting raw soldiers in front of masked batteries that could have been detected by proper outpost work. Then one of the staff reported a speech

Tyler had made when his troops rushed over the empty rebel breastworks and forts around Centreville. His officers were discussing the probable forces Beauregard had behind the crooked stream beyond.

"I believe we've got them on the run," Tyler said, exultingly, "from what we see here. I tell you the great man of this war is the man that plants the flag at Manassas, and I'm going through to Richmond to-night."

"Not much comfort in knowing we've got such a fool for a commander," Jack cried, thinking of the disgrace of the day before and of the small chance the regiment had under such a chief to redeem its prestige on the morrow. All personal griefs, everything but the pending battle, were driven from the men's minds as the signs of the momentous work of the morrow accumulated. The hospital corps was up in force. The yellow flag floated from an immense tent near the roadway. A great *cortége* of general officers rode away from McDowell's quarters about ten in the evening. The haversacks were filled with three days' cooked rations. One hundred rounds of ammunition to a man were dealt out to each company. Everything not absolutely necessary was ordered to the company wagons.

The talk in the camp that night was of home—of anything and everything but the dreadful to-morrow, so long looked forward to with eager hope, now regarded with uncertainty that was not so much fear as the memory of the panic at Blackburn's Ford. Jack was provided with a large atlas map of Virginia, and with the bits of information given by Dick he was able to conjecture the probable plan of the next day. The cronies of Company K listened in delight to his exposition of the action.

"Here," he said, "is the Bull Run. It makes two big elbows eastward toward us—one about four miles to the northwest of us, the other about eight miles to the southeast of that, and about four miles from our right hand here! The rebel we quizzed yesterday says that there are five fords between the Warrenton pike bridge—that's just ahead of us yonder at the end of the road we are on—the last one is McLean's Ford, at the very knuckle of the elbow that is crooked toward us a mile west of where we were yesterday. That is near the railway, which it is Beauregard's business to fight for and our business to get, for then he will have to fall back near Richmond to feed his army. Now from the railway where it crosses Bull Run near Mitchell's Ford to the Warrenton road, which Beauregard must also hold, is about nine miles. He must guard all these fords, and we must fight for any one or two of them that we need to cross by. The only problem is, whether our general is going to strike with his right arm at Mitchell's Ford, his left arm at this very Warrenton road we are on, or whether he means to butt the middle of the line of Beauregard's battle to break him into two pieces?"

"What would Frederick the Great or Napoleon do?" Nick asked, absorbed in Jack's confident predications.

"If Frederick had equal forces he would have a reserve just where we shall be in the morning—there at that point marked 'Stone Ridge,' and move a heavy mass to the southwest below McLean's Ford there, where you see the railway runs along the run for a half-mile or more. Or he would send this body to the northeast, over there where you see Sudley Springs marked in rather large letters, and he would by either one of these movements turn the enemy's flank—that is, get in behind him and force him to change front to fight, something that is rarely done successfully in battle. Napoleon would, on the contrary, mass all his best troops at the stone bridge, open the fight with every piece of artillery he could bring to bear, and in the panic send divisions ten deep across the bridge."

"Which would be the better plan?"

"Ah! that no one can say. The first is sure enough and less dangerous, if the commander is not certain of his men, because you notice that we felt excellent and confident all day, so long as we were marching forward and pushing the enemy from our path. The trial in battle is to be kept standing under fire, not sure where your enemy is; and then you noticed that our own guns behind us, sending shot and shells over us, were just as trying as the rebels'. Only soldiers of the very first class can be depended on in the Napoleon tactics. We are not soldiers of the first class; and you may be sure McDowell, who was many years in Europe, and who is a trained officer, will make use of the manœuvres best calculated to bring out whatever there is in his men. As a matter of opinion, I should say that, in view of the miserable affair on the right yesterday, he will strike out for Sudley Springs, where we shall have the rebels just as you would have me if you were at my side, held my left arm behind me, ready to break my back with your knee planted in it."

Jack was sergeant of the guard that night, and it was in the group of sentries awaiting their relief every two hours, re-enforced by his tent-mates of Company K, that these learned dissertations on war were carried on. It was a never-to-be-forgotten Saturday night to millions yet living. In Washington the President and his Cabinet sat far into the morning hours receiving the dispatches from the weary and disappointed chief—for, if Tyler had not made his miserable attempt to reach Manassas, the battle would have been fought that vital Saturday, and the result would have been another story in history. As the morning broke, red and murky, the army was up and in line, but without the usual noisy signals. The artillery-horses began to move first wherever it was possible. The heavy guns were pushed forward on the sward, to prevent the loud metallic clangor that penetrated the still air like clashing anvils. By half after six, the advance brigade, the Caribees in their old place, were within gunshot of the stone bridge.

"Ah ha, Jack! It is the Napoleonic plan!" Barney cried, as the artillery took places in front of the masses lying on the ground.

"Wait," Jack cried, owlishly. "The battle isn't fought always where the guns are loudest."

But the guns were now loud and quick. The rebels, behind a thick screen of trees, took up the challenge, and every sound was drowned in the roar of the artillery. A few far in the rear were wounded—those nearest the rebels were in the least danger, whether because the guns could not be sufficiently depressed, or because the gunners were poor hands, couldn't be determined. A breathless suspense, an insatiate craving to see, to move, to fly forward, or do anything, devoured the prostrate ranks. The firing had gone on two hours or more, which seemed only so many minutes, when to the group near General Tyler a courier, panting and dusty, rode in great excitement.

"General Tyler, the major-general has just learned that the enemy have crossed in force at Blackburn's Ford, below you. You are at once to take measures to protect your left flank."

"Ah ha, Jack; Frederick's on the other side, eh?" Barney said, as, standing near the group, these words reached their ears.

"Perhaps there are two Fredericks at work. Look yonder!" handing him his glass as he spoke.

"Thunder! our whole army is marching over there to the right, and we sha'n't even see the battle. They are four miles off. Why, what an immense army we must have! I thought this was the bulk of it, but we're not a brigade compared to that."

"Now, Barney, I feel confident that is the grand movement. Look how they fly along! The fields are as good as roads out there, and if it were not for the artillery they could make five miles an hour. Now, keep your ears open, my lad: you'll hear music off there to the northwest—music that will make Beauregard sick, if that courier's information is exact. For, don't you see, as we are placed here, with that gully to our left and the thick woods in front, we could hold this ground against six times our number."

Company K were now sent forward to the right to relieve a body of skirmishers that had been hidden on the margin of Bull Run, some distance to the westward of the stone bridge. Jack, going forward with his glass, noticed an officer among the men, but not catching sight of his face did not recognize him.

"Is that a rebel or one of our fellows?" one of the men

said, pointing to a horseman disappearing in the woods four hundred yards to the right and in front of the company, marching in a straggling line two abreast, "by the flank," as it is called. Jack took his glass to discover, but the rider had disappeared. An instant after from a knoll, Jack, glass at eye, was examining eagerly the field on the other side of the river, when a horseman suddenly shot into view, riding desperately.

"By George, it is the same man! I wonder how he crossed the stream? There must be a bridge down there among those thick trees and bushes," Jack said, excitedly.

"Are you sure, sergeant, that is the same man that was in the woods to the right there, five minutes ago?"

Jack turned; the officer was at his shoulder. He saluted respectfully, recognizing, with a thrill of joy, old Red Top, as the company called Sherman.

"Yes, colonel, it's the same man. He was in his shirt-sleeves and had a blue scarf tied about his arm. There can be no mistake; several of us saw him quite plainly."

"If that be true, we've gained a half-day's work in two minutes." He was looking diligently through the glass as he spoke, and his eye brightened as he marked the man until he disappeared. He turned to an orderly that was following at a distance leading a horse. Mounting this lightly the colonel rode to the head of the company and said in a short, decisive tone:

"Come ahead men, at a double-quick, until you strike the stream." He kept beside the men as they moved. In fifteen minutes they were at the water's edge. Then the company was deployed as skirmishers, two thirds halting where they struck the water and the rest keeping on up the bank of the river for a few hundred yards. Sherman was eying every inch of the bank until, suddenly reaching a break where fresh tracks of a horse were visible, he directed his orderly to follow, and plunged into the water. It was not up to the horses' knees from bank to bank. Riding back, his face aglow, the colonel ordered the captain to cross half his men and station them up and down on the bank where they would not be seen by the rebels on the high ground above. Then, addressing Jack, he said:

"Sergeant, select two or three trusty men. Follow the bank of the stream until you come to General Hunter's division, which may be a mile, perhaps more, to the right yonder; you can tell by the firing soon. Tell General Hunter that we have discovered a ford and shall not have to fight for the stone bridge. We shall be across in no time and take the enemy in the rear. If you can't find Hunter, give this intelligence to any officer in command. Stay."

He scribbled a line on a sheet of his order-book, saying: "This will be your authority. It's better not to write the rest for fear you should be captured. In case you are in danger tell each man with you what to say, so that there will be more chances of getting the information where it will do good; and remember, sergeant, that this news in Hunter's hands will be almost equivalent to victory. Ah!"

He paused again. Reverberating crashes came from the high grounds up the river. "You will have no trouble in finding him now. Those are Hunter's guns. Hurry."

Glowing, grateful, big with the fate of the battle, Jack had Barney, Nick, and another, whom he charged with the duty of historian, detailed for this duty of glory. The group set off with a fervent Godspeed from the company sheltered among the thick pines and oaks.

"Now, boys," Jack said, every inch the captain, "we must spread out like skirmishers. Our chief danger will be from the left, as no one will be likely to be in the water but our own men, and we must look as sharply for them as for the enemy. I will take the center; you, Barney, the left, next to me; and you, Nick, four paces farther to the left. Jack looked at his watch. It was just 9.30, Sunday morning, July 21, 1861. The crash of musketry ahead now became one unbroken roar, with a *crescendo* of artillery that fairly shook the ground the messengers were darting over, for all were on a dead run. The bushes grew thick on the hillside and their branches were stubborn as crab thorns. Hell, as Barney afterward remarked, would have been cool in comparison to the heat as the adventurers tugged and wrestled forward. Now guns were roaring on every side save the river. Behind, before, to the left, the thunders played upon the parched land. At the end of a half-hour the bullets and shells passed over the group as Jack and his squad pushed along the hilly way. Twice, commands, and even the clicking, of what Jack knew must be rebel guns sounded not twenty paces away, but, thanks to the thick bushes, the scouts passed unseen, and, thanks to the noise of battle, unheard. But now the danger is from friends, not enemies. Balls come hurtling through the trees across the stream, and in a low voice Jack bids Barney summon Nick. Then all slip down to the water's edge, and make their way painfully through the marshy swamps,.the cane-like rushes that fill the narrow valley. The run has been a fearful strain upon Nick, and at length he falls, gasping, in a clump of cat-tails.

"What is it, old fellow?" Jack cries in alarm.

"O Jack! I can't go a step farther. You go on and leave me. I shall follow when I get breath."

He was white and gasping. Barney filled his canteen from the running water, and, wetting his handkerchief, laid it on Nick's parboiled head and temples.

"Rest a few minutes," Jack said, soothingly. "I will reconnoitre a bit." Stripping off his accoutrements, he clasped a tall sycamore growing at the crest of the ravine, and when far up brought his glass to bear. A third of a mile to the left and southward, he could see a regiment with a flag bearing a single star, surrounding a small stone farm-house, on the brow of a gentle hill. They were firing to the west and toward the north, where the black clouds obscured his view. But the red gleam in the smoke told of at least a dozen guns, and he knew that the main battle was there, though the fury of it reached far to the east, near the stone bridge which he had quit an hour before. Then through the veil of smoke long, deep masses of blue emerge and make for the rebel front on the brow of the hill, fairly at Jack's feet ; the enemy redoubles the fire ; two guns at their left pour canister into the advancing wall of blue. It never wavers, but, as a group falls to the earth, the rest close together and the mass whirls on.

Jack feels like flying. Oh, the grandeur of it, the fearlessness, the intoxication! He almost falls from the tree in his excitement. But he takes a last sweep of the belching hill. Hark! Loud cheers in the trees back of the rebels, far to the southeast, perhaps a mile and a half ; then the flaunting Palmetto flag flying forward in the center of deep masses of gray. Which will reach the hill first? He can not quit the deadly sight. Ah! the blue lines are pressing on now ; the cannon-shots pass over their heads into the devoted line of gray, desperately thinned, but clinging to the key of the battle-field. But, great God! Perhaps his delay is aiding the enemy. He sees the route now clear—straight to the west—and no rebels near enough to intervene. He descends so fast that his hands and legs are blistered, but he is down.

"Look sharp, boys; you must follow me as best you can. I know the route—there is a forest path directly to our lines, and we shall be there in twenty minutes—I shall, at least." He doesn't stop to see whether he is followed or not, but dashes on, and the rest after him. He is far out of sight in an instant. It is only by the crackling of the branches that the others keep his course. The way is between steep, precipitous hills, which explains how they could be so near the battle and yet not in it, nor harmed by the missiles flying sometimes very near them. At a deep branch of the stream the three rearmost came in sight of Jack, up to his arm-pits in water and pushing for the shore.

While they are hailing him exultantly he sinks out of sight ; an awful anguish almost stops the others, but Barney, flinging his musket and impediments off as he runs, leaps far into the stream, and when the rest reach the spot he has Jack by the hair, dragging him to the bank. He is fairly worn out by the stress, and the others loosen his coat, stretch him on the brown sward and rub his hands, his body. It is ten minutes, it seemed an hour, before he is able to get up, and the rest insist on carrying his accoutrements. Then the wild race is begun again, every instant bringing them nearer the ·pandemonium of battle. Suddenly the sharp commands of officers are heard in front and to the left. Is it the enemy, or is it friends? The group halts in an agony of doubt. How can they find out? Barney takes out his handkerchief and puts it on his gun, which he was careful to go back and recover when Jack was on the bank. A ray of bright red suddenly flits above the thick tops of the scrub-oaks.

Yes, God be praised, there is the flag of stars, and there are blue uniforms! With a wild hurrah, drowned in the musketry to the left, they rush forward, are halted by a picket guard, exhibit Sherman's order, and are directed to the commanding officer. That personage has no knowledge of General Hunter's whereabouts, but Colonel Andrew Porter is just beyond, commanding the brigade. To him Jack makes known Sherman's message, and is directed farther to the southwest, the Union right now facing nearly to the east in the execution of McDowell's admirable flank manœuvre.

Now among their own, Sherman's couriers run more peril than when skirting the edge of the battle, for the shells are directed at the line they are pursuing. They push to the rear and continue southeastward, where Hunter's headquarters are supposed to be. But Jack is easy on the score of his mission, since the general, who is nearest the stone bridge, has been apprised, and well knows that the fire which has been coming near his left flank is Sherman's. Until, however, he has executed his orders literally Jack won't be satisfied, and plunges on, the others following, nothing loath. But it is a way of pain for the lads now. Every step they come upon the dead and dying. The air is filled with moaning men, whinnying horses, the hurried movement of stretchers, the solemn solicitude of the hospital corps. The line of foremost battle is less terrifying, less trying than this inner way of Golgotha, and the four are well-nigh unnerved when they reach a group where the commanding officer has been pointed out.

" General Hunter ? " Jack says, addressing an officer with a star.

" My name is Franklin. General Hunter was wounded an hour ago. What's the matter ? "

Jack gave his message, and Franklin said, cheerfully : " That's good news. You're a very brave fellow. Go a few yards in the rear yonder and you'll find General McDowell. He'll enjoy your message."

On the hill they halt electrified.

Thick copses of scrub-pine dot the gently sloping sward. Here and there clumps of tall pines stand in the bare, brown sod as if to guard the young outshoots clustering about them in wanton dispersion. Cow-paths, marked only by the worn edges of the bushes, run in zigzags across the hillside and up to the plateau. The remnants of rail fences strew the ground here and there. The low roof of the farm-house can be seen far back even from the depression, where the lines of blue are now resting a brief, deadly half-hour.

The sun is now behind the halted line of blue ; the bay-onets, catching the light, make a sea of liquid, mirror-like rivulets hovering in the air, with the bushy branches of pine rising like green isles in the shimmering tide. The men are filling their cartridge-boxes ; new regiments are gliding into the gaps where death has cut the widest swath. From the woods, cries, groans, commands, clashing steel as the men hustle against each other in the rush into line, prelude the Vulcan clamor soon to begin. Men, bent, sometimes crawl-ing, with stretchers on their shoulders, glide through the maimed and shrieking fragments of bodies, picking out here and there those seeming capable of carriage. Other men, prone on their faces, hold canteens of tepid, muddy water— but ah! a draught to the feverish lips which seems godlike nectar. Against the stout bodies of the trees, armless men, legless trunks, the maimed in every condition of death's fan-tastic sport, hold themselves limply erect, to gain succor or save some of the vital stream pouring from their gaping wounds.

Couriers dash up to the impassive chief, calm-eyed, keen,

alert, surveying the line, dispatching brief commands, receiving reports. It is Franklin. With the air of a marshal on a civic pageant, perplexed only by some geometrical problem denying the possibility of two right lines on the same plane, he glances upward toward the brow of the plateau. The four flags had been increased by half a dozen. Ah, they have received aid! A tremendous crash comes from the left. That must be Sherman. He is on the rebel rear. One strong pull, and the two bodies will be united, his left arm reaching Sherman's right. The shining mirage of steel above the green isle sinks. The clash of hurtling accoutrements comes up musically, tranquilly from the low ground. The blue mass, first deliberately, then in a quiet, regular run, passes like a moving barricade up the sloping hillside. Then from one end of the long wall to the other white puffs as of some monster breathing spasmodically.

The air is a blur of sulphurous blackness. The bullets are as thick as if a swarm of leaden locusts had been routed from the foliage, and taken wing hillward. Then behind, through the gaps in the trees, big, whining, screeching swarms of another-caliber shells fly over the wall of blue. In a moment the ground of the plateau is torn, the red clay flying far into the air. But now the blue wall is girdling the very crest of the hill; it stops, shrivels. Long gaps are cut in its broken surface. The hillside is dotted with sprawling figures. The crest is a ragged edge of writhing bodies and struggling limbs. Forward! The wall is advancing, but shorter. It is within reach of the shining guns —spouting flame and iron in the very face of the dauntless wall. Then there is a pause. The smoke hides everything but the maimed and quivering heaps that strive to crawl backward, back to the crest, back to the deeps that are not rest nor security. The hillside is like a field, covered with sheaved grain—with a thousand mangled bodies that had been men.

Then to these wrestling specters—for in the dim smoke and Tartarean atmosphere the actions of loading and aiming take the shape of huge writhing, convulsing, monstrous, grappling—come quick-moving lines of help. They rush through them, over them. The thirteen cannon behind the struggling hydra of gray seem one vortex—sulphurous, flaming, spitting, as from one vast mouth, scorching fire, huge mouthfuls of granite venom. Back—back, the gray masses break in sinuous, definite, slow-yielding disruption.

Then a sudden inrush from the left of the broken gray, where smoke and space play fantastic tricks with the sunshine. Miraculously a dark mass is projected on the shimmering spectrum, and a ringing voice is heard:

"We are saved; we are re-enforced. We will die here!" Then high above the din, in the exultant tumult of the deadly won ground, the nearest in blue hear a stentorian voice—grim, deliberate, exultant:

"Look where Jackson stands like a stone-wall! At them, men! Let us determine to die here, and we will conquer."

Die he did, when the yelling horde in the sudden outrush grazed the edge of the Union besom sweeping over the plain in a rush of death. Then behind these spectral shapes came others—thousands—with wild, fierce shouts. The blue mass is thinned to a single line. Men in command look anxiously to the rear. Where is Burnside? Where are the twelve thousand men whom Hunter and Heintzelman deployed in these woods two hours since? Back, slowly, fiercely, but backward, the slender wall of blue is forced; not defeated, but not victorious. All this Jack sees, and he turns heart-sick from the sight.

When the straggling couriers reached the point designated as McDowell's headquarters, he had gone to the eastward of the line, and, faithful to the command given him, Jack set out with Barney, leaving the others to deliver the message in case he missed the general. They emerged presently on the edge of a plateau, whence nearly the whole battle could be seen. Jack climbed a tall oak to reconnoitre the ground for McDowell, but, as his glass revealed the battling lines, he shouted to Barney to climb for a moment, to impress the frightful yet grandiose spectacle upon his mind. Far off

7

toward the stone bridge, now a mile or more northeast of
them, they could see the Union flags waving, and mark the
white puffs of smoke that preceded the booming of the cannon. Every instant the clouds of smoke came southward,
where the rebel lines were concealed by the thick copses.
But they were breaking—always breaking back anew. In
twenty minutes more, at the same rate, the hill upon which
the rebel lines nearest the tree held the Union right at bay
would be surrounded on two sides.

This, for the moment, was a sulphurous crater, the fire-
belching demons, invisible in the smoke. Through the glass
Jack could see the lines clearly—or the smoke arising above
them. The enemy had been pushed back nearly two miles
since he had left Colonel Sherman a few rods above the
stone bridge. The Union force, as marked by the veil of
smoke, curved about the foemen, a vast crescent, seven miles
or more from tip to tip. The bodies opposing were scattered
like a gigantic staircase, with the angles of the steps con-
fronting each other step by step. But now the Union ranks
at Jack's feet rush forward; a group of riders are coming to
the tree, and Jack descends hastily to meet the general. He
is again disappointed. It is not McDowell. At a loss what
to do, he salutes one of the officers and states his case, recognizing, as he turns, General Franklin.

"I don't see that you can do better than remain where
you are, or, still better, push to the brow of that hill yonder
and act as a picket. In case you see any force approaching
from this side, which is not likely, give warning. Our cavalry ought to be here, but it isn't. If you are called to account when the battle is done, give me as your authority.
I take it your brigade will be around here pretty soon, if
they make as rapid work all the way as they have made
since eleven o'clock. If the cavalry come, you can report to
the nearest officer for assignment."

CHAPTER XI.

THE LEGIONS OF VARUS.

THE two free lances set out now, relieved of all responsibility, and determined to watch the open fields and woods to see that this part of the field was not surprised. The hill to which the general had directed them was farther from the battle than they had yet been, but the work going on to the northeast showed that this would soon be the western edge of the combat if Sherman continued advancing. They are soon on the hill, and Jack posts himself in a tree with his glass. There is a lull in the quarter they have just quit. The smoke rolls away, and now he can see streams of graycoats hurrying to the edge of the plateau, where, two hours before, he had encountered Porter's brigade. Can it be possible that Porter's troops do not see these on-rushing hordes? They are moving on the right point of the crescent, and unless the Union commander is alert they will break in on the back of the point; for Jack, without knowing it, was virtually in the rebel lines—that is, he was nearer the rebel left flank, the foot of the long, bow-shaped staircase, than he was to the tip of the Union crescent.

But no! The Stars and Stripes fly forward; they are on the very crest whence the defiant guns spat upon them. But now the smoke covers everything. Then there is a calm. The ground is clear again. The gray masses are pouring up to the crest in still greater numbers; a large body of them march down the hill in the rear of the Union line concealed by the woods; they march right up to the ranks where the red-barred flag is flying! What can it mean? Neither side fires. There must surely be some mistake. Hark! now the blue line discovers—too late—that the mass is the enemy, and half the line withers in the point-blank discharge. They are swept from the ground. Jack is trembling—demoniac. The gray mass springs forward; they have seized the guns—four of them—and turn them upon the disappearing blue. Then a hoarse shout of delirious triumph. The guns are lost; the day is lost, for now there are no blue-coats in sight. But no ! A still wilder shout—electrifying, stentorian—comes across the plateau. The blue mass reappears; they come with a wild rush in well-ordered array; they are the regulars, Jack can tell by their movements. It must be the famous Rickett's battery he saw at Centreville in the morning. In five minutes the tale was retold, and the guns, snatched from the worsted gray-coats, are safe in the hands of their masters. Again the smoke obscures the picture; again it clears away, and now the gray are in greater force than before, and the horseless batteries are again the prize of this rapacious grapple. Swarming in from three sides, the gray again hold the contested pieces. The blue vanish into the thick bushes. Another irruption, another pall of smoke, and Jack's heart bounds in exultant joy, for he sees the New York flag in the van. Sherman has reached the point of dispute. But alas ! the guns are run back, and as the gray lines sway rearward in billowy, regular measure, they retain the Titanically contested trophies.

The sun is now far beyond the meridian. The Union lines are closing up compactly. One more such grapple as the last and the broad plateau where the rebel artillery is massed, pointing westward, northward, eastward, will be won. But a palsy seems to have settled on the lines of blue. They are motionless, while their adversaries are hurrying men from some secret place, where they seem to be inexhaustible. The whole battle is now within the compass of a mile. But where can these hordes come from ? Surely, General McDowell has never been mad enough to leave them disengaged along the fords! No; they do not come from that direction. They come at the very center of the rebel rear. Can it be that troops are arriving from Richmond ? The Southern lines are longer than the Northern, but they have been since the first moment Jack got a glimpse of them. He could see, too, that they were thinner; that on the spur of the plateau in front of the massed rebel artillery a single brigade was holding the Union mass at bay. He can almost

hear the rebel commands as the re-enforcements pour in.
But now the thunder breaks out anew, rolls in vengeful
fury around the western and northern base of the plateau.
The gray lines stagger; the falling men block the steps of
the living. Surely now McDowell is going to do or die.
Yes. The iron game goes on ; the blue lines jostle and
crush forward. They are at the last wall of resistance. But
what is the sound at his very feet ? As Jack looks down in
the narrow way between the hill he is on and the plateau on
the very edge of the Union line—in fact, behind it now, for
it has moved forward since he took post—a rushing mass of
gray-clad soldiery is moving forward on the dead run. In
one instant the head of the column is where General Franklin
rode but an hour or two before. He looks for Barney. He
can see him nowhere. He climbs down in haste and discovers his comrade soundly sleeping against the base of
the tree.

"Barney, the army is ruined!"

"Is the battle over ?"

"Oh, no, no, but it will be in a moment. Hark, hear
that!"

A roar of musketry—it seemed at their very feet. Then
an outbreak of yells, so sharp, so piercing, so devilish the
sound, that the marrow froze in their veins, arose, as if from
the whole thicket about them.

"Is it too late to warn General Franklin ?" Barney
asked, trembling.

"Ah, Barney, we are as bad as traitors; we ought to have
seen these rebels before they got near. If we had done our
duty this would never have happened. Perhaps it is not too
late to get back. Let me go up and see where we can find
a way without running into the enemy."

Reaching his perch again, Jack cast his despairing eyes
toward the fatal hill. It was now clear of smoke, and there
wasn't a regiment left on it. His heart leaped for an instant, the next it was lead, for the ranks that had disappeared were down on the brow of the hill—in the valley—
rushing forward, unresisted, the red and blue of the Union,

mixed with the stars and bars of the rebellion; but, worse than all, the ranks of gray were sweeping in overwhelming masses quite behind the lines of blue, cutting them down as a scythe when near the end of the furrow. To the eastward Sherman still clung desperately to the crests he had won, but Jack saw with agony that, slipping between him and the river, a great wedge of gray was hurrying forward. His last despairing glance caught a body of jet-black horses galloping wildly into the dispersing ranks of blue. He came down from the tree limp, nerveless, unmanned.

"Well ?" Barney asked.

"It's all over—we are ruined!"

"The army, you mean ?"

"Ah, yes! the army and we too."

"But what's going to become of us ?"

"I don't much care what becomes of us—at least I don't care what becomes of me!"

"But if we don't get back to our regiment, they'll think we're deserters."

"Good God, yes! I forgot that; I think I can find the way back. But we'll have to be careful, the enemy are all around us. I can hear them plainly, very near. Follow me, and don't speak above a whisper."

Then, with swift movement, always as near the thick bushes as they could push, they fled faster and faster, as fear fell more and more heavily upon their quickened fancies. The thought of the repute of deserters lent them endurance, or they must have broken down before the weary shiftings of that dreadful flight. They are now near the spot where they had met Porter's pickets in the morning. The sounds of battle had died out at intervals, renewed now and again by an outcry of cheers, a quick fusillade, then more cheers, and then an ominous silence. But now there is a continuous roll of musketry near the knoll, back of the Warrenton road. The two wanderers, breathless, with torn uniforms, swollen faces, halt, gasping, to take their bearings. They can see the turnpike far beyond the stone bridge half-way to Centreville; they see crowds fleeing in zigzag lines over the open fields, see horses plunging wildly, laden down by two and even three men on their backs; they see vehicles overturned at the roadside, whence the horses have been cut or killed by the rebel shells; they see an army, in every sense a mob, swarming behind the deserted rebel forts; they see orderly ranks of shining black horses this side the stone bridge charging the fleeing lines of blue; they see shells whirling like huge blackbirds in the sky, suddenly falling among the skurrying thousands; they see a shell finally burst on the bridge, shiver a caisson to fragments, and then all sign of organized flight comes to an end.

But near them, meanwhile, a sullen fire replies with desperate promptitude to the rebel shots.

"If we can get over to the men fighting at the edge of the woods, we may be killed or captured, but we won't be disgraced!" Jack cries.

Again they make a wide circuit through the woods, and now the firing is near at hand, coming slowly toward them. They have only to wait and they will be among the forlorn hope. Ah, with what fervent joy Jack marks the Union banner, flapping its twin streamers among the hurtling pines! They are near it; they are under it! Their own guns are no longer available; hundreds are lying at hand; they seize them. The line is firing in retreat. It is a sadly depleted battalion of Keyes's regulars, steadfast, imperturbable, devoted. A handful of them has been forgotten or misdirected. The rebels, uncertain whether it was not a trap to snare them, move with caution, while far to the left a turning column is hurrying to hem the Union group in on every side. There are hardly three hundred blue-coats in the mass, but their volleys are so swift, so regular, so steady, that they make the impression of a thousand. The enemy felt sure, as was afterward learned, that there was at least a regiment.

A young captain, soiled, ragged, his sleeves hanging in ribbons, the whole skirt of his coat gone, moves alertly, composedly in the center, seizing a gun when one comes handy on the ground, where there are plenty scattered.

"Steady, men, steady! We shall be at the water's edge, soon, and then we can give them hell!"

Never music sounded sweeter in Jack's ear than that jaunty epithet "hell"! How inspiring! How little of the ordinary association the word brought up! Now they were travers- ing slowly the very ground Jack and his comrades had flown over in the morning. Still firing—still working with all his heart in the deadly play, Jack sidles to the officer and cries out:

"Captain, I know a ford that will take us across above the stone bridge. We discovered it this morning. Shall I guide that way?"

"Guide if you can; but fire like seven devils, above all!" the captain cried, seizing two or three pouches lying in a mass and emptying the cartridges into his pockets.

"There, keep to the left sharp, and we shall come to a deep gully where the water is only knee-deep," Jack cries, also replenishing his cartridge-box, which had shrunk under the rapid work of the last half-hour.

"What regiment are you, sergeant?" the captain cries, looking for a moment at the tattered recruit.

"Caribees of New York, Sherman's brigade."

"And how came you off here? Your brigade was near the right of the line at the stone bridge." The captain asked this with a shade of suspicion in his voice.

Jack explained his mission, and the officer, who had been dealing out the timely windfall of ammunition, nodded.

"Poor Hunter was shot early in the advance. It would have been victory to our flag if the poor old fellow had been wounded before the action began. He lost three hours in the attack, and gave the rebels a chance to come up from Winchester."

Now Jack understood the mysterious legions that seemed to spring from the earth. They were Johnston's army from the Shenandoah.

"Keep up heart, men; Burnside and Schenck are near us somewhere. They are in reserve, and they'll give these devils a warm welcome, if they push far enough after us."

Then the steady volleys grew swifter, if that were possible, the enemy moving steadily after the slowly retiring group. But now there is a clear field to cross, so wide that the smallness of the force must be detected. The captain halts the line, takes his bearings, divides the little army into two bodies, orders one to move at a double-quick directly across the open; the rest are stretched out as skirmishers. He retires with the first squad across the field, directing the skirmishers to hold the ground until they hear three musket-shots from the wood behind. The rebels can now be seen closing in very near. But the skirmish-line, spreading over a wider front, evidently perplexes them, and they halt. The three shots are presently heard, then the skirmish-line flees in groups across the bare downs, the vociferating yells of the gray-coats fairly drowning the hideous clamor of the muskets.

"Ah! we're saved," a lieutenant cries, waving his cap like a madman. "Look! there are men in the wood yonder, to our right; they are coming this way!"

Jack turned, he was near the captain; and he marked, with deadly panic, a look of despair settle down on the heroic, handsome face. What could it mean? Didn't he believe that there were men there? Jack handed him his own glass—the captain had none.

"By Heaven, our flag! But what troops can they be in that quarter? They must be surrounded, like ourselves.—Sergeant, can you undertake a dangerous duty?"

"With all my heart," Jack cried, heartily.

"What's your name and company?"

"John Sprague, Cariboes, Company K."

"Slip around the edge of the skirt of bushes. You'll be within an arm's length of the enemy all the way. Reach the place where we saw those men a moment since. When you get there, if they are friendly, fire a shot. Here, take this pistol. Fire that; I shall recognize it from the musketry. If they are the enemy, fire all the barrels as fast as you can and retreat. You run great danger; you can only by a miracle escape capture; but it is our only resource for the next charge. We must surrender or die," he added, looking wofully at the meager remnant of his company. Before the words had fairly ended, Jack is off like a shot, forgetting Barney, forgetting everything but the extrication of this grand young Roman. As he skurried along, sometimes on hands and knees, he blames himself for not learning the captain's name. He feels sure that a day will come when the world will know and admire it. He has gained the other corner, and in a moment he will be in the thick copse where the Union flag had been seen, but as he makes a dash through a clump of laurel he is confronted by two men, muskets in hand.

"A Yank, by the Lord! Surrender, you damned mudsill!"

For answer Jack raised the pistol in his hand and fired. The man fell, with a frightful yell. The other leveled his musket fairly in Jack's face; but before he could pull the trigger a report at his ear deafened Jack, and the second man staggered against the tree.

"Ah, ha! me boy, the rear rank did the best work there," Barney cried, as Jack turned to see whence the timely aid had come. "A day after the fair's better than the fair itself, if the rain has kept the girls away," and Barney laughed good-humoredly.

"Well, 'pon my soul, Barney, it's a shameful thing to say, but all thought of you had gone from my mind. I should not have let you come if you had proposed it, but now we're in for it. Ah!"

As he spoke the Union flag he had seen came forward, but it was in the hands of a rebel bearer, and was upside down in mockery. The sight was enough. He fired the shots as agreed upon, firing two at the group marching heedlessly forward, as the skirmish-line was far ahead, or they supposed it was, for the two men disabled by Jack and Barney were the advance, as it was not supposed that any but stragglers were near at hand, and the company were returning to their regiment. In an instant a fierce volley is returned, and Barney, who is fairly in the bush behind a huge tree, hears a low groan. He looks where Jack had been and sees him lying on the ground, stifling an agonized cry by holding his left arm over his mouth. Barney might have escaped, at least he might have delayed capture, but coming from behind the tree, he holds up his hands, and flinging himself on the ground beside his comrade takes his head upon his knee and awaits the worst.

BOOK II.

THE HOSTAGES.

CHAPTER XII.

THE AFTERMATH.

THERE were not so many millions of Americans in 1861 as there are to-day. But they were more American then than they are now. That is, the Old World had not sent the millions to our shores that now people the waste places of the West. It was not until after the civil war that those prodigious hosts came—enough to make the populace of such empires as fill the largest space in history. That part of the land that loved the flag cherished it with a fervor deeper than the half-alien race that first flung it to the breeze under Washington. They loved the republic with something of that passionate idolatry that made the Greek's ideal joy—death for the fatherland ; some of that burning zeal and godlike pride that made the earlier Roman esteem his citizenship more precious than a foreign crown. But until the battle on that awful 21st of July proved the war real—with the added horror of civil hate—Secretary Seward's epigram of ninety days clung fast in the public mind.

Up to Bull Run there was a vague feeling that our army, in proper time, would march down upon the rebels like the hosts of Joshua, and scatter them and the rebellion to utter-most destruction in one action. It was upon this assumption that the journals of the North satirized, abused, vilified Scott, and clamored day by day for an " advance upon Richmond." The damnation of public clamor, and not the incompetency of the general, set the inchoate armies of Scott upon that fatal adventure. But that humiliating, incredible, and for years misunderstood Sunday, on the plateaus of Manassas, where, after all, blundering and imbecility brought disaster, but not shame, upon the devoted soldiery, aroused the sense of the North to the reality of war, as the overthrow at Jemmapes in 1793 convinced the Prussian oligarchy that the republic in France was a fact.

It was a dreadful Monday in the North when the first hideous bulletins were sent broadcast through the cities and carried by couriers into every hamlet. For hours—sickening hours—it was not believed. We have awakened many a morning since 1861 to hear of thrones overturned, armies vanquished, dynasties obliterated ; to hear of great men gone by sudden and cruel death : but the anger and despair when Booth's cruel work was known ; the shuddering horror over Garfield's taking off ; the amazement when the hand of Nihilism laid an emperor dead ; the overthrow of Austria in a single day ; the extinction of the Bonapartes— these things were heard and digested with something like repose compared to the bewildering outbreak that met the destruction of our army at Manassas.

It was not the dazed, panic-stricken, panic anguish that followed Fredericksburg or the second Bull Run. It was not the indignant, fretful wrath that rebuked official culpability for the destruction of the grand campaign on the Peninsula. It was a startled, incredulous, angry amazement, in which blame afterward visited upon generals or Cabinet, was humbly taken on the people's shoulders and echoed in a moaning *mea culpa*. For days all the people were close kin. In the streets strangers talked to strangers ; the pulpit echoed the inextinguishable wrath of the streets ; the journals, for a moment restrained into solemnity, echoed for once the real voice of an elevated humanity and not the drivel of partisanship nor the ulterior purposes of wealth and sham. Even schoolboys, arrested in the merry-making of youth, looked in wonder at the sudden reversal of conditions. Boys well remember in the school that Monday, when the northern heavens were hung in black and grief wrung its crystal tresses in the air, the master began the work of the day with a brief, pathetic review of the public agony, and dismissed the classes that he was too agitated to instruct. There were no games on the greensward, no swimming in the river, no excursion to the Malvern cherry groves. The streets were filled with blank faces and whispering crowds unable to endure the restraint of routine or the ordinary callings of life. Parties were obliterated, or rather from the flux of this white heat, came out in solidified unity that compact of parties which for four years breathed the breath of the nation's life, spoke the purposes of the republic, and amid stupendous reverses and triumphs held the public conscience clear in its sublime duty. The woes of bereavement were not wide-spread ; the killed at Manassas were hardly more than we read of now in a disaster at sea or a catastrophe in the mines. The whole army engaged hardly outnumbered the slaughtered at Antietam, Gettysburg, or Burnside's butchery at St. Mary's Hill.

Hence the marvel of the instant fusion, the swift resolve of the Northern mind. The battle was the sudden grapple of aggressive weakness—catching the half-contemptuous strong man unaware and rolling him in the dust. Brought to earth by this unlooked-for blow, the North arose with renewed force and the deathless determination that could have but one issue. The people, when the benumbing force of the surprise was mastered, flew together with one mind, one voice, one impulse. The churches, the public halls, the street corners, moving trains, and rushing steamers, were such hustings as the Athenian improvised in the porticoes, when her orators inflamed the heart of Greece to repel the barbarians, to die with Leonidas in the gorges of the Thermopylæ.

Ah, what an imposing spectacle it was! The blood of wrath leaped fiercely in the chilled veins of age; the ardor of youth became the delirium of the Crusaders, the lofty zeal of the Puritans, the chivalrous daring of Rupert's troopers, and the Dutch devotees of Orange. A half-million men had been called out; a million were waiting in passionate eagerness within a month; two hundred and fifty millions of money had been voted—ten times that amount was offered in a day. Every interest in life became suddenly centered in one duty—war. It touched the heart of the whole people, and for the time they arose, purified, contrite, as the armies of Moses under the chastening of the rod.

In Acredale there were sore hearts as the dreadful news became more and more definite. For days the death lists were mere guess-work; but when the routed forces returned to their camps in Washington the awful gaps in the ranks were ascertained with certainty. The Caribees were nearly obliterated. Of the thousand men and over who had marched from Meridian Hill only four hundred were found ten days after the battle. Elisha Boone had hurried at once to Washington, charged by all the fathers, mothers, brothers, and sisters of the regiment to make swift report of the absent darlings. Kate was besieged in the grand house with tearful watchers, waiting in agonizing impatience for the fatal finality. Olympia, to spare her mother the distress of the vague responses her telegrams brought from Washington, spent most of the time at the Boones', where, thanks to the father's high standing with the Administration, the earliest, most accurate information came. Finally he wrote. He had seen Nick Marsh, who gave the first coherent narrative of Jack, Barney, and Dick Perley. They had been seen—the first two in the last desperate conflict. An officer (the hero whom Jack had so much admired, and who turned out to be Gouverneur K. Warren) had escaped from the forlorn hope left to dispute the rebel charge upon the flying columns. He gave particulars that pointed with heart-breaking certainty to the death of the two boys. Young Perley had been lost sight of since noon of the battle. He had followed the path taken by Jack and his comrades across the flank of the enemy. He had been seen at Heintzelman's headquarters, but after that no one could trace him. Wesley, too, had been left near the stone bridge with a ball in either his arm or thigh, the informant was not quite sure which, as he fell in a charge of the line. Boone telegraphed to Kate that he was going through the lines with a flag of truce so soon as the affair could be regulated, and proffered his best offices for the Acredale victims.

Everything had been prepared by Olympia and her mother for an instant departure so soon as positive information came. With them Marcia Perley went, trembling and tearful, and Telemachus Twigg, to extricate his son from danger, for it was uncertain what his status was in the forces. Kate, too, joined the melancholy pilgrimage that set out one morning followed to the station by weeping kinsmen imploring the good offices of these ambassadors of woe. The sleeping-car gave the miserable company seclusion, if not rest. They were not the only ones in quest of the missing, for as yet there was no certainty as to the fate of those left on the field of battle. Later reports had been more encouraging, for hundreds who were set down as prisoners or missing began to be heard from as far northward as the Maryland line. In the station at Washington Boone met his daughter. Twigg hurried to him and asked:

"Any further news, Mr. Boone? We're all here—about half Acredale."

"Yes, I see; but there is no more news of the Caribees. We learn that the wounded have been sent to Richmond, and I shall set out for there to-morrow."

Mrs. Sprague, with Olympia and Merry, drove to the house of a friend she had known years before, whose husband was a Senator. The Boones—or rather Kate—bade them a cordial adieu as they drove off to the National Hotel.

Then the most trying part of the quest began. The War Department was besieged with applicants, mostly women. Orders had been issued to forbid all crossing the lines, and the despairing kinsfolk of the lost were in a panic of impatient terror. In vain Olympia called upon eminent Senators who had been friends of her father; in vain she invoked the aid of the Secretary of State, who had been the family's guest at Acredale. Once she penetrated, by the aid of strong letters, to the Secretary of War. He was surrounded by a hurried throng of orderlies, officers, and clerks, and even after she had been admitted to his office Olympia was left unnoticed on a settee, waiting some sign to approach the dreaded presence. His imperious and abrupt manner, his alternation of deferential concern for some and disdainful impatience for others, gave her small hope that he would heed her prayer. She waited hours, sitting in the crowded room, ill from the oppressive air, the fixed stare of the officers, and the sobbing of others like herself waiting a word with the autocrat. At length, late in the afternoon, when the crowd had quite gone, she heard the Secretary say in an undertone:

"Send an orderly to those women and see what they want."

Each of the waiting women handed credentials to the young man, and each in turn arose trembling and stood before the decisive official at the great, paper-strewn desk. There was no attempt to soften the refusal, as he turned curtly from the pleaders ; and Olympia, shrinking from the ordeal, was about to step out of the room, when a tall, care-worn man shambled in, glancing pityingly at her as she arose, half trembling, recognizing the President.

She stepped in front of him in a desperate impulse, and, throwing up her veil, cried piteously:

"O Mr. Lincoln, you are a father, you have a tender heart ; you will listen to the bereaved!" He stopped, looking at her kindly, and put his left arm wearily on the desk by his side.

"Yes, my poor girl, I am a father and have a heart; the more's the pity, for just now something else is needed in its place. I suppose your father is over yonder," and he nodded toward the Virginia shore.

"O Mr. Lincoln, my father is farther away than that. My father was Senator Sprague—you served with him in Congress—I—I—thought that perhaps you might take pity on his widow, his daughter, his son, if the poor boy is still living, and—and—"

"Send you across the lines ?"

"Oh, if God would put it in your heart!"

8

"It's in my heart fast enough, my poor child, but—"

"Impossible, Mr. President! The enemy, as it is, can open a Sabine campaign on us, and tie our hands by stretching Northern women out in a line of battle between the ranks!"

It was the weary, discouraging voice of the Secretary, imperiously implying that the Executive must not interpose weakness and mercy where Draconian rigor sat enthroned. The President smiled sadly.

"Ah, Mr. Secretary, a sister—a mother—give a great deal for the country. We can not err much in granting their prayer. Make out an order—for whom?"

Olympia, speechless with gratitude—reverence—could hardly articulate:

"My mother, myself, and Miss Marcia Perley."

"Another mother?"

"Her boy is not of age, and ran away to join my brother's company." She had a woman's presence of mind to answer with this diplomatic evasion.

"I'm afraid you will only add to your distress, my poor child; but you shall go." He inclined his head benignantly and passed into the inner sanctuary behind the rail, when Olympia heard the Secretary say, grimly:

"I shall take measures to stop this sort of thing, Mr. President. Hereafter you shall only come to this department at certain hours. At all other times the doors shall be guarded."

A gray-haired man in undress uniform presently appeared, and as he handed Olympia the large official envelope he said, respectfully:

"You never heard of me, Miss Sprague? Many years ago the Senator, your father, did a kind turn for my brother —an employé in the Treasury. If I can be of any aid to you in this painful business, pray give me a chance to show a kindness to the family of a great and good man. My name is Charles Bevan, and it is signed to one of the papers in this letter."

Within an hour all was ready, but they could not set out until the next morning, when, by eight o'clock, the three ladies were *en route*. There was a large company with them, all under a flag of truce. They passed through the long lines of soldiery that lay intrenched on the Virginia side of the Potomac, and pushed on to Annandale, where the rebel outpost received them. Olympia's eyes dwelt on the wide-stretching lands of pine and oak, remembering the pictures Jack had given in his letters of this very same route. But there were few signs of war. The cleared places lay red and baking under the hot August sun ; the trees seemed crisp and sapless.

At Fairfax Court-House, where the first signs of real war-like tenure were seen, the visitors were taken into a low frame house, and each in turn asked to explain the objects of her mission. Then the hospital reports were searched. In half a dozen or more instances the sad-eyed mothers were thrown into tremulous hope by the tidings of their darlings' whereabouts. But for Olympia and Aunt Merry there was no clew. No such names as Sprague or Perley were recorded in the fateful pages of the hospital corps. But there were several badly wounded in the hospital at Manassas, where fuller particulars were accessible.

They were conducted very politely by a young lieutenant in a shabby gray uniform to an ambulance and driven four miles southward to Fairfax Station on the railway, when, after despairing hours of waiting, they were taken by train to Manassas. An orderly accompanied them, and as the train passed beyond Union Mills, where the Bull Run River runs along the railway a mile or more before crossing under it, the young soldier pointed out the distant plateau, near the famous stone bridge, and, when the train crossed the river, the high bluffs, a half-mile to the northward, where the action had begun at Blackburn's Ford. He was very respect-ful and gentle in alluding to the battle, and said, ingenuous-ly, pointing to the plateau jutting out from the Bull Run Mountains:

"At two o'clock on Sunday we would have cried quits to McDowell to hold his ground and let us alone. But just as we were on our heel to turn, Joe Johnston came piling in here, right where you see that gully yonder, with ten thousand fresh men, and in twenty minutes we were three to one, and then your folks had the worst of it. President Davis got off the train at the junction yonder, and as he rode across this field, where we are now, the woods yonder were full of our men, flying from the Henry House Hill, where Sherman had cut General Bee's brigade to pieces and was routing Jackson—'Stonewall,' we call him now, because General Bonham, when he brought up the reserves, shouted, 'See, there, where Jackson stands like a stone wall!' He's a college professor and very pious; he makes his men pray before fighting, and has 'meetings' in the commissary tent twice a week."

"Did Mr. Davis join in the battle?" Olympia asked, more to seem interested in the garrulous warrior's narrative than because she really had her mind on the story.

"Oh, dear, no. Old Johnston had finished the job before the President (Olympia noticed that all Southerners dwelt upon this title with complacent insistence) could reach the field. He was barely in time to see the cavalry of 'Jeb' Stuart charge the regulars on the Warrenton road."

The train came to a halt, and the young man said, cheerfully:

"Here we are. The hospital's still right smart over yonder in the trees."

"But you will go with us, will you not?" Olympia asked in alarm, for it was wearing toward night.

"Oh, yes; I'm detailed to remain with you until you have found out about your kinsfolk."

In the mellow sunset the three women followed the orderly across the fields strewed with armaments, supplies, and the rough depot paraphernalia of an army at rest. The hospital consisted of a large tent for the slightly hurt, and a few old buildings and a barn for the more serious cases. The search was futile. There were two or three of the Caribees in the place, but they knew nothing of their missing comrades. Indeed, Jack's detail by Colonel Sherman had effectually cut off all trace of his movements after the battle began.

Mrs. Sprague's tears were falling softly as the orderly led them to the surgeon's office. They were there shown the records of all who had been buried on the field. Many, he informed them, sympathetically, had been buried where they fell, in great ditches dug by the sappers. In every case the garments had been stripped from the bodies before burial, so that there was absolutely no means of identification. Most of the wounded had, however, been sent to Richmond with the prisoners. "It would not do," he added, kindly, "to give up all hope of the lost ones, until they had seen the roster of the prisoners and the wounded in the Richmond prisons and hospitals."

Quarters were given to them in a tent put at their disposal by the surgeons, and in the long, wakeful hours of the night Olympia heard the guard pacing monotonously before the door. The music of the bugles aroused them at sunrise—a wan, haggard group, sad-eyed and silent. The girl made desperate efforts to cheer the wretched mother, and even privily took Merry to task for giving way before what was as yet but a shadow. 'Twould be time enough for tears when they found evidence that the stout, vigorous boys had been killed. As they finished the very plain breakfast of half-baked bread, pea-coffee, and eggs, bought by the orderly at an exorbitant rate, he said, good-naturedly:

"The train don't come till about ten o'clock. If you'd like to see the battle-field, I can get the ambulance and take you over."

Olympia eagerly assented—anything was preferable to this mute misery of her mother and Merry's sepulchral struggles to be conversational and tearless. They drove through bewildering numbers of tents, most of them, Olympia's sharp eyes noted, marked " U. S. A.," and she reflected, almost angrily, that the chief part of war, after all, was pillage. The men looked shabby, and the uniforms were as varied as a carnival, though by no means so gay. Whenever they crossed a stream, which was not seldom, groups of men were standing in the water to their middle, washing their clothing, very much as Olympia had seen the washer-women

on the Continent, in Europe. They were very merry, even
boisterous in this unaccustomed work, responding to rough
jests by resounding slashes of the tightly wrung garments
upon the heads or backs of the unwary wags.

"Why, there must be a million men here," Merry cried,
as the tents stretched for miles, as far as she could see.

"No; not quite a million, I reckon," the orderly said,
proudly; "but we shall have a million when we march on
Washington."

"March on Washington!" Merry gasped, as though it
was an official order she had just heard promulgated. "But
—but—we aren't ready yet. We—" Then she halted in
dismay. Was she giving information to the enemy? Would
they instantly make use of it? Ah! she must, at any cost,
undo this fatal treason, big with disaster to the republic. "I
mean we are not ready yet to put our many million men on
the march."

The orderly laughed. "I reckon your many million will
be ready as soon as our one million. You know we have a
big country to cover with them. You folks have only Washington to guard and Richmond to take. We have the Mississippi and fifteen hundred miles of coast to guard. Now, this
corner is Newmarket, where Johnston waited for his troops on
Sunday and led them right along the road we are on—to the
pine wood yonder—just north of us. We won't go through
there, because we ain't making a flank movement," and he
laughed pleasantly. They drove on at a rapid rate as they
came upon the southern shelf of the Mansassas plateau.

"This," the orderly said, pointing to a small stone building in a bare and ragged waste of trees, shrubs, and ruined
implements of war, "is the Henry House—what is left of it
—the key of our position when Jackson formed his stone
wall facing toward the northwest, over there where your
folks very cleverly flanked us and waited an hour or two,
Heaven only knows what for, unless it was to give us time
to bring up our re-enforcements. Your officers lay the blame
on Burnside and Hunter, who, they declare, just sat still
half the day, while Sherman got in behind us and would

have captured every man Jack of our fellows, if Johnston hadn't come up, where I showed you, in the very nick of time."

The women were looking eagerly at the field of death. It was still as on the day of the battle, save that instead of the thousands of beating hearts, the flaunting flags, and roaring guns, there were countless ridges torn in the sod, as if a plow had run through at random, limbs and trees torn down and whirled across each other, broken wheels, musket stocks and barrels, twisted and sticking, gaunt and eloquent, in the tough, grassy fiber of the earth.

"In this circle of a mile and a half fifty thousand men pelted each other from two o'clock that Sunday morning until four in the afternoon. Up to two o'clock we were on the defensive. We were driven from the broad, smooth road yonder that you see cutting through the trees, northward a mile from here. Jackson alone made a stand; if it hadn't been for him we should have been prisoners in Washington now, I reckon. You see those men at work? They are picking up lead. We reckon that it takes a ton of lead to kill a man."

"A ton of lead?" Olympia repeated.

"Yes. You wouldn't believe that thousands of men can stand in front of each other a whole day and pour lead into each other's faces, and not one in fifty is hit?"

"Ah!" Olympia commented, thinking that, after all, Jack might not have been hit.

"These are the trenches of the dead. Our dead are not here. They were all taken and sent to friends. There are five hundred of your dead here and near the stone bridge yonder. We lost three hundred killed in the fight."

"And are there no other marks than this plain board?" Olympia pointed to a rough pine plank, sticking loosely in the ground, with the words painted in lampblack: "85 Yanks. By the Hospital Corps, Bee's Brigade."

"That's all. They were all stripped—no means of identifying them. The sun was very hot; the rain next day made the bodies rot, and the men had to just shovel them in—"

"Oh, oh! don't, pray don't!" Olympia cried, as her mother tottered against the ambulance.

"I ask your pardon, ladies; I forgot that these are not things for ladies to hear." He spoke in sincere contrition.

To relieve him Olympia smiled sadly, saying, "Won't you take us back, please?"

The ambulance drove on into the Warrenton pike, and, if Olympia had known it, within a stone's-throw of Jack's last effort, where the cavalry picket came upon him. It was noon when they reached the station. The orderly returned the ambulance to the hospital, brought down the luggage, and the three women made a luncheon of fruit and dry bread, declining the orderly's invitation to eat at the hospital. The train came on three hours late. It was filled with military men, most of them officers; but so soon as the orderly entered the rear coach, ushering in his charges, two or three young men with official insignia on their collars arose with alacrity and begged the ladies to take the vacant places. At Bristow Station many of the officers got out and a number of civilians entered from the coach ahead and took their places. Mrs. Sprague, worn out by the fatigue of the journey and the strain upon her mind, quite broke down in the hot, ill-ventilated car. There was no water to be had, and Olympia turned inquiringly to the person opposite her, asking:

"Could we possibly get any water—my mother is very much overcome?"

"Certainly, madam. There must be plenty of canteens on the train. I will bring you some in a moment."

An officer who had been sharing the seat with Merry arose on hearing this and said, kindly:

"Madam, if you will make use of your seat as a couch, perhaps your mother will feel more comfortable reclining. I will get a seat elsewhere."

Olympia was too much distressed to think of acknowledging this courteous action, but Merry spoke up timidly:

"We are most grateful to you, sir."

"Oh, don't mention it. Are you going far?"

"Yes, we're going to Richmond, to—to find our boys, lost in the battle two weeks ago."

"Oh, you're from the North." He was a young man, perhaps thirty, evidently proud of his unsoiled uniform and the glittering insignia of rank on the sleeve and collar.

"Yes, sir ; we're from Acredale, near Warchester," Merry said, as though Acredale must be known even in this remote place, and that the knowing of it would bring a certain consideration to the travelers.

"Oh, yes, Warchester. I fell in with an officer from there after the battle, a Captain Boone. Do you know him ?"

"Oh, dear me, yes. He is from Acredale. He is captain of Company K of the Caribee Regiment—"

"Caribee ? Why, yes, I remember that name. We got their flags and sent them to Richmond ; we—"

"And, oh, sir, did you take the prisoners ? I mean the Caribees—were there many ? Oh, dear sir, it is among them our boys were ; they were mere boys."

"Yes, ma'am, there were a good smart lot of them, and as you say all very young. Boone himself can't be twenty-five."

"And are they treated well ? Do they have care ? Of course you did not ask any of their names ?" Merry asked eagerly, comforted to be able to talk with some one who knew of the Caribees, for heretofore, of· the scores they had questioned, no one had ever heard of the regiment.

"Oh, as to that, ma'am, you know a soldier's life is hard, and a prisoner's is a good deal harder. Most of your men are in Castle Thunder—a large tobacco warehouse." He hesitated, and looked furtively at Olympia administering water to her mother. "Perhaps," he said, heartily, " if you would put a drop of whisky in the cup it would brace up your mother's nerves. We find it a good friend down here, when it isn't an enemy, he added, smiling as Olympia looked at the proffered flask hesitatingly.

"I assure you, madam " (Southerners, in the old time at least, imitated the pleasant continental custom of addressing all women by this comprehensive term), "you will be the better for a sip yourself. It was upon that we did most of our fighting the other day, and it is a mighty good brace-up, I assure you."

But Olympia shook her head, smiling. Her mother had taken a fair dose, and was, as she owned, greatly benefited by it. The young man sat on the arm of the opposite seat, anxious to continue the conversation, but divided in mind. Merry was trying to hide her tears, and kept her head obstinately toward the window. Olympia, with her mother's head pillowed on her lap, strove to fan a current of air into circulation. She gave the young man a reassuring glance, and he resumed his seat in front of her, beside the distracted Merry.

"You are from Richmond?" Olympia asked as he sat puzzling for a pretext to renew the talk with her.

"Oh, no; I am from Wilmington, but I have kinsfolk in Richmond. I am on General Beauregard's staff. My name is Ballman—Captain Ballman."

She vaguely remembered that Vincent Atterbury was on staff duty. Perhaps this young man knew him.

"Do you know a Mr. Atterbury in—in your army?" she asked, blushing foolishly.

"Atterbury—Atterbury—why, yes! I know there is such a man. He is in General Jackson's forces—whether on the staff or not I can't say. Stay. I saw his name in *The Whig* this very day." He took out the paper and glanced down the columns. "Ah, yes ; is this the man?" And he read: "Major Vincent Atterbury, whose wounds were at first pronounced serious, is now at his mother's country-house on the river. He is doing excellently, and all fears have been removed."

"Yes, that is he. We know him quite well." And she turned her head window-ward, with a feeling of confidence in the mission, heretofore so blank and wild. Vincent would aid them. He could bring official intervention to bear, without which Jack might, even though alive and well, be hidden from them. She whispered this confidence to her mother as the train jolted along noisily over the rough road, and, a good deal inspired by it, Mrs. Sprague began to take something like interest in the melancholy country that flew past the window, as if seeking a place to hide its bareness in the blue line of uplands that marked the receding mountain spurs.

The captain was much more potential in providing a supper at the evening station than the orderly, who was looked upon with some suspicion when he told the story of his *protégés*. The zeal of the new Confederates did not extend to aiding the enemy, even though weak women and within the Confederate lines. It was nearly morning when the train finally drew up in the Richmond station, and the captain, with many protestations of being at their service, gave them his army address, and, relinquishing them to the orderly, withdrew. It had been decided that the party should not attempt to find quarters in the hotels, which their escort declared were crowded by the government and the thousands of curious flocking to the city since the battle.

He could, however, he thought, get them plain accommodations with an aunt, who lived a little from the center of the town. They were forced to walk thither, no conveyance being obtainable. After a long delay they were admitted, the widow explaining that she had been a good deal troubled by marauding volunteers. The orderly explained the situation to his kinswoman, and without parley the three ladies were shown into two plain rooms adjoining. They were very prim and clean ; the morning air came through the open windows, bearing an almost stupefying odor. It may have been the narcotic influence of the flowers that brought sleep to the three women, for in ten minutes they were at rest as tranquilly as if in the security of Acredale.

CHAPTER XIII.

A COMEDY OF TERRORS.

WHEN Jack, the day after the battle, found himself able
to take account of what was going on, he closed his eyes
again with a deep groan, believing in a vague glimpse of
peaceful rest that his last confused sensation was real—that
he was dead. But there were no airy aids of languorous
ease to perpetuate or encourage this delusion. Sharp pains
racked his head ; his right arm burned and twinged as
though he had thrust it into pricking flames. Loud voices
about, but invisible to him, were swearing and gibing. He
was lying on his back, his head on a line with his body. A
regular movement, broken by joltings that sent torturing
darts through his whole frame, told him without much conjecture that he was in an ambulance. The accent of the
voices outside told him that it was a rebel ambulance and
not a Northern one he was in. He tried to raise his head
to see his companions, but he might as well have been
nailed to the cross, so far as pain and helplessness went.
Then he lost the thread of his thought. He heard, in a
vague, far-off voice, men talking:

"We'll catch old Abe on our next trip ef we go on like
this—eh, Ben ? "

"I reckon. I'm jess going to take a furlough now.
Hain't seen my girl fo' foah months."

"How much did you pick up ? "

"I've got five gold watches and right smart o' shinplasters. I don't reckon they'll pass in our parts, but I'm
going to trade 'em off with some of these wounded chaps.
They'll give gold for 'em fast enough."

"I got a heap of gold watches, jackknives, and sech. I
don't know what in the land to do with 'em. Suppose we
can sell 'em in Richmond ? "

"Yes—but how are we going to get to Richmond ? We're
ordered to dump these Yanks at Newmarket and go back.
Ef we don't get to Richmond, our watches ain't worth a red

cent. Jess like's not old Bory'll issue an order to turn everything in. I'm blamed if I will!"

"Look yere, Ben, do you see that road off there to the right?"

"Yes, I do, but I don't see that it's different from any other road."

"Don't you? Well, honey, it's mitey sight different from all the roads you ever saw. It takes you where you don't want to go."

"What do you mean, Bob?"

"I jess mean that ar road goes to Newmarket, where these Yanks are ordered, but we've lost it and we shall come out in about an hour and a half at the junction, whar th' train goes on to Richmond. See?"

"Bob Purvis, you are a general, suah," and then there followed low, rollicking laughter, mingled with a gurgling as of a liquid swallowed from a flask. "But how'll we manage at the junction? We can't go right on the cars? There is some hocus-pocus about everything you do in the army."

"Oh, jess you keep your eye on your dad, and you'll see things you never saw afore. The minit them cavalry sneaks left us back thar, I made up my mind I'd skip Newmarket. They've gone back to pick up more loot. No one at the junction knows what our orders was. Besides, it'll be dark when we get thar. The trains'll be full of our wounded. We'll slip these Yanks in as if under orders. No one will know but we're hospital guards on a detail for the wounded. When it is found out we shall be in Richmond, and, if the provost folk get hold of me afore I've been home and planted my haul, then I'm a Yank."

"By mitey, Ben, you are a general, suah." Then suppressed laughter and the gurgling of the flowing enlivener. Jack blissfully fell into dreams, wherein home things and warlike doings mingled in grotesque medley. Relapses into consciousness followed at he knew not what intervals thereafter. He was conscious of cruel torment and a clumsy transfer into another vehicle, confused sounds of groans, curses, waving lights, and the hissing of escaping steam almost in his very ears. Then the anguish of thundering wheels, until his cracked brain reeled and he was mercifully unconscious. How long? His eyes opened on a clean white wall, flowers hung from the windows in plumy festoons, birds sang in the yellow dazzling sunlight. What could it mean? Was he at home? Surely there was nothing of war in these comfortable surroundings. His left arm was free, there was no one lying near to impede its movement. So it wasn't a hospital. He took vague note of all this before he tried to lift his arm. He raised his hand to rub his eyes and to assure himself that it was not a cruel delusion. When he took it away, a kind face—the face of a woman—was bending over him.

"You are feeling better, aren't you, lieutenant?"

"Lieutenant"? Why did she call him lieutenant? Had he been promoted on the battle-field? Was he in the Union lines? Oh, yes; else he would have been in a hospital, with moaning men all about him. He tried to speak. The woman put her finger to her lips, warningly.

"The doctor says you must not speak or be spoken to until you get strong."

Days passed. He couldn't tell how many, for he lay, long hours at a time, unconscious, the mental faculties mercifully dead while the wounded ligatures knit themselves anew. His right arm had been cut by a saber-stroke, and a pistol-ball had entered above the shoulder-blade. Prompt attention would have given him recovery in a few days, but the twenty-four hours in a cart and the cars made his condition, for a time, serious.

But now he is visibly stronger, and his nurse brings people into the room to see him. They look at him with wonder and admiration, while the good lady is all in a flutter of delight. He hears himself spoken of always as the "lieutenant," and hesitates to ask an explanation. The physician comes but seldom, the lady explaining that all the doctors in town are busy in the hospitals. The truth flashed upon him one morning, when his hostess came bursting in to say:

"The provost guard has come to take your name. I don't know it, for when you were brought here my son only heard you called lieutenant."

"My name is John Sprague"—Jack lifted himself to his elbow in excitement and disregard of everything—"and my regiment is the—ah!" He fell back, and the frightened dame hurried to him as she saw his changed look and deadly pallor.

"Oh, how careless of me; how unthinking! There, lie perfectly still. I will send the guard away and come back."

She was gone before he could recover his speech or enough coherence to say what was in his mind. She informed the orderly that the ailing man was John Sprague, a lieutenant in the First Virginia Volunteers, for that was the regiment the hospital guards had named, when, on the night of the arrival, the eager citizens swarmed at the station to take the wounded to their homes, the hospitals being sadly unready. Jack instantly suspected the situation, the conversation in the ambulance coming back to him now distinctly. What should he do? He was in honor bound to undeceive the kind-hearted and unwitting accomplice of the fraud practiced on herself as well as on him. She came in presently with an officer. Jack was not familiar with the rebel insignia, and could not discover his rank or service, but he expected to hear himself denounced as a spy or anything odious.

"Our surgeon has been sent to Manassas, and Dr. Van Ness is come to take care of you in his place," the matron said, as Jack stared silent and quavering at the new-comer. That gentleman examined the patient, shook his head dubiously and declared high fever at work, and ordered absolute quiet for at least twenty-four hours, when, if he could, he would return. "Continue the prescriptions you have now, Mrs. Raines. All he needs is quiet. The hospital steward will come to dress his wounds as usual."

Mrs. Raines came in with tea and toast in the evening, and as she spread the napkin on the bed she prattled cheerily.

"I'm so happy to-night. I've just received a letter from my son. He's at Manassas. He's been promoted to lieuten-

ant from sergeant. It was read at the head of the regiment
—for gallant service at the Henry House, where he captured
part of a company of Yankees with a squad of cavalry. He's
only twenty-two, and if he lives he may be a general—if those
cowardly Yankees will only fight long enough. But I'm
afraid they won't. *The Whig* says this morning that that
beast Lincoln has to keep himself guarded by a regiment of
negroes, as the Northern people want to kill him. I hope
they won't, for if they did then they might put some one in
his place that has some sense, and then the war would come
to an end and we should be cheated in a settlement, for the
Yankees are sharper than our big-hearted, generous men.
No, sir, no; you mustn't talk. I've promised to keep you
quiet, so lie still. I'll read *The Whig* to you."

She ran over the meager dispatches made up of hearsay
and speculation—how the North had fallen into a rage with
the Washington authorities; how Lincoln's life wasn't safe;
how the Cabinet had all resigned; how the Democrats had
arisen in Congress and in the State Legislatures and demanded negotiations with "President Davis"; how England
was drawing up a treaty with the new Confederacy. Then
she turned to the local page. She ran over a dozen paragraphs recounting the deeds of well-known Richmond heroes, but these made no impression upon the listener, until
she read:

"Major Vincent Atterbury, whose gallantry at the battle of
the 21st Richmond is a subject of pride to his friends, was
transferred to his country home, on the James, yesterday.
He is still very low, but the surgeons declare that home quiet
and careful nursing will restore him to his duties in time
for the autumn campaign—if the Yankees do not surrender
before that time."

Jack's eyes were so bright when Mrs. Raines looked at
him, as she lowered the sheet, that she arose, exclaiming
quickly:

"There, I have brought the fever back! Your eyes are
glittering and your cheeks are flushed. No, do not speak."

She moved precipitately from the room, and Jack sank

back with a groan. His danger, if not his difficulties, might be overcome now. He would write to Mrs. Atterbury, and through Vincent arrange for an exchange. But a still deeper trouble had been on his mind. Where were Barney and Nick, and, worse than all, young Dick Perley? If any mishap had befallen that boy, he would shrink from returning to Acredale. And his mother, what must her state of mind be? How many days had passed since the battle? He had no means of knowing. Ah, yes! The paper was there on the stand, where Mrs. Raines had thrown it. He raised himself slowly and seized it. Heavens! Saturday, August 4th? Two weeks since that fatal Sunday! And his mother? Oh, he must find means to write, to telegraph. "Mrs. Raines," he called, hoarsely, "Mrs. Raines!" She came running to his side in alarm.

"Oh, what has happened? You are worse!"

"I am very comfortable; but, my kind friend, I must—I must let my mother know that I am alive; she will think me dead."

"That's what I meant to ask you—just as soon as you seemed able to talk. I would have gladly sent her word and invited her to come here, but I didn't know the name nor the address. You didn't have a stitch of clothes when you came except your underwear; the rest had been taken off, the men said, because they were soiled and bloody, and there wasn't a clew of any sort to your identity, except that you were a lieutenant in a Virginia regiment. I thought we should find out when the provost came, but they have sent to Manassas, and no answer has come back yet."

"The men who brought me here deceived you, Mrs. Raines. I do not belong to a Virginia regiment; I belong to a New York regiment, and I am a—a—Union soldier."

"Great Father! A Yankee?" The poor woman sank on the nearest chair, as some one who has been nursing a patient that suddenly turns out to have small-pox or leprosy.

"Yes, Mrs. Raines: if you prefer that name, I'm a Yankee—but we call only New-Englanders Yankees." He

9

waited for her to speak, but as she sat dumb, helpless, over-come, he continued: "I tried to explain the mistake before, but your kindness cut me off. I can only say that, though you have given me a mother's care and a Christian's consid-eration under a misunderstanding, I trust you will not blame me for willful deception nor regret the goodness you have shown the stranger in your hands."

"And those men that brought you here—were they Yan-kees, too?" she asked, her mind dwelling, womanlike, on the least essential factor of the problem in order to keep the grievous fact as far away as possible.

"Oh, no! they were your own people. There was no collusion, I assure you." Jack almost laughed now, as the dialogue in the ambulance recurred to him, and the adroit use the men had made of their unconscious charges to secure a furlough. "No; I was more amazed than I can say when I came to myself in this charming chamber—a paradise it seemed to me, a home paradise—when your kind face bent over my pillow."

"It's a cruel disappointment," she said, rising and hold-ing the back of the chair as she tilted it toward the bed. "We were so proud of you—so proud to have any one that had fought for our dear State in our own house to nurse, to bring back to life. Every one on the street has some one from the battle, and oh, what will be said of us when people know that we—we—" But here the cruelty of the conclu-sion came too sharply to her mind, and she walked to the window, sobbing softly.

"I can understand, believe me, Mrs. Raines, and I am going to propose a means to you whereby I shall be taken from here, and your neighbors shall never know that you entertained an enemy unawares, though God knows I don't see why we should be enemies when the battle is over. If your son were in my condition I should think very hard of my mother if she were not to him what you have been to me."

"But I can't believe you're a Yankee; you were so gen-tle, so patient in all the dreadful times when the surgeon was cutting and hacking. Oh, I can't believe it! Oh, please say you are joking—that you wanted to give me a fright. And you have a mother?" She came over near the bed again and stood looking at him dismally, half in doubt, half in perplexed wonder; for Yankee, in her mind, suggested some such monster as the Greeks conjured when the Goths poured into the peninsula, maiming the men and debauching the women. "I said Sprague wasn't a Virginia name," she murmered, plaintively, in a last desperate attempt to fortify herself against the worst; "but there's no telling what names are in Virginia now, since Norfolk has grown so big and folks come in that way from all over the world."

Jack could scarcely keep a serious face, as this humorous lament displayed the pride of the Dominion and the unconscious Bœotianism of the provincial.

"Now, Mrs. Raines, here is what I propose: Major Atterbury, of whom you read to me, is my nearest friend. We have been college comrades; he has passed weeks at my home, and I have been asked to his, and meant to come this autumn vacation, if the war had not broken out. I will write to his mother, and she will have me removed to her house, and it need never be known that you gave aid and comfort to the enemy."

"But the Atterburys will never receive you. They were the first to favor secession, when all the rest of us opposed it. To tell you the truth, Mr. Sprague, it is partly because we were abused a good deal for holding back when the secession excitement was first started, that I am so—so anxious about the story getting out that we entertained a Yankee prisoner. My husband is in the service of the government in Norfolk, and my son is in the army. But you know what neighborhood gossip is."

So, after a friendly talk in which the poor lady cried a great deal and besought Jack's good-will for her darling William, if ever he were luckless enough to be captured, the note was written and dispatched to the Atterburys, whose city house was near the capital square. The messenger returned a half-hour later, reporting the family out of town;

that they had taken the major to their country-place near Williamsburg, on the banks of the James. The messenger had given the letter to the housekeeper, who said that it would go out an hour later with the mail sent daily to the family.

"Williamsburg is two hours' ride on the train," Mrs. Raines explained, "and we sha'n't hear from them until to-morrow."

Jack said nothing; his mind was on his mother and the misery she must be enduring. He turned restlessly on his pillow that night, and woke feverish in the morning. Mrs. Raines now took as much pains to keep people who called from seeing her hero as she had before put herself out to display the invalid. Even the doctor, calling about nine o'clock, was sent away on some pretext, and the poor lady waited with an anxiety, almost as poignant as Jack's own, for the response to his note. About noon it came. Mrs. Raines went to the door herself, not daring to trust the colored girl, who had lavished untold pains on Jack's linen and the manual part of his care. Jack heard low voices in the hallway, then on the stairs, and he knew some one had come.

"Here is Miss Atterbury sent to fetch you, lieutenant," Mrs. Raines said, now very much relieved, and impressed, too, by the powerful friends her dangerous *protégé* was able to summon so promptly by a line.

"You are Rosalind?" Jack said, smiling at a pair of the brownest and most bewitching eyes fixed soberly on him. "I should have known you if I had met you in the street, although you were a small girl when I saw you last."

"You needn't take much credit for that, sir, since Vincent probably had my portrait in all his coat-pockets and his room frescoed with them—it's a trick of his. So you needn't pretend that it was family likeness—I know better. Vincent has all the good looks of the family, and I have all the good qualities."

"That's why you've come to console the afflicted?"

"Yes, duty—you know how disagreeable that is. Vincent declared he would come himself, if I didn't, and mamma wouldn't hear of your being moved by servants alone, so I am here. But I give you fair warning that I am a rebel of the most ferocious sort. You shall ride under the 'bonnie blue flag' to Rosedale, and you shall salute our flag every morning when it is hoisted."

"I am the most docile of men and the easiest of invalids. I will ride under Captain Kidd's flag and salute the standard of the Grand Turk, to be near Vincent just now."

When Rosalind's colored aids had placed him in the big family carriage, and he had bidden Mrs. Raines farewell, the young lady resumed : "Ah, I know you ! Vincent has told me about your Yankee ways. Not another word, sir. I'll act as guide, and tell you all we see of note as we go on. There where your eyes are resting now is the Confederate Hall of Independence ; that modest house on the corner is President Davis's. We are going to build him another by and by—after we capture Washington and get our belongings—no—no—you needn't speak. I know what you want to say. That's Washington's monument, and there is our dear old Jefferson. Doesn't it quicken even your slow ·Yankee blood to pass the walls that heard Jefferson at his greatest, that held Patrick Henry, that covered Washington ? Ah ! if you Northern Pharisees were not money-grubbers and souless to everything but the almighty dollar, you would join hands with us in creating our new Confederacy. Yes, sir, you're my prisoner. We shall see that one Yankee is kept out of mischief—if the war lasts—which is not likely, as your folks are quite cowed by the victory at Bull Run. Wasn't it a splendid fight ? I shall never forgive Vin for not letting me know it was coming off. Vin, you know, is on General Early's staff. He knew two days before that there was to be a fight, for he started from Winchester to keep the railway clear and lead the troops to the Henry House when they got off the cars. He was in the thickest of the fight, near Professor Jackson—Stonewall, they call him now. He—Vin—had three horses killed, and was made a major on the field by General Joe Johnston. What ?—"

"Please let the carriage stop a moment. I want to absorb that lovely view."

He pointed to the James, debouching from the hills over which the carriage was slowly rolling. The afternoon sun was behind them ; but far, far to the eastward the noble river wound through masses of dark, deep green until it was lost in a glow of shimmering mirage in the low horizon.

"Isn't it lovely ? We shall have a nobler capital city than Washington, with its horrid red streets, its wilderness of bare squares, its interminable distances—"

"Carcassonne," Jack murmured.

"Carcassonne—what's that ? "

"An exquisite bit of verse and a touching story. I—"

"There, there—stop. You are talking again. You shall read the poem to me—that is, if it isn't a glorification of the North."

"No ; Carcassonne was a city of the South."

"Really—you must not talk. I'm not going to open my lips again until we get to the boat."

She settled back in her place and took out a book, looking over the top at him from time to time. The motion of the vehicle, the warmth of the day, and the odorous breath of flowers and shrubs gradually dulled his mischievous spirits, and he slept tranquilly until the carriage drew up at the wharf at Harrison's Landing, whence, taken on a primitive ferry, they in an hour or more arrived at a long wooden pier extending into the river. It was nearly six o'clock when the carriage entered a solemn aisle of pines ending in a labyrinth of oleanders and the tropic-like plants of the South. Then an old-fashioned porticoed mansion came into view, and on signal from the driver a *posse* of colored servants came trooping out noisily to carry the invalid in. Mrs. Atterbury was on the veranda, and stepped down to the carriage to welcome the guest. She greeted him with the affectionate cordiality of a mother, and asked :

"How have you borne the fatigue ? I hope Rosa hasn't let you talk ? "

"If I may speak now it will be to bear testimony that I

have been made a mummy since noon. I haven't been permitted to ask the local habitation or name of the scenic delights that have made the journey a panorama of beauty and my guide a tyrant, to whom, by comparison, Caligula was a tender master!"

"Since you slept most of the way you must have dreamed the beauty, as you certainly have invented the tyrant," Rosa retorted, as the brawny servants lifted Jack bodily and carried him up the three steps and into the sitting-room.

"Your quarters are next to my son's, if you think you can endure the constant outbreaks of that locality. We are with him in all but his sleeping hours, so you will do well to reflect before you decide."

"Oh, I shall insist on being near Vincent. He's too badly hurt to overcome me in case we are tempted to fight our battles over again."

"But he has allies here, sir, and you must remember that you are a prisoner of war," Rosa cried from the landing above, *en route* to minister to her hero before the Yankee invaded him. Vincent was propped up in the bed with a mass of pillows, and the two friends embraced in college-boy fashion, too much moved for a moment to begin the flood of questions each was eager to ask and answer.

"Before I say a word of anything else, Vint, I want you to do me a great service. It is two weeks since the battle. I am sure my mother can not have any certain information about me. Can you manage any way to get a letter or telegram sent her?"

"Of course I can. Nothing easier. Write your telegram. I will send it under cover to General Early. He will forward it by flag of truce to Washington, and it will be sent North from there."

But Jack's letter was never sent, for when the post came from Richmond the next day, Vincent read in the morning paper a surprising personal item:

"'Among the distinguished arrivals in the city within the week, we have just learned of the presence of Mrs.

Sprague, wife of the famous Senator, a contemporary with
Clay and Webster. Mrs. Sprague has come to Richmond in
search of her son, who was captured or killed on the field
near the Henry House. She comes with her daughter under a safeguard from General Johnston, who knew the
family when he was at West Point. Mrs. Sprague is stopping with Mrs. Bevan, on Vernon Street, and is under the
escort of Private William Bevan of the general headquarters.' "

CHAPTER XIV.

UNDER TWO FLAGS.

THAT modest paragraph in the morning paper wrought
amazing results in the fortunes of many of the people we are
interested in. A regiment of cavalry encamped near the
outskirts of the city on the line of the Virginia Central had
broken camp early in the morning to march northward.
One company detailed to bring up the rear was still loiter-
ing near the station when the newspapers were thrown off
the train and eagerly seized by the men, who bestrewed
themselves in groups to hear the news read aloud.

"Here, you Towhead, you're company clerk; you read so
that we can all hear."

In response to this a stripling, in the most extraordinary
costume, came out from the impedimenta of the company
with a springy step and consequential air. You wouldn't
have recognized the scapegrace, Dick Perley, in the carnival
figure that came forward, for his curling blond hair was
closely cropped, his face was smeared with the soilure of
pots and pans, and it was evident that the eager warrior had
exchanged the weapons of war for the utensils of the company kitchen. He read in a high, clear treble the tele-
graphic dispatches, the sanguinary editorial ratiocinations,
Orphic in their prophetic sententiousness, and then turned
to the local columns.

Any one listening to the lad would never have suspected that he was not a Southron. He prolonged the *a's* and *o's*, as the Southern trick is, and imitated to such perfection the pleasant localisms of Virginian pronunciation, that keener critics of speech and accent than these galliard troops would have been deceived. But suddenly his voice breaks, he falls into the clear, distinct enunciation of New York—the only speech in the Union that betrays no sign of locality. He is reading the lines about the distinguished arrivals. Fortunately at the instant there is a blast from the bugles—"Fall in!"—and the men rush to their horses. In twenty minutes the company is clattering out on the Mechanicsville road, and at noon, when the squadron halted for dinner, the company cook had to rely on the clumsy ministrations of his colored aides. "Towhead" had disappeared.

Olympia, after a night of anguish, began the new day with a heavy burden on her mind. Mrs. Sprague was delirious. The physician summoned during the night shook his head gravely. She was suffering from overexertion, heat, and anxiety. He was unable to do more than mitigate her sufferings. He recommended country air and absolute repose. Merry, too, though holding up bravely, gave signs of breaking down. The two women—Olympia and Merry—under the escort of young Bevan, had gone through the prisons, the dreadful Castle Winder, and through the hospitals, with hope dying at every new disappointment. They came across many of the Caribees, and saw a member of Congress, caught on the battle-field, who knew the regiment well.

Jack had been traced to Porter's lines, then far to the left, where Nick had been told to wait. Nick was among the sweltering mass at Castle Winder, but he could trace the missing no farther. He told of Jack's persistent valor to the last, and the dreadful moment, when he, Jack, had been separated. Dick he had not seen at all. Olympia made intercession for Nick's release, but was informed that nothing could be done until a cartel of exchange had been arranged. The Yankee authorities had in the first five

months of the war refused to make any arrangement, while
the Union forces were capturing the Confederate armies in
West Virginia and Missouri. Now that the Confederates
held an equal number, they were going to retaliate upon
the overconfident North. Olympia placed five hundred
dollars at Nick's disposal in the hands of the comman-
dant to supply the lad with better food than the commissary furnished, and, promising him strenuous aid so
soon as she got back to Washington, she resumed the quest
for the lost. She had written out an advertisement, to be
inserted in all the city papers, and was to visit the offices
herself with young Bevan that evening. She had her bon-
net on, and was charging Merry how to minister to the ailing mother, when the hostess knocked at the door. "A lady
is in the parlor who says she must see Mrs. Sprague immediately." Olympia followed Mrs. Bevan down tremblingly,
far from any anticipation of what was in store for her;
rather in the belief that it was some wretched mother from
Acredale who had learned of their presence and hoped to get
aid for an imprisoned son, husband, or brother. But when
she saw the kind, matronly face of Mrs. Raines beaming
with the delight of bearing good news, she sank into a
chair, saying faintly:

" Did you wish to see me, Mrs.—Mrs.—"

" You are not Mrs. Sprague ? "

" No; my mother is very ill. I am Mrs. Sprague's daughter. Can I—"

" Well, Miss Sprague, I think I can cure your mother. I—"

She arose and walked mysteriously to the door and looked
into the hallway.

"I know what the disease is your mother is suffering
from."

She couldn't resist prolonging the consequence of her
mission. All women have the dramatic instinct. All love
to intensify the unexpected. But Olympia's listless manner
and touching desolation spurred her on. She put her fingers to her lips warningly, and coming quite near her whispered, as she had seen people do on the stage:

"Don't make any disturbance; don't faint. Your brother is alive and well! There, there—I told you."

Olympia was hugging the astonished woman, who glanced in terror over her shoulder to see that feminine curiosity was not dangerously alert. "You will ruin me," she whispered, "if you don't be calm." Then Olympia suddenly recovered herself, sobbing behind her handkerchief. "He has been at my house two weeks. He left yesterday and is now with Major Atterbury's family on the James River, near Williamsburg. Miss Atterbury came herself to take him there yesterday morning. I saw your name in *The Examiner* only an hour ago, and I came at once to relieve the distress I knew you must be suffering."

Then the kind soul told the story, charging the sister never to reveal the facts. She withdrew very happy and contented, for Olympia had said many tender things; she almost felt that she had done the Confederacy a great service, to have laid so many people under an obligation that might in the future result in something remarkable for the cause.

Olympia's purpose of breaking the news gradually to the invalid was frustrated by her tell-tale eyes and buoyant movements.

"O Olympia, you have seen John!" she screamed, starting up—"where is he? Oh, where is he? I know you have seen him!" And then there were subdued laughter and tears, and mamma instantly declared her intention of flying to the hero. But there was considerable diplomacy still requisite. Mrs. Raines must not be compromised, and young Bevan must get transportation for them to the Atterburys. It was past noon when the carriage came for them. Olympia had come down-stairs to give Mrs. Bevan final instruction regarding letters and luggage, when a resounding knock came upon the door. Mrs. Bevan opened it herself, and Olympia, standing in the hall, heard a well-known voice, quick, eager, joyous :

"Is Mrs. Sprague, here ?

"O Richard," Olympia cried, rushing at him—"ah, you darling boy !—Aunt Merry—Aunt Merry ! Come—come quick! He is here." But Aunt Merry at the head of the stairs had heard the voice, and Dick, tearing himself ungallantly from the embrace of beauty, was up the stairs in four leaps and in the arms of the fainting spinster.

"It is Miss Perley's nephew," Olympia said, joyously, to the amazed lady of the house, who stood speechless. "We had given up all hope of seeing him, as his name was not on our army list. He ran away to be with my brother, and we felt like murderers, as you may imagine, and are almost as much relieved to find him as our own flesh and blood."

The subsequent conversation between the matron and the young girl seemed to put the mistress of the house in excellent humor, and when the carriage drove off she kissed all the ladies quite as rapturously as if she had never vowed undying hatred and vengeance upon the Yankee people. In the carriage the prodigal Dick rattled off the story of his adventures. He had come to Company K after Jack had been sent out on the skirmish-line. He had followed in wild despair the direction pointed out to him. He had lost his way until he met Colonel Sherman's orderlies. They had told him where the company was halted on the banks of the stream.

When he reached the place indicated he learned of Jack's detail to the extreme right of the army. He dared not set out openly to follow. He ran back in the bushes, out of sight, and then by a *détour* struck the stream far above to the right. The volleys away to the west guided him, and he tore forward, bruising his flesh and tearing his raiment to tatters. The stream seemed too deep to cross, for a mile or more, but finally, finding that the firing seemed to go swiftly to the southward, he plunged in. The banks on the other side were rugged and precipitous, and he was obliged to push on in the morass that the stream wound through. But nature gave out, and on a sunny slope he sat down to rest. He soon fell into a sound sleep, and when he woke there was noise of men laughing and shouting about him. He started to his feet.

"Hello! buster," a voice said near him. "What are you

doin' away from yer mammy? Reckon she'll think the Yanks have got you if you ain't home for bedtime."

The man who said this was lying peacefully under a laurel-bush. Others were sprawled about, feasting on the spoil of Union haversacks.

"I knew then that I was in a rebel camp," Dick continued, "but I wasn't afraid, because my clothes were not military; and, even if they had been, they were so torn and muddy, no one would have thought of them as a uniform. But, for that matter, a good many of the rebels had blue trousers; and, as for regimentals, there really were none, as we have them. I made believe that I lived in the neighborhood, imitated the Southern twang, and was set to work right away helping the company cook. The firing was still going on very near us, to the south, west, and east. But the men didn't seem to mind it much. In about a half-hour there was a sudden move.

"A volley was poured into us from the east, and in an instant all the graybacks were in commotion. I heard the officers shout: 'We are surrounded! Die at your post, men!' But the men didn't want to die at their posts, or anywhere else, but made off like frightened rabbits. In a few minutes we were all marching between two lines of Richardson's Union brigade. I had no trouble in stepping out, and then I pushed on in Jack's direction. But I could not find him when I got to Hunter's headquarters. An orderly remembered seeing him, or rather seeing the men that brought the good news that Sherman was on the rebel side of the stone bridge early in the battle. There I found an orderly of Franklin's, who had seen two men I described, sent off to the right to picket, until the cavalry could be sent there. I came upon Nick Marsh near the general's headquarters, and he told me the direction the others had gone, but urged me to remain with him—as Jack would surely be back there, horsemen having ridden out in that direction to relieve him. I don't know how far I went, but it must have been a mile.

"There I had to lie in the bushes, for two columns of troops were coming and going, the flying fellows that Sher-

man had routed near the stone bridge and the re-enforcements that were tearing up from the Manassas Railway. The
men coming were laughing and singing as they ran. The
men flying were silent, and seemed too frightened to notice
the forces coming to their support. I broke out of the bushes and ran toward the line of thick trees that seemed to mark
the course of the river. As I came out on a deep sandy road
I ran right into troops, halting. There were great cheering
and hurrah ; then a cavalcade of civilians came through
the rushing ranks at a gallop. 'Hurrah for President Davis! Hip, hip, hurrah!' I saw him. He was riding a splendid gray horse, and as the men broke into shouts he raised
his hat and bowed right and left. He was stopped for a few
minutes just in front of where I stood, or, rather, I ran to
where he halted. There were long trains of wounded filing
down the road, and men without guns, knapsacks, or side-
arms, breaking through the bushes on all sides.

"'They've routed us, Mr. President,' a wounded officer
cried, as the stretcher upon which he was lying passed near
Jeff Davis.

"'What part of the field are you from ?' Davis asked,
huskily.

"'Bartow's brigade, stone bridge. They've captured all
our guns, and are pouring down on the fords. You will be
in danger Mr. President, if you continue northward a hundred yards.'

"Sure enough, there was a mighty cheer, hardly a half-mile
to the north of us, and clouds of dust arose in the air. Davis
watched the movement through his glass, and, turning to a
horseman at his side, cried, exultantly:

"'The breeze is from the northwest; that dust is going
toward the Warrenton Pike. Johnston has got up in time;
we've won the day!'

"With this he put spurs to his horse, and the squadron
halted on the road set off at a wild gallop. The words of
the President were repeated from man to man, and then a
mighty shout broke out. It seemed to clip the leaves from
the trees, as I saw them cut, an hour or two before, by

the swarming volleys of musketry. A horseman suddenly broke from a path just behind where I was.

"'Is President Davis here?' he asked, riding close to me, but not halting.

"'He has just ridden off yonder.' I pointed toward the cloud of dust east and north of us.

"'Split your throats, boys! General Beauregard has just sent me to the President to welcome him with the news that the Yankees are licked and flying in all directions! Not a man of them can escape. General Longstreet is on their rear at Centreville.'

"There were deafening, crazy shouts; hats, canteens, even muskets, were flung in the air, and the wounded, lying on the ground, were struck by some of these things as they fell, in a cloud, about them. The shouts grew louder and louder, they rose and fell, far, far away right and left. Everybody embraced everybody else. Men who had been limping and despondent before broke into wild dances of joy. Everybody wanted to go toward the field of battle now, but a provost guard filed down the road presently, and in a few minutes I saw a sight that made tears of rage and shame blind me. Whole regiments of blue-coats came at a quick-step through the dusty roadway, the rebel guards prodding them brutally with their bayonets. The fellows near me, who had been running from the fight, set up insulting cheers and cat-calls.

"'Did you'ns leave a lock of your hair with old Mas'r Lincoln?'

"'Come down to Dixie to marry niggers, have ye?' and scores of taunts more insulting and obscene. Our men never answered. They were worn and dusty. They had no weapons, of course, for the first thing the rebels did was to search every man, take his money, watch, studs, even his coat and shoes, when they were better than their own. Hundreds of our men were in their stocking-feet, or, rather, in their bare feet, as they tramped wearily through the burning sand and twisted roots. I heard one of the rebels near me, an officer, say that the prisoners were all going to the junction to take

the cars. President Davis had ordered that they should be
marched through the streets of Richmond to show the people
of the capital the extent of the victory. Then the thought
flashed into my head that if our army had been captured,
my best chance of finding Jack would be to follow to Richmond and watch the bluecoats. I easily slipped among the
prisoners, came to the city and saw every man that went to
Castle Winder. But no one that I knew was among them,
and I made up my mind that Jack had escaped. I saw Wesley Boone's father and sister at the Spottswood House yesterday, but I was too late to catch them, and, when I asked the
clerk at the desk, he said they had taken quarters in the
town—he didn't know where."

"That's a fact," Olympia exclaimed; "they left Washington before us. I wonder if they found Wesley?"

"I don't know," Dick continued. "The officers were
brought in a gang by themselves, and I didn't see them.
Well, I hung about the town, visiting all the places I thought
it likely Jack might be, and then I joined a cavalry company
that belonged to Early's brigade, at Manassas. I was going
there with them this morning to get back to our lines and find
Jack, when I saw the paragraph in *The Examiner*, telling
of your coming and whereabouts."

CHAPTER XV.

ROSEDALE.

"WHAT an intrepid young brave you are, Dick!" Olympia cried, as the artless narrative came to an end.

"What a cruel boy, to leave his family and—and—run
into such dreadful danger!" Merry expostulated.

"What a devoted boy, to risk his life and liberty for our
poor Jack!" Mrs. Sprague said, bending forward to stroke
the tow-head. The carriage passed down the same road that

Jack had gone the day before, whistling sarcasms at his keeper. At Harrison's Landing there was a delay of several hours, and the impatient party wandered on the shores of the majestic James—glittering, like a sylvan lake, in its rich border of woodland. The sun was too hot to permit of the excursion Dick suggested, and late in the afternoon the wheezy ferry carried them down the lake-like stream. On every hand there were signs of peace—not a fort, not a breastwork gave token that this was in a few months to be the shambles of mighty armies, the anchorage of that new wonder, the iron battle-ship; the scene of McClellan's miraculous victory at Malvern, of Grant's slaughtering grapplings with rebellion at bay, of Butler's comic joustings, and the last desperate onslaughts of Hancock's legions. The air, tempered by the faint flavor of salt in the water, filled the travelers with an intoxicating vigor, lent strength to their jaded forces, which, while tense with expectation, could not wholly resist the delicious aroma, the lovely outlines of primeval forest, the melody of strange birds, startled along the shore by the wheezy puffing of the ferry. There were cries of admiring delight as the carriage ran from the long wooden pier into the dim arcade of sycamore and pine, through which the road wound, all the way to Rosedale. Then they emerged into a gentle, rolling, upland, where cultivated fields spread far into the horizon, and in the distance a dense grove, which proved to be the park about the house. The coming of the carriage was a signal to a swarm of small black urchins to scramble, grinning and delighted, to the wide lawn. There was no need to sound the great knocker; no need to explain, when Rosalind, hurrying to the door, saw Olympia emerging from the vehicle. They had not seen each other in four years, but they were in each other's arms—laughing, sobbing—exclaiming:

"How did you know? When did you come?"

"Jack, Jack! Where is he? How is he?"

"Jack's able to eat," Rosa cried, darting down to embrace Mrs. Sprague, and starting with a little cry of wonder as Aunt Merry exclaimed, timidly:

10

"We're all here. You've captured the best part of Acredale, though you haven't got Washington yet."

"Why, how delightful! We shall think it is Acredale," Rosa cried, welcoming the blushing lady. "And—I should say, if he were not so much like—like 'we uns,' that this was my old friend, the naughty Richard," she said, welcoming the blushing youth cordially. (Dick avowed afterward, in confidence to Jack, that she would have kissed him if he hadn't held back, remembering his unkempt condition.) Mamma and Olympia were shown up to the door of Jack's room, where Rosalind very discreetly left them, to introduce the other guests to Mrs. Atterbury, attracted to the place by the unwonted sounds. When presently the visitors were shown into Vincent's room, Jack called out to them to come and see valor conquered by love; and, when they entered, mamma was brushing her eyes furtively, while she still held Jack's unwounded hand under the counterpane. Master Dick excited the maternal alarm by throwing himself rapturously on the wounded hero and giving him the kiss he had denied Rosalind. Indeed, he showered kisses on the abashed hero, whose eyes were suspiciously sparkling at the evidence of the boy's delight. He established himself in Jack's room, and no urging, prayer, or reproof could induce him to quit his hero's sight.

"I lost him once," he said, doggedly, "and I'm not going to lose him again. Where he goes, I'm going; where he stays, I'll stay—sha'n't I, Jack?"

"You shall, indeed, my dauntless Orestes; you shall share my fortunes, whatever they be."

He insisted on a cot in the room, and there, during the convalescence of his idol, he persisted in sleeping—ruling all who had to do with the invalid in his own capricious humor, hardly excepting Mrs. Sprague, whom he tolerated with some impatience. Letters were dispatched northward to relieve the anxiety of Pliny and Phemie, as well as the Marshes. But it hung heavily on Jack's heart that no trace of Barney had been found. Advertisements were sent to the Richmond papers, and he waited in restless impatience for some sign of the kind lad's well-being.

"Well, Jack, this isn't much like the pomp and circumstance of glorious war," Olympia cried, the next morning, coming in from an excursion about the "plantation," as she insisted on calling the estate, attended by Merry, Rosa, and Dick. "I never saw such foliage! The roses are as large as sunflowers, and there are whole fields of them!"

"Yes; I believe the Atterburys make merchandise of them."

"But who buys them about here? They seem to grow wild—as fine in form and color as our hot-house varieties. Surely they are not bought by the colored people, and there seems to be no one else—no other inhabitants, I mean."

"Oh, no; they are shipped North in the season for them; but I don't think the family has paid much attention to that branch of the business of late years. Their revenues come from tobacco and cotton. Their cotton-fields are in South Carolina and along the Atlantic coast."

"And are these colored people all slaves?" Her voice sank to a whisper, for Vincent's door was ajar.

"Yes, every man jack of them. Did you ever see such merry rogues? They laugh and sing half the night, and sing and work half the day."

"They don't seem unhappy, that's a fact," Olympia said, reflectively, "but I should think ownership in flesh and blood would harden people; and yet the Atterburys are very kind and gentle. I saw tears in Mrs. Atterbury's eyes, yesterday, when mamma was sitting here with you."

"Yes," Jack said, unconsciously, "women enjoy crying—"

"You insufferable braggart, how dare you talk like that? Pray, what do you know about women's likes and dislikes?"

"Oh, I beg pardon, Polly; I'm sure I didn't mean anything—I was taking the minor for the major. All women like babies; babies pass most of their time crying; therefore women like crying."

"Well, if that is the sum of your college training, it is a good thing the war came—"

"What about the war? No treason in Rosedale, remember!" Vincent shouted from the next room. "You pledged me that when you talked war you would talk in open assembly." The voice neared the open doorway as he spoke. The servant had moved the invalid's cot, where Vincent could look in on Jack.

"There was really no war talk, Vint, except such war as women always raise, contention—"

"I object, Jack, to your generalization," Olympia retorted. "It is a habit of boyishness and immaturity.—He said a moment ago" (she turned to Vincent) "that women loved crying, and then sneaked out by a very shallow evasion."

"I'll leave it to Vint: All women love babies; babies do nothing but cry; therefore, women love crying; there couldn't be a syllogism more irrefutable."

"Unless it be that all women love liars," Vincent ventured, jocosely.

"How do you prove that?"

"All men are liars; women love men; therefore—"

"Oh, pshaw! you have to assume in that premise. I don't in mine. It is notorious that women love babies, while you have only the spiteful saying of a very uncertain old prophet for your major—"

"Whose major?" Rosa asked, appearing suddenly. "I'll have you to know, sir, that this major is mamma's, and no one else can have, hold, or make eyes at him."

"It was the major in logic we were making free with," Jack mumbled, laughing. "I hope logic isn't a heresy in your new Confederacy, as religion was in the French Constitution of '93?"

Rosa looked at Olympia, a little perplexed, and, seating herself on the cot with Vincent, where she could caress him furtively, said, with piquant deliberation:

"I don't know about logic, but we've got everything needed to make us happy in the Montgomery Constitution."

"Have you read it?" Jack asked, innocently.

"How insulting! Of course I have. I read it the very first thing when it appeared in the newspapers."

"Catch our Northern women doing that!" Jack interjected, loftily. "There is my learned sister, she doesn't know the Constitution from Plato's Dialogues."

"Indeed, I do not; nor do I know Plato's Dialogues," Olympia returned, quite at ease in this state of ignorance.

"Wherein does the Montgomery Constitution differ from the old one?" Jack asked, looking at Vincent.

"I'm blessed if I know. I've read neither. I did read the Declaration of Independence once at a Fourth-of-July barbecue. I always thought that was the Constitution. Indeed, every fellow about here does! You know in the South the women do all the thinking for the men. Rosa keeps my political conscience."

"Well, then, Lord High Chancellor, tell us the vital articles in the Montgomery document that have inspired you to arm Mars for the conflict, plunge millions into strife and thousands into hades, as Socrates would have said, employing his method?" Jack continued derisively.

"Our Constitution assures us the eternal right to own our own property."

"Slaves?"

"Yes."

"No one denied you that right, so far as the law went, under the old; it was only the justice, the humanity, that was questioned. The right would have endured a hundred years, perhaps forever, if you had kept still—"

"Come, Jack, I won't listen to politics," Olympia cried, with a warning look.

"No, the time for talk is past; it is battle, and God defend the right!" Rosa said, solemnly.

"And you may be sure he will," Jack added, softly, as though to himself.

"But we've got far away from the crying and the babies," Vincent began, when Jack interrupted, fervently:

"Thank Heaven!"

"You monster!" the two girls cried in a breath.

"No, I can't conceive a sillier paradox than 'A babe in the house is a well-spring of joy.' A woman must have written it first. Now, my idea of perfect happiness for a house is to have two wounded warriors like Vincent and me, tractable, amiable, always ready to join in rational conversation and make love if necessary, providing we're encouraged."

"Really, Olympia, your Northern men are not what I fancied," Rosa cried, with a laugh.

"What did you fancy them?"

"Oh, ever so different, from this—this saucy fellow—modest, timid, shy; needing ever so much encouragement to—to—"

"Claim their due?" Jack added, slyly.

"Well, there is one that doesn't require much encouragement to claim everything that comes in his way," Rosa retorts, and Olympia adds:

"And to spare my feelings you won't name him now."

"Exactly," said Rosa.

"How touching!" exclaimed Vincent.

"I left all my blood to enrich your soil, or I'd blush," replied Jack.

"Oh, no; it won't enrich the soil; it will bring out a crop of Johnny Jump-ups, a weed that we don't relish in the South," retorted Rosa.

"Ah, Jack, you're hit there!—Rosa, I'm proud of you. This odious Yankee needs combing down; he ran over us so long at college that he is conceited in his own impudence," and Vincent exploded in shouts of laughter.

"I fear you're not a botanist, Miss Rosa. It's 'Jack in the pulpit' that will spring from Northern blood, and they'll preach such truths that the very herbage will bring the lesson of liberty and toleration to you."

"What is this very serious discussion, my children?" Mrs. Atterbury said, beaming sweetly upon the group. "I couldn't imagine what had started Vincent in such boisterous laughter; and now, that I come, Mr. Jack is as serious as we were at school when Madame Clarice told us of our sins."

"Jack was telling his, mamma, and that is still more

serious than to hear one's own," Vincent said, grinning at the moralist.

" But, to be serious a moment, I have written to my old friend General Robert Lee, of Arlington, about Miss Perley. I know that he will grant her permission to take Richard home with her, and the question now is whether it is safe to let them go together alone ? " Mrs. Atterbury addressed the question to Olympia, making no account of Jack.

" Oh, let us leave the decision until you get General Lee's answer. If they get the message in Acredale that Dick is safe and sound, I don't see why they need go back before we do. I shall be able to travel in a few weeks. If the roads were not so rickety I wouldn't be afraid to set out now," Jack answered.

"Impossible ! You can't leave for a month yet, if then," Vincent proclaimed, authoritatively. " I know what gun-shot wounds are : you think they are healed, and begin fooling about, when you find yourself laid up worse than ever. There's no hurry. The campaign can't begin before October. I'm as anxious to be back as you are, but I don't mean to stir before October. Perhaps you think it will be dull here ? Just wait until you are strong enough to knock about a bit ; we shall have royal rides. We'll go to Williamsburg and see the oldest college in the country. We'll go down the James, and you shall see some of the richest lands in the world. We'll get a lot of fellows out from Richmond and have our regular barbecue in September. We wind up the season here every year with a grand dance, and Olympia shall lead the Queen Anne minuet with mamma's kinsman, General Lee, who is the President's chief of staff."

" This doesn't sound much like soldiering," Jack said, dreamily.

"No. When in the field, let us fight ; when at home, let us be merry."

" A very proper sentiment, young men. We want you to be very merry, for you must remember the time comes when we can't be anything but sad—when you are away and the night of doubt settles upon our weak women's hearts." It was Mrs. Atterbury who spoke, and the sentence seemed to bring silence upon the group.

Meanwhile, all the inquiries set on foot through the agency of the Atterburys failed to bring any tidings of Barney Moore. It suddenly occurred to Jack that the poor fellow was masquerading as a rebel in the bosom of some eager patriot like Mrs. Raines and he reluctantly consented to let Dick go to Richmond to investigate. Perhaps Mrs. Raines might know where the wounded men were taken that had come with him. Some of the stragglers could at least be found. The advertisement asking information concerning a wounded man arriving in Richmond with himself was kept in all the journals. But Merry wouldn't consent to let Dick go on the dangerous quest without her. She would never dare face her sisters if any mishap came to the lad, and, though Vincent put him under the care of an experienced overseer, and ordered the town-house to be opened for his entertainment, the timorous aunt was immovable.

"You must go and call on the President, Miss Merry. He receives Thursdays at the State-House. Then you'll see a really great man in authority, not the backwoods clowns that have brought this country into ridicule—such a man as Virginia used to give the people for President," Rosa said in the tone a lady of Louis XVIII's court might have used to an adherent of the Bonapartes.

" Ah, Rosa, we saw a gentle, tender-hearted man in Washington—the very ideal of a people's father. No one else can ever be President to me while he lives," Olympia said, seriously.

"Lincoln?" Rosa asked, a little disdainfully.

"Yes, Abraham Lincoln. We have all misunderstood him Oh, if you could have seen him as I saw him—so patient, so considerate ; the sorrows of the nation in his heart and its burdens on his shoulders ; but confident, calm, serene, with the benignant humility of a man sent by God," Olympia added almost reverently. " It was he who came to our aid and ordered the rules to be broken that our mother might seek Jack."

Rosa was about to retort, but a warning glance from Vincent checked her, and she said nothing.

"I say, Dick, don't try to capture Jeff Davis or blow up the Confederate Congress, or any other of the casual master strokes that may enter your wild head. Remember that we have given double hostages to the enemy. We have accepted their hospitality, and we have made ourselves their guests," Jack said, half seriously, as the young Hotspur wrung his hand in a tearful embrace.

"Above all, remember, Mr. Yankee, that you are in a certain sense a civilian now; you must not compromise us by free speech in Richmond," Rosa added.

"Ah, I know very well there's none of that in the South; you folks object to free speech ; they killed poor old Brown for it ; that's what you made war for, to silence free speech," Dick cried hotly, while Merry pinched his arm in terror.

Dick began his campaign in the morning with long-headed address. He visited the prison under ample powers from General Lee—procured though Vincent's mediation. There were a score of the Caribees in Castle Winder, and to these the boy came as a good fairy in the tale. For he distributed money, tobacco, and other things, which enabled the unfortunates to beguile the tedious hours of confinement. The prisoners were crowded like cattle in the immense warehouse in squads of a hundred or more. They had blankets to stretch on the floor for beds, a general basin to wash in, and for some time amused themselves watching through the barred windows the crowds outside that flocked to the place to see the Yankees, and, when not checked by the guards, to revile and taunt them.

Dick was enraged to see how contentedly the men bore the irksome confinement, the meager food, and harsh peremptoriness of the beardless boys set over them as guards. Most of the prisoners passed the time in cards, playing for buttons, trinkets, or what not that formed their scanty possessions. Dick learned that all the commissioned officers of

the company with Wesley Boone had been wounded or killed
in the charge near the stone bridge. Wesley had been with
the prisoners at first. He had been struck on the head, and
was in a raging fever when his father and sister came to the
prison to take him away. No one could tell where he was
now, but Dick knew that he must be in the city, since there
were no exchanges, the Confederates allowing no one to
leave the lines except women with the dead, or those who
came from the North on special permits.

Then he visited the provost headquarters, and was shown
the complete list of names recorded in the books there ; but
Barney's was not among them. At the Spottswood Hotel,
the day after his coming, he met Elisha Boone, haggard, depressed, almost despairing. Dick had no love for the hard-
headed plutocrat, but he couldn't resist making himself
known.

"How d'ye do, Mr. Boone ? I hope Wesley is coming on
well, sir."

Boone brought his wandering eyes down to the stripling
in dull amazement.

"Why, where on earth do you come from? How is it
you are free and allowed in the streets ?"

"Oh, I am a privileged person, sir. I am looking up
Company K. You haven't heard anything of young Moore,
Barney, who lives on the Callao road south of Acredale ?"

"No, my mind has been taken up with my son"; his
voice grew softer. "He is in a very bad way, and the
worst is there is no decent doctor to be got here for love or
money ; all the capable ones are in the army, and those that
are here refuse to take any interest in a Yankee."

The father's grief and the unhappy situation of his whi-
lom enemy touched the lad ; forgetting Jack's and Vincent's
warning, Dick said, impulsively :

"Oh, I can get him a good doctor. We have friends
here." He knew, the moment he had spoken the words,
that he had been imprudent—how imprudent the sudden,
suspicious gleam in Boone's eye at once admonished him.

"Friends here ? Union men have no friends here. There

are men here with whom I have done business for years, men that owe prosperity to me, but when I called on them they almost insulted me. If you have friends, you must have sympathies that they appreciate."

Dick knew what this meant. To be a Democrat had been, in Acredale, to be charged with secret leanings to rebellion. He restrained his wrath manfully, and said, simply:

"An old college friend of Jack's has been very kind to us."

"Us? I take it you mean the Spragues. They are stopping with Jeff Davis, I suppose? It's the least he could do for allies so steadfast."

"You shouldn't talk that way, sir. Every man in the Caribees, except old Oswald's gang, is a Democrat, but they are for the country before party."

"Yes, yes, it may be so—but, the North don't think that way. Well, I'm going to Washington to see if I can't get my boy out of this infernal place, where a man can't even get shaved decently."

"And Miss Kate, Mr. Boone, where is she?"

"She is nursing Wesley, poor girl. She is having a harder trial than any of us; for these devilish women fairly push into the sick-room to abuse the North and berate the soldiers that fought at Manassas."

"I should like to call on Wesley—if you don't mind," Dick said, hesitatingly.

"I shall be only too glad; and I'll tell you what it is, Richard, if you'll make use of your friends here, to get Kate and Wesley some comforts, some consideration, I'll make it worth your while. I'll see that you do not have to wait long for a commission, and I'll pay you any reasonable sum so soon as you get back North."

Dick restrained his anger under this insulting blow, perceiving, even in the hotness of his wrath, that the other was unconscious of the double ignominy implied in dealing with soldiers' rewards as personal bribes, and proffering money for common brotherly offices. It was only when Jack commended his astuteness, afterward, that Dick realized the adroitness of his own diplomacy.

"Thank you, Mr. Boone. I shouldn't care for promotion that I didn't win in war; and, as for money, I shall have enough when I need it. But any man in the Caribees shall have my help. Under the flag every man is a friend."

"True. Yes; you are quite right. Kate will be very glad to see you."

They walked along, neither disposed to talk after this narrow shave from a quarrel. Boone led the way to the northern outskirts of the city, until they reached a dull-brown frame building, back some distance from the street. A colored woman, with a flaming turban on her head, opened the door as she saw them coming up the trim walk—lined with shells and gay with poppies, bergamot, asters, and heliotrope.

"This woman is a slave. She belongs to the proprietor of the hotel who refused to receive Wesley. It was a great concession to let him come here, they told me. But the poor boy might as well be in a Michigan logging camp, for all the care he can get. But I'm mighty glad I met you. I know you can help Kate while I am gone. I hated to leave her, but I can do nothing here, and unless Wesley is removed he will never leave this cussed town alive. I sha'n't be gone more than ten days."

Kate had been called by the turbaned mistress, and came into the room with a little shriek of pleasure.

"O, Richard, what a delightful surprise! Have you seen your aunt? Ah! I am so glad; she must be so relieved! And Mr. Sprague—have they found him?"

Dick retailed as much of the story as he thought safe, but he had to say that the Spragues were all with the Atterburys in the country.

"How providential! Ah, if our poor Wesley could find some such friends! He is very low. He recognizes no one. Unless papa can get leave to take him North—I am afraid of the worst. Indeed, I doubt whether he could stand so long a journey. You must stay the day with us. I am so lonely, and I dread being more lonely still when papa leaves this evening."

Dick remained until late in the afternoon, sending word to Merry, who came promptly to the aid of the afflicted. The next day Dick left his aunt at the cottage with Kate, and warning them that he should be gone all day, and perhaps not see them until the next morning, he set off for Rosedale, where he told Jack Kate's plight. Vincent heard the story, too, and when it was ended he said, decisively:

"Jack, we must send for them. It would never do to have the story told in Acredale that you had found friends in the South—because you are a Democrat, and Boone was thrust into negro quarters because he is an abolitionist."

It was the very thought on Jack's mind, and straightway the carriage was made ready, with ample pillows and what not. Dick set out in great state, filled with the importance of his mission and the glory of Jack's cordial praises. He was to stop on the way through town and carry the Atterbury's family physician to direct the removal. When he appeared before Kate, with Mrs. Atterbury's commands that she and her brother should make Rosedale their home until the invalid could be removed North, the poor girl broke down in the sudden sense of relief—the certainty of salvation to the slowly dying brother. The physician spent many hours redressing the wounds. Gangrene had begun to eat away the flesh of the head above the temple, and poor Wesley was unrecognizable. He was quite unconscious of the burning bromine and the clipping of flesh that the skillful hand of the practitioner carried on. When the little group started on the long journey, the invalid looked more like himself than he had since Kate found him. The drive lasted many hours. Wesley was stretched in an ambulance, Kate sitting on the seat with the driver, the physician and Dick following in the carriage. Merry went back to the city house, where her nephew was to return as soon as Wesley had been delivered at Rosedale. Her charge placed in the hands of the kind hostess, Mrs. Atterbury, Kate broke down. She had borne up while her head and heart alone stood between her brother and death; but now, relieved of the strain, she fell into an alarming fever. A Williamsburg veteran,

who had practiced in that ancient college town, since the
early days of the century, took the Richmond surgeon's
place, and the gay summer house became, for the time, a
hospital.

Meanwhile the rebel provost-marshal had simplified Dick's
task a good deal. An order was issued that all houses where
wounded or ailing men were lying should signalize the fact
by a yellow flag or ribbon, attached to the front in a conspicuous place. Thus directed, Dick walked street after
street, asking to see the wounded; and the fourth day, coming to a residence, rather handsomer than the others on the
street, not two blocks from Mrs. Raines, Jack's Samaritan,
he found a wasted figure, with bandaged head and unmean-
ing eyes, that he recognized as Barney.

"We haven't been able to get any clew as to his name or
regiment. The guards at the station said he belonged to the
Twelfth Virginia, but none of the members of that body in
the city recognize him. You know him?"

"Yes. He is of my regiment," Dick said, neglecting to
mention the regiment. "I will send word to his friends at
once and have him removed."

"Oh, we are proud and happy to have him here. Our
only anxiety was lest he should die and his family remain in
ignorance. But, now that you identify him, we hope that
we may be permitted to keep him until his recovery."

It was a stately matron who spoke with such a manner, as
Dick thought, must be the mark of nobility in other lands.
He learned, with surprise, that the Atterbury physician was
ministering to Barney, though there was nothing strange in
that, since the doctor was the favorite practitioner of the
well-to-do in the city. That night he wrote to Jack, asking
instructions, and the next day received a note, written by
Olympia, advising that Barney be left with his present hosts
until he recovered consciousness; that by that time Vincent
would be able to come up to town and explain matters to the
deluded family. The better to carry out this plan, Dick was
bidden to return to Rosedale, and thus, six weeks after the
battle and dispersion, all our Acredale personages, by the

strange chances of war, were assembled within sight of the
rebel capital, and, though in the hands of friends, as absolutely cut off from their home and duties as if they had been
captured in a combat with the Indians.

CHAPTER XVI.

A MASQUE IN ARCADY.

IN the latter days of September, the life at Rosedale was
but a faint reminder of the hospital it had seemed in August.
The young men were able to take part in all the simple
gayeties devised by Rosa to make the time pass agreeably.
Wesley was still subject to dizziness if exposed to the sun,
but Jack and Vincent were robust as lumbermen. Mrs.
Sprague and Merry sighed wearily in the seclusion of their
chambers for the Northern homeside, but they banished all
signs of discontent before their warm-hearted hosts. There
was as yet no exchange arranged between the hostile Cabi-
nets of Richmond and Washington. Even Boone's potent
influence among the magnates of his party had not served
him to effect Wesley's release nor enabled him to return to
watch over the boy's fortunes. There was no one at Rosedale sorry for the latter calamity outside of Wesley and
Kate. I believe even she was secretly not heart-broken, for
she knew that her father would be antipathetic to the out-
spoken ladies of Rosedale.

There had been an almost total suspension of military
movements East and West. Both sides were straining every
resource to bring drilled armies into the field, when the
decisive blow fell. In his drives and walks about the James
and Williamsburg, Jack saw that the country was stripped
of the white male population. The negroes carried on all
the domestic concerns of the land. In these excursions, too,
he marked, with a keen military instinct, the points of de-

fense General Magruder, who commanded the department, had left untouched. He wondered if the Union arms would ever get as far down as this. If they did, and he were of the force, he would like to have a cavalry regiment to lead! Vincent was to rejoin his command at Manassas in October. Jack looked forward to the event with the most dismal discontent. To be tied up here, far from his companions; to seem to enjoy ease, when his regiment was indurating itself by drills, marches, and the rough life of the soldier for the great work it was to do, maddened him.

"I give you fair warning, Vint, if an exchange isn't arranged before you leave here, I shall cut stick the best way I can."

"Good! How will you manage? It's a long pull between here and our front at Manassas. How will you work it? Just as soon as you quit the shelter of Rosedale, you are a suspect. Even the negroes will halt you. If you should make for Fortress Monroe, you have all of Magruder's army to get through. You would surely be caught in the act, and then I could do nothing for you. You would be sent to Castle Winder, and that isn't a very comfortable billet."

Some hint of Jack's discontent, or rather of his vague dream of flight, came into Dick's busy head, and when one day they were tramping down by the James together, he said, owlishly:

"I say, Jack, when Vincent goes, let us clear out!"

"I say yes, with all my heart, but how can it be done? We are more than forty miles from the nearest Union lines. Whole armies are between us. Any white man found on the highway is questioned, and if he can't give a clear account of himself is sent to the provost prison. You remember the other day, when we left the rest to go through the swamp-road near Williamsburg, we were hailed by a patrol, and if Vincent hadn't been within reach we would have been sent to the provost prison. Even the negroes act as guards."

"Don't be too sure of that. I've been talking to some of

them. They are 'fraid as sin of the overseers, but you notice they shut up all the negroes in their own quarters at night, don't you? If they were all right, why should they do that?"

"Good heavens! you haven't been trying to make an uprising among the Rosedale servants, Dick? Don't you know that no end of ours could justify that? These people have been like brothers—like our own family to us. It would be infamous—infamous without power in the language for comparison—if we should requite their humanity by stirring up servile strife. I should be the first to take arms against the slaves in such revolt, and give my life rather than be instrumental in bringing misery upon the Atterburys."

"Oh, keep your powder dry, Jack! I never dreamed of stirring 'em up. What I mean is, that they are all restless and uneasy. They have an idea that 'Massa Linculm' is coming down with a big army to set them free. Many of them want to fly to meet this army. Many, too, would almost rather die than leave their mistress. None of them—but the very bad ones—could be induced under any circumstances to lift their hands against the family or its property."

"I should hope not—at least through our instrumentality. The time must come when they will leave the family, for the one call only and in one way; that is, by cutting out slavery root and branch. However, that's for the politicians to manage; all we have to do is to stand by the colors and fight."

"I don't see much chance of standing by the colors here," Dick retorted, wrathfully. "If you'll give me the word, I'll arrange a plan, and, as soon as Vincent goes—we'll be off."

"I'm not your master, you young hornet; I can't see what you're doing all the time. All I can do is to approve or reject such doings of yours as you bring me to decide on."

Dick's eyes sparkled. "All right, I'll keep you posted, never fear."

They were a very jovial group that prattled about the long Rosedale dining-table daily now, since every one was able to come down. The house was furnished in the easy

11

unpretentiousness that prevailed in the South in other days. Cool matting covered all the floors, the hallways, and bed-chambers. The dining-room opened into a drawing-room, where Kate and Olympia took turns at the big piano. The day was divided, English fashion, into breakfast, luncheon, dinner, and supper, the latter as late as nine o'clock in the night. Jack being unprovided with regimentals, Vincent wore civilian garb, to spare the "prisoner" (as Jack jocosely called himself) mortification. Gray was the "only wear" obtainable in Richmond, Mrs. Atterbury enjoying with gentle malice the rueful perplexities of her prisoner guests, Jack, Wesley, and Richard, as they surrounded the board in this rebel attire.

"I shall feel as uncertain of myself when I get back to blue, as I do in chess, after I have played a long while with the black, changing to white. I manœuvre for some time for the discarded color," Jack said, one evening.

" Oh, you'll hardly forget in this case," Rosa said, saucily; " it is for the blacks you are manœuvring constantly."

Jack looked up, startled, and glanced swiftly at Dick. Had that headstrong young marplot been detected in treason with the colored people? No. Dick met his glance clear-eyed, unconstrained. The shot must have been a random one.

"I think you do us injustice, Miss Rosa," Wesley said. "I, for one, am not interested in the blacks. All I want is the Union; after that I don't care a rush!"

"I protest against politics," Mrs. Atterbury intervened, gently. "When I was a girl the young people found much more interesting subjects than politics."

Rosa: "Crops, mamma?"

Vincent: "A mistress's eyebrow?"

Dick: "Some other fellow's sister?"

Olympia: "Some other girl's brother?"

Mrs. Sprague: "Giddy girls?"

Merry: "Bad boys?"

"Well, something about all of these," Mrs. Atterbury resumed, laughing. "I don't think young people in these times are as attached to each other as we used to be in our day—do you, Mrs. Sprague?"

"I don't know how it is with you in the South; but we no longer have young people in the North. Our children bring us up now—we do not bring them up."

"That accounts for the higher average of intelligence among parents noted in the last census," Olympia interrupts her mother to say.

"There, do you see?" Mrs. Sprague continues, with a smile, and in a tone that has none of the asperity the words might imply. "No reverence, no waiting for the elders, as we were taught."

"It depends a good deal, does it not, whether the elders are lovers?" Vincent asked, innocently.

"Oh, don't look at me, Mrs. Sprague, for support or sympathy. Vincent is your handiwork; he was formed in the North. He is one of your new school of youth; he is Southern only in loyalty to his State. For a time I had painful apprehensions that that, too, had been educated away."

"It was his reason that kept him faithful there," Rosa ventured, and catches Vincent dropping his eyes in confusion from the demure glances of Olympia.

"Oh, no; pride. A Virginian is like a Roman, he is prouder to be a citizen in the Dominion than a king in another country," Mrs. Atterbury says, with stately decision. "No matter where his heart may be," and she glanced casually at Olympia, "his duty is to his State."

"Politics, mamma, politics; remember your young days. Talk of kings, courts, romance, madrigals—but leave out politics," Rosa cried, remonstratingly.

"Let's turn to political economy. How do you propose disposing of your tobacco and cotton this year?" Jack asked, gravely.

"We are under contract to deliver ten thousand bales at Wilmington to our agent," Vincent replied. "As for tobacco, we expect to sell all we can raise to the Yankee generals. We have already begun negotiations with some of your commanders who are too good Yankees to miss the main chance."

"You're not in earnest?" Jack cried, aghast.

"As earnest as a maid with her first love."

"But who—who—is the miscreant that degrades his cause by such traffic?"

"Oh, if you wait until you learn from me, you'll never be a dangerous accuser. I learn in letters from friends in the West that all the cotton crop has been contracted for by men either in the Northern army or high in the confidence of the Administration. You see, Jack, we are not the Arcadian simpletons you think us. This war is to be paid for out of Northern pockets, any way you look at it. We've got cotton and tobacco, you must have both; you've got money, we must have that. What we don't sell to you we'll send to England."

All at the table had listened absorbedly to this strange revelation, and Jack rose from the table shocked and discouraged.

Olympia seated herself at the piano, and, slipping out, as he supposed, unseen, Jack strolled off into the fragrant alleys of oleander and laurel. Dick, however, was at his heels. The two continued on in silence, Dick trolling along, switching the bugs from the pink blossoms that filled the air with an enervating odor.

"I say, Jack, I've found out something."

"What have you found out, you young conspirator?"

"Wesley Boone's trying to get the negroes to help him off."

"The devil he is!"

"Yes. Last night I was down in the rose-fields. Young Clem, Aunt Penelope's boy, was sitting under a bush talking with a crony. I heard him say, 'De cap'n'll take you, too, ef you doan say noffin'. He guv Pompey ten gold dollars.'

"'De Lor'! Will he take ev'ybody 'long, too, Clem?'

"'Good Lor', no! He's goin' to get his army, and den he'll come an' fetch all de niggahs.'

"'De Lor'!'

"Trying to get closer, I made a rustling of the bushes, and the young imps shot through them like weasles before I could lay hands on them. Now, what do you think of that?"

"If it is only to escape, all right; but if it is an attempt to stir up insurrection, I will stop Wesley myself, rather than let him carry it out!"

"Wouldn't it be the best thing to warn Vincent? It would be a dreadful thing to let him go and leave his poor mother and sister here unprotected."

"Let me think it over. I will hit on some plan to keep Wesley from making an ingrate of himself without bringing danger on our benefactors."

Kate was dawdling on the lawn as the two returned to the house. Jack challenged her to a jaunt.

"Where shall it be?" she asked, readily, moving toward him. "The garden of the gods?"

"The garden of the goddesses, you mean, if it is the rosefield."

"That's true; a god's garden would be filled with thorns and warlike blossoms."

"I don't know; a rose-garden grew the wars of the houses of York and Lancaster."

"Do you remember the scene in Shakespeare where Bolingbroke and Gaunt pluck the roses?"

"Quite well. There is always something pathetic to me in the fables historians invent to excuse or palliate, or, perhaps it would be juster to say, make tolerable, the stained pages of the past. It is brought doubly nearer and distinct by this miserable war, and the strange fate that has fallen upon us—to be the guests of a family whose hopes are fixed upon what would make us miserable if it ever happened."

"It never will. That's the reason I listen with pity to the childish vauntings of these kind people. They have, you see, no conception of the Northern people—no idea of the deep-seated purpose that moves the States as one man to stifle this monstrous attempt."

They walked on in silence a few paces, and Kate continued:

"I don't know how you feel, Mr. Sprague, but I am wretched here. I feel like a traitor, receiving such kindness, treated with such guileless confidence, and yet my heart is filled with everything they abhor. It is not so hard for you, because you and Vincent have been close friends. He has made your house his home, but I certainly feel that Wesley and I should go elsewhere, now that he is able to be about."

"Does Wesley feel this—this embarrassment?"

"Passionately. He said, last night, he felt like a sneak. He would fly in an instant, if he could see any possible way to our lines."

"Pray, Miss Boone, tell him to be very circumspect. I know the Southern nature. When they give you their heart they give entirely. But the least sign of—of—distrust will turn them into something worse than indifference. We may see our way out soon. Caution Wesley against any act —any act"—he emphasized the words—"that may lead these kind people to think that he doesn't trust them, or that he would take advantage of servile insurrection to gain his liberty. Of course, they know that we are all restive here; that we shall be even more impatient when Vincent goes— but they could not understand any surreptitious movement on our part, to enable us to get away."

He hoped that, if she were in Wesley's confidence, she would understand his meaning. But she gave no sign. She assented with an affirmative movement of the head, and they walked through the fragrant paths, plucking a rose now and then that seemed more tempting than its fellows. At the end of the field of roses a Cherokee hedge grew so thick and high that it formed a screen and rampart between the house land and a dense grove of pines which was itself bordered by a stream that here and there spread out into tiny lakelets. On the larger of these there were rude "dug-outs," made by the darkies to cut off the long walk from their quarters to the tobacco and corn fields.

"Was there ever an Eden more perfect than this delicious place?" Kate cried, as the flaming sun sent banners of gold, mingled in a rainbow baldric with the blooming parterres of roses.

"I don't know much about Eden, and the little I do know doesn't give me a sympathetic reminiscence of the place; but I agree with you that Rosedale is about as near a paradise as one can come to on this earth," Jack qualifiedly replied.

"And yet we want to fly from it ? "

"Ah, yes; because the tree of our life, the volume of our knowledge, or, in plain prose, our hearts, are not here, and scenic beauty is a poor substitute for that. Duty, I am convinced, is the key of the best life. There are hearts here, noble ones—duties here, inspiring ones. But they do not satisfy us; they are become a torment to me. I feel like a soldier brought from duty; a priest fallen into the ways of the flesh."

"Your rhapsodies are like most fine-sounding things, more to the hope than the heart," Kate murmured, gazing dreamily into the purple mass of color hovering changefully over the opaque water at their feet. "You mean they do not reach your heart; that your soul is far away as to what is here. I think Vincent and Rosa would not agree that life has any more or narrower limitations here than we recognize at Acredale."

"Let us go on the water." He pulled the rude shallop to her feet and they got in and went on, Jack not heeding her gibe. "These brackish, threatening deeps remind me of all sorts of weird and uncanny things; Stygian pools—Lethe—what not mystic and terrifying. See, the tiny waves that curl before our boat are like thin ink; a thousand roots and herbs and who knows what mysterious vegetable mixture colors these dark deeps ? I could fancy myself on an uncanny pilgrimage, seeking some demon delight."

There was but one oar in the boat, which the negroes used as a scull. Jack made a poor fist with this, but there was no need of rowing. Kate, catching a projecting limb from the thick bushes on the margin, sent the little, wabbling craft onward in noiseless, spasmodic plunges. Deep fringes of wild columbine fell in fluffy sprays from the higher banks as the boat drifted along the other side. The thickets were musical with the chattering cat-birds and whip-poor-wills, mingled with a score of woodland melodists that Jack's limited woodcraft did not enable him to recognize.

"Who would think that we are within a half-mile of a completely appointed country house? We are as isolated here from all vestiges of civilization as we should be in a Florida everglade," Kate said, as the little craft swam along in an eddy.

"It seems to me typical of the people—this curiously wild transition from blooming, well-kept gardens, to such still and solemn nature. The place might be called primeval: look at those gnarled roots, like prodigious serpents; see the shining bark of the larch—I think it is larch—I should call it 'slippery' elm if it were at Acredale; but see the fantastic effects of the little lances of sunlight breaking through! Isn't it the realization of all you ever read in 'Uncle Tom' or 'Dred'?"

Kate glanced into the weird deeps of foliage, where a bird, fluttering on the wing, aroused strange echoes. "Ugh!" she said, in a half whisper, "I can imagine it the meeting-place of 'Tam o' Shanter's' eldritches seeing this—but, all the same, do you know it is fascinating beyond words to me? Should you mind going in a little farther—I should like the sensation of awe the place suggests, since there can be no danger—while you are here?"

He gave her a quick glance, but her eyes were fastened on the dark recesses beyond.

"I should be delighted, but I won't insure your gown, nor—nor half promise that we shall come out alive."

"Oh, as to that, I'll take the risk."

"I don't know the habits of Southern snakes; but if they are as well-bred as ours, they retire from the ken of wicked men at sundown, so we needn't fear them, as the sun is too far down for the snake of tradition to see or molest us."

They stepped out of the boat at a green, sedgy point, extending from a labyrinth of flowering vines and creepers.

Once inside the delicious odorous screen, they found themselves in an archipelago of green islets, connected by monster roots or moss-covered trunks that seemed laid by elfin hands for the penetration of this leafy jungle.

"Yes; I was going to say," Jack continued, "this swift transposition from the cultivation of civilization to the handiwork of Nature is whimsically illustrative of the people. Did you ever see or hear or read of such open-handed, honesthearted hospitality as theirs; such refinement of manners; such sincerity in speech and act ? Contrast this with their fairly pagan creed as to the slaves; their intolerance of the Northern people; their clannish reverence for family."

"But isn't the inequality of the Southern character due to their strange lack of education ? Few of them are cultivated as we understand education. Do you notice that among the people we met at Williamsburg—officers as well as civilians —none of them were equal to even a very limited range of subjects ? All who are educated have been in the North. Ah—good Heavens! "

Kate's exclamation was due to a sudden sinking in the mossy causeway until she was almost buried in the tall ferns. Jack helped her out, shivered a moment, doubtingly, as he exclaimed:

"The sun is nearly down now, though the air is transparent, or would be if we were in the free play of daylight. I think it would be better to go back." But they made no haste. Such trophies of ferns and lace-like mosses were not to be plucked in every walk, and they dawdled on and on skirmishing, with delighted hardihood, against the pitfalls of bog that covered morass and pitch-black mud. When the impulse finally came to hasten back, they were somewhat chagrined to discover that they had lost their own trail. The point where they had quit the stream could not be found. Clambering plants, burdened with blossoms, fragrant as honeysuckle, grew all along the bank, and the bush that had attracted them was no longer a landmark.

"Well," Jack said, confidently, "the sun disappeared over there; that is southwest. The house is in that direction

—northeast. Now, if you will keep that big sycamore in your eye and follow me, we shall be nearing the house, as I calculate."

They pushed on in that direction, but had only gone a few yards when the ground became a perfect quagmire of black loam, that looked like coal ground to powder, and was thin as mush.

"This is a brilliant stroke on my part, I must say," Jack cried, facing Kate ruefully. "We must go back and examine the ground, as Indians do, and find our entrance trail in that way. I will watch the ground and you keep an eye on the shrubs. Wherever you see havoc among them you may be sure my manly foot has fallen there."

Suddenly they were conscious of an indescribable change in the place. Neither knew what it was. It had come on in the excitement of their march into the morass—or it had come the instant they both became conscious of it. What was it? Kate turned and looked into Jack's blank face!

"I'm blessed if I know what it is, but it seems as if something had suddenly gone out of the order of things! What is it? Do you feel it; do you notice it?"

"Feel it—see it—why, it is as palpable, or, rather to speak accurately, it is as clearly absent as the color from an oil-painting, leaving mere black and white outlines."

"How besotted I am!" Jack cried; "why, I know. The sun has wholly gone, and the birds and living things have ceased to sing and move."

"That's it; could you believe that it would make such a change? Why, I thought, when we came in, the place was a temple of silence, but it was a mad world compared to this."

"Yes, and we must hurry and get out while we have daylight to help us. I take it you wouldn't care to swim the lagoon. Let us call it lagoon, for this place makes the name appropriate."

"Call it whatever you like, but don't ask me to swim it," Kate cried, pushing on.

"Ah! I have our trail," Jack cries in triumph. "By

George, it is wide enough!" he added, bending over where the thick grasses were crushed and broken. "See the advantage of large feet. Now, if you had been alone, 'twould have been as hard as to trace a bird's track."

"Is that an implication that I have Chinese feet?"

"No, too literal young woman. It was meant to show you that I am very much relieved, for, 'pon my soul, I was afraid we were in a very disagreeable scrape."

"And you are now quite sure we are not?"

"Quite sure. Don't you want to take my arm?"

"Oh, no, thank you. I'm not at all tired. I'm used to longer walks than this."

"Longer, possibly, but not over such trying ground."

"Oh, yes. I've gone with Wesley and his friends to the lakes in the North Woods."

"Ah! I've never been there. Are they as bad travel as this?"

"Infinitely worse— Why, what was that?"

"It sounded very like the report of a pistol."

Both stopped, Kate coming quite close to the young man, who was bent over with his hand to his ear, trumpet-fashion.

"Do you—" He made a warning gesture with his hand, and motioned her to stoop among the ferns. A halloo was heard in the distance; then a response just ahead of where the two crouched in the breast-high ferns, through which the path made by their recent footsteps led. When the echoing halloo died away, a bird in the distance seemed to catch up the refrain and dwell upon the note with an exquisite, painful melody.

"Why, it's the throat interlude in the Magic Flute! How lovely it is!" Kate whispered. "If you were my knight, I should put on you the task of caging that lovely sound for me."

The distant bird-note ceased, and then suddenly, from the bushes just ahead of them, it was caught up and answered, note for note, in a wild pibroch strain, harsher but inexpressibly moving. Jack turned to Kate, his face quite pale, and whispered:

"It is not a bird. They are negroes. I have read of these sounds. They are marauding slaves, and we must not let them see us. We must get to those thick clumps of bushes. Do you think you can remain bent until we reach them ? If not, we will rest every few paces."

"Go on. I can try."

The pibroch strains still continued, rising into a mournful wail, then sinking into the soft cries of the whip-poor-will. In a few minutes the perplexed fugitives were deep in a clump of wild hawberries, invisible to any one who should pass. The strains had ceased as suddenly as they began. Then a faint hallo-o-o sounded, being answered in the bushes, as it seemed, just in front of where Jack and his companion stood ; voices soon became audible farther along, ten or more paces. Motioning to Kate, Jack crept along noiselessly, and fancied he could distinguish forms through the thick screen of bushes. A voice, not a negro's, said :

"I went to the cove for you—what was the matter ?"

"I had the devil's work to get through the posts. For some reason or other they're getting mighty sharp. I must be back before twelve ; what's been done ?"

"Well, the mokes consent to go, but they won't touch the ranch. You'll have to bring up a few hands; the fewer the better. If them damned feather-bed sojers wasn't there, we could do the job ourselves."

"When does the boss get out ?"

"Next week. I don't know what day. They'd pay high for him both ways."

"No, we can't nibble there. The cap'n'll pay well. That's square. We can't afford to try the other now, at any rate. Is the skiff here ?"

"Yes; well, get in."

There was a plash and the receding sound of voices. Jack darted through the screen of branches, but he could not distinguish the figures, for it was growing every instant dimmer twilight. He turned to Kate. She was at his side.

"Who were they—what were they planning ? Were they soldiers ?" she asked.

"Never mind them now. We must find a way out of this. Our boat can't be far off. We must follow this line of bushes until we come to the spot we left. I know I can recognize it, for there was an enormous tree fallen a few steps from the sedge bank we landed on."

It was a very toilsome journey now, obliged as they were to hug the obstinate growth of haws, wild alder, and dog roses, which tore flesh and garments in the hurried flight. They came to the dead tree finally, and Jack almost shouted in grateful relief:

"You were a true prophet, Miss Boone. You gave utterance to some Druid-like remarks as we crossed the Stygian pool. The worst your fancy painted couldn't equal what we've seen and heard."

"I have seen nothing dreadful, and I can't say that I understand very much of what we heard."

"There is some ' caper ' going on to give these cut-throats a chance to get booty or something of the sort."

"They are probably rebel soldiers planning to sack the commissary."

They were in the boat now, and Jack was sending it forward by lusty lunges against every protruding object he could get a stroke at; when these failed he managed to scull after a fashion. They found the household in consternation when they got back, but Jack gave a picturesque narrative of their escapade, omitting the encounter with the negroes which he had charged Kate to say nothing about, as it would only alarm Mrs. Atterbury. The garments of the explorers told the tale of their mishaps, and when they had clothed themselves anew supper was announced. The feast was of the lightest sort : sherbet or tea for those who liked it; fruit and crackers, honey or marmalade—a triumph in the cultivation of dyspepsia, Jack said when he first began the eating. But it was observed that the disease had no terrors for him, for he sat at the table as long as he could get any one to remain with him, and did his share in testing all the dishes. He outsat everybody that night except Dick, who never got tired of any place that brought him near his idol.

"I'm going up-stairs in a moment, Towhead. Come up after me."

Dick nodded, a gleam of delightful expectation in his eyes. He was just in the ardent period when boys love to make mysteries of very ordinary things, and Jack's *sotto voce* command was like the hero's voice in the play, "Meet me by the ruined well when midnight strikes." He followed Jack up the wide staircase and into his own room, for greater security, as no one would think of looking for them there.

"Now, tell me all you have found out," Jack commanded as he shut the door. "Have you been among the darkys?"

"I've found out this much. The old negroes are opposed to going away or in any shape annoying their masters. The young bucks and the women are very eager to fly. It seems that some one has spread the story among them that Lincoln has sent Butler to Fort Monroe to receive all the negroes on the Peninsula. They have been assured that they are to have 'their freedom, one hundred acres of land, and an ox-team.' Where the report comes from, I can't find out: but there is some communication between here and the Union lines, I'm positive."

"Has Wesley been with the negroes again?"

"No. I have kept an eye on him all day."

"Where does he go at night?"

"The doctor has forbidden him to be in the night air for the present."

"Well, you keep an eye on Wesley," and then Jack narrated the strange scene in the swamp, the mysterious calls, and the conversation.

Dick listened in awe, mingled with rapture. "Oh, why wasn't I there? Just my blamed luck! I would have followed them, and then we should have known what they were up to. Did you know that a company of cavalry had gone into camp just below the grove?"

"No—when?"

"This evening. Vincent is down there now."

"Well, you may be sure they suspect something. I wonder if it wouldn't be better to speak to Vincent?"

"Of course not ! What have we to tell him ? Simply my suspicions and Clem's chatter. The little moke may have been lying ; I can't see that any of them do much else."

"The worst of it is, these Southerners are very sensitive about any allusion to the negroes. They would pooh-pooh anything we might say that was not backed by proof. It's a mighty uncomfortable fix to be in, Dick, my boy ; though, 'pon my soul, I believe you enjoy it !"

Dick grinned deprecatingly.

"I think you do, you unfledged Guy Fawkes. I know nothing would give you greater joy than to put on a mask, grasp a dagger in your hand, and go to Wesley, crying, 'Villain, your secret or your life !' Dick, you're a stage hero ; you're a thing of sawdust and tinsel. Come to the parlor and hear Kate play the divine songs of Mendelssohn ; perhaps, night-eyed conspirator, to whirl Polly or Miss Rosa in the delirium of the ' *Blaue Donau*.' Come."

But there was neither dance nor music when they reached the drawing-room. Everybody was there; Vincent had just come, and the first words Jack and Dick heard glued them to their places.

"Yes, all the negroes on the Lawless', Skinner's, and Lomas's plantations have gone. Butler has declared them contrabands of war, and a lot of Yankee speculators have been sneaking through the plantations, filling their ignorant minds with promises of freedom, a farm, and a share of their masters' property. Their real purpose is to get the negroes and hold them until the two governments come to terms, and then they will get rewards for every nigger they hold. Oh, these Yankees can see ways of making money through a stone-wall," and Vincent laughed lightly, as though the incident in no way concerned him. "Captain Cram, who is in camp just below in the oak clearing, is ordered to scour the river-bank to the enemy's lines near Hampton, so we need have no fear of these enterprising apostles of freedom interfering with our niggers."

"I don't think one of them could be induced to leave us if offered all our farms," Mrs. Atterbury said, a little proudly.

"There isn't one of them that I haven't brought through sickness or trouble of one sort or another, and there isn't one that wouldn't take my command before the gold of a stranger."

"I don't know, Mrs. Atterbury," Mrs. Sprague ventured, mildly. "Gold is a mighty weight in an argument. I have known it to change the convictions of a lifetime in a moment. I have known it to make a man renounce his father, dishonor his name, belie his whole life, deny his family."

" When a fortune beyond reasonable dreams was placed upon the head of Charles Stuart, for whom our ancestors fought and beggared themselves, his secret was in the keeping of scores of peasants, and the blood-money lay idle. I could cite hundreds of similar proofs, that gold is not God everywhere. I mean no offense, but you will agree with me that you Northern people are given up to the getting and worship of money. It is not so with us. Perhaps because we have it, and with it something that makes it secondary— birth. I have no fear of the infidelity of any of my people. I would as soon doubt Rosa or Vincent as the smallest black on my estate."

She spoke with mild, high-bred dignity, not a particle of assertion or captious intolerance, but as a prelate might assert the majesty of the word on the altar, neither looking for dissent nor dreaming that the spirit of it could exist.

"I'm glad to hear your mother express such confidence, Vint," Jack said as they walked out on the veranda to take a good-night smoke; "but just let me give you a maxim of my own, the lock's not sure unless the key is in your pocket."

"Sententious, my boy, but vague. My mother is perfectly right. Our niggers are fidelity itself. But since we are so near the Butler lines, where his agents can sneak up on the river and kidnap the new sort of contraband, I think it better to take some precaution. Hereafter General Magruder will have a picket post within two miles of us, between here and the creek, which offers a convenient point for smuggling."

"I am heartily relieved to hear it," Jack cried, giving something too much fervor to his relief, for Vincent turned and looked at him in surprise, but it was too dark in the shadow of the clematis to see his face, and after a silence Vincent said:

"Mamma has told you that the President is coming to Williamsburg to review Magruder's troops?"

"No; she hadn't mentioned it. Is he?"

"Yes; he will be there Thursday afternoon, and we shall have the ball the same evening. He will be here with General Lee, his chief of staff, and remain all night; so that you will be able to say when you go back North—something that few Yankees will be able to say during the war—that you have broken bread with the first President of the Confederacy."

"I will strive to bear my honors with humility," Jack said.

"It befits the conquered to be humble."

"If I hadn't come in time, you two would have been in a squabble—own it!" and Rosa drew a chair between them as a peacemaker.

CHAPTER XVII.

TREASON AND STRATAGEMS.

ROSEDALE was, indeed, Eden in the most orthodox sense to the group so strangely billeted in its lovely tranquillity. No sooner was the anguish concerning the invalids off Kate's, Olympia's, and Rosa's minds, than new perplexities beset them. Rosa was barely eighteen, Kate and Olympia older by three or four years, but the younger girl was in many essential things quite as mature as her Northern comrades. But Jack could not comprehend this, and quite innocently did and said things to arouse the young girl's dreams. I think I have said that Jack was a very comely fellow? He

12

was big and brawny, and tireless in good-humor, and the attractive little gallantries that women adore. He looked as sentimentally sincere, uttering a paradox, as another vowing eternal fidelity. He gave every woman the impression that his mind was lost wondering how he should exist until she gave him the right to call her his own. Though, as a matter of fact, it is the man who is the woman's own—when the final word comes.

Rosa was not long in discovering Vincent's happy tumult in Olympia's presence, and she secretly misunderstood Jack the more that he was so lavish and open in his adulations. If he rode, he exhausted eulogy in describing her pose, her daring, her skill; if they danced, as they did nearly every night—until poor Merry's fingers ached from drumming the unholy strains of Faust, Strauss, and what not, in the old-fashioned waltzes—he pantingly declared that she made the music seem a celestial choir by her lightness; in long walks in the rose-fields he exhausted a not very laborious store of botanical conceits, to make her cheeks resemble the roses. This assurance, this recklessness, this *aplomb*, quite bewildered the girl, who posed in Richmond for a passed mistress of flirting. She had, unless rumor was badly at fault, jilted an appalling list of the striplings who believed that beard-growing and love-making were conventionally contemporaneous events. But they had "mooned" about her and made themselves absurd in vain, while this unconscious Adonis calmly walked, talked, and acted as if she could know nothing else than love him, and one day she started in delicious misery to find that she did—that is, she thought she might if—if? But there her dreams became nebulous—they were rosy in outline, however, and she was content to rest there.

The morning after the coming of the cavalry-troop, Wesley was discussing the never-ending theme of how he was going to get home—with Kate busy arranging the ferns she had brought from the swamp.

"Really, Wesley, just now you ought to be content. There is no likelihood of any movement; besides, philoso-

phy is as much a merit in a soldier as valor—it is valor, it is
endurance. You complain of your unhappy fate, housed
here with a lot of women and idlers. How would you bear up
in Libby Prison ? There are as good men as you there, my
dear; shall I say better or older soldiers, Brutus ? You may
take your choice, and 'count on a sister's blind partiality to
justify you !' "

"Oh, don't always talk nonsense, Kate. You're worse
than Jack Sprague. He doesn't seem to have a serious
thought in his head from daylight till bedtime."

"Perhaps he keeps all his sober thoughts for the night,
to give them good company."

"No, but do say what I ought to do."

"You ought to study to make yourself tolerable to your
sister, dear, and agreeable to the other fellows' sisters. I
have remarked that the young man who does that, keeps
out of despondency and other uncomfortable conditions that
too much brooding on an empty head brings about."

"I'd like to know what heart I can have to make myself
agreeable to other fellows' sisters when you are always lam-
pooning me ; you delight in making me think I am nobody."

"Don't fear, my dear; if that were my delight I should
die an old maid, never having known delight, for it would
need more force than I can muster to make Wesley Boone,
captain U. S. A., anything else than he is—his father's pride
and his sister's joy. No, dear, my delight is to see you gay
and open and frank and manly, self-dependent, grateful for
the consideration shown you, and recognizant of the constant admonition of your sagacious sister."

"You talk exactly like the woman in George Sand's
stupid stories ; they always remind me of men in petticoats."

"That's a weak and strained comparison; not, however,
unworthy a soldier. We always compare, in speech, to
strengthen assertion or adorn it, and when we do we compare what is equivocal or vague, with what is well known
and usual. Now, I do not remember any men in petticoats,

unless you mean the Orientals, who wear a sort of skirt, and the Scots, who used to wear kilts—but strictly speaking—"

"Do, Kate, for Heaven's sake, be serious for a moment! I have a chance to escape, no matter how, but I can make my way to our lines without running any great risk. Now, is it or is it not dishonorable for me to do it ?"

"Seriously, Wesley, just now it would be, while Vincent is here, for he is in a sense pledged for you to his superior. Further, there is no need to hurry. You are barely recovered. If you were North you would be in Acredale; if you were, there is no immediate want of your presence in the army. The articles we see in the Richmond papers every day, copied from Northern journals, show that this new general, McClellan, means to bring a trained, drilled, disciplined army down when he moves. It took six months to prepare McDowell's useless mass. It will certainly take a year to put the million men now arming in shape to fight. I may be wrong, but at the earliest there can be no movement before late in October. By that time we shall probably have the problem solved by the Government, and you will go North, having made delightful friends of all this charming family."

Wesley was even more afraid of Kate's strong sense of honor than of her biting sarcasm, and he ended the interview without daring to tell her how far he had compromised himself with the secret agents that were surrounding the plantation. Dick, running down-stairs in his wake, encountered Rosa, with her garden hat covering her like the roof of a disrupted pagoda. She arrested his stride as he was darting toward the door.

"Here—you—Richard, just come and be of some use to me. I'm housekeeper to-day, and I want to go to the quarters. Come along."

Now Dick had a double grievance against this imperious young person. He had fallen into the most violent love with her brown eyes and pink cheeks the moment he saw her; he had assiduously striven both to conceal and reveal this maddening condition of mind. But he remarked with ungovernable wrath that, whenever Jack or Wesley came about, the heartless young jilt, made as if she didn't know him; quite ignored him, and cared no more for his simple adoration than she did for the frisky gambols of Pizarro, the mastiff. But she was so adorable; her Southern accent was so bewitching; she put so much softness in those amusing idioms " I reckon " and " Seems like," " You others," and the countless little tricks of the Southern vernacular, that Dick passed sleepless hours and delicious days dreaming and sighing and groaning and doing all manner of unreasonable things—that we all do when we meet our first Rosas and they light the torch for other feet more favored than our own.

So, when Rosa called him to accompany her, Dick took the round basket she held out to him, and walked sulkily ahead of her, never opening his mouth. When he had stalked along through the currant bushes, he half turned his face; she was walking demurely behind him, and he made a pretext of picking a currant to give her a chance to come abreast. She did, and passed him trippingly, saying, as she cast a sympathetic side glance at him :

"Toothache ? "

He stood rooted to the spot with indignant amazement. The heartless little minx ! How dare she talk like that to a soldier ?

" Did you call some one, Miss Atterbury ? " he said, with chilling dignity. Usually he called her plain Rosa.

" I thought may be you had the toothache—you kept so quiet."

" No; I haven't got the toothache." Poor Dick! He said, to himself, that he had much worse. But he wouldn't gratify her with the acknowledgment of her triumph, and he stalked along with the basket over his head, as he had often seen the darkeys in the sun. There was a faint little appealing cry from behind.

" Oh—oh—dear ! "   ·

" What is it; are you hurt ? " he cried, rushing to where Rosa stood, balanced on one foot.

" There is a crab thorn an inch long in my foot; it's gone

through shoe and all. That wretched Sardanapalus never clears the limbs away when he cuts the hedge. I'll have him horsewhipped. Oh, dear !"

"Let me hold you while I look for the thorn."

Dick cleverly slipped his arm about her waist and set the basket endwise for her to sit on. Then kneeling, he picked out the thorn, which was a great deal less than the dimensions Rosa had described. But he said nothing to her about picking the torment out and slipping it in his vest pocket. He held the foot, examining the sole critically. Finally, as she moved impatiently, he asked :

"Does it hurt yet ?"

"Of course it does, you stupid fellow. Do you suppose I would sit here like a goose on a gridiron and let you hold my foot if it didn't hurt? Men never have any sense when they ought to."

He affected to examine the sole of the thin leather of the upper still more minutely. As she gave no sign of ending the comedy, he said :

"I'm sure, Rosa, if it relieves the pain to have me hold your foot, I'll sit here in the sun all day—if you'll bring the rim of your hat over a little—but, as for the thorn, it has been out this ten minutes."

She gave him a sudden push and darted away. He followed laughing, admonishing her against another thorn. But she deigned no answer. Coming to the bee-hives, she stopped a moment to watch the busy swarm, and Dick stole up beside her. She turned pettishly, and he said, insinuatingly:

"Toothache ?"

"You know, Dick, you're too trying for anything—holding my foot there like a ninny in the hot sun. You haven't a thimbleful of sense."

"Well, now we'll test these propositions, as Jack does, by syllogisms. Let me see. All men are trying. Dick Perley is a man; therefore he is trying."

"No; your premise—isn't that what you call it ?—is wrong. Dick Perley is only a boy."

" I'll be nineteen in January next."

" Well ? "

" Well, your father was married at nineteen. You've said it yourself, Rosa, and thought it greatly to his credit—at least Vint does."

" You can't imitate my father in that, at least."

" I might."

" How ? "

" You could help me, Rosa."

" How ? "

" Would you if you could ? "

" That depends."

" On what ? "

" On the girl."

" Ah ! she's a perfect girl, but she's very young," and Dick eyed Rosa with ineffable complacency.

" That's bad."

" But she's older than she looks."

" That's worse; you'd grow tired of her."

" No, no; I don't mean she's older than she looks; her mind is older than her looks."

" Women with minds make troublesome wives. I have refused to let Vincent marry several of that kind."

" But, my girl hasn't got that kind of mind; it is all sweetness and wit and gayety and loveliness and—and—"

" Your girl ? Who gave her to you ? "

" Love gave her to me."

" Oh, well, since love gave her to you, I don't see how I can be of any service. Down here the mother always gives the girl, unless she have no mother; then some other kin gives her. But if your girl has all these qualities you describe, I advise you to get her into your own keeping just as soon as you can, for that's the sort of girl all the fellows about here are seeking."

" Very well, I'm ready. Will you help me ? It comes back where we started."

" But you evaded my question."

" What question did I evade ? I answered like an encyclopædia !" Dick cried, immensely satisfied with his own readiness.

"That convicts you; an encyclopædia has nothing about living people."

"Oh, yes; the new ones do." Dick was now very near her as she stood contemplating the bees, swarming in the comb. "O Rosa—Rosa, you know I love you, and you know I can never love anybody else. Why will you pretend not to understand me ? I don't want you to marry me now, but by and by, when I shall have made a name as a soldier, or—or something," he added in painful turbulence of joy and fear—over the great words—which he had been racking his small wits to fashion for weeks past, and, now that they were spoken, were not nearly so impressive as he had intended they should be.

"My dear Richard, you are a perfect boy—a very delightful boy, too, and I am extremely fond of you—oh, very, very fond of you—but you really must not make love to me. It isn't proper," and Rosa glanced into his eyes with a tender little gleam, that gave more encouragement than rebuff—for it came into her mind, in a moment, that it was not a time to hurt the bright, eager love—so winning, if boyish.

"Nonsense, Rosa, it is perfectly proper; everybody makes love to you; Jack makes love to you, and he is as good as engaged—" But here it suddenly flashed in Dick's mad head that he was meddling, and he stopped short. Rosa had turned upon him with a flash of such scorn, such indignant pain, that he cried:

"No, no; I don't mean that; but you know fellows do make love to you, and why mayn't I ?"

She flirted away from him too angry or mortified to speak. He could not see her face, for she pulled the ample breadth of the hat-brim down, which served at once as a veil to shut out her visage and a sweeping sort of funnel to keep him far from her side, as she tripped determinedly to the pleasant group of clean, whitewashed cabins, where the negroes abode. Poor Dick, vexed with himself—angry at her for being irritated—waited in the hot sun until she had ended her commands, and when she came out to return he repentantly sidled up, imploring pardon in every movement. She couldn't resist the big, pleading blue eyes, and said, quite as if there had been deep discussion on the point:

" I don't think you mean to be a bad boy."

" I'm not a boy, I'm a soldier. It isn't fair in you to call me a boy."

" You're not a girl."

" If I were I wouldn't be so heartless as some I know."

" And if I were a boy I wouldn't be so silly as some I know."

" Yes, I think Southern boys are quite soft."

" Come, sir, my brother *was* a Southern boy."

" Yes, but he always lived North, and is like us."

" Jackanapes! "

" Dear Rosa."

" How dare you, sir ? "

" Oh, just as easy, I dare do all that becomes a man—who dares do more is none. You are Rosa, and you are dear—"

" Not to you."

" You cost me enough to be dear and you are lovely enough to be 'Rosa' in Latin, Rose in English, and sweetheart in any tongue."

" You're much too pert. Boys so glib as you never really love. They think they do and perhaps they do—just a little."

" Ah ! a ' little more than a little,' dear Rosa."

" You're quoting Shakespeare, I suppose you know ? I'll quote more: ' A little more than a little is much too much.' "

" A little less than all is much too little for me. So, Rosa, give all or none."

" I don't understand you."

" That's proof you love me. Girls never love fellows they understand."

" Prove that I love you."

" Well, you don't hate me. You don't hate Vincent. Therefore you love him. Ergo, you love me."

" Simpleton."

"True love is always simple.   Here, take this white rose as a sign that you don't hate me."   He plucked a large half-opened bud from a great sprouting branch and held it toward her.

"But the red rose is my favorite."

"Well, here is a red one.   Give me the white.   That is my favorite.   Now we've exchanged tokens.   The rose always goes before the ring.   I'll get that."

"If you were a true lover you would wear my colors."

"These white leaves will grow red resting on my heart."

"When they do I will listen to you."

"Will you, though?   It is a promise; when this white rose is red you will love me?"

"Oh, yes, I can promise that."

"Dear Rosa!" He was very near her as she disentangled an obtruding vine from her garments, and before she was aware of his purpose he had audaciously snatched a kiss from her astonished lips.

"You odious Yankee! I haven't words to express my disgust—abhorrence!"

"Don't try, love needs no words; but I'll tell you: let me put this white rose to your lips; it will turn red at the touch, and in that way you can take your kiss back, if you really want it; then there'll be a fair exchange.   I—"

"Hello, there! are you two grafting roses?"

It was Wesley, coming from the lower garden, where the stream was narrowest beyond the high wall of hedge.

"Oh, no, Mr. Boone: Richard here is studying the color in flowers.   He has a theory that eclipses Goethe's 'Farbenlehre.'"

"Oh, indeed!" Wesley was quite unconscious of what Goethe's doctrine of colors might be, so he prudently avoided urging fuller particulars regarding Dick's theory, and said, vaguely:

"You have color enough here to theorize on, I'm sure."

"Yes, we have had very satisfactory experiments," Dick assented naïvely, stealing a glance at Rosa.

"But quite inconclusive," she rejoined, moving onward, the two young men following in the penumbra of her wide hat.

CHAPTER XVIII.

A CAMPAIGN OF PLOTS.

MEANWHILE, there were curious events passing and coming to pass on the seven hills upon which the proud young capital of the proud young Confederacy stood. Rome, in her most imperial days, never dreamed of the scenic glories that Richmond, like a spoiled beauty, was hardly conscious of holding as her dower. Indeed, such is the necromantic mastery of the passion of the beautiful that, once standing on the glorious hill, that commands the James for twenty miles—twenty miles of such varied loveliness of color, configuration, and *mis en scène*, that the purple distances of Naples seem common to it—standing there, I say, one day, when the sword had long been rusting in the scabbard, and the memory of those who raised it in revolt had faded from all minds save those who wanted office—this historian thought that, had it been his lot to be born in that lovely spot, he, too, would have fought for State caprices—just as a gallant man will take up the quarrel of beauty, right or wrong !

Thoughts of this sort filled Barney Moore's mind too, that delicious September afternoon as he stood gazing dreamily down the river, toward that vague morning-land of the sun's rising, where his mind saw the long lines of blue his eyes ached to rest on. Barney had left the kindly roof where he had been nursed back to vigor. He had quit it in a fashion that left a rankling sorrow in his grateful heart. Vincent had represented to Jack the inconvenience it would be, the peril, rather, for him to assume the guardianship of so many enemies of the Confederacy. Scores of the old families of the city were under the ban simply because they had pleaded for deliberation before deciding on the secession ordinance. The Atterburys had their enemies too. It was pointed out that Vincent and Rosa had been educated in the North; that Mrs. Atterbury had spent many of her recent summers there. Their devotion to the Confederacy must be shown by deeds. It was true they had given twenty thousand dollars to the cause, but what was that to threefold millionaires? General Lee, their kinsman, had shaken his Socratic head solemnly when Rosa, at the War Department, told him, as an excellent joke, the strange chance that had brought Vincent's college chum and his family under the kind Rosedale roof.

Richard Perley was, therefore, deputized to rescue Barney from his false position and give him a chance for exchange when the time came. He journeyed up to Richmond, and, one day, laid these facts before Barney, who instantly saw his friend's dilemma, and at once set about inventing a *ruse* that should extricate him, without mortifying the kind people who had befriended him. When he was able to be about, he feigned a desire to go to his friends in Arrowfield County, south of the James, and was bidden hearty Godspeed. Then, with funds supplied by Jack, he gained admittance to a modest house far out on Main Street, where the city merges into the country. They were simple people, and his thrilling tale of being a refugee from Harper's Ferry was plausible enough to be accepted by more skeptical people than the Gannats.

Day after day Barney skirted furtively about the uncompromising walls of Libby and Castle Thunder, where once or twice he had gone with his hosts to make a mental diagram of the place for future use. Little by little he became familiar with Richmond, which, like a new bride, gave the visitor welcome to admire her splendid spouse, the Confederate government. He learned all the plots of the prison, and became the confidant of Letitia Lanview, known to every exile in Richmond as the friend of the suffering—St. Veronica she was called—after a poem dedicated to her by a young Harvard graduate, rescued by her perseverance from death in Libby Prison. With this lady he drove all about the environs of Richmond, and several times far out toward the meditated route of flight, in order that he might be able to lead the bewildered refugees. He got the whole landscape by heart, and could have led a battalion over it in the dark. Then he passed days wandering over the Libby Hill, down in the bed of the "Rockets," as the bed of the James was known in those days; he learned the ground to the very beat of the patrols that guarded the wretched prisoners in the towering shambles. One whole night, too, he spent in marking the course of the guards as they changed in two-hour reliefs. With his facts well collected he visited Mrs. Lanview, and at last he was confronted by Butler's agent. This agent was a middle-aged man, who had evidently once been very handsome, but dissipation had left pitiable traces upon his fine features, and his once large, open eyes, that perplexingly suggested some one Barney tried in vain to recall—vainly? The man didn't say much in the lady's presence, but when the two were in the open air, facing toward the center of the town, he divulged a good deal that surprised Barney.

"You are from Acredale, young man. I lived there when I was younger than I am now. My name? People call me a good many names. I don't mind at all, so that I have rum enough and a bed and a bite to eat. No man can have more than that, my boy. I am plain Dick Jones now. It's an easy name, and plenty of the same in the land; and if I should die suddenly there would be lots o' folks to feel sorry, eh? But as you are from Acredale I don't mind telling you that it is Elisha Boone that foots the bill. Butler is a friend of Boone's, and he has given me authority to summon all the troops within reach to my aid. My business is to carry young Wes Boone to Fort Monroe. Butler doesn't know that. He thinks I am spying Jeff Davis and piping for the prisoners. He didn't say that he wanted me to kill Davis, but if we could carry him to Fort Monroe, my boy, there'd be about a million dollars swag to divide! How does that strike you?"

"It doesn't strike me at all. I think it is for the interest of the Union that Davis should be where he is. He is vain, arrogant, silly, and dull. He will alone wreck the rebel cause if he is given time. There couldn't be a greater misfortune for the North than to have Davis displaced by some one of real ability, such as Stephens, Lee, Benjamin, Mason, Breckenridge, or, in fact, any of the men identified with secession."

"You surprise me, my son. Still, admitting all you say, the men who should surprise the North some fine morning with a present of Jeff Davis on their breakfast-plates, wouldn't be without honor, to say nothing of promotion and profit?"

"Oh, if we can carry Jeff off without compromising the safety of the prisoners, I'll join you heartily. But first of all we must rescue them."

"Unquestionably; now, here's the programme: Butler's forces will be within gunshot of Magruder's lines on Warwick Creek Thursday—that's three days from now. The prisoners will be out of the sewer Wednesday after midnight. You know the roads eastward. You will lead them to the swamps near Williamsburg. There we will have boats to take part down the river; the rest will make through the swamps under my lead. I have been spying out the land for a week. At a place called Rosedale we pick up young Boone, who is really the object of my journey. I couldn't find him for weeks, and inquired of all the prisoners. Mrs. Lanview finally put me on the track, and I saw Wes Boone as I came up here. He thought the chances were better with a big party than alone. I saw him again yesterday, and he told me that Davis and Lee, his chief of staff, were to be at a party in the Rosedale house on Thursday next. Now, we can pick up Davis just as well as Boone. There is the whole plan."

"Oh, that's a different matter. Davis will not be near the city, and his keeping will not add to our danger. I see no reason why we shouldn't grab him. Heavens, what a sensation it will make! We shall be the wonder of the

North—we shall be like the men that discovered André and Arnold—Paulding and—and"—but here Barney's historical facts came to an end—"we shall be famous for—forever!"

"For a week, my son; wonders don't live long in these fast days. For a week the North will glorify us; then, if they find that we voted for Douglas, as I did, they will say we had some sinister design in bringing Davis North, and likely send us to Fort Lafayette."

Barney stopped dead; they had come under a gas-lamp between Grace and Franklin Streets. He looked at the man. He was quite sober. His eyes answered the young man's indignant protesting glance, openly, unshrinkingly, humorously.

"I should be sorry to think that, Mr. Jones."

"Well, wait. When you get North you will see a mighty change in things. Sentiment, my boy, follows the main chance. It's money, my boy, money. Enough money would have made Judas respectable; he was fool enough to put his price too low."

"Ugh!—you almost make me hate the North! Who can have heart to fight for such heartless traffickers?"

"The North doesn't ask your heart. It has counted the cost, and finds that it can pay a million of men thirteen dollars a month for three years, and still make a good thing out of it—that's about the breadth of it. Here's an oasis in the desert of darkness. Come and have a drink?"

But Barney—not caring for a drink, the cynic—gave him his address, and, dreadfully cast down in spirit, the eager partisan moped up the long hill homeward. The next day Mrs. Lanview gave him the details of the meditated escape. There were only sixty or a hundred in position to avail themselves of the subterranean way that had been toilsomely dug, by a few devoted spirits, with tools casually dropped among them by the guileless Veronica during her daily visits. The plotters counted on at least six hours' start before discovery. The guards were not to be disturbed, and the evasion would not be known until eight o'clock, when the miserable breakfast ration was distributed.

Of that amazing exploit, the digging through twenty solid feet of earth and stone, I do not propose to tell. It is to be found in the journals of the day: it is contained in the hundred pathetic narratives of the men who took part. It has nothing to do with this history beyond the use made of it to mislead the ingenious Barney, and in the end complicate the careers of those in whom we are interested. Suffice it, therefore, to say that in the dim morning mist, as arranged, a shadowy host emerged on the river-bottom, now dry and footable; that each man, as he crawled from the pit, was directed into the thick willows bordering the banks; that when six score or more had clambered out they obeyed a whispered command, for which Veronica had prepared them, and noiselessly, in shadowy single file, they followed the bed of the stream, even where the water flowed deep and dangerous, until they came to the gentle slopes of Church Hill. Then, under guidance of Barney, those who were wise followed swiftly down the river-road until daylight, when they hid in the dim recesses of the white-oak swamps, where they lay concealed many hours. As night fell they faced hopefully forward down the Williamsburg road, until a flaming wave in the air admonished them to strike to the right, and they plunged into the pathless swamps of the Chickahominy. Here they were secure. No force able to cope with them could enter; no force at the command of Magruder could surround them. But Barney's guiding hand was now replaced by another. Jones had appeared, and with him men bearing Butler's commission. The prisoners of Libby set up a defiant cheer. They were once more under the flag. Father Abraham was again their commander.

There were sedate, fatherly men among these rescued bands. There were men with gray hairs and sober behavior; men who could bow meekly under the chastening rod; but the antics of the juvenile group, in which we are mainly interested, were grave and decorous compared with the abandoned, delirious joy of these grave men as they reached the recesses of a swamp that denied admission to all save practiced explorers. Why, here they could subsist for weeks! The rebels might spy them, might surround them, but they need not starve—the buds were food, the bushes refreshment, the pellucid pools drink and life. Barney stared in speechless amazement at the unseemly gambols of the motley mass.

Delirium! it was a mild term for the embracing, the prancing, the Carmagnole-like ecstasy of the half-clad madmen running amuck in the almost unendurable joy of liberation. Barney knew that this condition of things would never do. All who bore commissions in the army were selected from the men. The highest in rank, who proved to be a colonel, was invested with the command, Barney serving as adjutant, and Jones as guide. The rabble, having made a good meal from the spoil of a sweet-potato patch, pushed forward through the fretwork of fern, rank morass, and verdure, toward security. But the march was a snail's pace, as may be imagined. The men, worn to skeletons by months of captivity, insufficient food, and stinted exercise, were forced to halt often for rest in such toilsome marching as the half-aquatic surface of the swamp involved.

By Thursday noon they were still far from the river. Foragers were detailed to procure food, and pending their return the wearied band sank to the earth to rest. In less than two hours the predatory platoon returned with a sybaritic store—chickens, young lamb, green corn, onions. Only the stern command of the colonel suppressed a mighty cheer. When the march was resumed the colonel led the main column south by east. Jones, with Barney and a dozen men, struck due east. In answer to Barney's surprised question, Jones informed him they were to pick up "Wes" Boone by taking that route. Difficult as the way had been heretofore, it now became laborious in the extreme for this smaller band. The bottom was all under water, and before they had proceeded a mile half the group were drenched. In many cases an imprudent plunger was compelled to call a halt to rescue his shoes — that is, those who were lucky enough to have shoes—from the deep mud, hidden by a fair

13

green surface of moss or tendrils. It was a wondrous journey to Barney. The pages of Sindbad alone seemed to have a parallel for the awful mysteries of that long, long flight through jungles of towering timber, whose leaves and bark were as unfamiliar as Brazilian growth to the troops of Pizarro or the Congo vegetation to the French pioneer. Jones and his comrades saw nothing but the hardships of the march and the delay of the painful *détours* in the solemn glades. The direction was kept by compass, many of the men having been supplied with a miniature instrument by the prudent foresight of Mrs. Lanview, who was niggard of neither time nor money in the cause she had at heart. In spite of every effort a march so swift that it would have exhausted cavalry, Jones's ranks did not reach the rendezvous until midnight. At about that hour the exhausted fugitives came suddenly upon a wide, open plain, and far below them, in the valley, a vision of light and life shone through the dark.

"There, boys, we're at the end of our first stage. Unless I'm much mistaken, that bit of merry-making yonder will cost the Confederacy a chief."

"But is it certain that Davis is there?" asked the man Jones called Moon, who seemed to be his intimate.

"Ah, that we will learn so soon as Nasmyd reports. We will give the signal when we reach that fringe of wood yonder. It's back of the grounds, separated from them by a hard piece of swamp and water.—Men, you must follow now in single file, and when we get in the swamp, mind, a single step out of line will cost you your lives, for, sucked into that morass, wild horses can't pull you out."

Then, as they plunged anew in the gloomy deeps of swamp and brake, the friendly lights were lost and the depressed wayfarers struggled on with something of the feeling of a crew cast away at sea, who, thrown upon the crest of a rising billow, catch a near glimpse of a great ship, light and taut, riding serenely havenward to lose it the next in the dire waste. Presently the melancholy bird-notes that had puzzled Jack in the same vicinity days before broke out just in front of Barney, who was clambering along, the third man from the head of the little column. Again, after a long pause, the sweet, plaintive note was re-echoed from a distance.

"Ah, all is well!" he heard Jones ejaculate triumphantly. "We are in time and we are waited for.—Now, men, put all the heart that's in you to the next half-hour's work. No danger, but just cool heads and strong arms."

This good news was conveyed from man to man, and the toilsome movement briskly accelerated under the inspiring watchword. Shortly afterward the larger growth—cypress and oak—diminished, as the band straggled into the open, starry night at the margin of what they could tell was water by the croaking of frogs and plashing of night birds and reptiles. Then the train was halted. Jones left Nasmyd in command and plunged into a thick skirt of bushes. Now Barney, hot and dirty from the march, had shot ahead when he heard the ripple of the water. He had taken off his shoes to bathe his blistered and swollen feet, and sat quite still and restful under the leafy sprays of an odorous bush that even in the dark he knew to be honeysuckle.

"Well," he heard Jones cry in an exultant whisper, "we've done it. The woman is a trump. There are a hundred nearly of the prisoners gone to the boats. Now we are ready for Boone. Is Davis here?"

"Yes; he came over from Williamsburg at eight o'clock; they were feasting when Clem came away a three or more ago."

"Any cavalry at the house?"

"A squadron; but they are ordered to be in saddle for their quarters at midnight. There's the bugle for boots and saddles now."

"Yes; by the Eternal, what luck! Davis will sleep there."

"So Clem says; the state chamber has been prepared for him; all the rest except Lee go back to Williamsburg."

"We couldn't have arranged it better if we had been given the ordering of it. Are all the boats here?"

" Yes."

" And the negroes—how many have you?"

"I can't say. They've been dropping across in twos and threes since ten o'clock. The curious thing is that the women are more taken with the idea of fight than the men. We shall have enough—too many, I fear."

" We'll make them our safety, Jim, my boy ; we'll divide them up, and, in case of pursuit, send them in different directions to confuse the troops."

" How many men are you going to take to the house?"

"Six, with you and me. It will be unsafe to take more, as the boats are small. I will go back and select the men. You get the boats ready."

Barney hurried on his shoes, crawled through the bushes, and was in his place when Jones presently appeared. The men, dead tired, were disposed about on the ground asleep, not minding the damp grass or the heavy dew that made the air fairly misty.

"Wake four of the men," Jones whispered, and when they were aroused he said to a tall, reeling shadow, idly waiting orders :

" We'll be back in a half-hour, or an hour at the farthest. Let the men sleep ; they need it. Sleep yourself if you want to. Moon or I will come to rouse you, and we will bring you plenty of bacon and hominy. Have no fears if you hear movements just beyond you ; there are a couple of contrabands here who go with us. Here's a ration of tobacco for the men when they wake, and a gallon of whisky, which you must serve out gradually."

Revived by this stimulating news quite as much as by the whisky, Barney and his three comrades followed Jones to the boats. There were four—the dug-outs we saw Jack manœuvring in the same waters a few nights before. A negro sat silent, shadowy in each, and, when Jones gave the word, " Let drive!" the barks shot through the waters, propelled by the single scull, as swiftly as an Indian canoe. In a few moments all debarked on the grassy knoll behind the black line of hedge. Jones made straight for the high doorway, and inserting a key it was noiselessly opened.

"Men," he whispered, "no names must be used in any case. I'm number one, Jim here is number two, Moore number three, and so on. Each one remember his number. Clem will remain here with number six to guard the gate. All the rest follow me."

Two negroes joined the party that stole forward through the rose-field to the negro quarters. All was silent. As they reached the great kitchen behind the house and connected with it by a trellised pavilion, only an occasional light could be seen in the house. All were apparently there. The ball had ended. Leaving Barney in charge of the rest, Jones and Number Two crept along the trellis toward the house and soon disappeared around the southern corner. Jones presently returned and said, exultingly:

"The cavalry is gone; we have nothing to fear.—Plato, you go with Number Two to the stables and bring the horses out; hold six and send the rest scattering in the fields, so that in case of anybody's being in the mind to follow he'll have to use his legs, and we can beat them at that game. Where are the ropes?" he asked the black man left in the group.

"In de kitchen, massa."

"Get them!"

"Must I go alone, massa?"

"That's a fact.—There, Moore, you go with the boy—don't be a minute."

Barney followed the sable marauder through the grounds to the rear of the trellis, and crept with him through a window which stood open. The kitchen was dark, but the negro seemed perfectly familiar with the place. He made directly for a dark panel in the northern wall, opened a cupboard-door, knelt down and began to grope among bottles, boxes, and what not that housewives gather in such receptacles.

"Oh, de lor'! dey ain't no rope! It's done gone!"

"Have you a match ?" Barney asked.

" No, massa, but dey is some yondah."

"Find them."

The boy crept cautiously in the direction of the passage leading into the house ; he fumbled about, an age, as it seemed to the impatient Barney, and at last uttered an exclamation:

"Got 'em ?"

" No, massa, but Ise suah deys kep dar."

"Take my hand and lead me."

"It's molasses, massa, and Ise all stickem," the voice in the dark whispered, delightedly, and Barney could see a double row of glistening white ivory in the dim light that came through the window. He came nearer the clumsy wight, and saw that it was a pan of batter the cook had left on the table, probably the morning griddle-cakes. The negro was a mass of white, pasty glue, and knelt on the floor, licking his hands passively.

"Where are the matches ?"

"Under de clock, in a tin safe, massa—right da."

Barney groped angrily about the table, on the clock-shelf, knocking down a tin dish, that fell with the clatter of a bursting magazine in the dense stillness of the night. Both drew back in shadow, waiting with heart-beats that sounded in their ears like tramping horses on thick sward. The clamor of rushing steeds in the lane suddenly drowned this; a loud, joyous whinny sounded in the very kitchen it seemed, and there was a rush houseward past the pantry as of a troop of cavalry. Then a blood-curdling outcry of voices, then shots. Barney, leaving the negro writhing in convulsions under the table, darted to the window—to the rendezvous. It was deserted.

CHAPTER XIX.

"HE EITHER FEARS HIS FATE TOO MUCH."

WHEN Vincent visited the stables on the morning of that eagerly-looked-for Thursday, he found three of the horses clammy with perspiration and giving every sign of having been ridden! The awkward and evasive answers of the stablemen would not have been enough for any other than a man preoccupied by love. When Rosa went to the kitchen, if her head had not been taken up with the love in her heart, she must certainly have remarked that the stores of food prepared for the household were curiously diminished and the kitchen girls unwoutedly reserved. Indeed, in any other condition than that in which the family now found themselves, they must have remarked a singular change in the black brigade in kitchen and garden. But, preocupied each with a different interest, as well as the preparation for the President's *fête*, the Atterburys remarked nothing sinister in the distracted conduct of their servants, and had only a vague feeling that the great event had in some sort paralyzed their wonted noisy activities and repressed their usual chatter. Kate's uneasiness and restless vagaries, her disjointed talk and half-guilty evasions, would have been remarked by her prepossessed hosts; while Wesley's shifting and moody silence would have warned his comrades that he was suffering the pangs of an evil done or meditated. Precursive signs like these—and much more, which need not be dwelt on—the kind hosts of Rosedale made no note of. But when Vincent opened the mail-bag—brought by an orderly from Williamsburg every morning, the first surprise and shock of the day was felt—though in varying degrees by all the diverse inmates of the house.

" Hah! glory to the Lord of hosts!" the exultant reader cried, as he passed to his mother a large official envelope at the breakfast-table.

"I'm ordered to the field." he cried, as Jack looked inquiringly; " I'm to set out to-night and report for duty with

General Johnston to-morrow at Manassas. No more loiter-
ing in my lady's bower; Jack, my boy, the carpet will be
clear for your knightly pranks after to-night."

"If it were Aladdin's magic rug, I should caper nimbly
enough, I warrant you."

"What would you wish—if it were under your feet, with
its slaves at your command?"

"I should whisk you all off—North—instanter."

"Ingrate!—plunge us into the chilly blasts of the North,
in return for our glorious Southern sun? Fie, Jack! I'm
surprised at such selfish ingratitude. We expected better
things of our prisoners," Mrs. Atterbury murmured, and
affected a reproving frown at the culprit, as she handed her
son back the order, with a stifled sigh.

"The sun of the South is not the sun of York to us, you
know; all the clouds that lower on our house are doubly
darkened by this Southern sun; even the warmth of Rosedale hearts can not make up for our eclipsed Northern star,"
Jack said, sadly, with a wistful look at the rival warrior
reading with sparkling eyes the instructions accompanying
the order to march.

"Since Vincent is going so far northward, I think it will
be a good time for us to go home," Mrs. Sprague began,
tentatively.

"Oh—no—no! Oh, we could never think of such a
thing," Rosa cried—"could we, mamma?"

"Why should you go?" Mrs. Atterbury asked. "Until
Jack is exchanged, you've certainly no duty in the North so
important as watching over this headstrong fellow. We
can't think of your going—unless you are weary of us."

"O Mrs. Atterbury, pray don't put it in that way!
You know better. Our visit here has been perfect. But
you can understand my anxiety to be at home; to be where
I can aid my son's release. I have been anxious for some
time to broach the subject, but I saw that our going would
be a trouble to you; now, since fortune offers this chance,
we must seize it—that is, those of us who feel it a duty to
go"; and she looked meaningly at Merry and her daughter.

"Nonsense! You are hostages for Vincent, in case he is captured, as long as you are here; I can't let you go—under the laws of war—I can not. Can I, Vincent?"

Vincent looked at Jack solemnly, but made no answer.

"Mamma is quite right. While you are with us no harm can come to Vincent; for, if he should be taken prisoner, we can threaten the Yankee Government to put you to torture unless he is well treated," Rosa interrupted, reassuringly.

"We should be far more aid and comfort to Vincent if we were in the North than we could be here. If he were taken prisoner and wounded, we could return him the kindness we have received here. In any event, we could lessen the hardships of prison life."

"Oh, you would have to minister to a mind diseased, if such a fate should befall me!" Vincent cried, sentimentally; with a glance into Olympia's eyes, which met his at the moment. Both blushed; and Olympia, to relieve the embarrassment, said, decisively:

"Mamma is right. Jack must have his family on the ground, to watch over his interests. I am sure there is some underhand work responsible for this long delay in his case, for I saw by *The Whig*, last week, that exchanges of prisoners had been made; I think that—" But, suddenly remembering the presence of Kate and Wesley, she did not finish the thought, which implied a belief in the intervention of the elder Boone—to Jack's detriment. In the end—when the two mothers talked the matter over—Mrs. Sprague carried the point. She convinced Mrs. Atterbury that there was danger to Jack in a longer stay of his family in the Confederate lines. Vague reports had already reached them from Acredale of the suspicious hostility in which the Democrats were held after Bull Run. The Northern papers, which came through the lines quite regularly, left no doubt that Democratic leanings were universally interpreted in the North as evidences of rebel sympathy, if not partisanship. Such a charge, as things stood, would be fatal to Jack; and the mother's duty was plain. She had friends in Washington, once powerful, who could stand between her son and

calumny—perhaps more serious danger—when she was present in person to explain his conduct. If she could not at
once secure his exchange, she could save him from compromise in the present inflammable and capricious state of the
public mind. Understanding this, and the enmity of Boone,
Mrs. Atterbury not only made no further objection, but acknowledged the urgent necessity of the mother's presence in
the North. The idle life of Rosedale had grown unbearably
irksome to Merry, too.

"I feel as if I were a rebel," she confided to Mrs. Sprague
in the evening talks, when the piano sounded and the young
people were making the hours pass in gayety. "It's a sin for
us to laugh and be contented here, when our friends are bearing the burdens of war. I shall be ashamed to show my face
in Acredale. Oh, I wish I could carry a musket!"

"You might carry a canteen, my dear. I believe the
regiments take out *vivandières*—there would be an outlet
for your warlike emotions," Mrs. Sprague said, with the
purpose of cheering the unhappy spinster.

"Ah, no; I must not give encouragement to that dreadful
Richard. But we shall go now, thank Heaven, and it will
comfort my sisters to have the boy back on Northern soil,
even if he persists in being a soldier."

She had a long talk with Jack on the subject. That tem-
pest-tossed knight convinced her that it would only incite
the boy to more unruliness to persist in his quitting the army,
or to urge him northward now, before an exchange was
properly arranged. Indeed, he was a prisoner—taken in
battle—though his name did not appear on the lists. So
Vincent's sudden going was welcomed as a stroke of good
fortune. The Atterburys, understanding the natural feelings
of the family, made only perfunctory opposition. Olympia
and Kate were to remain until their brothers' fates were decided. Vincent, who had been for weeks wildly impatient
to return to the field, was divided in mind now—by joy and
despair. He had put off and put off a last appeal to Olympia. He had not had an opportunity, or rather had too much
opportunity—and had, from day to day, deferred the longed-

for yet dreaded decision. When ready to speak, prudence
whispered that it would be better to leave the question open
until it should come up of itself. She would learn every day
to know him better in his own home, where all the artificiali-
ties of life are stripped from a man, by the concurrent abra-
sions of family love and domestic *devoirs*. She would see
that, however unworthy of her love he might have seemed
in the old boyish days at Acredale, now he could be a man
when manliness was demanded; that he could be patient, reticent, humble in the trials her caprice or coquetry put upon
him. She had, it seemed to him, deepened and broadened
the current of his love during these blissful weeks of waiting.
Her very reserve, under the new conditions surrounding her,
had made more luminous the beauty of her heart and mind.
She was no longer the airy, capricious Olympia of his college
days. The pensive gravity of misfortune and premature responsibility had ennobled and made more tangible the traits
that had won him in her Northern home. She had not
avoided him during these weeks of purifying probation, as he
feared she would. Of late—Jack's state being secure—she
had revived much of the old vivacity, and deepened the thrall
that held him.

But now the merry-making season which had opened before them was at an end. The madrigals that welled up in
his soft heart must sing themselves in the silence of the night,
in the camp yonder, with no ears to comprehend, no heart to
melt to them. He should probably not get a chance to see her
again during the conflict. How long ? Perhaps a year—for
it would take two campaigns, as the rebel leaders reckoned,
to convince the North that the Confederacy was unconquer-
able! And what might not happen during those momentous
months ? Perhaps Jack's death ?—and then they would be
divided as by fire—or, if the conflict resulted victoriously for
the South, as he knew it must, he foresaw that the soldier of
the conquering army would not be received as a wooer in the
family of the defeated. He knew her so well! She would,
in the very pride of outraged patriotism, give her love to one
of the defeated, rather than add to the triumphs of the hated

South. She had strong convictions on the war. She hated slavery, and she could not be made to see that the South was warring for liberty, not to sustain slavery. These thoughts ran through Vincent's troubled mind as his mother directed the preparations for the *fête* of the President.

Kate, Jack, and Dick were pressed into the service of decorating the apartments. Olympia left the room with her mother, to advise and assist in making ready for the journey North; and Vincent, aiding his mother with a sadly divided mind, kept furtive watch on the hallway. She held him hours in suspense, he thought, almost wrathfully, of deliberate purpose; for she must have read in his eyes that he wanted to talk with her. The artless Dick finally gave him a chance.

"I say, Vint, get Polly to show you the roses needed for the tables; I'll be with you by-and-by to cut the ferns. Do you think you could make yourself of that much use? You're not worth a straw here."

"Send for Miss Polly and I'll do my best," Vincent said, with a gulp, to conceal his joy. She appeared presently; and, as they were passing out of the door, Rosa cried, imperiously:

"Oh, yes, Vint, we need ever so much honeysuckle; you know where it hangs thickest—in the Owl's Glen. Olympia will like to see that—the haunt of her favorite bird"; and the busy little maid laughed cheerily, like a disordered goddess, intoxicated by the exhaling odors of the floral chaos.

"*En route* for Roumelia, then," Vincent cried in military cadence, as the florists set out. Roumelia was the name Jack had given the rose-lands near the stream, in fanciful allusion to the Turkish province of flowers. Halting at the gardener's cottage, Vincent procured an immense pair of shears, like a double rapier in size, and, bidding the man follow to gather the blossoms, he pushed into the blooming vineyard.

"With such an instrument I should say it was the golden fleece you were after," Olympia cried, as he reached her side, "though I believe Jason didn't do the shearing."

"No, the powers of air worked for him, and he found his quest ready to his hand."

"I'm sure the powers of air have not denied you; look at those radiant ranks of blossoms bending to be gathered."

"Ah, yes, beauty stoops sometimes to welcome the trembling hand of the suitor."

"Your hand is rather unsteady—infirm of purpose ; give me the blades." She took them laughingly, and snipped the green stems rapidly and dexterously.

"Yes, I believe men are infirm in moral purposes, as compared to women. It is only in the brutalities of life that men are decisive."

"Do you mean that women approach the trials of life less thinkingly and act less rationally than men ? "

"Yes and no. The daring too much is always before a man; the daring too little is, I think, the only trouble a woman has."

"Oh, that is a large question, involving too much mental strain in a garden of roses, where the senses sleep and one is content with mere breath and the faintest motion."

"There are enough roses; now we will go for the wild smilax and honeysuckle; perhaps the cool air of the pools will restore your mental activities."

They left the dismembered roses scattered in fragrant heaps on the shaded path and walked slowly toward the dense hedge.

"What a perfect fortress this green wall makes of the gardens!" Olympia said, glancing around the great square, where the solid green wall could be seen running up much higher than their heads.

"Yes, as I said the other day, it would take hard work for an invading force to get at the house unless traitors within gave up the gates. This one," he added, unlocking a massive oak door, crossed with thick planks and studded with iron bolts, "alone admits from the creek and swamp. It is locked all the time; no one has the key except the gardener, who delivers it to mamma every night."

"A feudal demesne; it takes one back to the so-called days of chivalry."

"Why do you say 'so-called'? To me they are the delight of the past—when men went to battle for the smile of the women they loved, when knights rode the world over in search of adventure, and my lady, in her donjon, listened with pleasure to the lover's roundelay. Ah, it was a perfect life, an enchanting time. We are living in a coarse, brutal age; chivalry was the creed of civilization, the knights the priesthood of the higher life."

"There's the Southerner through and through in that sentimentality. To me chivalry means all that is narrow, cruel, and rapacious in man. The philandering knights were sensual boobies, the simpering dames soulless wantons. Life meant simply the rule of the strong, the slaughter of the weak. Servitude was its law and robbery its methods. Have you ever traveled in out-of-the-way places in Germany, Austria, or Italy?"

"No, I've never been abroad."

"You would know better what I mean if you had seen the monstrous relics of the age you admire. The few ruled the many; the knights were simply a brotherhood of blood and rapine; men were slaves, women were worse. The bravest were as unlettered as your body-servant, the most beautiful dames as termagant as Penelope the cook. At the table men and women ate from a common dish, without forks or spoons. Men guzzled gallons of unfermented wine. A bath was unknown. Cleanliness was as unpracticed as Islamism in New York. Ugh! anything but chivalry for me."

"But surely the great lords were not what you represent. They were gentle born, gentle bred. They could not be robbers; they lived from great estates."

"They were the 'Knights of St. Nicholas,' which, in the slang of the middle ages, meant what they call in the West road agents; indeed, plain highwaymen they were called in England in Bacon's day."

Vincent bent over discomfited, and held the little shallop

until Olympia was seated, and then pushed off into the murky stream.

"Do you see those streamers of loveliness waving welcome to you, fair damsel—Nature knows its kind?"

"That's one word for me and one for yourself," she cried, seizing the dainty pink sprays that now trailed over her head and shoulders as the boat glided along the fringe of bushes supporting the clinging vines.

"Oh, no, Olympia; I can't speak even one word for myself. I have been trembling to do it this six weeks, but your eye had none of the invitation these starry blossoms offer us. I am going to say now, Olympia, what I have to say—for after to-day there will be no chance; what has been on my mind you have long known. You know that I love you; how much I love you, how impossible it is to think of life without you, I dare not venture to say to you, for you distrust our Southern exaggeration. But I do love you; ah, my God! all the world else—my mother, my sister, my duty seem nothing compared to the one passionate hope in my breast. Do you believe me, Olympia—do you doubt me?"

"Far from it, Vincent—dear Vincent—no—no—sit where you are and listen to me—" She was deeply moved, and the lover in his heart cursed the luckless veils of blossom that she apparently, without design, drew before her face. "I do believe all you say; I knew it before you said it. But you remember we went over this very same ground before. Since then, it is true, you have been the means of saving us much misery; how much I hardly dare think of when I look back to that dreadful day, when mamma lay in the fever of coming disease and the hopelessness of despair. All I can say, dear, dear Vincent, is what I said before. Wait until thine and mine are no longer at war. Wait until one flag covers us—"

"But that can never be!"

"Wait! I have faith that it will be!"

"If one flag should cover us—my flag—would you—would you—?"

"Ah, Vincent! don't ask me; don't force me to say something that will make you unhappy, since I don't know my own mind well enough yet to answer as you wish me to answer—"

"But you can tell me now whether you love me, or, at least, whether there is any one you love more ?"

"I don't think I love you. I know, however, that I think no more of any one else than I think of you; pray, let that suffice."

"But how cruel that is, Olympia ! It is as much as to say that you won't wait and see whether you may meet some one that you can be surer of than you are of me ?"

"I must distress you whatever I say, Vincent ! Frankly, I don't think you can decide just now whether your heart is really engaged. I think you do not know me as a man should know the woman he makes his wife. I am certain I do not know you. If you had been born and bred in the North, I should have no difficulty in deciding; but your ways are so different here: women are accorded so much before marriage, and made so little of a man's life after marriage, that I shrink from a promise which, if lightly or inconsiderately given, would bring the last misery a woman can confront."

"What, Olympia ! you think Southern men do not hold marriage to be sacred ?"

"I think that the Southern man has a good deal of the knight you spoke of in him, and, like the Frenchman, marries inconsiderately, and does penance in infidelity, at least to the form, if not the fact, of the relation."

"O Olympia ! where do you get such repulsive ideas of us; who has been traducing us to you ?"

"I judge from the Southern men I have seen North; pardon me, Vincent, I do not see how it can be otherwise in a society based upon human servitude. To live on the labors of a helot people blunts the finer sensibilities of men and women alike; when you can look unshrinkingly at the separation of husband and wife on the auction-block, when you can see innocent children taken from their mothers and sold into eternal separation, I think it is not unnatural in me to

fear that a woman with my convictions would not be happy
mated with a Southerner. All this is cruel, I fear you will
think, but it would be crueller for me to encourage a love
that, under present circumstances, would bring misery to
both of us."

"You are an abolitionist?"

"Yes; every right-thinking person in the North is an
abolitionist to this extent; we want the South to take the
remedy into its own hands, to free its slaves voluntarily;
the radical abolitionists prefer a violent means. That I do
not seek or did not; but now, Vincent, it is bound to
come."

"And, if it should come, what would you answer to my
question?"

"Here is a white rose: I picked it with my hand, and, you
see, a drop of my blood is on it; when you can give me a
rose with a drop of your blood on it as free from taint as the
stain mine makes, I shall have an answer that will not be
unworthy your waiting for!"

"Unworthy! I don't understand you. Surely, you don't
think me a profligate?"

"When the time comes that no human being acknowl-
edges your ownership, perhaps you may receive a voluntary
bond-maid, bound to you by stronger ties than the chattel of
the slave."

"But you love me, then, Olympia?"

"I can not love where I do not reverence."

"But it is not my fault that slaves are my inheritance!"

"It will be your fault if they are your support when you
are your own master."

"You love an idea better than you love a man who would
die for you!"

"I love manliness and the sense of right, which is called
duty, better than I love a man who is blind to the first
impulse of real manhood—"

"Would you ask a Jew to give up his synagogue to gain
your hand?"

"The synagogue is the temple of a creed as divine as my
14

own, and the faith of the man I loved would never swerve me in accepting or refusing him."

"We of the South believe slavery a divine institution—that is, first established by the fathers!"

"The tribes in the Fiji Islands believe man-eating an ordinance of the gods!"

"Well, this sort of discussion leads to nothing," Vincent said, ruefully. "The world is well lost for the woman one loves, when I come to you shorn of my world!"

"Ah! then, Vincent, you will find another!"

He drew her hand from the clinging vines and kissed it.

"I am very happy. I shall lose my world with a very light heart."

"The world is a very tough brier; we sometimes bring it closer, when its thorns prick us more painfully in the struggles to cast it off."

"Then I'll cut the brambles, and not risk tearing my flesh!"

"That's the soldier's way—the heroic way; but wait for the future; I am young and you are not old."

Vincent's gayety when they returned to the drawing-room attracted the observant Dick, and he slyly whispered to the warrior, "Been practicing the Roman strategy with the Sabines?"

"No, I've been at the Temple of Minerva and taken a pledge to hold my tongue."

"Ah! the goddess of the owls; but, as they see light only in darkness, I fear you groped in blackness."

The whole household were to meet President Davis and his party in Williamsburg, assist at the review, and get back with the distinguished guests in time for a state dinner. Merry and Mrs. Sprague were reluctant to go, but they feared a refusal would be misunderstood. Poor Merry was very tearful and disconsolate at the thought of leaving Dick, but she strove heroically to hide her grief when the cavalcade set out, the elder ladies driving, the young people mounted. The ancient capital of Virginia was aflame with the new rebel bunting. President Davis, with Generals Lee

and Magruder, were in place on the pretty green before the
old colonial college edifice when the Rosedale people came
up. Davis saluted Mrs. Atterbury with cordial urbanity;
but, as the troops were already in column, there was only
time for hasty presentation of the strangers.

Jack watched the rather piebald pageant with absorbed
interest. The infantry marched wretchedly. The arms
were as varied as the uniforms, and the artillery seemed a
relic of Jackson's time. But the cavalry was superb. Never
had he seen such splendid ranks, such noble horses. At
sight of the tall, elegant figure of the President, the troops
broke into the peculiar shrill cheer that afterward became a
sound of wonder, almost terror, to unaccustomed Northern
ears. It was a mingling of the boyish treble of college cries
and the menacing shriek of the wild-cat. Jack was secretly
very much delighted with the review. More than half the
rank and file were mere boys; and he could see that they
were unruly, almost to point-blank disregard of their officers'
commands, or the prescriptions of the manual. It would
take short work for the disciplined hosts the new Northern
general was training, to sweep such chaff from the field of
war. Vincent saw something of this in his comrade's eye,
and a good deal nettled himself by the slovenly march and
humorous abandon of the men, he said :

"You must remember, Jack, our army is made up of
gentlemen's sons; the gentry of the South are all in arms,
and we can't at once reduce them to the mere machines a
more heterogeneous soldiery can be made. The men who
won Manassas passed in review a day or two before the
battle, and they made the same impression upon me—upon
Beauregard himself—that I see these men have made on
you. Depend upon it, in a fight they will be good soldiers."

"Let me have the poor comfort of underrating my enemy, the thing above all others that a wise man shuns and a
fool indulges."

"Oh, on that theory revile them if you like."

"No, indeed; I'm far from reviling them. The cavalry
is magnificent. I don't think we have a regiment in our

army that can compare with that brigade. Who commands
it?"

"Jeb Stuart—the Murat of the South," Vincent said,
proudly. "I'm going to tell the President what you said of
the brigade; you know he is passionately fond of the army,
and really wanted to be the commander-in-chief, when they
made him President at Montgomery."

At sunset the President and General Lee entered the carriage with Mrs. Atterbury and Mrs. Sprague, Merry driving
in a phaeton with Kate, who didn't enjoy so long a ride on
the horse.

"I'm glad we've got such important hostages as yourself
and son," Davis said gallantly to Mrs. Sprague, as the carriage passed out of the clamor of acclamation the crowd set
up. "I knew the Senator, your husband, intimately. If he
had lived, I doubt whether we should have been driven out
of the Union. He was, in my mind, one of the most prudent
statesmen that came from the North to Congress."

"He certainly never would have consented to break up
the Union," Mrs. Sprague said, in embarrassment.

"Nor should I, madam, if there had been any further
security in it. The truth is, there was nothing left for us
but to go out or be kicked out. The leaders of the Abolition
party long ago proclaimed that. However, war settles all
such problems. When it is settled by the sword we shall be
satisfied."

Mrs. Atterbury changed the conversation by asking how
Mrs. Davis liked Richmond.

"Oh, she has been treated royally by the people there.
I declare Richmond is as Southern a city as Charleston. I
have been agreeably surprised by the absolute unanimity of
gentle and simple in the cause. My wife receives a clothes-
basketful of letters every morning from the mothers of the
Confederacy proffering time, money, and service wherever
she can suggest anything for them to do. I propose later
on establishing an order something like the Golden Fleece,
which shall confer a certain social precedence upon the
wearers. I have thousands of letters on the subject, and as

the society of the South is, as a matter of fact, a society of gentle-folk—for the most part lineally descended from the nobility of older countries—I think it proper and right that lineage should have certain acknowledged advantages in the new commonwealth. But I propose to go further, and institute an order of something like nobility for women—who have thus far given us great help and encouragement. Indeed, there are many in the Congress—a dozen Senators I could name—who think that we ought to make our regime entirely different from the North, and that we should adopt a monarchical form—"

" I'm sure, I think we should," Mrs. Atterbury exclaimed, delightedly. We are really as unlike the Northern people as the French or the Germans."

"The strongest argument for declaring the Confederacy an empire is the one that weighed with Napoleon I. We should at one stroke secure the alliance of all the monarchies. They have never looked with favor on the experiment of a powerful republic over here, and it is almost certain they would befriend us for transforming this mighty infant state into an empire. However, that is for future action. Our agents abroad have sent us full reports on the matter."

" I doubt the wisdom of ever hinting such a thing," General Lee said, gravely. " We must show that we are able to act independently in selecting our form of government. I doubt very much whether the masses would listen favorably to an empire established by foreign aid."

" Possibly, general, possibly. As I said before, there will be time enough for that when, like Napoleon, we have made our armies the masters of this continent. Then, with boundaries embracing Mexico, Canada, and the Western States—for they can never exist independent of us—we can choose empire, republic, or a Venetian oligarchy."

As they came in sight of Rosedale, Davis stood up in the carriage to get a better view of the landscape, which showed swift alternations of dense thickets and wood and rolling acres of rich crops.

" What a State Virginia is ! " he exclaimed with enthusiasm. " It has the climate and soil to support half of Europe. Mother of Presidents in the past, it will be the granary and magazine of the Confederacy in ten years. My own State, Mississippi, is rich in land, but the climate is hard for the stranger. It enervates the European at first. But we are an agricultural people, or rather we give our energies to our staple, cotton; that is to be the chief treasure of the Confederacy."

Dinner was ready for the table when the guests came from their rooms. Davis excused his lack of ceremonial dress, saying, pleasantly:

" I am something of a soldier, you know, and travel with a light train. Lee, there, has the advantage of me. A soldier's uniform is court costume the world over."

" But you are the commander-in-chief, Mr. President. Don't you have a uniform ? "

" No. I am commander-in-chief only in law. Congress is really the commander-in-chief. The man that assumes those duties can attend to them alone. He is, of course, subject to the executive; but only in general plans, rarely in details."

Davis was placed at Mrs. Atterbury's right, Mrs. Sprague at her left. General Lee sat at Vincent's right, *vis-à-vis* to Jack, who was lost in prodigious admiration of the Socratic-like chieftain—Lee was as yet unknown to all but a discriminating few in the Confederacy. He was as tall as Davis—fully six feet—but more rounded and symmetrical. He spoke with great gravity, but seemed to enjoy the jests that the young people found opportunities to indulge in, when it was seen that the President devoted his talk exclusively to the hostess or Mrs. Sprague. Davis was a good talker, and charmed the company with reminiscences of old times in Congress.

" I don't remember Lincoln distinctly," he said, concluding a reminiscence, " but I think he's the man that used to be so popular in the House cloak-room, telling stories which were said to be extremely droll."

"Mrs. Lincoln is in some sort kin to Mrs. Davis, isn't she?" Mrs. Atterbury asked. "I have read it somewhere."

"Very distant. Mrs. Lincoln is of the Kentucky Tods, and they were in some way kin of my wife's family, the Howells. Not enough to put on mourning, if Mrs. Lincoln should become a widow."

"Is it true, Mr. President, that a society in the North has offered a million dollars for your capture—abduction? I heard it in Williamsburg, and saw an allusion to it in *The Examiner* the other day."

"Oh, I'm sure I can't say. If the offer were authenticated, I should be tempted to go and get the reward myself. With a million dollars I could do a good deal more for the cause in the North than I can here, making brigadiers and settling questions of precedence between Cabinet ministers, judges, and Senators."

"Mr. President, give me an exchange North, and I will ascertain the facts in the million-dollar offer and write you faithfully how to set about getting the money," Jack said, very soberly, from his end of the table.

"Ah! the Yankee spoke there—nothing if not a bargain. Sir, you deserve your clearance papers, but I'm too good a friend of Mrs. Atterbury and her daughter to bring about the loss of company that I am sure must be agreeable. Then, too, there's no telling the miracles of conversion that may be brought about by such ministers as Miss Rosa there."

Rosa blushed, Jack felt foolish, and everybody laughed except Dick, who looked unutterable things at his adored, and boldly entered the lists against the great personage by asking, in a quivering treble :

"Doesn't the Bible say that the wife shall cleave to the husband ; that his people shall be her people, his God her God, where he goes she goes?"

"It is so said in the Bible, sir ; but it was a woman that uttered it, and she was in love. When you know more of the sex, you will understand that women in love are like poets ; they say much that they don't mean, and more that they don't understand."

"But, Mr. President, what the one woman said in the Bible all women practice. You never knew a woman that didn't believe her husband's beliefs, hate his hates, love his loves."

Davis smiled, and his eyes twinkled kindly on his boyish inquisitor.

"I know only one woman. That is as much as a man can speak for. She doesn't hate my hates, love my loves, or enter unprotestingly into all my ways. Indeed, I may say that, being a peaceful man, I wanted to remain in Washington, for I believed that Seward was sincere in pleading for a compromise; but the woman I speak of had her own opinion, convinced me that she was right, and I came to my own people."

At this moment there was a diversion. A soldier, booted and spurred, entered the room, walked to the head of the table, and bending deferentially to the President, said :

"I am ordered to deliver this message wherever you may be found." He handed Davis a large envelope and retreated respectfully two or three paces backward. Everybody affected to resume conversation as the President, breaking the seal, said :

"Pardon me a moment, madam." But he had no sooner ran over the lines than he turned to the courier, crying, in visible discomfiture :

"When did you leave the war office ? "

"At five o'clock, sir."

"General, we must return instantly to Richmond; a hundred or more of the prisoners have broken out of Libby ! It is reported that a column of the enemy with gunboats have passed up the James.—Madam, this is one of the exigencies of a time of war. I needn't say to an Atterbury that everything must give way to public business ! " He called Lee aside, spoke rapidly to him, and the latter, beckoning Vincent, left the room. He returned in ten minutes, announcing that everything was in readiness to set out. The carriage with Mrs. Sprague's and Merry's small luggage was ready when the cavalcade set out, Davis riding with them

and the cavalry company from below, divided into squadrons before and behind the carriage. It was eleven o'clock
as the last dark line of the troop disappeared. Olympia and
Jack stood at the great gate in mournful silence. The swift-
ness of the parting had lessened the pain, but their minds
were full of the sorrow that follows the inevitable. Mrs.
Sprague had herself declined to postpone the ordeal when
Mrs. Atterbury pointed out the untimely hour. No, it was
better to suffer this slight inconvenience to have Vincent's
protecting presence all the way to the Union lines ; and
Jack, acknowledging this, didn't say a word to dissuade her.
Vincent's last act was to call Jack to his room.

"I wanted to tell you, Jack, what a great joy it has been
to me—it has been to all of us—to have you in our home at
this trying time. I can not tell you how much comfort it
has been to me now, but some time you shall know," Vincent stammered, and began to open a drawer in the bureau.
"Here is something I want you to accept as a keepsake from
me." He drew forth a pistol-case and opened it. "It will
be a melancholy pleasure for me to feel, in the dark days to
come, that these weapons may prove your friend in battle,
where I must be your enemy."

"By George, they're beauties!" Jack cried, taking the
weapons out.

"Yes; they were bought last year, and I have had J. S.
cut on one, and V. A. on the other. I meant them for your
Christmas last year, but they were mislaid."

"What a kind fellow you are, Vint! I don't think I
ought to take these."

"Why not ? I have others! I shall feel easier, knowing
that you have them. You can stow them about you easily,
they are so small."

"But it's against the laws of war for a prisoner to be
armed."

"That's just the reason I haven't asked you to take them
before. You can leave them here in my room until you are
exchanged, and then you can carry them with impunity."

The household assembled at the gate leading into the

roadway as the cavalcade took up the march. There were sad, sobbing farewells spoken—the kindly night covering the tears, and the loud neighing of the horses drowning the sobs.

The Northern group remained in the roadway, straining their eyes to catch the last glimpse of the wanderers as they disappeared in the misty foliage, far up the roadway.

The horizon to the zenith was full of shimmering star-points. Olympia, with Jack, turned slowly toward the house, silent and not wholly sad. Dick, in a low treble, could be heard just behind them, quoting melancholy verses to Rosa; and the brother and sister returned slowly up the dewy, odorous path. At the porch Rosa exclaimed, in surprise:

"I wonder where Pizarro is? I haven't seen him while we have been out. It can't be possible he has followed Vincent! What shall we do if he has?"

"Make Dick take his place. A terrier is sometimes as faithful as a mastiff," Jack said, quickly.

"Oh! Miss Atterbury wants something with a bite, rather than a bark, and a terrier wouldn't do," the boy answered.

"I want Pizarro. I shall never sleep a wink all night if he isn't here," Rosa said, in consternation; "he is better than a regiment of soldiers, for he won't let a human being come near the house after the doors are closed, not even the servants."

An expedition, calling upon Pizarro in many keys, set out and wandered through the grounds, back to the quarters, to the gates leading to the rose-fields, to the stable, but Pizarro was not to be found. Lights were burning in the hall only when the four re-entered, and with a very grave face Rosa bade the rest good-night.

CHAPTER XX.

A CATASTROPHE.

ROSEDALE had been a bed of thorns to Wesley Boone since his recovery. He felt that he was an incongruous visitor among the rest, as a hawk might feel in a dove-cote. He would have willingly returned to Richmond—even at the risk of re-entering the prison—if Kate had not been on his hands. The life of the place, the constant necessity of masking his aversion to the Spragues, his detestation of Dick, the simple merry-making and intimate amenities of such close quarters, tasked his small art of dissimulation beyond even the most practiced powers. The garment of duplicity was gossamer, he felt, after all, in such atmosphere of loyalty and trust as surrounded him at Rosedale.

He knew that in the daily attrition and conventional intimacies of the table, the drawing-room, or the promenade, the cloak covering his resentful antipathy, his moral perversities, his thinly veiled impatience, was worn to such thin shreds that eyes keen as Jack's must see and know him as he was. What was hatefulest and most unendurable of all was the bondage of truce in which the Atterburys held him. Wesley was no coward, and he ached to meet Jack face to face, arm to arm, and settle with that thoughtless insubordinate a rankling list of griefs heaped up in moments of over-vivacious frankness. He would make Jack smart for his arrogance, his insolence, his cursed condescension so soon as they were back among the Caribbees.

But meanwhile, here, daily tortured by harmless things —tortured by his soul's imaginings—Wesley was becoming a burden to Kate, who saw too plainly that he was in misery, and realized that it was largely through his own inherent weakness and insincerity. He had all the coarse fiber of his father without the same force in its texture. With merely superficial good manners, he was never certain whether the punctilious niceties observed toward him by

the Spragues and Atterburys were not a species of studied
satire. Vincent, who had never shown him the slightest
consideration in Acredale, treated him here with the chivalrous decorum that the code of the South demanded in those
days to a guest. Wesley ground his teeth under the burden, not quite sure whether it was mockery or malevolence.
He watched with malignant attentiveness the imperceptible
change of tone and manner that marked the family's treatment of the Spragues. There was none of the grave cere-
moniousness he resented in the Atterburys' behavior with
them.

Jack was a hobbledehoy son of the house, almost as
much as Vincent. Kate, too, was, he felt certain, treated
with a reserve not shown to Mrs. Sprague or Merry. Brooding on this, brooding on the unhappiness of his own dispo-
sition, which denied him the privilege of enjoying the best
at the moment, indifferent to what might be behind, Wesley had come to hate the Atterburys for the burden of an
obligation that he could never lift. He hated Mrs. Atterbury for her high-bred, easy ignoring of all conditions save
those that she exacted. He hated Rosa for her gayety, her
absorption in the young scamp Dick. He hated Vincent
because he seemed to think there was no one in the North
but the Spragues worthy a moment's consideration. It is in
hate as in love—what we seek we find. Every innocent
word and sign that passed in the group, in which he did not
seek to make himself one, Wesley construed as a gird at
him or his family. Constantly on the watch for slights
or disparagements, the most thoughtless acts of the two
groups were taken by the tormented egotist as in some
sense a disparagement to his own good repute or his family
standing.

Nor were the marked affection and confidence shown
Kate by everybody in the house a mitigation of this malign
fabric of humiliation. Jack's fondness for Kate had not
escaped the observant eyes of Dick, who had confided the
secret to Rosa, who had likewise unraveled it to mamma,
and, as she kept nothing from Vincent, the Atterburys had

that sort of interest in Kate that intimate spectators always show in love affairs, where there are no clashing interests involved. It was a moot question, however, between the three, when, after weeks of observation, Mrs. Atterbury declared that Jack was not in love with Miss Boone. "He can't be," she declared. "He doesn't seek her alone; he doesn't make up to her in the evening. Half the time when they come together it is by Dick's arrangement. *He* seems to be in love with Kate."

"How absurd!" Rosa cried, with a laugh; "a boy like him! Why, he would be in school, if there were no war."

"Well, Rosa, I fancy that Dick hasn't found war very much different from school, so far. He seems to recite a good deal to the mistress, and occupies the dunce's block quite regularly," Vincent retorted, with a provoking significance that set mamma in a brown study and suspended the comments on Kate's and Jack's probable sentiments.

Mrs. Sprague and Wesley were the only people in the house who had no suspicion of a deeper feeling than mere passing goodfellowship between Jack and Kate. Both were blinded by the same confidence. The mother could never conceive a son of the house of Sprague making such a breach on the family traditions as a union with a Boone. Wesley could not conceive a sister of his giving her heart to the son of a family that had insolently refused to concede social equality to her father. Something of Wesley's miserable inner unrest could not fail to be visible to the Atterburys, but the less congenial he became the more watchfully considerate they made their treatment of him. He was their guest, with all the sacred rights and immunities that quality implies, in the exaggerated code of the Southern host. Kate was the single power that Wesley had bent his headstrong will before, ever since he was a boy. His father he obeyed, while in his presence, trusting to wheedling to make his peace in the event of disobedience. But Kate he couldn't wheedle.

She was relentless in her scorn for his meannesses and follies, and, though he did not always heed her counsels, he proved their justness by finding his own course wrong. Kate, however, hesitated about remonstrating with him on his deepening moodiness, for she was not quite sure whether it was mad jealousy of Dick's favor in Rosa's eyes, or a secret purpose to attempt to fly from the gentle bondage of Rosedale. Wesley with Rosa it was remarked by Kate, was, or seemed to be, his better self, or rather better than the self with which others identified him. It was, however, she feared, more to torment Dick, than because she found Wesley to her liking, that the little maid often carried the moody captain off into the garden, pretending to teach him the varied flora of that blooming domain. Dick remarked these excursions with growing impatience, and visited his anger upon Rosa in protests so pungent and woe-begone that she was forced to own to him that she only pretended an interest in the captain, so that he might not think he was shut out of the confidence of the circle.

"And who cares if he does think he is shut out, I should like to know? He is a sneak, and I don't like to have you talking with him alone," Dick cries, quite in the tone of the Benedict who has passed the marriage portal and feels safe to make his will known.

"I should like to know what right you have to order what I shall or shall not do?" Rosa protests, half angry, half laughing. "Why, you talk like a grown man—like a husband. How dare you?"

Dick pauses confused, and looks guiltily about at this.

"Ah, if you put it that way I have no right except this: My whole heart is yours. You know that. You may not have given me all yours." (Protesting shrug from Rosa's shoulders.) "Well, all the same; if my heart is all your own you have a duty in the case. You ought to spare your own property from pain." (Rosa laughs softly.) "Of course you are right. You are always right. How could such a beautiful being be wrong!" The artful rogue slips his arm about her waist at this, and, after a feeble struggle, he is permitted to hold this outwork unprotested.

"And, Rosa, if I speak like a man, it is because I am a

man. Wasn't it the part of maids in the old times to inspire the arm of their sweethearts; to make them constant
in danger, brave in battle, and patient in defeat? Are you
less than any of the damsels we read of in chivalry? Am I
not a man when I look in your dear eyes and see nothing
worldlier than love, nothing earthlier than truth there?"

"What a blarney you are! I must really get Vint to
send you away, or he will have a Yankee brother-in-law."

"And the Perleys will have a rebel at the head of the
house."

Now, this silly prattle had been carried on in the arbor
near the library, and Wesley, sitting under the curtain, had
heard every word of it. Neither the words nor the unmis-
takable sounds that lips meeting lips make, which followed,
served to soothe his angry discontent. This was early on
the great Davis gala day, and thereafter he disappeared from
the scene. He made one of the party to Williamsburg,
and, though distraught in the conversation, was keenly alert
to all he saw.

Rallied upon his reticence, he had snubbed Kate and
turned disdainfully from Jack's polite proffers to guide him
through the review. He had studied Davis all through the
manœuvres with a furtive, fascinated attention, which Mrs.
Atterbury remarked with complacency, attributing it to awe.
At the dinner-table, seated between Kate and Merry, he had
never taken his eye from the chief of the Confederacy.
Twice the President, courteously addressing him, he had
blushed guiltily and dropped his gaze. Before the dinner
was half over he pleaded a severe headache, and, bidding
his hostess good-night, hurried from the room. The wide
hall was deserted; the moon threw broad swaths of light
on the cool matting, and he halted for an instant, breathing
rapidly. Something lying on the rug at the door moved
languidly. Wesley, looking carefully about, moved swiftly
to the spot and stopped. Pizarro raised his head, whining
amicably, and, as Wesley bent over to pat him, wagged his
tail with a spasmodic thud against the floor, in sign of goodfellowship.

" Come, Pizarro, come with me," Wesley said, coaxingly.
But the dog, redoubling the tattoo with his tail, remained
obstinately at his post.   Wesley stole to the end of the hall
and listened, then, hearing the busy clamor of the servants
moving from the kitchen to the dining-room, he retraced his
steps to the stairs, bounded lightly up and in three minutes
reappeared, and, keeping his eyes on the half-closed doors,
slipped softly to Pizarro.   The dog sniffed excitedly, and as
Wesley took a thick parcel from his coat-pocket the beast
leaped up and attempted to seize it.

"Follow me, Pizarro, and you shall have it."   He held
up the packet, a red, glistening slice of raw beef.   The dog
whined ecstatically and Wesley, holding a morsel of it just
out of his reach, retreated up the stairs.   Pizarro bounded
after him as if construing the by-play into a challenge, and
frisking in all sorts of fantastic shapes to win the savory
prize.   The door of Wesley's room was open, and as the
dog came abreast of it he flung a piece into the apartment.
Pizarro, lowering his sniffing nose, looked at the tempting
bit sidewise, and then wagging his tail in modest deprecation
of his boldness, made a start inward.   It was swallowed in
an instant, and then, as Wesley entered, the door was closed.
Pizarro, by the humility of his manner, the lowered head
and sidelong glance, asked pardon for intruding upon the
privacy of a guest, but argued with his ears and by short
yelps, in extenuation, that such a feast as a bit of meat—
after an active day, when the servants had forgotten to feed
him—no dog with a healthy appetite could resist, no matter
how perfect his breeding.   He was ready for the larger ration Wesley held in his hand.

Wesley held the temptation in his hand until he had
lured the dog into a large closet communicating with the
bedroom by a locked door.   Once in, the door was shut, and
the young man sank on a seat in a thrill of grateful relief.

"That danger's over," he muttered.   "Now to see who is
in the upper rooms."

Perfect silence on the upper floor ; only the solemn
shadows of the night, as the moon rises higher and higher,

and the plaintive cries of the night-birds alone betoken life.
Through the windows the white-jacketed house-servants are
rushing gayly to and from the dining-room. All the rooms
are dimly lighted. The President's apartment is fragrant
with blossoms, and the lace counterpane turned down. Re-
tracing his steps, Wesley enters Vincent's room on the corridor with his own. The candle is burning dimly on the
mantel. He seems to know his whereabouts very well, for
he makes straight for a bureau between the bed and the window. He takes from the top drawer a pistol-case, which he
has evidently handled before, as he touches the spring at
once. He takes out one pistol, and, rapidly extracting the
loads, puts it back. He has taken four out of the five barrels
of the second when a sound of footsteps in the hall startles
him. He has barely time to replace the weapons, close the
case, put it in the drawer and crawl under the bed, when
Vincent and Jack enter.

His suspense and terror are so overmastering that he can
only hear an occasional word. His own heart-beats sound
in his ears like the thumping of a paddle. Is Vincent going
to bed? Are Jack and he going to sit and smoke, as they
often do? No, relief beyond words, they are going out!
Perhaps to Jack's room? They often sit there until very
late, and then Vincent slips in stocking-feet to his own room.
But they are gone, and he must fly. He dares not return to
extract the last charge. But one ball can't do much hurt
in the dark, and, if his plans are carried out with care,
there will be no chance for any one to use the weapons
on the rescuing party, even if he were disposed to. In a
moment Wesley is back in his room, marking, with surprise, that there is no sound from Jack's or Dick's room.
But all is well. He is in his own room and secure from
surprise.

He sat down to think. He must keep everything in mind.
One whippoorwill cry from outside would mean that all was
well; two that he must hurry to the rendezvous. It seemed
like a dream. Davis, the arch-rebel, the chief architect of
the Confederacy, under the same roof; in an hour, if no hitch

15

come, the traitor would be bound and flying in trusty Union hands. And when they got North ?—when he, Wesley Boone, handed over to the authorities in Washington this hateful chief of a hateful cause, what fame would be his ! No one could dispute it. He had informed Butler's agent; he had watched day and night; had given the Unionists plans of the grounds; was now periling his own rescue to bring the arch-traitor to his doom. Ah ! what in all history would compare with this glorious daring ? He sat glowing in dreams of such delicious, roseate delight, that he took no heed of time, and was startled when he heard Dick and Jack bidding each other good-night. Then in a few minutes he heard Jack's door open and a tap at Dick's door.

"Come to my room. I want to show you a present I got to-night." Then silence. Wesley had no watch. The rebels had relieved him of that at Bull Run. But it must be quite midnight. He opened one of the windows softly. Oh, the glory of the night, harbinger of his high emprise, his deathless glory ! The wondrous, wondrous stillness of the scene —and to think that over yonder, in the dark depths of the forest, fifty, perhaps a hundred, men were waiting for him— for him ? Yes, the mighty arms of the Union were about him; the trump of a fame, such as no song had ever sung, was poised to blow to the world his daring. Hark ! Heavens, yes; the long, tender plaint of the whippoorwill. Ah ! now, now there was no doubt. In swooning delight he waits. Good Heaven ! What's that sound ? Angels and ministers of grace, the dead in wailing woe over the deed about to be done ? Ah ! he breathes.

Pizarro has grown tired of imprisonment and has set up an expostulatory wail, facetiously impatient at first, but now breaking into sharp yelps. This will never do. He must stop that ear-splitting outcry, or the household will be awakened. That sharp-eyed, razor-tongued young devil, Dick, is just across the hall. Wesley opens the closet door, and Pizarro bounds out, licking his jailer's hands in grateful acknowledgment. He frisks, appealing to the room door, inviting the further favor of being permitted to go to his post, his wagging tail explaining how necessary it is that a dog intrusted with such important duties as the guardianship of the household can not suffer the casual claims of friendlessness or the comity of surreptitious feeding to lure him into infidelity. The tail proving ineffectual in argument, Pizarro supplemented its eloquence by sharp admonitory yelps, tempered by a sharp *crescendo* whining, of which he seemed rather proud as an accomplishment.

"Damn the brute ! He will ruin everything. I must kill him." But how ? He had no weapon. He looked about the room in gasping terror—the dog accepting the move as a sign that the eloquence of the tail argument had proved overpowering, supplemented this by an explosion of ecstatic yelps of a deep, bass volume, that murdered the deep silence of the night, like salvos of pistols. The curtains to the windows were held in place by stout dimity bands. Whispering soothingly to the dog, Wesley knotted four of these together, and, making as if to open the door, slipped the bands like a lasso over the head of the unsuspecting brute. In an instant his howls were silenced. The dog, with protruding tongue and eyes—that had the piteous pleading and reproach of the human, looked up at him, bloodshot and failing. But now the second signal must be near ! He may have missed it in the infernal howling of the brute. Yes, that was it. He looks out of the window; his room is in view of the covered way to the kitchen. He sees moving figures; he hears voices. They are there. He has missed the signal; he must hasten to them. He puts out the lights and opens the door cautiously. All is invitingly, reassuringly still. He is at the hall door in a minute, in another he is with the shadows in the rear of the house.

"Jones, is it you ? "

"Ah, captain, we are waiting for ropes to secure the prize."

" There is no time to wait. The dog has made such a noise that I didn't hear your signal. I saw you from my window. Come, we must not lose a minute, for I couldn't fasten the brute very well. Davis is here, and we have only to take him from his room. The cavalry went about eleven; I heard them march away an hour ago."

"Now, give me the exact situation here, that there may be no surprise. How many men are we likely to encounter in the event of a fracas ?"

"Counting Davis and Lee, four in the house. How near the orderlies and guards are you know better than I. Besides Davis, there's Jack Sprague, young Atterbury, and Dick—but he don't count."

"No ! Why ?"

"He is not over his wound, and besides he's but a boy. They had two pistols loaded, but I managed to draw all the charges except one. So that if Jack and Atterbury should come to the rescue they could do no damage."

"They sleep at this end of the house ?"

"Yes, and our work is at the other."

"Well, then, in that case I will get ladders I saw near the carriage-house and put them up to Davis's window as a means of escape in case these young men get after us before we finish the job. Even with their unloaded pistols, two full grown men and the boy could make trouble."

He called Number Two and gave him orders to place a ladder at each of the two windows of Davis's room, and to have a man at the top of each—armed. When the men had hurried away, Jones continued:

"Here's a pistol for you. It is a six-shooter bull-dog, and will do sure work. Now move on to the stairway; others will join us in a moment. You're sure you know Davis's room ? It would be mighty awkward to poke into any of the others."

"Yes; everybody in the house was taken to see it. It is the old lady's room, occupied by mother and daughter, generally; but given up to the President for the night."

They are in the hall, stealing softly over the thick matting; they are in the broad corridor—running the whole length of the house—Jack's, Olympia's, Dick's, and Kate's rooms all behind them—southward. Wesley, with Jones touching his right arm and Number Two at his left, is moving slowly, silently northward to the left of the stairs.

"Great God! What was that?"

A sound as of a clattering troop of cavalry, the neighing of horses in the grounds! Wesley halted, trembling, dismayed.

"That's all right," Jones whispered. "I ordered the stables opened so that the horses wouldn't be handy, if any one should happen to be at hand who felt like pursuing us, or going for the cavalry."

"It was a mistake; the horses will arouse the house. We must hurry."

In a moment they were before the door of the Davis room. Wesley raised the latch. It was an old-fashioned fastening. Number Two was directed to stand at the threshold while Wesley and Jones secured Davis.

Now they are in the room. There is no sound; but from the open window, looking upon the carriage-road, there is the tramping of horses, drowning all sounds in the room. They are nearly to the large canopied bed between the open windows, when Jones, who is nearest, discovers a startled apparition half rising from the bed. He is discovered by the figure at the same instant, and a piercing scream, so loud, prolonged, and ear-splitting that it echoes over the house, ends the wild dream of the marauders. Wesley reels in panic. But Jones is an old campaigner. If he can't have victory, there must be no recapture. He rushes at the white figure, and snatches — Rosa, limp, nerveless, and swooning !

"See who's in the bed!—I'm damned if you haven't brought us to the wrong room—see, quick!"

But there was no necessity for seeing. Mrs. Atterbury uttered a stifled cry: "Help! help! murder!"

"You, Boone, know the place; stand by me and I'll see that we are not nabbed; but you've made a nice mess of the affair."

But the comments of the indignant Jones were suddenly drowned in a blood-curdling sound in the doorway: the savage, suppressed growl of a dog, and the responsive imprecations of Number Two. With this came the apparition of two figures, at sight of which Jones darted to the window, the two figures, Jack and Dick, following to his right and left.

"Save your powder, whoever you are. Fire at me, and you hit the young woman. I don't know who she is, but her body is my protection." Saying this, Jones coolly, determinedly retreated backward to the window; but Dick, hardly hearing, and certainly not comprehending, had come within arm's length of the two, somewhat to the left of Jones.

"Don't fear, Rosa," Dick exclaimed, between his teeth. "I can see you. Ah, ah!" Then four reports, that sounded as one, split the air.

Rosa broke from the thick cloud of smoke as a fifth report rang out, and a scream of death went up between the bed and the door where Jack stood.

At the instant Dick spoke, Jack, in the doorway, heard an exclamation at his side. He half turned, and as he did so his eye caught the outlines of a man, with a shining something raised in the air, coming toward him from the bedside. He pointed his own pistol at the figure, there were three simultaneous reports, and the oncoming figure fell with a hoarse cry of pain. The man at Jack's back now cried:

"Get through the window; they're coming through the house!"

"It's only a dog; come on."

Then there was a sound of flying feet in the wide passage.

"Are you hurt, Rosa? Tell me—did they hit you? Speak, oh, speak!" It was Dick's voice, in a convulsive sob. Now, the boy again, that danger was gone.

Jack meanwhile had struck a match, and soon found the candles on the night-table near the bed. There was, at the same instant, the audible sound of scurrying along the passage. He ran out. The man assailed by the dog had reached the head of the stairs. As Jack got half-way down the corridor, man and dog disappeared over the balustrade. When he reached the hall the dog was inside, growling furiously, the door was closed and the man gone. Jack opened the door. Pizarro bounded out, and Jack followed. The dog stopped a moment, sniffed the ground, and made for the kitchen. A loud bark, followed by a ferocious growl, and a scream of mortal pain broke on the air; then a pistol-shot, and a long, pitiful gasp, and silence.

" Well, that dog won't trouble any one now," Jack heard, and the voice made his hair rise into bristling quills.

" Barney! " he cried; " Barney Moore, is that you ? "

" It is; no one else. If I'm not drunk or dreaming, that's my own Jack. God be praised! "

" How in Heaven's name did you get here ? "

" I might ask you the same question, but you have priority of query, as they say in court. I came here first to help rescue Captain Wesley Boone, and second to capture his rebel Excellency Jeff Davis."

" O my God! my God! Barney, Barney, tell me all, and tell me quickly! "

Barney told all he knew, and told it rapidly, Jack catching his arm almost fiercely, as the miserable truth began to define itself in his whirling senses. Then the meaning of the two marauders in the ladies' apartments became plain. Jack and Barney were hurrying toward the chamber as the latter talked, Jack filled with an awful fear.

CHAPTER XXI.

THE STORY OF THE NIGHT.

Now, the timely—or untimely—appearance of Jack and Dick in the crisis of the plot came about in this way: Dick, on returning from Jack's room, had remarked, with quickening suspicion, a gleam of light under Wesley's door. Perhaps he is ill, the boy thought, compunctiously; if he were, he (Dick) ought to offer his services. He started to carry this kind thought into effect, when he heard suspicious sounds in the room. Some one was moving. He waited, now in alert anticipation. The plaintive signal of the whip-poorwill—bringing passionate energy to Wesley—reached Dick's ears; he heard the opening of the window; then silence. Could Wesley be descending thence to the ground ? He blew out his candle, drew the curtain, and cautiously raised the window. No; Wesley was not getting out. Then the sound of the Pizarro episode came dimly through the walls. He thought the dog's expostulatory growls a voice. There was some one in the room with Wesley. Perhaps it was Kate. It wouldn't do to act until he was sure that his suspicions were a certainty. Besides, Jack had warned him not to interfere with a mere escape on Wesley's part, unless it seemed to involve depredations upon the Atterburys. Then he heard the faint sound of the scuffle, when Wesley throttled the compromising mastiff. Should he slip over and warn Jack? He was moving toward the door, when, through the stillness of the night, a sound came up from the direction of the quarters. He ran lightly to the window again. His eyes, now accustomed to the darkness in his room, distinguished clearly in the pale starlight. He thrilled with a sudden sensation of choking. Yonder, stealing houseward from the rose-gardens, he could plainly discern two—four—six—moving figures. Heavens, the slaves were out ! There was to be a servile uprising. Now he must go and warn Jack; but he must note first whither the assassins were directing their attack. Perhaps, with the aid of Jack's pistols, they could be frightened away by a few shots from the windows. He ran noiselessly to Jack's room, to his bed, and whispered in his sleeping ear :

"Jack, make no noise; dress yourself and come. The negroes are surrounding the house, and Wesley is in mischief."

Jack was awake and in his clothes in a few seconds. He handed Dick one of the pistols, and, armed with the other, hastened toward Wesley's room. The door was open and all was silent. Dick looked in hastily, marked the open window, and exclaimed:

"He is gone! Come to my room. I know exactly where to locate them from my window; it is nearer the point they halted at than Wesley's."

Yes; figures were moving swiftly against the trellised walls that led to the kitchen. They moved, too, with the precision of people thoroughly acquainted with the place. Then some one appeared swiftly from under the shadow of the house; then three came toward it and passed under the veranda near Wesley's window. Jack leaned far out to discover what this diversion meant. At the same instant the sounding gallopade of hoofs came from the tranquil roadway leading to the stables. The shrill whinny of horses broke on the air.

"They are mounted. There are a score of them!" Jack cried, desperately. "We can at least keep them out of the house."

"We can, if Wesley hasn't opened the doors to them," Dick said, shrewdly.

"That's a fact. But is it sure Wesley is not in his room? Bring matches and let us examine it."

There was no sign of Wesley in the room. The cool night air poured in from the open window.

"Draw the curtain before you strike the match," Jack whispered. "We must not let a light be seen from the outside."

"But the curtains are thin, the light will shine through."

"Sh! Come here. By Heaven, it is Wesley, and he is dead! No—the devil!—it is Pizarro—dead! Kneel down and strike a match, keeping between the light and the window. One glance will be enough."

One glimpse revealed the dog with distended tongue and half-glazed eyes, but still alive. Jack loosed the band from the neck. The dog gave a convulsive thrill and uttered a plaintive moan.

"Set a basin of water down here. He may recover. Poor fellow! This was a cruel return for his kindness to Wesley,"

Jack said, forcing the dog's nose into the basin. He began to lap the cool water greedily. But now Dick, in the doorway, uttered a cry.

"They are in the house. I hear them moving in the vestibule. Come, for God's sake, Jack ! They are making for Mrs. Atterbury's apartment. Evidently some one who knows that the family jewels are there, for what else can they want ?"

The dog staggered to his feet as the two stole softly from the room. They followed with high-wrought, loudly-beating hearts and tingling nerves. The marauders in front of them moved on like men accustomed to the house. They made, as the light footfalls indicated, straight for Mrs. Atterbury's door, which, unlike the others, fronted the length of the hall in a small vestibule sunk into the lateral wall. The invaders were thus screened from Jack and Dick when they had turned the corner, and the latter were forced to move with painful caution to get the advantage of surprise to offset superior numbers. But now a new peril menaces them. A shuffling in the long corridor behind them freezes the current of their blood. They have been caught in a trap. There are two forces in the house. They both turn and halt, silent and trembling, against the south wall and wait. The steps still advance, the scraping of the nailed boots tears the light matting.

"We will wait until the new-comer or new-comers are abreast," Jack breathes in Dick's ear, "and then fire a volley into them point blank."

At the instant Rosa's shriek, blood-curdling and electric, breaks from the corner. Dick is over the intervening steps in two mighty bounds, Jack at his heels and the foe in the rear following. Against the open window Dick catches the outlines of his darling in the brawny arms of Tarquin. He has the advantage of the light, and, as the ruffian retreats to the window, Dick is at his side, and in an instant deals him a stunning blow on the head. Jack, in the dim light, sees the dark figure dashing at him with the gleam of steel in his hand. He levels his weapon, three reports ring out at once, and the miserable Wesley falls with a dreadful gurgling gasp on the floor.

But there are interlopers in the rear as well! Jack turned to confront them. He realized vaguely hearing a struggle as he confronted the robbers. Ah! yes, the dog; the dog has come upon the scene. There is sound of low, fierce, growling, flying footsteps on the floor, and Jack, assuring himself by a quick glance that there were no more marauders in the room, hurried to see that the front door was closed before re-enforcements could come to the invaders. But Pizarro's lusty growls, denoting recovered strength, attracted him kitchenward, and he encountered Barney, and with Barney something of a clew to the hideous attempt. One prayer was in his heart—one hope—that Wesley had escaped; but with shuddering horror he hastened with Barney back to the scene of blood and death. The great candelabra on the mantel had been lighted, and the room was visible as in daylight. Jack halted, transfixed, horror-stricken, in the doorway. The women in hastily snatched robes were all there, and on the floor, wailing over the dead body of Wesley, Kate sat, prone and disheveled, calling to him to look at her, to speak to her, as she kissed the cold lips in incredulous despair. She paid no heed to Mrs. Atterbury, to Olympia, kneeling beside her—all her heart, all her senses benumbed in the agony of the cruel blow. Jack moved to the piteous group, and, dropping on his knees, felt the lifeless pulse, and sank back, pale and shrinking, with the feeling that he was a murderer. Mrs. Atterbury turned to him, crying convulsively :

"Oh, what does it mean, Mr. Sprague? what does it mean?"

"It is a dreadful game of cross-purposes. These unhappy men believed Mr. Davis to be in this room when they entered. They meant to capture him and carry him North."

"Ah, thank God! thank God! who carried our President away in time," and the matron clasped her hands fervently as she sank in a chair. But the sight of Kate, woe-begone, feverishly caressing the dead brother, brought the tenderer instincts back. She rose again, and, clasping her arms about the poor girl, said pleadingly:

"Let him be carried to his room; you are covered with blood."

"Ah, it is his blood, his innocent blood! Murdered, when he should have found mercy."

Jack found tongue now. He was hideously calm—the frightful calm of great-hearted men, who use mirth, levity, and indolency to hide emotion.

"Miss Boone—Kate—it was perhaps the shot from my pistol that killed Wesley. I did it in defense of women in peril, in defense of my own life. It was an accident in one sense. Had I known the circumstances I certainly shouldn't have fired, but you must put the blame on me, not upon this guiltless household."

She looked up at him—looked with a wild, despairing, unbelieving gaze, pressing the handsome dead face to her bosom, and then, with a wild, wailing sob, bent her head until the shining dark mass of hair fell like a funeral veil over her own and the dead face. Rosa, who had disappeared in the dressing-room, now entered the chamber. Turning from the woful group on the floor, she glanced hastily about, as if in search of some one. Her eyes fell upon Dick, dazed and bleeding, on the couch. She ran to him with a tender cry.

"O Richard! are you hurt? Great heavens! your face is all blood. You are wounded. O mamma, come—come—Richard is dying!"

The boy tried his best to smile, holding his hand over his left side, as if stifling pain. He smiled—a bright, contented happy smile—as Rosa knelt, sobbing, by his side, and, opening his jacket, baring the blood-stained shirt, plucked a purplish rose from the bleeding bosom.

"The white rose is red now, Rosa."

"Oh, my darling! my darling!" Rosa sobbed; and the boy, smiling in the joy of it, tried to raise himself to fold her in his arms. But the long tension had been too much—he fell back unconscious.

Olympia saw that Mrs. Atterbury, the natural head of the house, was unequal to the dismal burden of control. She took the painful duty of order upon herself, sent Jack to summon the servants, called Barney to her aid in removing Dick to his room, and, when the terrified housemaids came, distributed the rest to the nearest apartments. Morning had dawned when the work was done, and then Jack set out to investigate the condition of the quarters. Twenty or more of the negroes had disappeared. It was easy to trace them to the swamp, but Jack made no attempt to organize a pursuit. Blood could be traced on the white shell path leading to the rose-fields, and the pond gate was wide open. He reported the state of affairs to Mrs. Atterbury. She begged him to take horse to Williamsburg, bring the surgeon, and deliver a note to the commanding officer. He returned in two hours with the surgeon, and a half-hour later a cavalry troop clattered into the grounds.

Dick's wound was first examined. The ball had entered the fleshy part of his chest, just under the armpit. It was readily extracted, and, if so much blood had not been lost, the boy would not be in serious danger. Wesley had died almost instantly. The ball entered his breast just above the heart. He had passed away painlessly. Jones was shot through the right shoulder, the ball passing clear across the breast, grazing the upper ribs, and lodging just above the left lung. He was, by Mrs. Atterbury's command, removed to the quarters and delivered to the commander of the cavalry troop as a spy, an inciter of servile insurrection. By order of the department commander, civilians were refused all communication with him, as the Davis cabinet meant to make a stern example so soon as he was able to bear trial. Mrs. Atterbury announced to Jack and Olympia that so soon as Dick could bear removal the house would be closed and the family return to Richmond. They heard this with relief, for the place had become hideous to all now. To Jack it was a reminder of his misfortune, and to every one of the group it was associated with crime, treason, and blood. The hardest part of poor Jack's burden was the seizure of

Barney, who was marched off by the cavalry commander. Vincent gone, Jack had no one to reach the ear of authority, and he shrank from asking the intervention of the mistress whose home had been invaded by the guiltless culprit. The case was stated with all the eloquence Jack was master of to the captain in command.

"You are a soldier, sir," the officer replied. "You know I have no latitude in the matter. This Moore has no status as a regular prisoner of war; he is found on the premises of a non-combatant aiding servile insurrection. Even President Davis himself could not intervene. The Southern people are deeply agitated by Butler's attempts to arouse the negroes. We have been weakened, robbed by the abduction of hundreds right here on the Peninsula. The gang that Moore came here with was led by this scoundrel Jones, who is Butler's agent. A very vigorous example must be made of these wretches, or the country-side will be deserted and the government will be without produce. We must inspire confidence in the owners of plantations, or the soldiers in the army will have to come back to guard their homes."

Jack saw the futility of further pleading. The officer was unquestionably right. Such scenes as Rosedale had witnessed would end in the desertion of the rural regions of the Confederacy. At Mrs. Atterbury's urgent intercession Kate was permitted to leave the lines with her dead. She was conducted to the rebel outposts in the Atterbury carriage, and under a flag of truce entered the Union lines near Hampton. Olympia accompanied her in the carriage, Jack riding with the escort. Kate refused every suggestion to see Jack ; refused his own prayerful message, and sternly, solemnly with her dead passed from the scene of her sorrows.

Youth and something else stronger than medicine, more tenacious than any other motive that keeps the life-current brisk and vigorous, made Dick's recovery swift and sure. Rosa had no torments for him now. The blood-red rose had proved a magician's amulet to confirm her mind in the sweet teachings of her heart. But the patrician mother was with difficulty brought to listen to the tying of this love-knot. She had looked forward to a grand alliance for the heiress of Rosedale—an alliance that should bring the family high up in the dominant hierarchy of the South. She listened silently to the young girl's pleading prattle of the boy's bravery, his wit, his manliness. She did not say no, but she hoped to find a way to distract her daughter from a *mésalliance*, which would not only diminish her child's rank, but compromise the family politically. Such a sacrifice could not be. Fortunately, both were mere children, and the knot would unravel itself without perplexities that maturer love would have involved. So the mother smiled on the happy girl, kissed Dick tenderly morning and night, for he had been a hero in their defense, and she was too kindly of heart, too loyal to obligation, to permit Dick's attitude of suitor to lessen her fondness and admiration for the bright, handsome lad. Olympia was the confidante of both the lovers, listened with her usual good-humor to the boy's raptures and the girl's panegyrics, and soon came to share Jack's high place in the happy lovers' devotion.

CHAPTER XXII.

A CARPET-KNIGHT.

JACK meanwhile sank into incurable gloom. The memory of Kate's mute, reproachful look, her heart-broken outcry, never quitted him. He woke at times with the dead eyes of Wesley staring into the night at him, the convicting gaze of Kate fastened upon him. He must fly, or he must die in this abhorred, guilt-haunted atmosphere. Olympia saw this, Mrs. Atterbury saw it, and the first week in November Rosedale was turned over to the military and the household re-established in the stately house in the official quarter of Richmond, where the bustle and movement of new conditions gave Jack's mind another direction, or, rather, took it from the bitter brooding that threatened madness.

When the sun accepted the wind's challenge to contest for the traveler's cloak, I dare say all the spectators of the novel highway robbery—the moon, the stars, the trees, birds and beasts, and others that the fable does not mention—took odds that the wind would snatch off the wayfarer's garment in triumph. However, the wind whipped and thrashed the poor man in vain. The stronger it blew and the more it walloped the cloak's folds, the tighter and more determinedly the traveler held on to it, as he plodded wearily over the hillside. But when the sun came caressingly, inspiring gentle confidence, bathing the body in warm moisture, the tenacious hold was relaxed, then the disputed coat was thrown over his arm, and, as the vista spread far away in golden light, the victim cast the garment by the wayside and the sun came off victor. Youth is despoiled of the garment of grief in this sort. Congenial warmth, the sunshine of friendliness, soon relax the mantle of woe, and the path that looks wintry and hard becomes a way of light and gayety.

It was by mingling—at first perfunctorily—in the gayety of the Confederate capital that Jack lost the melancholy in which the tragedy at Rosedale had clothed his spirits. At worst, the calamity was over; he had been a guiltless vengeance in the punishment of Wesley's treason. So he took bond in hope of better things to come. With a stout heart, strong limbs, a plowman's appetite, and a natural bent to joyousness, a youth of twenty-two or three is not apt to mistake his memories for his hopes and hang the horizon in black when the sun is shining in his eyes!

Richmond, always the center of a fascinating society, was at that time exuberant in her young metropolitan glories. It was the gayest capital in the Western hemisphere. To resist its seductions would have tasked the self-denial of a more constant anchorite than our dashing Jack ever aspired to be, in the lowest stage of his martial vicissitudes. There was nothing of the garishness of the parvenu in the capitol's display. The patrician caste ruled in camp and court. The walls that had echoed to the oratory of Jefferson, Henry, Washington, Randolph, now housed the young Congress of the new Confederacy. An hundred years of political, military, legal, and social precedence were the inheritance of the men chief in the cabinet, the council, and the camp. Stirring traditions clung about every quarter of the town, now devoted to the offices of administration, from the Mayo wharves to the lodgings of Washington and Lafayette. On the stately square yonder, where the musing eye of the rebel chief might study its history, stood the suggestive mansion where Burr's treason was brought home to that first great rebel.

Not far distant the disdainful pointed out the tenement where Fremont had instructed the Richmond youth in far other doctrines than those which made him the abolitionist choice for President in after-times. Royalist and republican glories mingled in the reliquary edifices that met the wondering eyes of the provincial Confederates drawn to the capital in the generous enthusiasm of that first prodigious achievement at Bull Run. Here a royal Governor had dwelt, yonder a Bonaparte had sojourned and beguiled the famous beauties of Powhatan, as the patriarchs loved to call the city. A Lee was the chief of the military staff, a Randolph ruled the war office; scions of the Washingtons family filled a dozen subordinate places; the kin of Patrick Henry revived their ancestor's glory by as zealous a devotion to the new revolution. With personages like these in every office the society of the new capital revived the brilliancy of the French Directory and also the character of the States-General, while Holland held the Spains at bay. The blockade had not yet pinched the affluent, nor beggared the industries of the well-to-do. Always famous for a brilliant bar, a learned judiciary, and a cultivated taste among its women, Richmond in 1861 was the ideal of a political, military, and social rendezvous of a young nation.

The raw legions had been victorious in the first pitched battle of the war on the plains of Manassas, and what might not be reasonably hoped from them under the training of

16

such master-minds as Johnston, Beauregard, Jackson, and
Lee? Wasn't it the common talk among diplomats, the
concurrent opinion of the French and English press, the
despairing admission of the half-hearted and panic-stricken
North, that one more such decisive victory would bring the
South peace and independence? Wasn't it, indeed, well
known among the favored juntas that those sagacious diplomats, Senators Mason and Slidell, had delayed their journey
to Europe in order to aid the President in the treaty of peace
that the victorious legions of Johnston were to exact in
Washington?

Jack was amazed and disheartened at what he saw and
heard. The activity, resources, gayety, and confidence of the
authorities and people, recalled to his mind, Oxford, the
jocund capital of Charles II and the royalists, while the
Commonwealth leaders were drilling their armies. But instead of the chaos of rapine, the wanton excesses, the pillage
of churches and colleges that marked the tenure of the miserable Charles, Richmond was as orderly, serene, the Congress
as deliberate, and the people as content, as the Rome of the
conquest of Persia or France after Jemmapes. The army
was hot for battle, and as confident of the result as the Guard
at Austerlitz or McClellan at Malvern. The work done and
the way of its doing showed that the populace, as well as
the rulers, were convinced of the destiny of the city to be
henceforth mistress of herself, the preordained metropolis
of half the continent—perhaps the whole continent—for,
would the North be able to resist joining States with a destiny so glorious—a regal republic where birth and rank
were tacitly enthroned? The city's greatness was taken by
the mass, as a matter of course—like an heir in chancery
who has won all but the final decree in the suit, or like a
great nobleman who has come to his inheritance.

Though it was the first week of November when the
Atterburys found home affairs going on smoothly in the
town-house, summer still disputed with winter the short
lovely days of fall, as Jack described the lingering May-day
mildness of this seductive Southern autumn. It was the first

season he had ever spent south of New York, and, like most
Americans, he realized, with wonder, that the wind which
brought ice and snow to New York, visited lower Virginia
with only a sharp evening and morning reminder that summer was gone. The balm and beauty of the climate came
with something of healing to the hurt his heart and hope
had suffered at Rosedale. If anything could have mitigated
the pangs of a young warrior perplexed in love and held in
leash in war, it was such an existence as the Atterburys in-
veigled him into leading. The part of carpet-knight is not
difficult to learn, and the awkwardness of it is to some extent atoned for when the service is constrained. At least
Jack took this philosophical view of it, and soon gave himself
up to the merry social life of his surroundings with an animation that led his hosts to hope that he might be won over to
the Confederate cause. Very young men do not sorrow long
or deeply, and Jack was young. He was neither reckless
nor trifling, but I am sure that none of the adulating groups
that made much of the handsome Yankee in Richmond that
season would have suspected that the young man looked in
his mirror night and morning, frowned darkly at the reflected image he saw there, and said, solemnly, "You are a murderer!" It was by no means a tragic accent in which this
thrilling apostrophe was spoken. It was very much in the
tone that a woman employs when she looks hastily in the
mirror and utters a soft "What a fright I am!" apparently
receiving comforting contradiction enough from the mirror
to make the remark worth frequent repetition.

As a matter of fact, however, Jack was not insensible to
the awkward complication of his predicament. Grief as a
mantle is difficult to adjust to the shoulders of the young.
It is melted by the ardor of companionship as swiftly as it
is spun by the loom of adversity. His interest in the strange
scenes that the war brought to pass, his association with people—intimate in a sense with the leading forces of rebellion,
the airs of incipient grandeur, these raw instruments of government gave themselves—all these things engrossed the
observant faculties of the young man, who looked out upon

the serio-comic harlequinade playing about him as a hostage
of the Roundheads might have taken part in the showy fes-
tivities of the Cavaliers, in the years when the chances of battle had not gone over wholly to the Puritans. Not that the
figure illustrates the contrasting conditions adequately. For,
if the South prided itself at all—and the South did pride itself vauntingly, clamorously, and incessantly—it made its
chief boast the point that its people were the gentry of the
land, and that under the rebel banner the hosts of chivalry
had assembled anew to make all manner of fine things the
rule of life. Jack, writing and talking of his few months'
experience, dwelt with wonder upon the curious ignorance
of the two peoples respecting each other. Mason and Dixon's
line separated two civilizations as markedly unlike as the
peoples that confront each other on either side the Vistula
or the Baltic Sea. The hierarchy not only seemed to love
war for war's sake; they possessed that feudal faculty, so in-
comprehensible in the middle ages, the power of making
those who suffered most by it believe in it too, and sacrifice
themselves for it.

The people—Jack sagaciously remarked, in discussing the
topic with Olympia—seemed made for such a climate, rather
than made by it. They would have been out of place in the
bleak autumn blasts, and wan, colorless seasons of Acredale,
where the sun, bleary and dim, furtively skirted the low
horizon from November until April, as if ashamed to be
identified with the glorious courser that rode the radiant
summer sky. Here the sun came up of a morning—a little
tardy, 'tis true, but quite in the manner of the people—warm
and engaging, and when he went down in the afternoon he
covered the western sky with a roseate mantle that fairly
kept out the chill of the Northern night. "No wonder,"
Jack said to his sister, watching this daily spectacle—"no
wonder these people are warm, impulsive, and even energetic; here is an Italian climate without the enervating lan-
guor of that sensuous sunshine."

The Atterbury house was the gayest in Richmond. Mrs.
Atterbury, though the mother of a son in the army and a

daughter with a coterie of her own in society, insisted on
maintaining the leadership she had long held among the
social forces of the capital. "All Richmond," and that
meant a good deal in a city whose women had been adored
for beauty and wit on two continents, received Mrs. Atterbury's bidding to her drawing-room with proud alacrity.
Never had her "teas," her *musicales*, her receptions, and
fêtes been merrier or more convivial than during this memorable autumn that Jack and Olympia passed as prisoners
of war. It was generally believed that the brother and sister were occult agents of the Federal power, negotiating
with the Davis Cabinet, and Jack's whimsical sobriety of
speech and manner, contrasting with his former high animal
spirits, carried out the notion of his being a secret ambassador.

It was at a reception given to the Cabinet by Mrs. Atterbury that the rumor of this accredited function came to
Jack's ears. "All Richmond" was among the guests. Olympia, in spite of her abhorrence of the cause, couldn't resist
a glow of sympathetic admiration of the women who, in
dress, in speech, in tact, in all the artifices which make feminine diplomacy so potent an agency in statecraft, bent every
faculty to inspire confidence in the new Administration.
Mrs. Davis herself was not the least of the factors that made
the President's policy the creed of the land. There was no
elaboration of costume—no obtrusive jewels. The most
richly dressed dame in the company was a Madame Gannat,
the deity of the most charming drawing-room at the capital.
At her house society was always sure to meet the European
noblemen traveling in the country, the *quasi* official agents
of France, England, and Austria, accredited to the new Confederacy, the generals of the Southern armies on leave in the
city, and the political leaders able to snatch an evening's re-
laxation. For some reason this potential personage let Olympia and Jack see that she was deeply interested in them.
She took the young man's arm late in the evening, and
whispering, "Find a place where we can have a little talk,"
accompanied him to a small apartment joining a conserva-

tory, where Mrs. Atterbury transacted business with her agents.

"You must take down a book, so that, in case the curious remark us, our *tête-à-tête* may not be regarded as conspiracy."

"No one would be apt to associate you with such a thing," Jack said, vaguely.

"I don't know. Like all conspiracies, this Confederate comedy is suspicious."

"Comedy, Mrs. Gannat? Why, I never saw people so earnest! I can't imagine the surroundings of Cromwell more methodic."

"Ah, yes; those who have all to lose by the crash, when it comes, are bending every energy to impress the North that we are all of one mind down here; we are not. I am talking frankly with you, because my friend Mrs. Lanview has made me fully acquainted with your circumstances. I have asked you for a talk here because I dare not have you at my house. No one suspects my loyalty to this Davis masquerade; but there are many of us who are doing, and shall do, all the better work for the Union cause. You are just the man needed for a great work here; you are believed to be secretly in favor of the Confederate cause—an ambassador, in short. Now, the special purpose of this talk is this: The men caught at Rosedale three weeks ago are to be tried before a military court. If you and this young man Perley could escape before the event, it would be impossible to convict them. Mrs. Lanview tells me that you are very closely allied to the younger prisoner, Moore, and that for his sake you will do all in your power to avoid testifying."

"I will cut out my tongue before a syllable from me shall bring danger to that noble fellow!"

"Exactly. I expected as much. Now, can you not manage to inspire Perley with the same sentiment? If you can, we feel confident that the court will be unable to secure evidence sufficient to convict. I leave the details to your own ingenuity. Your absence would deprive the judge-advocate of the vital witnesses, but your refusal to testify would only bring you into danger, and prolong the proceedings; and with time we hope to effect an escape. Sh! As I say, Mr. Sprague, the heart of the South beats with one impulse, the triumph of the noblest inspiration of a great people."

The warning and sudden change in topic were caused by the apparition of a dame who came rustling in, a vision of youthful charms and vivaciousness.

"Mrs. Didier Rodney—Mr. Sprague," Mrs. Gannat said, cordially. "You are sent by inspiration, for I am doing my poor best to convince this obdurate Yankee to turn from evil courses and do a duty by the country that will in future make his name illustrious."

"And I have no doubt you have shaken his obstinacy, if there be any left," Mrs. Rodney murmured, studying Jack attentively. "I have just been dining at the Executive Mansion, and Mr. Davis, hearing your name, lamented that women were not eligible to office. If they were, he declared that Mistress Gannat should be appointed ambassadress to France, and that, within ten days of her reception at the Tuileries, there would be a treaty of alliance signed between France and the Confederacy!"

"I take that as rather an admission of weakness on your President's part," Jack said, as the lady glanced inquiringly at him, "since it is a poor cause that requires the strongest advocates."

"Ah! a Southern man would never have said a thing so uncivil as that," Mrs. Rodney cried, reproachfully. "You pay Mrs. Gannat a compliment at the cost of the Confederacy."

"And Mr. Davis paid me a compliment at the expense of the truth, so the account is squared," the elder lady said, serenely.

"Well, Mr. Davis is here himself by this time, and you shall talk it out with him," Mrs. Rodney retorted, as a rustle at the door announced new-comers. A half-dozen ladies came trooping in, among them Mrs. Davis and several of the Cabinet ladies.

"We heard you were here, Madame Gannat," the President's wife murmured, graciously. "And since you wouldn't come to us, we have come to you."

Mrs. Gannat arose to receive the great lady, and when she had exchanged salutations with the rest she presented Jack.

"Ah! the hero of the Rosedale affair," and as Mrs. Davis said this she looked keenly at the young man. She was, he owned, an extremely graceful woman, of a mature beauty, admirable manner, and, as she talked, he remarked keen intelligence, with an occasional evidence of reading, if not high education. She was dressed in simpler taste than her "court," as it was the fashion then to style the Cabinet group. A few jewels were half hidden in the rare lace that covered her bodice, but she was ungloved, and in no sense in the full-dress understood in the North, at a gathering of the sort. The talk became general. Jack, not knowing the personages, simply listened. There was animated discussion as to whether Mistress Judge this, and Mistress General that, or Mistress Senator the other, would be in the capital in time for the opening of the new Congress in December.

"Mr. Davis is very anxious to have the occasion made a grand one, and I reckon that every one of account in the Confederacy will be here," Mrs. Davis said, with conviction.

"The scene will be worthy of a great painting, like the Long Parliament, or the meeting of the Three Estates, at Versailles," Mrs. Rodney added, in a glow of anticipation.

This amusing pedantry rather taxed the historical knowledge of most of the ladies, and to divert the talk Mrs. Monteith, a Cabinet lady, said:

"Who has read the account in the Yankee papers of Lincoln and his wife at a reception of the diplomatic corps? It is too funny. The Lincoln woman was a Southerner. She has some good blood, and ought to know better. She was dressed like a dowdy, and when the ministers bowed she gave them her hand and said, 'How d'ye do?'"

"It will really be a liberal education to the North to have a capital like ours near them, where their public men can learn manners, and where Northern ladies can see how to conduct themselves in public," Mrs. Rodney broke in, laughing. "It is not often a great people go to war for an idea, but we are taking up the gage of battle to teach our inferiors manners."

"We taught them how to run at Manassas," Mrs. Starlow, a Senator's dame, remarked.

"I'm afraid they have learned the lesson so well that we shall never teach them how to stand," Mrs. Davis added, gayly.

"Ah! friends, we are teaching each other how to die—let us not forget that," Mrs. Gannat murmured, gently, and there was a sudden hush in the exchange of vivacities. Before the strain could be renewed, Mrs. Atterbury entered hastily, crying:

"The gentlemen are all distracted. We are going to have an old-time minuet, such as my mother used to dance with Justice Marshall and Tom Mayo. The President is going to lead with Mistress Wendolph, and all the rest of you are assigned, by command of the Executive."

"Humph! a military despotism?" asked Mrs. Renfrew, a young bride of the Executive Mansion, whose husband was confidential adviser of the President. "I don't think I shall obey. I shall show the honesty of my rebel blood by selecting my own partner, unless some one asks me very humbly."

"Shall I go on my knees," Mrs. Renfrew?—I know no humbler attitude." Jack said, hastily presenting himself.

"Oh, yes, sir; there is something humbler than the knees."

"Yes? What, pray?"

"Repentance. Deny your name; no longer be a Montague—that is, a Yankee. Give me the hand of a rebel. Then I shall believe you."

"I am a rebel."

"Ah! you have been converted?"

"I never was perverted."

"You have been with us all the time?"

"I have been here a long time!"

"And you are a rebel. Oh, I must tell Mr. Davis!"

"He knows it, I think."

"Oh, no, he can not; for it was only a few moments

since that he said to Mrs. Atterbury that the son of Senator Sprague, the friend of Calhoun and the comrade of Hayne, should be in the ranks of the young nobility upholding our sacred cause."

"I am, however, a rebel—a rebel to all these fascinations I see about me, a rebel to your beauty, a rebel to all you desire."

"Pah! you odious Yankee; I felt certain that you had not come to your senses."

"I don't think I ever lost them—though I never had enough to make such a spirit as yours lament their loss." The rest of the ladies had passed out; and, as this repartee went on, Jack led his petulant companion into the large drawing-room, where he instantly recognized the President with Mrs. Wendolph on his arm. He towered above the mass of the dancers, eying the admiring groups with attentive scrutiny. He was in evening dress, but, unlike the larger number of the eminent partisans in the rooms, had no insignia, military or otherwise, to denote exalted rank.

As the President was to lead off, to keep up the character of a court minuet, the middle of the large room was left uncrowded. The music began what Jack thought at first was a funeral march, but with the first bars the tall, slender figure of the President bent almost double, while the lady seemed fairly seated on the floor, she bent down and back so far. She had adjusted a prodigious silken train, which swept and swirled in many bewildering folds as she slowly turned, courtesied, tripped forward and retreated, with such bending and twisting as would turn a ballet-master mad with envy. In all the movement of the overture the two dancers merely touched the tips of each other's fingers, and when the solemn measure came to a close the President slid across the floor in one graceful, immense pirouette, handing the lady who confronted him, bent nearly to the ground, into her seat. There was an outburst of applause, and then the assembly took places, repeating, in as far as the mass would permit, the stately evolutions of the leader.

Later, a Virginia reel followed, danced with old-time

verve, some of the more accomplished dancers bounding over the floor in pigeon-wings, such as were cut by the nimble a hundred years ago, when Richmond danced in honor of Washington and Lafayette. There was no end of drinking among the men, and as soon as the dancing seemed at its height the matrons began to gather into groups and send out signals to the younger ladies. The feast ended in drinking-bouts between dispersed bodies, who seemed to know the names of all the servants, and ordered as liberally as if in their own houses. In the *mêlée* of separation, Jack felt a hand on his shoulder.

"Remember, every moment is precious. Many lives, perhaps a great campaign, depend upon your discretion, promptitude, and loyalty. Be ready when the signal reaches you, and remember you do not know me beyond the civility of a presentation, and do not like me."

Jack had hardly turned as these words were whispered in his ear, and he gave the kind lady's hand a warm pressure, as she moved away unremarked in the throng.

Jack, confiding Mrs. Gannat's disclosures to Olympia, was elated by his sister's enthusiasm, and was strengthened in his conviction that he was doing right by her approval.

"But you know, Polly, that—I—I, too, must be of the party? I must fly to the Union lines."

"Of course you will! I should be ashamed of you were you to let such a chance pass. It is the only thing to do; it is your duty as a soldier to be with your flag; any means to get to it is justified. The Atterburys will feel hurt, perhaps outraged, but I can soon convince them that you have only done what Vincent would do, and whatever he would do they will soon see is right for you to do, even though it may bring them into temporary disgrace with the authorities. Of late I have begun to suspect that the Atterburys are to blame for your detention."

"What do you mean to blame? Surely they can not hasten the slow business of negotiation?"

"No; but I'm convinced that they have given out hopes that you can be seduced into a soldier of secession. It is common talk in the drawing-rooms I have visited, where I was not always recognized as your sister. The silly tale has angered me, but for prudence' sake I kept silent. I have heard in a score of places that the Atterburys were detaining you until another reverse to the Union arms should convince you of the uselessness of remaining in the service of the abolitionists."

"O Polly, it must be a joke! They little know me, who could suspect me of such dishonor ! Surely the Atterburys can't think me so base as that. What have I ever done to justify such a stigma ?"

"You wrong them there. They hold that you are wanting in loyalty to our father's memory in espousing the cause of men who were his enemies—men who strove to ruin his political life. It is in being a soldier of the Union that they look upon you as recreant to the traditions of your family and your party."

"Well, I shall make a hard struggle for escape. If I fail, they will at least see that I am in earnest—that I put country before family or party, or anything else that men hold dear. Heavens! to think of being held in such bondage! I could stand it with more patience if I were in prison sharing the hard lines of the fellows. But to be here; to be hand in glove with these boasting, audacious coxcombs, and forced to listen to their callow banter of us and our army, it makes me feel like a sneak and a traitor, and I'm glad that I see the end."

"But do you see the end ? Prudence is one of the wisest counselors in war. You are very rash, and you must take all your measures carefully. It won't do to rush into a trap, as you did at Manassas; and, O Jack, what is to become of Dick ? He is not in the lists. He has no standing here, and is at the mercy of any one who chooses to accuse him of being a spy."

"By George, you're right ! I hadn't thought of that. He must go with me. I had thought it better to leave him. He is so happy with Rosa that I fancied he would remain contentedly until the war ends. But he is in constant danger. He is forever tantalizing the people that visit the house, who make slighting allusions to the Northern armies, and very likely some rebel patriot will take the trouble to inquire about him."

"But even if this were not a peril, he would never consent to remain here if you were gone. I think he would give up Rosa rather than be separated from you."

"Yes, the impulsive little beggar, I believe he would," Jack said, his eyes glistening. "That will compel us to take him into the secret. In fact, I don't see how it can be managed without him; and then his testimony would convict the prisoners. I hadn't thought of that. But now, Polly, about yourself. What's to become of you?"

"I have my plans laid. Mrs. Myrason, the wife of one of Johnston's generals, is going to the front next week. I shall insist to-night on accompanying her, as some of our physicians are going to be sent through the lines at the same time. There is really no reason for my remaining here, now that you are well. I have already broached the subject to Mrs. Atterbury, and I shall inform her at once that I am decided. She will not suspect anything, as she knew I was half-tempted to go North when mamma went. The important thing for you, now, is to give your whole mind to the rescue, and have no fears for me. If you can convince Dick to go with you, all will be well. If he proves obstinate, hand him over to me." Jack laughed.

"Polly, you should have been the first-born of the house of Sprague; you have twice the sense that I have."

"It isn't sense that wins in war; it is daring and resolution, and you have all that."

When Jack had cautiously laid the situation before his young Patroclus, that precocious warrior at once justified the confidence reposed in him.

"Rosa has promised to marry me as soon as the war is over. She can't expect me to hang around here like a peg-top on a string. Besides, I wouldn't stay where you are not, Jacko, even if I lost my sweetheart for good and all."

There was a piteous quaver in the treble voice, and, forgetting that he was no longer a school-boy, he brushed his eyes furtively with his coat-sleeve, as Jack pretended pre-occupation with his shoe-string.

"You're a brick, Dick. I think I have confided that to you before—but you are a brick, made of the best straw in the field of life, and you shall be a general one of these days—your shrill voice shall let slip the dogs of war and cry havoc to the enemy. You shall return to Acredale—proud Acredale—your brows bound with victorious wreaths, and all the small boys perched on the spreading oaks to salute you."

"I think I have heard something like that before, my blarneying Plantagenet. You shall be the Percy of the North, and command the great battle. You shall meet and vanquish fifty Harrys, and cry, 'God for Union, liberty, and the laws.'"

"Bravo! You know your Shakespeare if you don't know prudence. However, we're plotters now, and you must take on your wisest humor. You must not breathe a word to Rosa. Love is a freebooter in confidences. It has no conscience, as it has no law. It is an immense friction on the sober relations of life. It is cousin to the god of lies—Mercury. So be warned that while your heart is Rosa's your reason's your country's, your friends', and you have a chance now to employ it to the profit of both! You must be ready to evade Rosa's infinite questioning with innocent plausibilities, for you must bear in mind that, however much she may love you, she, like you, loves her cause, her people—more, in fact, for you have seen that these passionate Southerners have made a religion of the war, and, like all enthusiasts, they will go any lengths, deny all ties; glory, faith, in personal sacrifices and heart-wrenchings, to make the South triumph. So, without being false to your love, you must deceive, to be true to your country; for to lull love's suspicions a man must regulate the two currents of his life, the heart and brain. Keep the heart in check and let the brain rule in such affairs as we have on hand."

"Phew Jack! you talk like a college professor. You're

deeper than a well; and what was the other thing Mercutio said?"

"Ah! Mercutio said so much that Shakespeare got frightened and let Tybalt kill him. So beware of saying too much. That's your great danger, Dick; your tongue is terrible—mostly to your friends."

"Is it, indeed? I have a friend who doesn't think so."

"No, because she considers your tongue part of herself now."

"I don't see why she should; she has enough of her own."

"In wooing-time no woman ever had enough tongue."

"How changed you are from what you were at Acredale, Jack! I never heard you talk so deep and bookish."

"I had no need at Acredale, Dick. There I was a boy—lived as a boy, romped as a boy, and loved boyish things. But a man ripens swiftly in war—you yourself have. You are no longer the mischief-maker and tom-boy that terrified your family and set the gossips agog in the dear old village. Mind broadens swiftly in war. That one dreadful day at Bull Run enlarged my faculties, or trained them rather, as much as a course in college. Something very serious came into my life that day. It had its effect on you too. It fairly revolutionized Vint; we may not have exactly put away boyishness and boyish things—please God, I hope to be a boy many a year yet—but we have been made to think as men, act as men, and realize that there are consequences and responsibilities in life such as we could not have realized in ten years in time of peace."

Dick listened during this solemn comedy of immature doctrinal induction, his eyes dilating with wonder and admiration. Jack, in the *rôle* of sage, delighted him, and he straightway confided to Rosa that he couldn't understand how any girl could love another man while Jack was to be had.

"He's so clever, so brave, so manly. He knows so much, and yet never takes the trouble to let any one see it. Ah, Rosa, I wish I were like Jack!"

"I think Jack's very nice, but I know somebody that's

much nicer," Rosa replied, busy with a rough material that was plainly intended for the Southern warriors.

"Ah! but if you really knew all about Jack, you wouldn't look at anybody else," Dick cried, pensively, tangling his long legs in the young girl's work.

"There, you clumsy fellow; you've ruined this seam, and I must get this work done before noon. We're all going to the provost prison to take garments to the recruits. You may come if you'll be very good and help me with these supplies."

"May I? I will sew on the buttons. Oh, you think I can't? Just give me a needle." And sure enough Dick, gravely arming himself from the store in Rosa's "catchall," set to fastening the big buttons as composedly as if he had been brought up in a tailor's shop. It was in this sartorial industry that Jack, coming in, presently discovered the pair.

"You've turned Dick into a seamstress, have you, Rosalind? You're an amazing little magician. Dick's sewing heretofore has been of the common boy-sort—wild oats."

"No, Mr. Jack, I'm no magician. Dick is a very sensible fellow, and, like Richelieu in the play, he ekes out the lion's skin with the fox's."

"I didn't come to add to the stores of your wisdom. This is the day set, as I understand it, for us to go to the prison and relieve the distress of the victims of war. Do I understand that we, Dick and I, are to go and have our patriotic hearts torn by the sight of woes that fortune, in the shape of the Atterburys, keeps us from?"

"Of course you are. We couldn't think of going without you. There, my work is done. We'll have lunch and then start," Rosa said, rising and directing Dick to fill the large wicker basket with the garments.

Fashion and idleness make strange pastimes. The recreation to which Jack and Dick were bidden was a visit to the melancholy shambles where the heterogeneous mass of unclassified prisoners were detained. It was a long, gabled building on the bank of the river, from whose low, grated windows the culprits could catch glimpses of the James, tumbling over its sedgy, sometimes rocky bed. A few yards from it arose the grim walls of what had been a tobacco-factory, now the never-to-be forgotten Libby Prison.

It was an animated and curious group that made up Jack's party. They were piloted by a young aide on the staff of General Lee, and, as his entire mind was engrossed in making his court to Rosa, the pilgrims were given the widest latitude for investigation. On the lower tier he pointed out the cells of the Rosedale prisoners, where, as you may imagine, Jack and Dick, without giving a sign, kept their wits alert. Jones—the "most desperate of the conspirators against the President, the special agent of Butler"—was in a cell by himself, constantly guarded by a sentinel.

"This, Sprague," said the young aide, lowering his voice as he came abreast of Jones's cell, "is the man the Government has the strongest proof against. He is proved to have come into our lines from the Warwick River, to have managed to escape from Castle Thunder, and to have led the miscreants to Rosedale. Your own and young Perley's testimony after that will swing him higher than a spy was ever swung before."

These words, begun in a low tone, were made clearer and louder by the sudden cessation of chatter among the visiting group. Jones, who seemed to have come to his grating when the suppressed laughter sounded in the dark corridor, heard every word of the official's speech. He was no longer the bearded desperado Jack had seen in the *mêlée* at Rosedale—there was a certain distinction in the poise of the head, an inborn gentility in the impassive contemplation with which he met the furtive scrutiny of the curious visitors. Jack he eyed with something of surprise, but when Dick pushed suddenly in front of the timorous group of young women, he started, changed color, and averted his face; then, as if suddenly recalling himself, turned and devoured the lad with a strange, yearning tenderness. Dick met the gaze with his habitual easy gayety, and, turning to Jack, said, impulsively:

17

"I should never recognize this man as the bandit who fired the shot that night—are you really the Jones that choked and wounded me at Rosedale?" Dick advanced quite close to the wicket as he asked this.

"And who may you be, if I am permitted to ask a question?" the prisoner replied vaguely, all the time devouring the boy with his dilating eyes.

"I am Richard Perley, of Acredale, a soldier of the Union and a friend of all who suffer in its cause." Dick murmured the last words so low that the group of visitors did not catch them, and, adding to them an emphasis of the eye that the prisoner seemed too agitated to notice, he continued, as Jack pushed nearer: "This is certainly not the man we saw at Rosedale. But I have seen you somewhere. Tell me, have I not?"

"I can tell you nothing—I—I—" As he said this Jones backed against the wall. The guard sprang forward in alarm. The women, of course, cried out in many keys, most of them skurrying away toward the staircase.

"Water!" Jack cried. "Guard, have you no water handy?"

"No, sir; the canteen was broken, and there is none nearer than the guard-room."

"Run and get some. I will see that the prisoner does not get out. Run!"

The aide had gallantly gone forward in the passage to re-assure the ladies, and Jack, seizing the chance, for which the prisoner seemed to be prepared, whispered:

"Here is an auger, a chisel, and a knife. Secrete them. Work straight out under your window. We shall be ready for you by Wednesday night. Don't fail to give a signal if anything happens that prevents your cutting through. There is only an old stone wall between you and the river. You must take precautions against the water, if it is high enough to reach your cut."

Jones played his part admirably. He remained limp and stolid in the supporting arms of Jack, while Dick, hovering in the doorway, kept the prying remnant of the visitors, eager to witness the scene, at a safe distance. When the water came Jack yielded his place to the guard and the party moved on.

"Here we have a real Yankee, a regular nutmeg," the young aide cried, as the party came to a room not far from Jones's. "This youngster was one of the chief devils in the attack on Rosedale. The judge-advocate has tried every means to coax a confession from him, but without result. He is as gay as a bridegroom, and answers all threats with a joke."

"Ah! the old Barney under all," Jack said, half sadly.

"Do you know him, Mr. Sprague?"

"Like a brother. He is from my town."

"Ah, perhaps you can convince him that his best course is open confession?"

"No, I fear not. He is very headstrong, and would rather have his joke on the gibbet than own himself in the wrong."

"But, Mr. Jack, if you should talk to him, show him the wickedness of conspiring against a peaceful family, inciting a servile race to murder, I'm sure you could move him, and it would be such a comfort to have the criminals themselves expose the atrocious plot."

This was said by Miss Delmayne, a niece of Mrs. Gannat. Jack caught her eye as she spoke, and instantly realized the covert meaning. How stupid he had been! Of course, Barney must be apprised of the rescue, and what time more propitious than the present? But, unfortunately, he had not provided himself with the tools for the emergency. What could be done? He suddenly remembered a bayonet he had seen near the guard-room. It was lying unnoticed on the bench.

"I must have a drink before I answer a plea so urgent. Amuse the prisoner while I slake my thirst."

Barney was lying at the far end of the narrow, boarded cage. He raised his head as the group halted before his door, but gave no sign of interest as this dialogue was carried on:

"Prisoner," said the aide, magisterially, "come to the door."

"Jailer, what shall I come to the door for ?" Barney mimicked indolently.

"Because I bid you, sir."

"Not a reason in law, sir."

"I'll have the guard haul you here."

"Then he'll have a mighty poor haul, as King James said when he caught the Orange troopers in the Boyne."

"I'll teach you, sir, to defy a commissioned officer !"

"I've learned that already; but if you're a school-teacher I'll decline the verb 'will' for you."

"Guard, hustle that beast forward."

"Guard, don't give yourself the trouble." And Barney arose nimbly and came to the grating. "O captain, dear, why didn't ye tell me there were ladies here ? You could have spared your eloquence and your authority if you had tould me that the star of beauty, the smile of angels, the—"

"Never mind, sir ; be respectful, and wait till you're spoken to."

"Then, captain, dear, do you profit by your own advice ; let the ladies talk. I'm all ears, as the rabbit said to the weasel."

But at this interesting point of the combat Jack returned, and, pushing-to the door, cried, as if in surprise, "Hello, Barney, boy, what are you doing here ?"

"Diverting the ladies, Jack, dear, and giving the captain a chance to practice command, for fear he'll not get a show in battle." The roar that saluted this retort subdued the bumptious cavalier, and he affected deep interest in the whispered questions of one of the young women in the rear of the group.

"You're the same old Barney. Marc Anthony gave up the world for a kiss, you'd capitulate a kingdom for a joke," Jack said, striving to catch Barney's eye and warn him to be prudent.

"Well, Jack, dear, between the joke and the kiss, I think I'd go out of the world better satisfied with the kiss ; at all events, it wouldn't be dacent to say less with so many red lips forninst me," and Barney winked untold admiration at the laughing group before him, all plainly delighted with his conquest of the captain.

"But, Barney, you should be thinking of more serious things."

"Sure I've thought of nothing else for three months. The trees can't go naked all the year ; the brook can't keep ice on it in summer ; the swan sings before it dies ; the grasshopper whirrs loudest when its grave is ready. Why shouldn't I have me joke when I've had nothing but hard knocks, loneliness, and the company of the prison for half the year ? "

"Poor fellow ! " Rosa murmured in Dick's ear, who had not trusted himself in sight of his old comrade. "I don't believe he's a bad man ; I don't believe he came to our house. Oh ! pray, Mr. Jack, do talk with him. Encourage him to be frank, and we will get Mr. Davis to pardon him."

"Pardon, is it, me dear? Sure there's no pardon could be as sweet as your honest e'en—God be good to ye!—an' if I were Peter after the third denial of me Maker, your sweet lips would drag the truth from me! What is it you would have me tell?"

"The captain, here, desires me to talk with you. He thinks that perhaps I can convince you of the wiser course to follow," Jack said, with a meaning light in his eye.

"Oh, if that's what's wanted, I will listen to you 'till yer arms give out, as Judy McMoyne said, when Teddy tould his love. I promise, in advance, to do what you advise."

"I knew you would," Jack said, approvingly.—"Now, captain, if you can give me five minutes—"

The captain beckoned the guard, whispered a moment, and then said, exultingly:

"The guard will stand in the passage until you have finished with the prisoner. We shall await you in the porch."

"Now, Barney, I must be brief, and you must not lose a syllable I say. Here, sit on the cot, so that I may slip this bayonet under the blanket. You can work through this wall with that. You must do it to-night and to-morrow. Be ready Thursday at daylight. You will be met on the outside either by Dick or myself. We have the route all arranged, and friends in many places to lull suspicion."

"But I won't stir a foot without Jones. Do you know who he is?" Barney whispered, eying Jack curiously.

"No other than that he seems a very desperate devil-may-care fellow. Who is he?"

"An agent and crony of Boone's."

"Good God!"

"It's a long story. I can't tell it now, but if your plan takes him in, I'm ready, and will be on hand."

"I have seen him, and have given him better tools than I have brought you for the work."

"That's all right. I ask nothing better than the bayonet. The other fellows that got out of Libby didn't have nearly so good."

"You know how I am fixed here. I have grown tired of this sort of hostage life, and I am going North with you. So, Barney, I beg of you to be careful, for other lives than your own are at stake. I should be specially hateful to the authorities if I were retaken—for the whole Southern people clamor to have an example made of the assassins of the President, as they call you."

"Don't fear, Jack ; I'll be quiet as a sucking pig in starlight. I'll be yer shadow and never open me mouth, even if a jug, big as Teddy Fin's praty-patch, stud furninst me!"

"It isn't your tongue I'm so much afraid of as your propensity to combat. You must resist that delight of yours—whacking stray heads and flourishing your big fists."

"My fists, is it? Then I'll engage to keep them still as O'Connell's legs in Phœnix Square."

"Now, I shall report that you are considering my advice. You must be very gentle and placating to the guard, and let on that you have something on your mind."

"Indeed, I needn't let on at all. I have as much on me

mind as Biddy McGinniss had on her back when she carried
Mick home from the gallows."

"O Barney, Barney, you would joke if the halter were
about your neck!"

"An' why wouldn't I, me bye? What chance would I
have if I didn't? I couldn't joke when I was dead, could I?"

"Well, well, think over what I've said, and remember
that penitence half absolves guilt."

This was said for the benefit of the guard, who had approached as Jack arose to take his leave.

CHAPTER XXIII.

ALL'S FAIR IN LOVE AND WAR.

OPPORTUNITY is an instinct to the man who dares. To
him the law of the impossible has no meaning. To him
there is no such thing as the unexpected. What he wants
comes to pass, because he can not see danger, difficulty,
nor any of the obstacles that daunt the prudent and the tem-
porizing. It is, therefore, the impossible that is fulfilled in
many of the crises of life. By the same token it is the fool-
hardy and preposterous thing that is most readily done in
determinate conjunctures. We guard against the possible,
but we take little note of the enterprises that involve fool-
hardiness or desperation. Daring has safeguards of its own
that are understood only when mad ventures have come to
successful issue. Helpless and hopeless as Jack's situation
seemed, the very poverty of his resources, helped the daring
scheme of escape that filled his mind night and day during
these apparently indolent weeks of pleasuring in the ranks
of his enemies. Then, too, the arrogant self-confidence of
his captors was an inestimable aid. Military discipline and
provost vigilance were at their slackest stage in the rebel
lines at this triumphant epoch in the fortunes of the Con-

federacy. The easily won combat at Bull Run had filled
the authorities—as well as the rank and file—with over-
weening contempt for the resources of the North, or the enterprise of its soldiers. It was not until long after the time
I am now writing about, that the prisoners were closely
guarded and access refused to the idle and curious. But, as
a matter of fact, nothing in the fortunes of our friends
equals the truth of the thrilling and desperate chances taken
by Northern captives to escape the lingering death of prison
in the South. Since the war, volumes have been written of
personal experience, amply attested, that would in romance
receive the derisive mark of the critics. Danger daily met
becomes a commonplace to men of resolution. Things which
appall us when we read them become a simple part of our
purpose when we live in an atmosphere of peril and put our
hope only in ending the ordeal.

The incidents I am narrating were the work of many
hands. Mrs. Gannat had from the first given her heart to the
Union cause. A woman of high standing in society, well
known throughout the State for her mind, her manners, and
her benevolence, it was not difficult for her, by adroit management, to aid such prisoners as fell into rebel hands during the early years of the war. Before Richmond became a
mart in the modern sense, the Gannat mansion, set far back
among the trees of a noble grove, was a shrine to the tradi-
tion-loving citizens, for, beyond any Southern city, save perhaps New Orleans, Richmond folk cherished the memory
of aristocratic and semi-regal ancestors. There were those
still living when the war began, who had heard their fathers
and mothers talk of the last royal Governor and the splendid state of the great noblemen who had flocked to the city
of Powhatan when Virginia was the gem of England's colonial coronet. The patrician caste of the city still held its
own, aided by the helot hand of slavery. Among the most
reverently considered in this sanctified group, Mrs. Gannat
was, if not first, the conceded equal. She was the dowager
of the ancient noblesse. The young Virginian received in
her drawing-rooms carried away a distinction which was

recognized throughout the State. The dame admitted to Mrs. Gannat's semi-literary *levées* was accepted as all that society demanded of its votaries.

In other years this great lady had been the admired center of the court circle in Washington. There she had known very intimately Senator — then Congressman — Sprague. Jack remembered vaguely the gossip of an engagement between his father and a famous Southern beauty; and when the lady in the course of the conspiring said, as they talked, "My son, I might have been your mother," he knew that this gentle-voiced, kindly-eyed matron was the woman his father had loved and lost. I don't propose to rehearse the ingenuities of the complicated plans whereby the group we are interested in were to be delivered. Mrs. Gannat's perfect knowledge of the city, her intimacy with the President, Cabinet, and leading men, her vogue with the officials, all tended to make very simple and easy that which would seem in the telling hare-brained and impossible. Jack's unique position, and Dick's attitude of the half-acknowledged *fiancé* of an Atterbury, broke down bars that even Mrs. Gannat's far-reaching sagacity might not have been able to cope with in certainty. The night chosen for the escape was fatefully propitious. The President was entertaining the newly arrived French delegate and the ministers Mason and Slidell, just appointed to the courts of St. James and the Tuileries. Everybody that was anybody was of the splendid company.

Jack, however, was tortured by a doubt of Dick's constancy when it came to an abrupt quitting of his sweetheart. Poor lad, he fought the battle bravely, making no sign; and when Rosa, the picture of demure loveliness, in her girlish finery, asked him maliciously as the carriage drove toward the Executive Mansion—

"Don't you feel like a traitor, you sly Yankee?" Dick gave a great groan and said:

"O Rosa, Rosa, I can't go! I do feel like a traitor. I am a traitor."

Jack, luckily, was sitting beside him, and brought his

heel down on the lad's toes with such emphasis that he
uttered a cry of pain. Rosa was all solicitude at this.

"What is it, Richard; have I wounded you ? Don't mind
my chatter ; I only do it to tease you. He shall be a Yankee; he shall make nutmegs; he shall abuse the chivalrous
South; he shall be what he likes; he sha'n't be teased—"
and she wound her bare arms about his neck, quite indifferent to the reproving nudges of mamma and the sad mirth-
fulness of Jack.

Dick found means in the noise of the chariot, and the
crush they presently came into, for saying something that
seemed to lessen the self-reproachful tone of the penitent,
and, when they entered the modest portals of the presidency,
Rosa was radiant and Dick equable, but not in his usual
chattering volubility.

"You are sure you do not repent ? You can stay if you
choose," Jack said, as they entered the dressing-room.

"Where you go, I go; what you say is right I know is
right, and I will do it." Dick looked away confusedly as he
said this. They were surrounded by young officers, all of
whom the two young men knew.

"Ah, ha, Mr. Perley ! I have stolen a march on you; I
have secured the first waltz from Miss Rosa," a young man
at the mirror cried, as Dick adjusted his gloves.

"Then, Captain Warrick, I'm likely to be a wall-flower,
for the second, third, and fourth were promised yesterday."

"Fortunes of war, my dear fellow—fortunes of war.
You must lay siege to another fortress."

"Dick," Jack whispered, "it's an omen. It will give us
time to slip out and change our garments without the danger of excuses, for, though nothing is suspected, any incau-
tious phrase may destroy us."

"Don't fear for me. I shall be prudent as a confessor.
We can't go, however, just yet. I must have a little talk
with Rosa. I may never see her again. If you were in
love and going from the light of her eye, perhaps never to
see her again, you wouldn't be so cool. We must, anyway,
take the ladies to the host and hostess for presentation; then

a few words and I am ready." Dick was trembling visibly
and blushing like a school-girl at first facing a class-day
crowd. Jack's heart went out to the lad, and he thought
the chances about even that when the moment of trial came
the boy's resolution would give way. The ladies were waiting for them when they emerged into the corridors—Rosa
began, prettily, to rally Dick on his tardiness. It took time
to thread the constantly increasing crowd in the hallways,
the corridors, and on the stairs, but they finally reached the
group in which Mrs. Davis was receiving the confused salutations of the throng at the drawing-room door. As soon
as this formality was ended, Rosa whisked Dick in one
direction while Mrs. Atterbury asked Jack to take her to
the library. Here, by a happy chance, she came upon a
group of dowagers—friends of her youth from other towns
—brought to the capital by the event, or their husbands'
official duties in the new government. Jack bowed low as
he relinquished the good lady's arm, feeling as if he were
embarking on some odious treason, in view of her persistent
and generous treatment of him and his.

"Now that you are among the friends of your youth, I
will leave you; who knows whether I shall see you again?"
he faltered, as she turned an affectionate glance upon
him.

"Oh, you needn't think that you can take *congé* for good,
Jack. I may want to dance during the night. If I do I
shall certainly lay my commands upon you. You may de-
vote yourself to the young people now, but I warn you I am
not to be thrown over so easily. Besides, I want to present
you to a dozen friends that you have not yet met at my
house."

"You will always know where to find me; but I am not
so sure that I shall be as able, as I am willing, to come to
you," Jack said, trembling at the double meaning of his
words.

"Oh, I know you're dying to get to the dancers."

"I can go to no one that it will give me more happiness
to please than you. Indeed, I'm going into danger when I

quit you. Give me your blessing, as if it were Vincent going to the wars."

She had turned from the throng of ladies, who were discussing a political secret, and her eyes melted tenderly as
Vincent's name passed Jack's lips. She touched his bowed
head gently, saying:

"Why, how serious you are ! One would think beauty a
battery, and you on the way to charge."

"You are right. It is a murderous ambush."

"Well, if you regard it so seriously—God bless you
in it."

Her gentle eyes rested tenderly on him; he seized the
kind hand, and, raising it to his lips in the gallant Southern
fashion, turned and hurried away among the guests.

"Ah, Mrs. Atterbury, conquests at your age, from hand
to lip, there's but short interval," and the President held up
a warning finger as he came closer to the lady.

"Oh, no, age makes a long route between hand and lip—
thirty years ago you kissed my hand, and you never reached
the lip."

"It wasn't my fault that I didn't."

"Nor your misfortune either," and Mrs. Atterbury
glanced archly at her rival, Mrs. Davis, the mature beauty
of the scene.

Dick, meanwhile, not so dexterous in expedients or ready
in speech as his mentor, became wedged in an eddy, just
outside the main stream, pouring drawing-roomward, so that,
returning to the spot where they had separated, Jack did
not, for the moment, discover him.

Rosa's gayety and delight deepened the depression that
made Dick so unlike himself. At first, in the exuberance
of the scene, the girl did not heed this. She knew everybody, and, though in daily contact with most of them, there
were no end of whispered confidences to exchange and
tender reassurances in ratification of some new compact.
Then there were solemn notes of comparison as to the fit
and form of gowns, or the fit of a furbelow, exhaustively
discussed, perhaps that very afternoon. Keen eyes, merry

and tantalizing, were lifted to Dick's sulky face during this
pretty by-play, but all the gayety of the comedy was lost to
him. When he could contain himself no longer, with another bevy of cronies in sight coming down the stairs, he
cried out, desperately:

"For Heaven's sake, Rosa, don't wait here like the statue
in St. Peter's, to be kissed by everybody on the way to the
pope; it's simply sickening to stand here like a shrine to be
slopped by girls that you see every day. Come away; I want
to say something to you."

Rosa turned her astonished eyes upon the railer, and,
with a comic movement of immense dignity, drew her arm
from his sheltering elbow, and, in tones of freezing *hauteur*,
retorted:

"And since when, sir, are you master of my conduct? I
am my own mistress, I believe. I shall kiss whom I please."

"O Rosa, Rosa, I didn't mean that; I don't know what
I meant. I—O Rosa, don't be fretful with me now! I can't
bear it. I am ill—I mean I am tired. Come and sit with
me."

Several on the outer edge of the flowing current turned
curiously as this sharp cry of boyish pleading rose above the
noisy clamor. It was impossible, however, to push backward, but in an instant the lovers were sheltered in an
alcove near the doorway. Rosa had taken his rejected arm
again in a panic of guilty repentance, and, looking at his
half-suffused eyes, cried, piteously:

"Oh, forgive me, Richard, forgive me—I did not mean
it! I forgot you were ill. Ah, please, please forgive me!
You know—I—I—"

But Dick, now conscious that inquiring eyes were fastened upon them, curious ears listening, seized her arm, and,
by main force, reached the hall doorway, now nearly deserted.

"Rosa, I am not well—that is, I have a headache, or heart-
ache—it's the same thing. I didn't mean to tell you, for I
didn't want to destroy your pleasure, and you have looked
forward so long to this; but I—I—can not dance. Jack and

I are going to walk a little while, and then we—we shall be more ourselves."

Poor Dick had only the slightest idea what he was saying, and Rosa listened with wide-open eyes and little appealing caresses, not quite certain what the distracted lover did mean.

"All your dances are taken up. Young Warrick just told me he had the first. You gave Gayo Brotherton two yesterday, so you will have no need of me for hours yet."

"But I will cut them if you say so. Only you know that it is our way here to give the first who ask."

"Yes, yes; that's right. I—I couldn't dance now. I shall be all right, presently, if—if I see you happy. Ah, Rosa, if—if I should die—if I should be carried away, would you always love me—would you always believe in me?"

"Why, Dick, you are really ill; let me feel your wrist." Rosa seized Dick's hand and began a convulsive squeezing. "Yes, you certainly have a fever. You must go home. I shall go with you. It is your wound. It has broken out again—I know it has. You shall go home this instant. I will send for the carriage. Come straight up-stairs, you wicked boy! To let me come here when you are so ill! I shall never forgive myself—never!"

"A large vow for a small maid."

"O Mr. Jack!"—for the voice was Jack's—"Dick is very ill, and he must go home at once. Will you not get the carriage and take us?"

"I will not take you. I am very experienced in Dick's ailments, and I have already summoned a physician, who is waiting for us. But he can not attend his patient if you are present."

"Yes, Rosa, Jack is right. I will leave you now, and when you see me again you will see that I am not ill—that I—I—"

"I will stop for you at the door, Dick. You know the physician can not be kept waiting, so make your parting brief. Short shrift is the easiest in love and war."

"A doctor is as dreadful to me as a battle, Rosa. Kiss

me as if I were going to the field," Dick whispered as Jack's
back was turned. A minute later he had joined his mentor,
and the two hurried through the square and down toward
the river.

"I can't do it, Jack," Dick suddenly broke out, as they
hurried through the dark street. "I must leave Rosa a line
telling her my motive. What will she think of me sneaking away like this without a word? Now, you go on to
Blake's cabin and change your clothes. I will get an old
suit of Vint's. It will really make no difference in the time,
and it will be safer for us to reach the prison separately than
together."

"No, Dick, be a man. Every line you write will add to
our peril. She will, of course, show it to her mother. Our
flight will be known in the morning. Mrs. Atterbury is too
loyal to the Confederacy to conceal anything. You will
thus give the authorities the very clew they need. No, Dick,
you must be guided by me in this; besides, you can send
Rosa letters through Vincent at headquarters as soon as we
reach Washington."

"I can't help it. I know you are right, but I must do it.
I will be with you in less than an hour. I'm off."

"Listen!—Good God, he's gone!" Jack ejaculated as Dick,
taking advantage of a cross-street, shot off into the darkness.
Jack halted. To call would be dangerous; to run after him
excite comment, perhaps pursuit and discovery. There was
nothing to be done but wait at the rendezvous. He would
come back—Jack tried to make himself believe that he could
depend on that. When, after a circuitous walk of half an
hour, he reached the cabin of Blake, the colored agent of
Mrs. Gannat, he found a note from his patroness warning
him that the prison authorities had become alert. A rumor
of a plot to escape had penetrated the War Department, and
orders had been given to increase the precaution of the
guards. The reception at the President's was a stroke of
good fortune for the prisoners, as all the higher officials
would be detained there until morning. Perhaps, in view
of the chance, it would be better to anticipate the hour of

flight, as, unfortunately, the horses that had been got together for the fugitives were in use for the Davis guests,
and on such short notice others could not be provided without exciting suspicion or pointing to the agency by which
the liberation had been brought about.

"Ah, if Dick were only here," Jack groaned, "we could
go to the square and lead away enough staff or orderly
horses to serve the purpose. The little wretch! It would
serve him properly to leave him here mooning over his
sweetheart." Then his heart took up a little tremor of protest.
He sighed gently. He, too, had loitered when his heart
pleaded. Why should Dick be firmer than he? It was
after midnight when he reached the sheltering, broken
ground along the river. The provost prison fronted the
water. It had been a tobacco warehouse, built long before,
and hastily transformed into its present military purpose.
It was set in what was called a "cut" in the heavy clay
bank, thus bringing the lower windows below the level of
the surrounding land. There were sentries stationed in front
and rear, who walked at regular intervals from corner to
corner. The sentinel on the high level to the rear could not
see the ground along the wall, and it was this fact which
Jack calculated upon to enable him to help the prisoners to
remove the *débris* of the wall through which they were to
presently emerge. The night was pitchy dark. This had
been taken into consideration long before. Heavy clouds
hung over the river, throwing the prison and its environs
into still more security for Jack's purpose. He reconnoitred
every available point, searched every corner of possible danger, and as the time passed he began to rage with impatience
against Dick, whose delay was now periling the success of
the enterprise.

It was twelve o'clock and after. He dared wait no longer.
Dick must shift for himself. Perhaps he had lost his way.
In any event it was safer to set the general prisoners free, as
they were only carelessly guarded. Lamps glimmered fitfully in the guard-room, throwing fantastic banners of light
almost to the water's edge. He made a final tour about the

broken ground, but there was no sound or suspicion of Dick.
He knew every inch of the ground. Dick and he had surveyed and resurveyed it for days. The coast was clear. No
one was on guard at the vital point, but still he lingered, his
breath coming and going painfully, as a break in the clouds
cast a moving shape over the undulating ground. Should
he give the boy another half-hour's grace? He makes a
circuit in the direction Dick must approach by and waits.
He will count a hundred very slowly, then wait no longer.
He counts up to fifty, hears a coming step, and waits alertly.
No—it passes on. He begins again—counts one hundred,
two hundred. No sign. "Pah! it is madness to delay for
him. The young poltroon has lost his resolution in his love-
sick fever. Very likely he has been unable to run the risk
of Rosa's anger—her mother's indignation—the possibility
of never seeing the girl again." Well, he had given him
ample grace. He had endangered his own and other lives
to humor a boyish whim. Now he must act, and swiftly.

The plan was too far gone in execution to be changed.
He must carry out the final measures alone. Now, one of
these details required some one to slip down on the ground
and crawl to the point between the windows where the prisoners were working and aid them to remove the thin shell
of brick. If it fell outward, the guard at the corner would
hear the noise, and might come down to see what it was
that made it. The removal of this wall released all confined
in the main prison. These he saw stealing out in groups of
ten or more. They had guides waiting on the bank of the
river. Jack gave them final orders. The most difficult
work was the getting out Jones and Barney, for they had
special cells. Jack was to guard Jones's exit and Dick Barney's, but now all the work would devolve upon him. It
was two o'clock, and he dared wait no longer. Raising
himself from the low wall where he had been crouching, he
started toward the corner of the prison farthest from the
guard-room. At the wall of the building he dropped flat on
his face and began to crawl forward, sheltered by the low
ground that formed a sort of dry ditch about the basement

18

of the prison. He had barely stretched himself at full length when a bright light was flashed on him from a deep doorway just beyond him, and a voice, mocking and triumphant, exclaimed:

"This is a bad place to swim, my friend ! There ain't enough water to drown you, but if you stir you'll run against a bullet."

Jack lay quite still and raised his eyes. Above him stood a trooper, with a revolver leveled at and within ten feet of him. Figure to yourself any predicament in life in which vital stakes hang on the issue; figure to yourself the shipwrecked seizing ice where he had hoped for timber; the condemned criminal walking into the jailer's toils where he had laboriously dug through solid walls; the captain of an army, leaving the field victor, to find his legions rushing upon him in rout; figure any monstrous overturn in well-laid schemes, and you have but a faint reflex of poor Jack's heart-breaking anguish when this jocular fate stood above him, with the five gaping barrels pointed at his miserable head. Oh, if Dick had only been there ! His quick eye and keen activity would have discovered this lurking devil; perhaps, between them, they would have averted the disaster. Where could Dick be ?

BOOK III.

THE DESERTERS.

CHAPTER XXIV.

BETWEEN THE LINES.

On quitting Jack, Dick had but one thought in mind—to make his departure less abrupt for Rosa. If he left her without a word, what would she think? Then, with an officer's uniform, he could be of much more help to Jack and the party than in the rough civilian homespun furnished at the cabin. Besides, he knew of certain blank headquarter passes lying on Vincent's desk. He would get a few of these; they might extricate the party in the event of a surprise.

He tore over the solemn roadway, under the spectral foliage, and in twenty minutes he was in his room in the Atterburys'. Vincent's old uniform he had often noticed in a spare closet adjoining his own sleeping-room. In an instant he was in it, and, though it was not a fit, he soon put it in order to pass casual inspection. The line for Rosa was the next delay. What should he say? He had had his mind full for days of the most tender sentiments and prettily turned phrases, but the turmoil of the last hour, the vital value of every moment to Jack's plans, left him no time to compose the proem he had meditated so long. Rosa's own pretty desk was open, and on a sheet of her own paper he wrote, in a scrawling, school-boy hand:

"Darling Rosa: You've often said that you would disown Vincent if he were not true to the South. Think of

Vincent in my place—dawdling in Acredale or Washington while battles were going on. You would not hold him less contemptible that he was in love; that he let his love, or his life, for you are both to me, stand as a barrier to his duty. You can't love where you can't honor, and you can't hate where you know conscience rules. I go to my duty, that in the end I may come to you without shame. I ask no pledge other than comes to your heart when you read this; but, whatever you may say, whatever you may decide, I am now and always shall be your devoted

RICHARD."

He sighed, casting a woe-begone glance into the mirror, dimly conscious that he was a very heroic young person. He kissed various objects dear to the little maid, and then, in lugubrious unrest, sallied out and mounted.

Again under the calm sky—again the fleet limbs of the horse almost keeping time to his own inward impatience. He holds to the soft, unpaved, outlying streets, that his pace may not attract remark. He passes horsemen, like himself spurring fleetly in the darkness. He is near the river at last—dismounts and reconnoitres. He easily finds a place to tie the horse, and, familiar with every inch of the outlying ground about the prison, crawls close to the wall, listening intently. He can hear no sound save the weary clank of the sentry on the wooden walk. He reaches the wall where the prisoners Jones and Barney were to emerge. There is no sign of a break! Where can Jack be? Some disaster must have overtaken him, for it is past the hour set and soon it will be dawn, and then all action will be impossible. Perhaps Jack has been caught reconnoitring? Perhaps he has gone with the main body, not venturing to try for Jones and Dick without help? No, that was not like Jack. This was his special part in the plan—if it were not done, Jack was still about. He can find out readily—thanks to the countersign. He steals back over the low hillock, mounts the horse, and by a *détour* reaches the sentry guarding the river front of the prison. He is challenged, but,

possessed of the countersign, finds no difficulty in riding up
to the guard-room doorway.

"Has Lieutenant Hawkins been here within an hour,
sentry?" he asks, in apparent haste.

"No, sir, I think he has been sent for—leastwise, the sergeant went away about an hour ago to report the taking of
a deserter, found prowling about the side of the prison."

"A deserter?"

"Yes, sir. He had a brand-new uniform on and no company mark, nor no equipments."

"What has been done with him?" Dick asked, breathlessly, dismounting. "I wonder if he isn't one of my company from Fort Lee? He went off on a drunk yesterday,
though he was sent here on a commissary errand."

"I dunno, sir. He's in the lockup there. He was very
violent, and the sergeant bound him with straps."

"I will go in and examine him; he may be one of my
men, and, as our brigade moves in the morning, I should
like to know."

"Very well, sir; the officer of the day is asleep in the
room beyond the first door. One of the men will call him."

"Oh, no need to disturb him until I have seen the prisoner.—Here, my man"—addressing a soldier asleep on a
settee—"show me to the deserter brought in to-night"

"Yes, sir," the man cried, starting up with confused alacrity; then, noticing the insignia of major on Dick's gray
collar, he saluted respectfully, and, pointing to a double
doorway, waited for his superior to lead the way. Dick,
who had been in the prison before, knew his whereabouts
very well, and it was not until the soldier reached the room
in which the deserter was detained that he seemed to remember that there were no lights.

"Here are the man's quarters, sir; but I'm out of matches.
If you'll wait a minute I'll bring a candle."

"All right," Dick responded, in a loud voice; "I'll stand
here until you come back."

The quest of the candle would take the guide to the closet
in the guard-room, and, risking little to learn much, Dick

struck a match and peered into the stuffy little room, more like a corn-crib than a prison-cell.

"Hist, Jack! is it you?" he called.

There was an exclamation from the farther end of the room, and then a fervent—

"Heavens, Dick! is it really you?"

"Sh—, sh—!"

The soldier's returning footfalls sounded in the passageway; but, as he re-entered the hall where Dick stood shading the flickering light, he could not see the hastily extinguished match in Dick's hand. As the man came slowly along the winding passage-way, Dick whispered:

"You are a recruit in Rickett's legion; you were drunk and lost your way, and I am your major; you are stationed at Fort Lee, near Mechanicsville, and you belong to Company G."

Jack pretended to be sound asleep when the soldier and Dick entered. He rubbed his eyes sleepily, and looked up in a vacant, tipsy way, leering knowingly at the soldier, who had caught him by the shoulder.

"What are you doing here, Tarpey? Why aren't you with your company? You'll get ball and chain for this lark, or my name's not James Braine."

"But, major, it—it wasn't my fault. My cousin, Joe Tarpey, came down from Staunton with a barrel of so'gum whisky, and—and—"

"You drank too much and was caught where you had no business to be. However," Dick added, sternly, "the regiment marches in the morning—you must get out of here. Soldier, show me to Captain Payne's quarters. Say to him that Major Braine, of Rickett's Legion, desires to speak with him a moment." But he had no sooner said this than he realized the danger he was running.

The captain might know Braine, and then how could he extricate himself from the dilemma? Luckily the captain was not in his quarters, and Dick, with calm effrontery, sat down and wrote out a statement of the case, where he was to be found, and his reasons for carrying the prisoner away.

The sergeant, having read this, made no objection to releasing the alleged deserter, since there had been no orders concerning him, and, without more ado, Jack walked away with his captain, the picture of abashed valor and repentant tipsiness.

"Now, Dick, there's no time to ask the meaning of your miraculous doings. We've still time to let our friends out and get away before daylight; but we mustn't lose a second. Sh! stand still, what's that? Troopers! Good heavens, they can't have found out your trick so soon! Ah, no! They are floundering about looking for quarters," he added, in immeasurable relief, as the voices of the riders sounded through the darkness, cursing luck, the road, and everything else. "O Dick, if we only had the countersign I could play a brilliant trick on these greenhorns! Perhaps I can as it is."

"I have the countersign. How do you suppose I could have managed to get to you if I hadn't? It is 'Lafayette.'"

"Glory! Now make all the clatter you can after I challenge."

They had by this time reached a row of tumble-down stables directly in the rear of the prison, and shut out from the open ground by a decrepit fence, broken here and there by negroes too lazy to pass out into the street to reach the river. The horsemen had turned into this lane-like highway—evidently misdirected. When within a few feet, Jack gave a sudden whack on the board and cried, sternly:

"Halt! Who comes there?"

There was a sudden clash of steel as the group halted in a heap, and then a weary voice replied:

"We have no countersign. We should have been at our destination long before sundown, but were misdirected ten miles out of our course on the Manchester pike."

"Very well. Dismount and come forward one man at a time," Jack answered, briefly. This the spokesman did with some alacrity. As he came up, Dick took the precaution of getting between him and his three companions, and then Jack said: "I suppose you are all right; but my orders are to arrest all mounted men, detain their horses here in these, the provost stables," and Jack pointed to Dick's horse dimly outlined against the sky. "I will give you a receipt for him, and you can get him back in the morning when you state your case to the provost marshal.—Stephen," he turned to Dick, "take that horse and put him with the others." He then made out a receipt, handed it to the astonished trooper, and, directing him where to go, carried out the same short shrift with the other three. The troopers were glad enough to be relieved of their beasts. This they did not attempt to deny, for they had seen a public-house in the street below, where they could procure much-needed refreshment, relieved as they now were from the necessity of reporting to their commander, whose whereabouts were far down the Rocett road.

"By George, Jack, what a crafty plotter you are! Now we have a mount for the party, and I needn't take poor Warick's crack stallion."

"Yes; we've doubled the chances of escape by this little stratagem; but we have lost time. Come. Have you tied the horses?"

"Yes. Lead on."

Over the turfy hillside, now moist and sticky with the heavy dew, they stole, half crouching, half crawling, until they were on a level with the prison basement. The sentry in front was no longer pacing his beat, and there was no sign of the man in the rear. In a few minutes the two crawling figures were at the preconcerted places in the wall. In response to their light taps, a square of brick-work large enough to leave a space for a man to crawl through crumbled upon Jack and Dick, who held their bodies closely pressed against the *débris* to prevent too loud a noise. There was no time to wait probabilities of discovery, and an instant later Barney and Jones emerged, panting and half smothered.

"I thought it was all up with me hopes, as Glory McNab said when her sweetheart ran away with the cobbler's daughter," Barney whispered, hugging Jack rapturously.

"Sh—! Down on your stomachs. Move that way until

you see me rise. Come." And Jack squirmed ahead as if he had been accustomed to the locomotion of snakes all his life. In ten minutes they were in the improvised stables. Dick had taken the precaution to place the horses where they could feed on a heap of fodder stacked in the yard, and when they mounted the beasts appeared refreshed as well as rested. Dick loosing Warick's horse so that he might make his way back to his master, the fugitives rode cautiously out of the lane, into the open fields, and, though it was not their shortest way, pushed along the river road to mislead pursuit. Jack's stratagem had resulted in better luck even than the possession of the horses. It not only secured a mount for the four, but, what was equally and perhaps, in view of unforeseen contingencies, more important disguises for the two prisoners.

They found an extra coat strapped to each saddle, and with these Barney and Jones were easily transformed into something like Confederate soldiers. Both Jack and Jones knew every inch of the suburbs, having made the topography a study. They struck for the less traveled thoroughfares until they reached the northeastern limits, then following the old Cold Harbor road they pushed decisively toward the Williamsburg pike. But, instead of following it, they traversed on by lanes and bridle-paths during the day. This was to divide pursuit, as the larger party had taken the river route where Butler's troops were waiting in boats for them. The saddle-bags proved a windfall, for in them were orders to proceed to Yorktown and report to General Magruder. With these Jack felt no difficulty in passing several awkward points, where there was no escaping the cavalry patrols, owing to miles of swamp and impenetrable forest.

They kept clear, however, of such places as the telegraph reached, though at one point they found a post in a great state of excitement over news brought from a neighboring wire, announcing the escape of two prisoners who had been traced to the York road. But with such papers as Jack presented and the number of the party double that described in the dispatch, the adventurers easily evaded suspicion. The great danger, however, was in quitting the Confederate lines to pass into Butler's. They chose the night for this, as the camp-fires would warn them of the vicinity of outposts, Union or rebel. They had purposely avoided highways and habitations, and, as a result, were limited in food to such corn-cribs as they found far from human abodes, or the autumn aftermath of vegetables sometimes found in the shadow of the woods. All were good shots, however, and a fat rabbit and partridge were cooked by Dick with such address, that the party were eager to take more time in halting since they need not starve, no matter how long the journey lasted.

Jack, by tacit consent, was considered commander of the squad, Barney remarking humorously that they would not ask to see his commission until they were in a country where a title meant authority. The commander ordered his small army very judiciously. They were to ride as far apart as the roads or woods or natural obstructions would admit. They thus moved forward in the shape of a triangle, the apex to the rear. Exchanges of position were made every six hours. They were at the end of the second day, toward sunset, approaching what they supposed was Warrick Creek, nearly half-way to Fort Monroe, when they suddenly emerged on an open plateau from which they could see a mile or two before them a tranquil waste of crimson water.

"Why, this can't be the creek!" exclaimed Jones, excitedly. "The creek isn't half a mile at its broadest."

"What can it be?" Jack asked, who had been the right wing to Jones's left. "It's certainly not the James, for the sun is setting at our back!"

"Blest if I can tell. It looks very much like the Chesapeake, only the Chesapeake is wider."

By this time Barney and Dick had ridden up, and began to admire the expanse of water spreading from the land before them to a green wilderness in the distance.

"I'm afraid we are in a fix," Jones said, resignedly. "If I'm not very much mistaken, the red line yonder, that looks like a roadway, is a breastwork, and behind that what looks like a plowed field is earthworks. My boys, we are before Yorktown and farther from our lines than we were yesterday. The nigger that showed us the way in the woods was either ignorant or deceiving us. We are now inside the outposts of the rebels, and we shall have to crawl on our hands and knees to escape them."

"I don't see what better off we'll be on our hands and knees than we are in our saddles," Barney cried, guilelessly "Sure we can go faster on the bastes than we can on our hands, and, as for me knees, 'tis only in prayer that I ever use them."

"Not in love, Barney?" Dick asked, innocently.

"No, me darlin'. The gurls I love think more of me arms than me knees, and I do all of me pleadin' with me lips."

"I should think they could hold their own," Jones remarked, dryly.

"Indeed, they can that, and a good deal more, as me best gurl'll tell you if she'll tell the truth, and no fear of her doing that, I'll go bail."

"Fie! Barney, if she won't tell the truth you should have none of her," Dick cried in stage tones.

"Indeed, it's little I have of her, for she's that set on Teddy Redmund that she leaves me to her mother, when Teddy comes to the porch of an evening."

"Well, friends, your loves are, no doubt, adorable, and it is a pleasant thing to talk over, but just now what we want is a way out of this trap"; and Jack, saying this, slipped from his horse and led him into the shelter of a thick growth of scrub-pines. The rest followed his example. They tied their animals and held a council of war. It was resolved that Jack and Jones should make a reconnaissance to find out the route toward the Warrick; that Dick and Barney should secrete and guard the horses and do what they could to obtain some food. This decision was barely agreed upon, when the shrill call of a bugle sounded almost among the refugees, and they sprang to their horses, waiting in silence the next demonstration. Other bugles sounded farther away ; a great cloud of dust arose in the direction of the water, and then Jack whispered :

"Remain here. I will climb one of these trees and see what it means."

He was in the leafy boughs of a spreading pine in a few minutes, and could descry a broad plain, with tents scattered here and there ; still farther on the broad uplands frame buildings with a red and white flag floating to the wind could be seen. Back of all this he could make out a broad expanse of water and a few ungainly craft, lazily moving to the current in the Yorktown roadstead.

"Yes, this certainly must be Yorktown. Why have they such a force here ? No one is threatening it," Jack murmured, his eyes arrested by a long line of cavalry in undress, leading their horses up a circuitous and hitherto concealed road to the plateau. Ha ! they go down there for water. Let me see. That is to the southeastward ; that is our point of direction. I think we may venture to push on now." He hastily descended from his survey, and making known what he had seen, added : "We must proceed with the greatest caution. There is no time to think of food until we get away from this dangerous neighborhood. We must keep well spread out, and move only over turfy ground or in the deep shade of the wood. In case of disaster, the cry of the night owl, as agreed upon, will be a warning."

The four had practiced the melancholy cry of the owl, as heard in the Southern woods both day and night, and they could all imitate it sufficiently well to pass muster if the hearer were not on guard against the trick, and yet so clever an imitation that none of the four could mistake it. So soon as they quit the plateau, seeking a way east by south, they plunged immediately into a dreary swamp, where progress was slow and difficult. The mosquitoes beset them in swarms, plaguing even the poor animals with their lusty sting. Hour after hour, until the woods became a hideous chaos of darkness and unseemly sounds, the four panting fugitives pushed on, fainting with hunger, worn out by the incessant battle with the corded foliage, the dense marshes, and quagmires through which their path to safety lay. But at midnight Jones gasped and gave up the fight.

"Go on ; leave me here. I am of no use at best. I should only be a drag on you. Perhaps you may find some darkey and send him back to give me a mouthful to eat. That would pick me up ; nothing else can."

The four gathered together for counsel. The horses, faring better than their masters, for they found abundance to allay hunger in the lush, dank grass of the morass, were corraled in a clump of white ash, and the jaded men, groping about, clambered upon the gnarled roots of the trees to catch breath. They had been battling steadily for five hours against all the forces of Nature. Their clothes were torn, their flesh abraded, their strength exhausted. They could have slept, but the ground offered no place, for wherever the foot rested an instant the weight of the body pushed it down into the oozy soil until water gushed in over the shoe-tops. Jones had found the struggle hardest because he had not the youth of the others nor their light frames. The striplings were spared many of his hardships and were still able to endure the ordeal, if the end were sure relief. Jack struck a match, and with this lighted a pine knot. He surveyed the gloomy brake carefully, and at last, finding a mound where a thick growth of underbrush gave assurance of less treacherous soil, he called to Barney to aid him. The little hillock was made into a couch by means of the saddles, and the groaning veteran carefully laid upon the by no means uncomfortable refuge. As Jack held the light above him, Jones's eyes closed and he sank into a lethargic sleep.

"He will be in a high fever when he awakes," Jack said, looking at Barney. "We must see that he has food, or the fever will be his death. Here is what I propose: you and I shall sally out from here, blazing the path as we go. We must find some sign of life within a circuit of five miles. That will take us say till daylight to go and come. We will leave Dick here to guard Jones, and if we do not return by noon to-morrow Dick will know that he must shift for himself."

"You command, Jack dear. What you say I'll do, as Molly Meginniss said to the priest when he told her to repent of her sins."

"Dick, my boy, do you think you are equal to a vigil? You must stay here with Jones. If he wakes and wants water, press the moisture of these leaves to his lips, it's sassafras; and, stay—here is a sort of plantain, filled with little globules of dew ; pour these into his mouth, and at a pinch give him a handful from the pool. In case of great danger fire two shots, but if any one should come toward you or discover you it will be better to surrender. In that event, you can make up a story to suit the case, which may enable you to finally escape. This man's life is in your hands. Remember that it is as glorious a deed as fighting in line. Keep up a stout heart. We will soon be back, or you may take it for granted all is up with us."

"Ah! Jack! Jack! To start so well and end so miserably. I can't bear it—I can't stay here. You stay and let me go."

"No, Dick, it can't be; you are already so worn out that we should have been obliged to halt for you if Jones hadn't broken down. It can't be that you would think of leaving a fellow-soldier in such extremity as this, Dick? I know you better."

"But I don't know him. I have no interest in him. With you I'll face any danger—I'll die without a word; but to stay here in this awful place, with the black pools of water, like great dead eyes, glaring in their hideous light" (the pine-torch flaring in the wind filled the glade with vast ogreish shadows, as the clustering bushes were swayed in the night air) "and these hideous night-cries—O Jack, I can't—I can't —I must go !"

"But the horses and the need of some one that can come back in case anything befalls me. I am disappointed in you, Dick. I am shocked; you are not the man of courage and honor I thought you."

"O my God, go—go—I will stay; but, Jack, if you find me dead, tell—tell—Rosa—that—that—" He gasped and sank down sobbing against the gnarled tree that crossed the mound above Jones's head.

"I will tell Rosa that you were the man she believed you were when the trial came," and with this Jack and Barney, with a flaming torch, set forward hastily through the fantastic curtain of foliage and night, which shut in the glimmering vista of specters, dark, sinister, and menacing.

CHAPTER XXV.

PHANTASMAGORIA.

To say that night is a time of terror is a commonplace. Night is not terrible of itself. It is like the ocean—peace and repose if there be no storm. But of all terrors there are none, outside a guilty mind, so benumbing as night in the unknown. It does not lessen the horror of darkness that fear makes use of the imagination for its agencies. Fancy, intuition, and the train that follows the inner vision, these make of night a phantasmagoria, compared to which Milton's inferno is a place of comparative repose.

If you would realize the wondrous necromancy of the sun, pass a night in some primeval forest, untouched by the hand of man. Until he stands in the awful silence of the midnight wood, or upon some vast waste of nature, no man can figure to himself the varied shapes the mind can give to terrors based upon the mysterious noises of nature, and the goblin motions of inanimate things. The lover thinking of his lass welcomes the night and the rapturous walks among well-known scenes and kindly objects. With glimmering lamps in the foliage and the not distant sounds of daily life, even the woods have nothing fearful to the meditative or the distraught. But in flight, with fear as a garment that can not be laid aside, the somber forms of the forest are more terrible than an army with banners, as a haunted

house is a more unnerving dread than burglars or any form
of night marauders. It was at night that the mutinous sailors of Columbus broke into decisive revolt; it was at night
that the iron band of Cortes lost heart, and were routed on
the lakes of Mexico; it was at night that the resolution of
Brutus failed before the disaster at Philippi.

That two-o'clock-in-the-morning courage, which is the
secret of soldierly success, comes only from companionship.
The night-wood is a world by itself, filled with its own atmosphere, as oppressive to valor as the electric reefs that
drew the nails from the ships of Sindbad. Among familiar
scenes and well-known shapes, it is all the delight the poets
sing—so tranquillizing, inspiring, fecund, that in comparison
the thought of day brings up garish hues, flaunting figures—
the hardness, harshness and unlovely in life. But night in
the goblin-land, where Dick found himself suddenly deserted,
with fantastic forms swaying in the lazy wind, would have
had terrors for the most constant mind; terrors such as filled
the soul of Macbeth, when Birnam wood came marching to
Dunsinane. In an instant, as it seemed to Dick's exalted and
painfully impressionable sense, every separate leaf, branch,
brier, copse, and jungle, was endowed with a voice of its
own—hateful, irritating, mocking. Swarms of peering eyes
hovered in the air, glowering uncanny menace into the boy's
wild, dilating vision.

Brave, even to recklessness, Dick was, as you have seen;
but no sooner had the glimmer of Jack's torch flickered and
fluttered into the black distance, making place for the monstrous shapes, the luring shadows, and threatening forms
encompassing him, than Dick threw himself, with a wailing
shriek, into the morass in a wild attempt to follow.

In an instant he was up to his middle in mud and water.
He seized the prickly branches coiling about and above him;
he gasped in prayerful pleading, the home teaching still
strong in him; but there was no answer, save the crooning
night-birds and the croaking frogs. Slimy things touched
his torn flesh; whirring birds shot past him, disturbed in
their night perches. The deadly odor, pungent and nause-

ous, of a thousand exhaling herbs, filled his nostrils. The darkness grew, instinct with threatening forms. He gasped, struggled, and in a fervent outburst of thanksgiving regained the dank mound. Ah, there was life on that! human life. Jones slept, the stertorous sleep of delirium. He murmured brokenly. Dick was too terrified to distinguish what he said. The blaze of the pine knot flared from side to side as the sighing breeze arose from the brackish pools, protesting the vitality of even this moribund hades. Ah ! if he could but lie down and bury his face. The horses ? They were feeding tranquilly yonder, standing up to their knees in mosses and water. The lines that tied them were long. They could move about. This was some comfort. They were more human than the dreadful specters that filled the place.

Ah! the blessed, blessed light that flamed out from the merry pine-torch; he didn't wonder that half the Eastern world worshiped fire. He adored it—blessed, blessed fire—the sign of God, the beacon of the human. Hark! What half-human—or rather wholly inhuman—sounds are these that alternate in unearthly measure ? Surely animal nature has no voice so strident, vengeful, odious. Can it be animals of prey ? No. The Virginia forests are dangerous only in snakes. Snakes ? Ah, yes! He shrinks into shadow against the oak at this suggestion; snakes ? the deadly moccasin, that prowls as well by night as day. Ugh! what's this at his feet—soft, clammy, shining in the flaring light ? He leaps upon the smooth tree-trunk, growing slantwise instead of perpendicular. What if the torch and the odor of flesh should draw the snakes to the sleeper ? The flame flares in wide, lurid curves, revealing the outlines of the sleeping man. Heavens, what a terrible face! He moves in spasmodic contortions. He is smothering. The veins of his neck will break if he is not awakened.

"O my God! my God! have mercy!" Dick buries his face in his hands, as he clings desperately to the smooth white-oak trunk. A strange, wild strain, like a detached chord of a vesper melody, sounds above him! It is the whip-

19

poorwill — steadily, continuously, entrancingly the dulcet measure is taken up and echoed, until the slough of despond seems transformed into a varying diapason of melancholy minstrelsy. He dares not raise his head. It will vanish if he moves. He crouches, panting, almost exultant, in the sense of recovered faculties, or rather the suspension of numbing fear. How long will it last? He must move; his limbs are cramped and aching. He raises his head. Mortal powers! the torch is flickering into ashes! Another instant and he will be in the dark. Dare he move? Dare he seek the distant pine, between him and which the black surface of the murky sheet shines, dotted with uncanny growth and reptilian things? Yes; anything is better than the hideous darkness of this hideous place.

The horse he rode has broken his leash and comes to him with a gentle whinny, as if asking why the delay in such a place. "Blessed, blessed God, that made a beast so human!" He caresses it, he clings to its neck and calls to it piteously. Ah, yes; the dying light. He must renew it. He slips down upon the bare back and urges the patient beast across the brackish morass. Ah, this is life again! He is not alone. This noble beast is human. It crops the tender leaves confidingly, and swings its head as much as to say: "Don't fear, Dick; I'm here. I'll stand by you; I don't forget the pains you took to get me water, and that particularly toothsome measure of oats you cribbed in the rebel barn near Williamsburg!"

But the pine knot that will burn is not so easily found. Dick was forced to go a long way before he came upon the resinous sort. He brought back a supply, having taken the precaution to provide matches in order to secure his way back. The quest had to some extent lessened the morbid or supernatural forms of his terrors. They all returned, however, when, having dismounted, he forgot to tie the horse, and it wandered off in search of herbage. He called, but the beast made no sign of returning. Alone again. Alone in the night; spectral forms about him; the sleeping man adding to the ghostliness of the scene by his incoherent mutterings, his hideous, gulping breath, his ghastly, blood-curdling outcries. Then through the gloom the shining outlines of the white oak, like shreds of shrouds hung on funeral foliage. Ah! he would go mad—he must break the brutish sleep of the sick man.

"Mr. Jones," he wails—and his own voice—the comically commonplace name, "Mr. Jones," even in the agony of his terror, the humor of the conjuncture glimmered in the boy's crazed intelligence, and he laughed a wild, maniacal laugh. But the laugh died out in a pulseless horror. The sick man uprose on his elbow. Dick, above him on the white-oak trunk, could see his very eyes bloodshot and wandering. He uprose, almost sitting. He passed his hand over his staring eyes, and began to murmur:

"Did you bring me here to do murder, Elisha Boone? You have bought my body, but you never bought my soul. No, no! I will not. I say I will not. Do you hear? I will not!"

He glared wildly; then, his eyes meeting the full flame of the torch, he laughed, a dreadful, marrow-freezing laugh, and broke out again in clearer tones: "I am yours, Elisha Boone, but my boy is not yours. He was born in my shape, but he has his mother's soul. He will be a man; he will be your vengeance; he will undo all his father has done. You've robbed me; you've made me rob others. But if you touch, if you look at my boy, my first-born, you might as well hold a pistol at your head. I'm no longer mad. You must treat with him. Ah! yes; I'll do your bidding with the others. I'll make young Jack as much trouble as you ask, but you must make a path of gold for my boy. You must give him what you have robbed from me. Felon? I'm no felon. It was you who plotted it. It was you that put the means in mad hands. I can face my family. I have no shame but that I was a coward. My son! He is no coward. He is a soldier. He is the pride of the Caribees. He is the beloved of—of—"

The gibbering maniac, exhausted in body, still incoherently raving, sank back in piteous collapse, a terrifying gurgle breaking from his throat, while his tongue absolutely protruded from his jaws.

Dick, his terrors all forgotten in a new and overmastering horror, bethought him of Jack's admonition about the water. He slipped down from the tree, gathered the large moist leaves that clustered near the pool and held them to the burning lips. Jones swallowed the drops with a hideous gurgling avidity, clutching the boy's hand ravenously to secure a more copious flow. There was a tin cup in the holster under the invalid's head. Taking this, Dick dipped up water from the black pool between the green leaves; the hot lips sucked it in at one dreadful gulp.

"More, more; for God's sake, more!"

Dick filled it again, and again it was emptied.

"More—more—I'm burning—more!"

The boy was cruelly perplexed. He remembered vaguely hearing that fever should be starved; that the thing craved was the dangerous thing; and he moved away in a sort of compunctious terror.

"More—more! Oh, in the name of God, more!"

The words came gaspingly. Dick thought of the death-rattle he had heard in Acredale when old man Nagle, the madman, died. He dared not give more water, but he gathered leaves from the aromatic bushes and pressed them to the fevered lips. Before he could withdraw them, the eager jaws closed upon the balsamic shrub. They answered the purpose better than the most scientific remedy in the pharmacopœia, for the patient called for no further drink, and presently fell into profound and undisturbed sleep. Again the boy was alone with the daunting forces of the dark in its grimmest and most terrifying mood. Alone! No; his mind was now taken from all thought of self. He was with a fellow-townsman. The man had mentioned Boone; had referred to deeds that he had heard all his life associated with the father he had never seen. A wild thought flashed upon him. Was the collapsed body at his feet his father's? He could not see any resemblance in the dark, handsome face to the portrait at home, though all through the flight from Richmond something in the man's manner had seemed like a memory. He strove to recall the image his young mind had cherished, the personality he had heard whispered about in the gossiping groups of Acredale. This was not the gay, the brilliant, the fascinating *bon viveur* who had been the life of society from Warchester to Bucepholo, from Pentica to New York. Ah! what were the mystic terrors of the night, what the oppressive surroundings of this charnel-house of Nature, to the awful spectacle of this unmanned mind, this delirious echo of past guilt, past cowardice, past shame?

To lessen the somber gloom, Dick had lighted many torches and set them about the high mound where the sleeper lay in a huddle. Taking little heed of where he set them, some of them, as the wind arose, flared out until their flames licked the decayed branches of the fallen white oak. As the boy crouched, pensive and distraught, he was suddenly aroused by a vivacious cracking. He looked up. Lines of fire were darting thither and yon, where dry wood, the *débris* of years of decay, had been caught in the thick clumps of underbrush and among the limbs of the trees. The fire had pushed briskly, and the uncanny glade was now an amphitheatre of crawling flames, stretching in many-colored banners in a vast circle about the point of refuge. Dick gazed fascinated, with no thought of danger. His spirits rose. It was something like life—this gorgeous decoration of fire. How beautiful it was! How it brought out the shining lines of the white oak, the glistening green of the cypress! Why hadn't he thought of this before? Then, as the curling waves of fire pushed farther and farther up the stems of the trees, and farther and farther endlessly into the undergrowth, an unearthly outcry and stir began. Birds, blinded by the light, whirred and fluttered into the open space above the water, falling helplessly so near Dick that he could have caught and killed a score to surprise Jack with a game breakfast, when he returned. Then—ugh!—horror!—great, coiling masses detached themselves from the tufts of sward, and splashed noisily into the putrid water, wriggling and convulsed. The invalid still slept—but, dreadful sight! the coiling monsters, upheaving themselves from the water, glided, dull-eyed and sluggish, upon the mossy island, about the unconscious figure.

Dick, fascinated and inert, watched the snaky mass, squirming in hideous folds almost on the recumbent body. Then, aroused to the horror of their nearness, he seized a torch and made at the slimy heap. The fire conquered them. They slid off the ground, with forked tongues darting out in impotent malice. But others, squirming through the water, wriggled up; and the boy, maddened by the danger, stood his ground, torch in hand, defending the sleeper.

But now the fire has widened its swath, and is enveloping the tiny island. The serpents, hedged in from the outer line, uprear in blood-curdling masses, their dull eyes gleaming, and their tongues phosphorescent, darting out in their agony. Dick doesn't mind them now, for he has, for the first time, begun to realize that his illumination has destruction as the sequel of its delight. Great clouds of smoke settle a moment on the water and then rise, impelled by the cold surface. Even the green verdure begins to roll back where the crackling flames play into the more compact wall of incombustible timber. The sleeper murmurs in his dreams. Dick casts about despairingly. He hears the horses—they have broken their tethers—he can hear them whinnying, upbraidingly, far off. Wherever he casts his eye, volumes of fire dart and sway, always coming inward, first scorching the green limbs, then fastening on the tender stems and turning them to glowing lines of cordage; only the great sheet of water, inky, terrible, and threatening a few hours before, protects him and his charge. The hissing snakes have sunk into it.

Bevies of birds, supernaturally keen of sight, have dropped upon the twigs that lie on the glittering bosom of the water. Dick, in all the agonized uncertainty of that night of peril, thinks with wonder on the mysterious resources Nature provides its helpless outcasts. The hideous shallows, black, glistening, are now a belt of safety, not only for himself and the sleeper, but a refuge for all manner of whirring birds and crawling things, intimidated and harmless in the stifling breath of the fire. The flame, leaping from sedge to sedge, from trunk to trunk, seems to seek, with a human instinct, and more than human pertinacity, food for its ravening hunger; far upward, where festoons of moss hung from the sycamores in the day, airy banners of starry sparks, swayed, coiled, and flamed among the branches. But Dick was soon reminded that the scene was not for enjoyment, however fantastically fascinating.

The smoke, at first rising from the burning brakes, lodged among the tree-tops; then, meeting the humid night-air in the matted leaves, descended slowly. Dick found himself nearly smothered when he had partly recovered from the spell-bound wonder of the demoniac *fête*. The ground under his feet felt gratefully cool. He bent down, and shudderingly laved his burning face in the inky water. The sick man had slept more peacefully during the last half-hour. He no longer breathed in gasping efforts; his sleep was unbroken by muttering or outcry. But now he must be aroused. He must be taken out of the circle of fire, for, sooner or later, the curling waves would lick downward from the dry vines above and scorch the mound. How to get away? The horses were long since gone. They might be miles from the spot! Dick touched the sleeping man, filled with a new suspense. He breathed so softly, or did he breathe at all?

"For God's sake, Mr. Jones, wake up! We must go from here; the swamp is burning!"

"Eh—who is it? Where am I? Was—I dreaming? I thought my boy was with me, and we were in the old home at Acredale."

He lay quite still, staring upward with unseeing eyes. Dick's heart gave a great throb of grateful, devout thanksgiving. The madness and fever were gone.

"You remember you were too worn out to go on, and Jack has gone to get food. But the swamp has caught fire, and we must move away."

Jones had risen to his elbow; then, with an exclamation

that sounded like an oath, to his feet, gazing on the flaming specters rising and falling, enlarging and shrinking, among the black tracery of limbs and trunks.

"You ought to have waked me before," Jones said, when he had swept the scene, with sane realization in his eye. "I'm afraid we can never break through the fire. It reaches a mile or more all about us, and I—I am in no condition to move. I feel as if I had been down months with illness."

"But if you could eat something you would be able to move," Dick ventured, cruelly hurt at the implied delinquency.

"Eat!" Jones held up one of the luckless torches that Dick had lighted in a circle about the mound, and began to examine the ground. "What is there to eat? Stay! By Heaven, I have it! The bushes are filled with fluttering game. There, see that! and that, and that!" As he spoke he had thrust the burning torch into a thick clump of bushes, dense and glistening as laurels, that looked like wild huckleberry. The branches were laden with birds, and in a moment he had seized three or four partridges.

"What better do we need? We have salt, water, and fire. I'll prepare them. Do you keep your face well bathed, and heap up embers at the foot of that ash."

Sure enough, sometimes hidden by billows of smoke, rising lazily among the burning bushes, Jones stripped the birds, spitted them on his bayonet, and, holding them in the hot coals, soon presented a well-browned portion to his companion.

"I have had a good deal worse fare than this, my young friend. I have been in the West, when fire, Indians, and hunger besieged us at the same time. But we should have a poor chance here if it were not for the wet grass and the everlasting water. If we can manage to keep clear of the smoke, we shall be all right, but the smoke seems to grow denser. Where can it come from?"

"Great Heavens! do you hear that? Shots—one—two! That's Jack's signal. He—he is near. He is in danger. I must go to him." Dick cried. "Listen; more shots. No, that can't be the signal. There, do you hear that? A volley. The rebels are after them, or we are near the outposts, and the two armies are skirmishing."

Yes; the shots now sounded more frequently, but they seemed to be fired not far away.

"It is Jack. I know it is Jack, and he is in peril. I must go to him. I can not stay here. Surely there is no danger in pushing toward the firing?"

"There is every danger. In the first place, the smoke will smother us. Then suppose we reached the spot? We might be nearer the rebels than our friends. They know where we are. If they are not taken, they will come back for us. If they are taken, we must do our best to get to our lines and send out a scouting party. Be guided by me, youngster. I am an older hand in business of this sort than you are."

The boy stood irresolute. Both listened intently. The firing had stopped. A great sough of rising storm came from the northwest, carrying a hot, blinding mass of smoke and flame into the little retreat. They flung themselves on the damp ferns to keep their breath. Still the breeze rose, until it became a wind—a spasm of hurricane. It was madness to linger, for the flames now licked the ground, driven down anew by the blast. Then Jones spoke decisively: "Strap a pine torch to your body. I will do the same. Take all you can carry and follow in my wake." Jones, as he spoke, seized a torch, extinguished it, and handed it to Dick. Equipped as he had directed, they set out, half crawling, half swimming, to avoid the volumes of smoke hovering in the thick, cactus-like leaves of the wild laurel. Presently they emerged, after toil and misery, that excitement alone enabled the boy to support, into what seemed a cleared space. But as soon as their eyes could distinguish clearly, they found themselves on the edge of a wide pond. The fire was now behind them. They could stand erect and breathe the pure, cool air.

"Ah, now we are in luck!" Jones whispered. "We will walk to the right, on the edge of this lake, and keep it between us and the fire. We have got out of that purgatory; now if we could only signal our friends."

"Hist!" whispered Dick, "I hear some one moving behind us."

They crouched down in the thick reeds and waited. The sky above was darkly overcast; an occasional burst of lightning revealed the dimensions of the pond, and they could see high ground on the eastern shore, covered by enormous pines.

"If we can only reach the pines we shall be all right. There the ground will be dry and soft and you can get some rest. I'm afraid, my boy, it will go hard with you if you don't."

"I don't mind what happens if we can only come up with Jack. There, do you hear that ?"

Yes, both could plainly hear voices ahead of them on the margin of the pond. They were talking in low tones, and the words were undistinguishable.

"We must crawl back toward the bush, and get as near these folks as we can," Jones whispered. They made their way easily into the high bushes and stole forward in the direction of the voices. But as they had to guard against breaking twigs or hurtling branches, which would have betrayed them, their advance was slow. When they reached the vicinity where they had fancied the voices to be, all was silent.

"Sound the call; perhaps that will lead to something," Jones whispered in Dick's ear.

But, unnerved by the trying experience of the night, or worn out by fatigue, Dick's call was far from the significant signal he had practiced with Jack. He repeated it several times, but there was no response. There was, however, something more startling. A few rods beyond them a flame suddenly shot up, lighting a group of cavalry patrols standing beside a fire just kindled.

"Rebels!" Jones whispered. "Now we must be slippery as snakes. If they have no dogs, we are all right. If you hear the whimper of a hound, follow me like lightning and plunge into the water. That'll break the trail. Stay here and let me reconnoitre a bit. Have no fear. I'll go in no danger."

Jones crept away, leaving Dick by no means easy in his mind, but he no longer felt the terror that numbed him in the deep wood. Here there was companionship. By pushing the branches aside he could see the figures lounging about the fire; he could see the dark vault of the sky, and was not oppressed by the hideous shapes and shadows of the dense jungle. Jones meanwhile had pushed within earshot of the group. He flattened his body against a friendly pine and listened.

"I reckon they ain't the Westover niggers, for they were traced to the Pamunkey; these rascals are most likely from the south side—"

"If Jim gets here with the dogs in an hour, we can be back to the barracks for breakfast."

"Ef it hadn't been for that blamed fire in the swamp, we should have had them before this. The rascal that fired at Tom wasn't a musket-shot from me when the smoke poured out and hid him."

"They've gone into the swamp. The dogs'll soon tree them. I'm going to turn in till the dogs come. One of you stay awake and keep a sharp eye toward the creek."

"All right, sergeant. You won't have more'n a cat-nap. Bilcox's dogs are over at the ford, I know, for they were brought there's soon as the news of the Yankee escape came."

"I hope they are; but I'm afraid they are not. If they are, we shall soon hear them."

Jones had heard enough. Hastening back to Dick, he asked:

"Can you swim?"

"Yes, I'm a good swimmer."

"Very well; throw away everything — no, stay — that would betray us. When we reach the water bury all you can't carry in the sand and then follow me."

They were forced to retrace their painful way through the bushes to reach a place as distant from the point of pursuit as possible. A half-mile or more from their starting-place they found themselves in a running stream. Jones examined it in both directions, and bade Dick enter it and follow in the water, pushing upward in the bed, waist-deep, a hundred yards. Then, climbing to the bank, he groped about until he found a slender white oak. Climbing this as high as he could get, he slowly swung off, and, the tree bending down to the very stream, he dropped back into the water and rejoined Dick. Both waded in the middle of the stream until they reached the pond, and then struck out toward the pine clump the lightning had revealed a little while before. There was no need of swimming, and, find-ing it possible to wade, Jones decided to retain the pistols and ammunition which he had at first resolved to bury as impeding the flight. The bottom appeared to be hard sand, a condition often found in Southern ponds near the inflow of the sea. They had gone a mile or more, keeping just far enough from the bank to remain undistinguishable, when the appalling baying of a hound sounded from the farther end of the pond, where the patrol fire gleamed faintly among the trees.

"Now, youngster, we must keep all our wits at work. The dogs will push on to where we hid. They will follow to the stream, and I think I have given them the slip there. Then they will beat about and follow our trail into the cy-press swamp. There the horses will mislead them, and if you can only hold out, so soon as daylight comes we can strike into the pines and make for the Union lines."

"I—I—think I can—ah!—"

Dick reeled helplessly and would have sunk under the water, if Jones had not caught him.

"Courage, my boy, courage! Don't give up now, just as we are near rescue!"

But Dick was unconscious, the strain of the early part of the night, the desperate fight through the brakes, all had told on the slight frame, and Jones stood up to his middle in the dark water, holding the fainting boy.

CHAPTER XXVI. .

IN THE UNION LINES.

IF there is reason as well as rhyme in the old song that danger's a soldier's delight and a storm the sailor's joy, Jack and his comrade were in for all the delights that ever gladdened soldier or sailor boy. When they left Dick and Jones, the eager couriers tore through the marshy lowlands, the stubbly thickets and treacherous quagmires, poor Barney, panting and groaning in his docile desire to keep up with his leader, as he had done often in boyish bravado.

"There'll not be a rag on me body nor a whole bone in me skin when we get out of this!" he gasped, as they reached high ground between two spreading deeps of mingled weeds and water. "The sight of us'd frighten the whole rebel army, if we don't come on them aisy loike, as the fox said when he whisked into the hen-house."

"He was a very considerate fox, Barney. Most of the personages you select to illustrate your notions seem to me to be gifted with little touches of thoughtfulness. Barney, you ought to write a sequel to Æsop. There never was out of his list of animal friends such wise beasts, birds, and what not as you seem to have known."

"Jack, dear, if a man lived on roses would the bees feed on him? If he ate honeysuckle instead of hard-tack would he be squeezed for his scents to fill ladies' smelling-bottles?"

"I don't know that sense is always a recommendation to women," Jack shifts his burden to say tentatively, as Barney, involved in a more than commonly obstinate brier, loses the thread of this jocose induction.

"Ah, Jack, dear, ye're weak in ye're mind when you fall to play on words like that."

"You mean my sense is small?"

"Not that at all. Sure, it's a hero's mind ye show when you can find heart to make merry at a time like this!"

"Yes—'he jests at love who never felt a throb.'"

"Then you've a hard heart—and I know I lie when I say

it, as Father Mike McCune said to himself when he tuk the
oath to King George in '98—if ye're heart never throbbed in
Acredale beyant, for there's many a merry one cast down
entirely that handsome Jack's gone."

"Come, come, Barney; it's dark, and I can't see the grin
that saves this from fulsome blarney."

"Indeed, then—"

"Hark!"

Through the monotonous noises of the night the clank-
ing of steel and the neighing of horses could be heard just
ahead.

"We must move cautiously now, Barney. Try to put a
curb on your tongue, and let your reflections mature in your
busy brain."

"Put me tongue in bonds to keep the peace, as Lawyer
Donigan cautioned Biddy Gavan when the doctor said she
was driving the parish mad with her prate."

"Sh!—sh!—you noisy brawl; we shall have a platoon of
cavalry upon us. Even the birds have stopped crooning to
catch your delicate brogue!"

"'Tis only the ill-mannered owl that makes game of me
—if—"

"Sh! Come on. Bend low. Do as I do—if you can see
me. If not, keep touch on my arm."

"As the wolf said to the lamb when he bid him take a
walk in the wather."

They had now emerged on the reedy margin of the dark
pool discovered by Dick and Jones later. All was silent.
The sky was full of stars—so full that, even in the absence
of the moon, there was a transparent clarity in the air that
enabled Jack to take definite bearings.

"This must be an outlet of the York River, the stream
we saw this afternoon. If it be, then we are not far from
our own outposts. The troopers we heard just now may be
Union soldiers. We must wait patiently to let them discover themselves. Keep abreast of me, and don't, as you
value your life, speak above a whisper—better not to speak
at all."

"That's what the priest said to Randy Maloney's third wife when she complained that he bate her."

"Barney, I'll throttle you if you don't keep that mill you call your tongue still."

"Ah, I'll hold it in me fist, as Mag Gleason held her jaw, for fear her tooth would lep out to get more room to ache."

Jack laughed. "If we're caught it will be through your jokes, for bad as they are I must laugh at some of them."

"Dear, oh dear no; you may save the laugh till a convenient time, as Hugh McGowen kept his penances, until his head was clear, and there was no whisky in the jar."

They had been pushing on rapidly—noiselessly, during this whispered dispute, and now found themselves at the reedy margin of a wide inlet, where, from the swift motion of the water and the musical gurgling, they could tell they were by the side of a main channel.

"We must push on southward, and see if there is a crossing. If we come to one, that will tell us where we are, for it will be guarded, you may be sure," said Jack, buoyantly.

"Yes, but I'd rather find a hill of potatoes and a drop than all the soldiers in the two armies."

"You are not logical, Barney. If we find soldiers, we'll find rations; though I have my doubts about the sort of 'drop' you'll be apt to find down here."

"There was enough corn in the field beyant to keep a still at work for a winter," Barney lamented with a sigh, recalling fields of grain they had passed near Williamsburg, which he vaguely alluded to as "beyant."

"I wish some of the 'still' were on the end of your tongue at this moment."

"With all me heart—'twould do yer sowl good to see the work it'd give me tongue to do to hould itself," Barney gasped, trying to keep abreast of his reviler. "Be the dark eyes of Pharaoh's daughter there's a field beyant—yes, and a shebeen; d'ye see that?"

They had suddenly emerged in a cleared place. Against the horizon they could distinctly distinguish the outlines of a cabin, the "shebeen" Barney alluded to.

"Yes, we're in luck. It's a negro shanty. We shall find friends there, if we find anybody. Now, do be silent."

"If the field was full of girruls, with ears as big as sunflowers, they wouldn't hear me breathe, so have no fear. A hill of potatoes all eyes couldn't see us in such darkness as this."

For dense clouds had swiftly come up from the west, covering the horizon. After careful reconnoitring, requiring a circuit of the clearing, Jack ventured to make directly for the dark outlines of the cabin. War had obviously not visited the place, for as they passed a low outhouse the startled cackle of chickens sounded toothsomely, and Barney came to a delighted halt.

"Sure we'd better get a bite to ate while we may, as th' ass said when he passed th' market car, for who knows what'll happen if we stop to ask by your lave?"

For answer Jack gave him a sharp push, and the discomfited plunderer hurried on with a good-humored grunt. All was silent in the cabin. The windows were slatted, without glass, and the door was unfastened. Jack pushed in boldly, leaving Barney to guard the rear. Peaceful snoring came from one corner, and Jack, shading a lighted match with his hand, looked about him. In the hurried glimpse he caught sight of an old negro on a husk mattress, and the heads of young boys just beyond. They were sleeping so soundly that the striking of the match never aroused them. Jack had to shake the man violently before the profound sleep was broken.

"I say, wake up! or can you wake?"

"What dat? Who's dar—you, Gabe? What you 'bout?"

The old man shuffled to a sitting posture, and Jack, renewing his match, held it in the negro's blinking eyes.

"Have you any food? We are Yankees, and want something for companions in the swamp. Are we in danger here? We heard cavalry-men on the other side of the pond; are they rebel or Yankee?"

At this volley of questions the bewildered man turned

piteously to the sleepers, and then stared at Jack in perplexity.

"'Deed, marsa captain, I don no noffin 'tall. I—I hain't
been to de crick fo' a monf. I'se fo'bid to go da—I—"

"Well, well, have you any food ? Get that first, and then
talk," Jack cried, impatiently.

But now the boys were awake, and Jack had to give them
warning to make no noise. Yes, there was food, plenty.
Cooked bacon, hoe-cake, and cold chicken, boiled eggs, and,
to Barney's immeasurable joy, sorghum whisky. The hunger of the invaders satisfied, each provided himself with a
sack to feed the waiting comrades ; and while this was going
on they extracted from the now reassured negroes that the
spot was just behind Warick Creek, near Lee's Mills ; that
parties of rebels from the fort at Yorktown had been at work
building lines of earthworks, and that every now and then
Yankees came across and skirmished in the woods a mile or
two up, in the direction whence Jack had come. The cabin
was only a step from the main road, upon which the rebels
were encamped—a regiment or more. Some Yankee prisoners had been captured early in the morning, and were in
the block-house, a short distance up the road.

"Can you lead us near the block-house ?" Jack asked.

"I reckon I can ; but ef I do they'll shu'ah' find it out,
and den I'se don, 'cos Marsa Hinton—he's in de cavalry—
he'll guess dat it was me dat tuk you 'uns dar."

"Do you want to be free ? Do you want to go into the
Union lines ?"

"Free ! oh, de Lor', free ! O marsa captain, don't fool
a ole man. Free ! I'd rudder be free dan—dan go to Jesus
—almost."

"Have you a wife—are these your children ?"

"My ole woman is up at Marsa Hinton's; she's de nuss
gal. Dese is my boys; yes, sah."

"Very well ; we're going into the Union lines. You
know the country hereabouts. Help us to find our friends
in the swamp, and we will take you all with us," Jack said ;
but feeling a good deal of compunction, as he was not so sure

20

that the freedom bestowed upon these guileless friends might not, for a time at least, be more of a hardship than their happy-go-lucky servitude. Meanwhile, in the expansion of renewed hopes and full stomachs, no watch had been kept on the outside ; a tallow dip had been lighted, and the whole party busied in getting together such necessaries as could be carried. One of the boys, passing the door, uttered a stifled cry :

"Somebody comin' from de road."

"Where can we hide? Don't put out the light; that will look suspicious!" Jack whispered, making for the window in the rear. "Is there a cellar, or can we get on the roof ?" But the dark group were too terrified to speak. They ran in a mob to the doorway, luckily the most adroit manœuvre they could hit upon, for with the dip flaring in the current of air, the room was left in darkness. Jack and Barney slipped through the low lattice, and by means of a narrow shed reached the low roof. They could hear the tramp of horses, how many they could not judge, and then a gruff voice demanding:

"You, Rafe, what ye up to ? What ye got a light burnin' this time o' night fo' ?"

"'Deed, marsa, it's nuffin'—fo' God. marsa! I was gittin'' de stomach bottle fo' Gabe—he eat some jelly root fo' supper and he's been powerful sick—frow his insides out—I—"

"Leave your horses, boys. Rafe's got some of Hinton's best sorghum whisky—you, there, nigger, get us a jug and some cups."

How many dismounted Jack couldn't make out, but presently there was a heavy tramping in the cabin and then a ferocious oath.

"What does this mean; why have you got all these traps packed ? Going to cut to the Yankees! Don't lie, now— you'll get more lashes for it."

Jack listened breathlessly. Would the quavering slaves have presence of mind to divert suspicion ? There was a pause, and then the old man cried, pleadingly:

"We'se gwine to lebe dis place; we's gwine up to de house

in de mornin'. My ole woman can't come down heah now,
case de sojers is always firin', and Mars' Hinton told us to
come to de quarters, sah."

"I don't believe a word of it, you old rascal. I'll see
whether Hinton has ordered you to leave here. Likely
story, indeed; leave one of his best fields with no one to
care for it. Git the whisky and stop your mumbling. You,
there, you young imps, step about lively—do you heah ?"

There was the sound of a sharp stroke, then a howl of
pain and a boisterous laugh.

"You keep an eye on the rear and I will see how many
horses there are," Jack's lips murmured in Barney's ear.
He slid cautiously down the slanting roof until he came to
the corner where he saw the dark group of horses. There
were three—tied to the peach-trees. He made his way back
to Barney and whispered:

"There are but three horses. If you are up to an adventure I think we can make this turn to our profit."

"I'm up to anything, as the cat said when Biddy Hiks's
plug ran her up the crab-tree."

"Very well. Come after me."

The sorghum, meanwhile, had been handed to the raid-
ers in the cabin, and the men could be heard making merry.

"You, Gabe, go out and mind the horses; see that they
don't twist the bridles about their legs."

Gabe sallied out and one of his brothers with him. As
they neared the horses Jack came upon them, and taking
the elder, Gabe, in the shadow of the house, he whispered:

"Have the soldiers' pistols ?"

"Yes, sah."

"Where are they ?"

"De put dem on de stool, neah de doah."

"Good. How many ?"

"Free."

"Have they swords ?"

"Yes, sah."

"Where are they ?"

"On de stool, too."

"That will do; keep with the horses, and don't be fright
ened if you hear anything. We'll give you freedom yet, if
you'll be prudent."

He could hear the men grumbling because the food was
not enough to go around. The liquor had begun to work
in their systems, drinking so lavishly, and without nour-
ishment to absorb its fiery quality. Jack let enough time
pass to give this ally full play in disabling the troopers, then
taking Barney to the rear of the cabin, whispered:

"I will dash in at the door, seize the weapons, and demand surrender. You make a great ado here; give command, as if there were a squad. The boys will make a loud
clatter with the horses, and we shall bag the game without
a blow. Now, be prudent, Barney, and we will go into the
Union lines in triumph."

Inside the men were laughing uproariously, mingling
accounts of love and war in a confused medley—how a
sweetheart in Petersburg was only waiting for the stars on
her lover's collar to make him happy; how the Yankees
would be wiped out of the Peninsula as soon as Jack Magruder got his nails pared for fight; how three Yankees
had been gobbled that day, and how others were in the net
to be taken in the morning. The bacchanal was at its highest when Jack, dashing into the open doorway, placed himself between the drinkers and their arms, and cried, sternly,
as he pointed his pistol at the group:

"Surrender, men! You are surrounded!"

"Close up, there! Keep your guns on a line with the
windows; don't fire till I give the order!" Barney could be
heard at the window in suppressed tones, as he, too, covered
the maudlin company. Gabe and his brother added to the
effect of numbers by clattering the stirrups of the horses, so
that the clearing seemed alive with armed men.

The troopers, sobered and astonished, half rose, and then
as these sounds of superior force emphasized the menace of
Jack's pistol in front and Barney's in the rear, they sank
back in their seats, the spokesman saying, tipsily:

"I don't see as we've much choice."

"No, you have no choice.—Sergeant, bring in the cords," Jack ordered.

Barney at this came in with a clothes-line Jack had prepared from the negroes' posts. The arms of the three men were bound behind them, and then Jack retired with his aide to hold a council of war. Without the negro they could never retrace their way to Dick. But how could they carry the prisoners with them ? Manifestly it could not be done. It was then agreed that Barney should take the prisoners, the horses, and the old man, with the younger boys, and make for the Union lines, not a mile distant. Jack, meanwhile, with little Gabe, would go to the rescue of Dick. If firing were heard later, Barney would understand that his friends were in peril, and, if the Union outposts were in sufficient strength, they could come to the rescue, and, perhaps, add to the captures of the night. Barney was now serious enough. He was reminded of no joke by the present dilemma, and remained very solemn, as Jack enlarged on the glories of the proposed campaign. How all Acredale would applaud the intrepidity of its townsmen snatching glory from peril ! Barney consented to leave him with reluctance, suggesting that the "ould nagur" could take the prisoners "beyant."

"Gabe has shown sense and courage, and I shall be much more likely to reach Dick and extricate him and Jones, alone, than if I had this cavalcade at my heels."

Jack and Barney were forced to laugh at the big-eyed wonder in old Rafe's eyes when he was informed of the imposing part he was to play in the warlike comedy. To be guard over "white folks," to dare to look them in the face without fear of a blow, in all his sixty years Rafael Hinton had never dreamed such a mission for a man of color. The troopers, too tipsy and subdued to remark the sudden paucity of the force that had overcome them, were tied upon their own steeds, Barney in front of the leader, and Rafe and his son in charge of the two others.

Rafe led the way in trembling triumph. He knew the ford, indeed, every foot of the country, and had no misgivings about reaching the Union lines. Jack watched the squad until it disappeared in the fringe of trees, and then, turning to the tearful Gabe, said, encouragingly:

"Now, we must do as well when we go among the Union soldiers. You know the point in the swamp I have told about. How long will it take us to reach that the shortest way?"

"Ef we had dad's dugout we could save right smart."

"You mean we could get there by water?"

"Yes, sah. We ken go all froo de swamp in a boat."

"Then I'm afraid it is not the place I mean, for we found as much land as water."

"Dey ain't no odder swamp neah heah, sah."

"Well, we'll try my route first. If that misleads us, we shall try the boat. Can you find it?"

"Suah."

"Where is it?"

"Ober neah the blockhouse. De sogers done tuk it to fish."

"Ah, yes, the blockhouse! I must look into that! Now, we must hurry. Skirt the edge of the water and make no noise."

This was a needless warning to the boy, who, barefooted and scantily clad, gave Jack as much as he could do to keep up with him. They had left the cabin a mile or more behind them to the southeastward, and were somewhere near the spot Jack had emerged from the cypress swamp, when both were brought to a halt by shifting clouds of smoke pouring out from the underwood.

"Where does that come from?" Jack asked, throwing himself flat to catch his breath.

"Dunno, sah. Most likely de sojers sot de brush on fiah."

When Jack was able to look again he saw far in among the trees a moving wave of light now and then, as the heavy curtain of smoke was lifted by the wind.

"Good heavens!" he ejaculated; "it was in there I left my friends. Can we get to them?"

"No, sah; der ain't no crick dah."

"Then !" Jack thought, "have I sacrificed Dick and Jones in my zeal to be adventurous ? Ten minutes sooner, and we could have gone in and brought them out. But I will find a way in, if I have to clamber over the tree-tops."

The noise of whirring wings, the rush of startled animals, now drowned all other sounds, until, through the tumult from the copse far in front of them, they heard the clatter of swords, and then gigantic figures breaking toward them, along the edge of the pond.

"Down, down; hug the ground!" Jack cried, pushing the boy down into the reeds. Almost as they sank, a group of troopers dashed by, talking excitedly.

"Fire at random, men; that will force them into cover! If we can keep them in ambush till daylight, the dogs will be here, and we shall nab them," Jack heard a voice say as the men rode past.

How could they have heard of the affair so quickly, for Jack took it for granted that it was his exploit that the troopers were afoot to balk ? Still another group passed, and they were talking of the dogs that were expected.

"You may depend upon it, they are in the swamp. They are making off that way and hope to mislead us by firing the place. We must keep our eyes peeled on the swamp. The creek will stop them down yonder, and we must watch this break in the brush. As soon as the dogs come we shall have no trouble. They'll run 'em down in no time."

Jack had heard enough to warn him that it was useless to try to penetrate the swamp. With half of his usual wit, Dick would have been *en route* long before this, for the fiery glow in the woods showed that the flames had been raging some time. Unless Jones's illness had handicapped him, Dick would be on his way, following Jack's route as closely as the darkness would permit. But now he must seek means to evade the dogs. This could be done only by reaching the water and getting into it far from the point where they proposed to leave it.

"Can you find the boat?" he asked Gabe, who chattered between his teeth.

"I fink so, sah."

"Very well; we must find a small stream running into the pond, and then lead me to the boat."

"Moccasin Brook is close yonder, sah. Shall I go dah?"

"Yes, like lightning."

In a few minutes they were in a sluggish current, running between masses of reeds and spreading lily-leaves, into the pond. Here Jack repeated Jones's manœuvre, except that he was not wise enough in woodcraft to make use of a tree to get into the water, and thus leave the dogs at the end of the trail at a point far removed from his real entrance into it. When they had reached the pond, Jack bade the boy lead to the boat. This they found moored under a bluff, and Gabe, pointing upward, said the blockhouse was there.

"Very well, you stay here in the boat and wait for me. Don't stir, don't speak, no matter what you see or hear. Will you do this?"

"Oh, yes, sah; 'deed, 'deed I will, sah!"

Jack crawled up the bank, keeping in the shadow of the uneven ground, until he reached a point whence he could make out the blockhouse. It was a half-finished structure of rough logs, and, from the stakes and other signs of engineering preliminaries, he saw that it was intended as the guard-house of a fortification. He could hear the drawl of languid, half-sleepy voices, and, as he pushed farther to the eastward, saw a group of troopers lounging about a dying fire. A sentry sat before the doorway, which had no door. He was dozing on his post, though now and then he aroused himself to listen to the comments of the men at the fire. While Jack waited, irresolute what to do, a volley sounded across the pond, evidently the fellows whom he had seen, keeping up the fusillade to distract the fugitives.

"They've wasted enough lead to fight a battle," he heard one of the men say, scornfully.

"Well, that's what lead's for," a philosopher remarked,

stirring the embers. " So it don't get under my skin, I don't care a cuss what they do with it."

" Oh, your skin's safe enough, Ned. You may adorn a gallows yet."

" If I do, you'll be at one end of the string—and I ain't a-saying which end, neither," the other retorted, taking a square segment of what looked like bark, but was really tobacco, and worrying out a circle with his teeth, until he had detached a large mouthful. This affording his jaws all the present occupation they seemed capable of undertaking, the other resumed when the haw-haw that met the sally had subsided:

" Yes, it takes two to make a hangin', just like it takes two to make a weddin', and you can't allus say just sartin which one has the lucky end."

This facetious epigram was duly relished, and the sage was turning his toasted side from the fire to present the other, when the clatter of a horse coming up the hillside sent the group scouring toward their guns, stacked near the unfinished walls.

" Sergeant Bland, the captain orders you to take four men and station them along the north shore of the pond. The rascals are in the cypress swamp, and are making their way out toward Moccasin Creek. One man can watch the block-house, and the rest come with me.—Guard, we shall be within a hundred yards of you. A shot will bring a dozen men to your assistance; but it isn't likely an enemy can reach this point. The whole regiment is deployed in the woods."

This was said to the sentry as the group, detailed for Moccasin Creek, filed off at a double-quick down the hill. In a few moments the blockhouse was deserted, save by the sentry, who had now risen and was vigorously pacing before the doorway. Now was Jack's time, if ever. If he could only whisper to one of the prisoners to call the sentry. But how ? He had nothing to fear in approaching the rear, and in a few moments he had examined the walls. There was no opening where he could get speech with those inside. What could he do? To boldly fall upon the sentry was risky, for the slightest noise would bring rescue from the front of the bluff. At the base of the wall, where the log-joists rested upon a huge bowlder, his quick eye detected an air-hole. He examined it hurriedly. It was evidently below the flooring. So much the better. Putting his mouth to this, he called out in a piteous tone:

"For God's sake, sentry, give me some water! I'm choking—oh—oh water! water!"

He waited to see if the sentry would heed the call. He knew that the men inside could not betray him, for, if they were not asleep, they could not be sure that the voice was not from among themselves. Sure enough, the sentry's step ceased. Was he near the door? Jack crept to the corner. Yes, he had halted at the aperture. Would he enter? Jack stepped back to his post, as the guard called out:

"Where are you? Which of you wants water? Sing out!"

"Here!" Jack cried. "Here!" Then darting back to the corner, he was just in time to see the man lean his gun against the door-post, and disappear in the hut. In an instant the gun was in Jack's possession, and he was behind the Samaritan in quest of the suffering victim. It was dark as a tunnel. Jack's victim still gave him the aid he needed, for, as he groped along the wall, he said, good-humoredly:

"Sing out again, my friend; I haven't got cat's eyes."

Jack's grasp was on his throat and Jack's mouth was at his ear.

"One sound, one word, and this knife goes to the hilt in your heart!"

The astounded man half reeled at this awful apparition in the black darkness, and he limply yielded to his captor under the impression that the prisoners were loose and upon him. Jack tied the man's unresisting hands with his own canteen-straps; then seated him near the wall and lighted a match. Four men, undisturbed by this swift and noiseless coup, were stretched on the board floor, breathing the heavy, deep sleep of exhaustion. Jack aroused them with the greatest difficulty, and found it still harder to make them understand that, with courage and resolution, they would be back in their own lines by daylight. When this became clear to them they were as eager and energetic as their rescuer. The men were to remain near the blockhouse, but not in it, until Jack returned for the negro, and then under the lad's guidance they could find their way to the Union outposts. Just as this was decided, a blood-curdling baying of bloodhounds echoed across the pond from the distant cabin. Jack trembled, his mind at once on Dick, so near and yet so far from him now, in this new danger. There was not a moment to be lost. Perhaps even now all the night's hard-won victories were to be turned to worse than defeat—prison, death; for the liberation of slaves was at that time punishable by hanging in the rebel military code.

"Courage," he said to himself, grimly; "courage, a dog's no worse than a man. We've overcome them to-night, we ought to be able to tackle the dogs." This new danger changed his plan slightly. Instead of leaving all the men, he took one of the rescued four, Tom Denby by name, with him, and set out for the water. But here another check met him. He suddenly recalled that the guard at the blockhouse had been scattered along the shore to watch the debouch from the swamp. This enforced a wide *détour*, bringing him out in the rear of the boat and nearer the point where Moccasin Creek emptied into the pond. They reached it finally, and skirting along the shore kept a keen eye on the water for the boat. They had skurried along half-way back toward the bluff, listening for a sound on the water and peering into the black surface, when Denby suddenly touched Jack's arm.

"There's a horse or cow standing in the water yonder. I've seen it move; there, look!"

Yes, outlined against the low horizon, a monstrous shape could be plainly seen. The yelp of the hounds suddenly broke through the air back of them toward the creek. The

monstrous figure started, moved heavily forward, then
seemed as if coming toward them. Both waited, wondering, curious, terrified. It was within a rod of them, stagger-
ing, gasping.

"Oh, God help us! I can go no farther; better be taken
than both drown together."

Jack could hardly repress a cry:

"Jones—Dick! Is it you ?"

But whoever it was or whatever it was had no speech to
answer this eager inquiry. They would have sunk in the
shallow water if Jack and Denby had not caught them.
Jack had food with him, and, better than all, the bottle of
sorghum whisky. With this restorative, both were soon
able to sit upon the ground and eat. Jack left Denby to
feed them, while he went in search of the boat. He found
it just where he had left it, and in a few minutes, at the head
of his little band, he was back at the blockhouse. The food
and Jack's hastily told news had restored Dick to something
like his old friskiness.

"Jericho!" he cried, as the released prisoners, having
held back warily until the color of the new-comers was
known, ran forward. "The whole army is here. I feel as
if I were in the Union lines."

"Well, you ain't, by a long shot," Denby cried. "We've
got a good hour's march, and if you're wise, Captain Sprague,
you won't waste time for any frills."

"No time shall be wasted.—Jones, you and Dick take
the rear. I, with Denby, will skirmish ; and you, Corporal
Kane, shall command the center. No firing, remember,
unless superior force assails us.—Gabe, stick to the water-
side as closely as you can, but make the shortest cut to the
bridge."

Gabe was the most delighted darkey in all Virginia for
the next hour. He led them swiftly and surely, and why
shouldn't he ? He had passed all his life in the vicinity,
and with the first beams of the sun he pointed to a narrow
wooden bridge.

"Dar's whar de pickets fire across."

As they passed the bridge a loud sound of rushing horses could be heard in the distance.

"Dick, you take two men and hurry down the road to assure our pickets that we are friends. We'll take up the planks to give them time!" Jack shouted, and Dick, with two of the rescued prisoners, dashed away. Many hands and high hope made short work of the light timbers. As the pursuing cavalry turned the bend in the road, in sight of the bridge, Jack's squad gave them a volley and then dashed into cover. The fire was returned. Dick, coming back at a run, with a dozen dismounted men, heard the bullets whistling over his head and saw Jack's *posse* dispersing to the right and left in the bushes. All were forced into the woods, as the rebels commanded the highway.

"Where is Jack?" Dick asked, rushing among the men. No one had noticed him in the panic. He was not in the huddle that cowered in the reeds to escape the balls, still hurtling viciously over the open. With a cry of rage and despair, Dick flew into the road, and there, not a hundred yards from the bridge, he saw the well-known figure prone on the red earth motionless — dead? Heedless of the warning cries of the others, Dick tore madly to the body, and with a wild cry fell upon the lifeless figure, weltering in blood.

CHAPTER XXVII.

"THE ABSENT ARE ALWAYS IN THE WRONG."

UNDER Vincent's ardent escort Mrs. Sprague and Merry traveled from Richmond northward in something like haste and with as much comfort as was possible to the limited means of transportation at the command of the Confederate commissary. Even in those early days of the war, the railway system of the South was worn out and inadequate.

Such a luxury as a parlor-car was unknown. The trains were filled with military personages on their way to the field. Mrs. Sprague and Merry were the only women in the car in which they passed from Richmond to Fredericksburg. The route brought them through a land covered with hamlets of camps, drilling squadrons, and the panoply of war. While the elder lady gave a divided mind to the strange panorama, Merry watched everything eagerly, amused and interested by this spectacle of preparation. Such soldiers as she could see distinctly looked like farmers in holiday homespun ; the cavalry like nondescript companies of backwoods hunters. There seemed to be no uniformity in infantry equipment or cavalry accoutrements, and the discipline struck her as in keeping with this diversity of dress and ornament. The men could be seen hurrying in boyish glee toward the train as it drew near the temporary station, where mail-bags were thrown out and sometimes supplies of food or munitions of war. Jocular remarks were passed between the soldiery at the windows when the wistful groups gathered along the railway line.

"I say, North Cal'ina, you'n's goin' straight through to Yankee land ?" a man in the throng shouts to some one on the train.

"Straight."

"Send us a lock o' Lincoln's hair to poison blind adders, will you ?"

"No—promised his scalp to my sweetheart to cover the rocking-chair."

Then, as the laugh that met this sally died away, another humorist piped out :

"Tell Uncle Joe Johnston we're just rustin' down here for a fight ; ef he don't hurry up we'll go ahead ourselves. We're drilled down so fine now that we can't think 'cept by the rule o' tactics."

"Jest you never mind, boys. Uncle Joe'll do enough thinkin' fur ye when he gets ready to tackle the Yanks."

"Hurrah for Uncle Joe !" And as the cheery cry swelled farther and farther, the train drew out, everybody looking from the windows as the patient soldiery straggled back campward.

"Your soldiers seem very gay, Vincent. One would think that war, the dreadful uncertainty of their movements, absence of friends, and lack of good food would sadden them," Mrs. Sprague said wistfully at one of the stations when raillery like this had been even more pointed and boisterous.

"A wise commander will do all he can to keep his men gay ; if they were not jovial they'd go mad. Think of it ! Day after day, week after week, who knows but year after year, the wearisome monotony of camp and march! Where the men are educated, or at least readers, they make better soldiers, because they brood less. Brooding saps the best fiber of the army. Your Northern men ought to have an advantage there, for education is more general with you than it is with us. It is not bravery that makes a man eager for the campaign, it is unrest. As a rule, the best soldiers in action are those who have a mortal dread of battle."

"That surprises me."

"It is true. I always distrust men that clamor to be led on ; they are the first to break when the brush comes. Jack will tell you that, for we are agreed on it."

"Jack himself was eager for battle," Mrs. Sprague said, sighing.

"No, Jack was eager for the field. When the battle comes he meets it coolly, but he has no hunger for it, nor have I. General Johnston is as brave a man as ever headed an army, yet he has often told us that his blood freezes when the guns open. I'm sure no one would ever suspect it, for he is as calm and confident as if he were in a quadrille when he rides to the field."

"We in the North have heard more of Beauregard than Johnston, yet I never hear you mention him. Wasn't it he who commanded at Bull Run ?"

"Yes and no. General Beauregard is a superb soldier. He is, it has been agreed among us, better for a desperate charge, or some sudden inspiration in an emergency, than the complicated strategy that half wins a battle before it is begun. For example, at Manassas he would have been defeated, our whole army captured, if fortune had not exposed General McDowell's plans before they were completed. As it was, we should have been driven from the field if General Johnston had not come up in time and rearranged the Confederate lines."

"Yes, Jack has described that. Battles, after all, are decided by luck."

"And genius."

"Luck won Waterloo."

"Partly, but genius, too, for Wellington and Blücher practiced one of Napoleon's most perfect maxims, and won because he despised them both so much that he didn't dream them capable of even imitating him. Nor, left to themselves, would they have been equal to it. But renegade Frenchmen, taught under Napoleon's eye, prompted them."

"General Johnston was very considerate to us when we came down. I wish you would make him know how grateful we are."

"Oh, he couldn't be anything else ; he is the ideal of a chivalrous knight."

"Yes, I believe you claim chivalry as your strong point in the South, and accuse us of being a race of sordid money-getters."

"I don't, for I know better, but our people do. They will learn better in time. Men who fought as your army fought at Manassas must be more than mere sordid hucksters."

"And yet it is curious," Mrs. Sprague continued, musingly, "it is we who are warring for an idea and you are warring for property."

"How do you mean ?" Vincent said, quickly.

"You are fighting to continue slavery, to extend it ; we to abolish it or limit it. But even I can see that slavery is doomed. No Northern party would ever venture to give it toleration after this."

" But if we succeed, it will exist in our union at least."

" Ah, Vincent, can't you see that such a people as ours may be checked, beaten even, but they will never give up the Union ? Why, much as I love Jack, I would never let him leave the colors while there was an army in the field. Don't you know every Northern mother has the same feeling ? "

" And every Southern mother, too."

" Yes, I believe that, but there's this difference : Your Southern mothers are counting on what doesn't exist—a higher physical courage—a prowess in battle, I may call it, that you must know the Southern soldier has not, as distinguished from the Northern. As time goes on and the war does not end ; as our armies become disciplined, the confidence that supports your side will die, and then the struggle, though it may be prolonged, will end in our triumph."

" I don't think it. I can't think it. But don't let us talk about it. We, at least, are as much friends as though Jack and I were under one flag, and if it depends on me it shall be always so."

" If it depends on us, it shall never be otherwise." She gave the young man a kind, scrutinizing glance, which made his heart beat joyously and his handsome cheeks mount color. At Fairfax Court-House they said farewell, the ladies continuing the journey in an ambulance under Federal guard.

They passed over the long bridge three days after the famous night at Rosedale, of whose exciting sequel they were profoundly ignorant. In her husband's time Mrs. Sprague had lived in hotels in the capital, as the sessions were short; she had never remained in the city when the warm weather set in, no matter how long the term lasted. But on her arrival at the old hotel now, she was a good deal disturbed to learn that she could not be accommodated in her former quarters. The military crowded not only this but every hotel in the city, and it was only after long search that a habitable apartment was found in Georgetown. On

21

the whole, the necessity that drove her thither was not an unmitigated adversity, for Georgetown then was far more desirable for residence than Washington. Nothing could be more depressing than the city at that epoch. Every visible object in the vast circumference of its spreading limits was then naked—unkempt. Even the trees, that ranged themselves irregularly in the straggling squares and wide street areas, stretched out a draggled and piebald plumage, as if uncertain whether beauty or ugliness were their function in the *ensemble*.

The photographic realism of the later newspaper correspondent had not come into play in these earlier years of the war, and, as a consequence, the thousands who poured down to the Army of the Potomac beheld the city with something of the incredulous scorn with which the effeminate Byzantines regarded the capital of the Goths, when the corrupt descendant of Constantine made the savage Dacians his allies, rather than fight them. Patriotism, however, not pride, marked the common mold of the men of the civil war. It may have been that many an honest plowman, marching through the muddy quagmires of Pennsylvania Avenue, bethought himself that such a capital was hardly worth while marching so far to protect—more emphatically so when the enemy was really to be found on lines far north of it! Sentiment is the heart and soul of war; if it were not, there would be no war, for war never gained as much as it loses ; never settled as much as it unsettles ; never left victor or vanquished better when the last gun was fired! In old times the capture of a nation's capital meant the end of the war, but we have seen capitals captured and the war not modified a bit by it. Washington was seized and burned by the British in 1814, and the war went on ; Paris was held by the Germans for half a year, and the war went on.

Our civil war would have been three campaigns shorter —Burnside's, Hooker's, and the stupid massacre of Pope— to say nothing of the saving of untold treasure, had the political authorities abandoned a capital which must be defended for a secure seat like New York or Philadelphia. The sagacious Lincoln, whose action in army matters was paralyzed by cliques, in the end saw through sham with an inspired clarity of vision, and proposed the measure, but the backwoods Mazarin, Seward, prepared such voluminous "considerations" in opposition that the good-natured President withdrew his suggestion, and, as a consequence, the dismal Ilium on the Potomac became the bone of a four years' contention, whose vicissitudes exceed the incidents of the Iliad. Great armies, created by an inspired commander, were wasted upon the defense of a capital that no one would have lamented had it been again burned, and of which to-day there is scarcely a remnant, save in the public buildings and the topographical charts. A new race entered the sleepy city. The astute, far-seeing Yankee divined the possibilities of the future, where the indolent, sentimental Southerner had never taken thought of a nation's growth and a people's pride! The thrifty and shifty patriots sent from the North at once took a stake in the city, and thenceforward there was growth, if not grace, in the capital.

Lincoln's Washington was to the capital of to-day what the Rome of Numa was to the imperial city of Augustus. Never, in its best days, more imposing than a wild Western metropolis of to-day, the sudden inrush of armies and the wherewithal to supply and house them, soon gave the vast spaces laid out for the capital the uncouthness and incompleteness of an exaggerated mining town or series of towns. Contrasted even with its rival on the James, Washington was raw, chaotic, squalid.

Long tenure of estates and little change in the people had given Richmond the venerableness we associate with age. Many of her picturesque seven hills were transformed into blooming fields or umbrageous groves, under which vast villa-like edifices clustered in Grecian repose. Save in the bustling main streets none of the edifices were new or raw, or wholly unlovely in design or fabric. In Washington nothing of this could be seen. Staring brick walls, buildings of unequal height and fatiguingly ugly designs, uprose here and there in morasses of mud that were meant for streets. Disproportionate outline, sharp conjunctures of affluence and squalor, accented the disheartening hideousness of the scene.

But upon this uncouth stage a great drama was going on; great figures were in action; momentous events were hourly taking form and consequence; men and women at their best and worst were working out the awful ends of Fate. In the large mansion yonder, the wisest, greatest, simplest of mankind—by times Diogenes and Cromwell, Lafayette and Robespierre—was, in jest and joke, mirth and sadness, working out his own and a people's sublime destiny. It was to this curiously unequal personage that Mrs. Sprague, after fruitless pleading with her husband's friends, came finally to secure action on behalf of her son. There was little of the ceremonial needed to gain access to the Chief Magistrate which is now the fashion.

She found a care-worn man, deeply harassed, standing in the low-ceiled room, in which the Cabinet had met a few moments before. A sweet, wan smile—the instinctive, inborn sensitiveness of a noble nature—flickered over the rugged lines of the face as the usher, retiring, said:

"Mr. President, this is Mrs. Sprague, whom you ordered to be admitted."

"I am both glad and sorry to meet you, madam. I knew your husband, the Senator, in other and happier times. I wish that it were in my power to do for him or his what he was always doing for the unhappy or distressed."

"Ah! how kind you are! How—"

She was going to say different from what she expected, but bethought herself of the ungraciousness of this form, since at that time Mr. Lincoln was the object of almost universal misreport and caricature.

"How can I say what a mother should say?"

While she spoke he began pacing the apartment, each time, as he came to the double window near which she sat, peering out with a yearning, far-away look toward the river and the red lines of the hills beyond it. Then turning back,

he strode the length of the long baize-covered table, sometimes
absently picking up a document, until, facing her again as she
narrated the story of Jack's misfortunes, he would fling it
hastily on the scattered heaps and fix his mild eye upon her.

"I know all this already, dear madam. It has come to
me from the boy's friends, and"—he hesitated a second—
"and from his—or from those who are not his friends."

"Not his friends?" the mother cried, half rising. "Why,
Mr. President, Jack hasn't an enemy in the world!"

"You came through from Richmond last week? Have
you heard nothing from your son since you saw him?"

"Nothing. Oh, is there anything about him?"

"You have not even read the newspapers, I see."

"No, no; I have been so uncertain, so agitated, so constantly in attendance upon our members, that I have had no
time to read or even talk. But, pray tell me! Your manner
indicates that something has happened. O Mr. President,
think of my anxiety! My only son!"

"Ah, Mrs. Sprague! It is I that should be pitied here.
You came to me for comfort. You came in reliance on my
power to restore your son, and I—I have the burden of telling you very grievous news. No, no, your son is not dead,
have no fear of that, if in the end it prove a comfort. Last
night your townsman, Elisha Boone, came to me with his
heart-broken daughter, demanding vengeance for his son's
death, whom your boy had slain the very night you left him
on the James. He shot Captain Boone in the house you visited, and defeated a well-arranged plan to capture the rebel
chief, Davis. Not only this, but he endangered the escape
of a number of sorely-worn prisoners who had succeeded in
reaching the Rosedale place and halted only to make Davis's
capture certain."

"My son shot Wesley! oh no, no; it can not be; or, if he
did, it was because his own life was in peril. Ah! no, no,
Mr. President, do not believe this. I know my son. I know
the misery he endured in Wesley's company; endured like
a hero; endured like a Sprague. He must have been in
peril of his life."

"Dear madam, I feel for you. I feel with you, but these facts are all in the possession of the Secretary of War. Mr. Boone will no doubt give you all the details. If it can be made to seem as you say, have no fear that I will wink at mere revenge, or make the machinery of justice an instrument of family feuds. Get your lawyer; have the matter investigated, and rely upon me for every proper clemency and aid in your hard lot."

She had arisen long before, and, recognizing this as a dismissal, she bowed, unable to speak, and, with blinded eyes, staggered toward the two steps leading upward from the room. She would have fallen had the ready arm of the President not been near to support her. In the anteroom he said, huskily:

"Captain, send an orderly to accompany this lady to her carriage."

Merry was in the carriage. One glance at Mrs. Sprague's face told that dire news had been heard. She did not ask a question, but, embracing and supporting the sobbing mother, awaited patiently for the dreaded revelation. When at length the miserable story came in gaspings and sobs, the spinster exhibited an unexpected firmness.

"I don't believe a word of it. If Jack shot Wesley, it was because he was in some sort of treacherous business. You may depend upon it, that, when we get the true story, Jack's part will prove him in the right. I am going this instant to Boone to learn his source of information. He can have nothing but rumors."

"I will go. It is better for me to see Mr. Boone. He will not venture to misrepresent to me."

At Willard's, where Boone was stopping, the ladies were obliged to wait a long time, and, in the end, it was Kate who appeared before them in deep black, with a half-yearning, half-defiant expression in the sadly worn face. They would never have recognized her, and, as it was, Merry started with a slight scream as the dark figure stopped before them.

"Papa begs to be excused. He supposes that you want

to hear the particulars of the—the affair at Rosedale, and bids me tell you."

"O Kate, Kate, it is not true! it can not be true. Oh, you who knew Jack so well, you know that he never could have—have—"

Kate had seized a chair and drawn it before the two who sat on one of the long sofas that filled without adorning the vast hotel parlor, dim even at noonday in its semi-subterranean light.

"Yes, Mrs. Sprague, your son shot Wesley deliberately; shot him as deliberately as if I should draw a pistol and take your life now and here."

"And—and killed him?"

"He never spoke again. He—he—ah! I can not, I can not! We brought him here. His body is in the cemetery, waiting the military formalities."

"But tell us how it happened, Kate," Merry sobbed, entreatingly. "We know nothing but what you have told us. Tell us all. It is so startling, so awful, that we can not comprehend such a thing happening where we left everybody in the most friendly spirit."

Kate, struggling with her tears, told the story so far as she knew it, but of course she knew little beyond the mere fact that Wesley had come to his death in Mrs. Atterbury's room; that Jack stood over him with the smoking pistol, and owned that he had fired in the darkness. She told the tale as gently as might be, her own heart secretly pleading for everything of extenuation that might lessen Jack's guilt, but she had insensibly taken the darker view her father had instantly adopted, that Jack's enmity had led him to seize the chance to rid himself of a rival and enemy under cover of defending the Atterburys. She did not hint this to the mother, but Merry, knowing Boone, at once saw what the President's words meant. Boone had charged Jack with deliberate murder. Dreading the realization of this by Mrs. Sprague at this time, Merry made a sign to Kate, who, comprehending at once, arose and begged to go back to her father, who was in need of her.

"Oh, if Olympia were here! she has so much self-control! she would advise so well what should be done!" the mother moaned, as she passed down through the long, barrack-like parlor.

"But, dear Mrs. Sprague, Olympia is just where her good sense is most needed. She is near Jack. He needs comfort and counsel. You can have your lawyer, and you shall see the case isn't so bad as we have heard. You must remember that the Boones are not likely to take an impartial view. It is only human nature that they should think the worst of the—the—death of son and brother. Wait till we hear Jack's story, and you will see that it puts a different face on the matter."

"But it's Jack's disgrace and death they want. That was what the President meant. I didn't understand it then; I do understand it now. They shall not murder him! I shall command him to remain in Richmond. I shall command him to join Vincent. The North is unworthy of such men as my son. He is too pure, too innocent, too high-minded to be understood by the coarse natures that have come to power in the country. I shall not let this odious Boone destroy him as he ruined your brother."

"O Mrs. Sprague, think what you are saying! Think how fatal such words would be, if Jack were brought to trial! You see every day in the press how all are suspected of treason who were Democrats in the old days. I know very well that you do not mean this. Much as I love Jack, I would rather see him in his grave with the Union flag over him than in the rebel lines, a soldier of that bad cause. As to my poor brother, Boone was only an accident in his ruin. If it had not been Boone, it would have been some one else. Put the whole matter in the hands of Simon Brodie. He is almost a Sprague. He will see that the son of his old patron has justice."

Simon Brodie, of Warchester, was the chief advocate of the three counties. He had studied law with the late Senator Sprague, and, at his death, from partner succeeded to his lucrative law practice. He came at once to Washington at

Mrs. Sprague's summons, and set about learning the status
of the case. The affair was no easy matter to trace, but, after
inconceivable delays and persistent misleading, he found
that Jack was in the military archives charged with desertion, murder, and treason: desertion in quitting his company
and regiment without orders, treason in consorting with
armed rebels, and murder in joining with the enemies of
the country to take the life of his commanding officer.
Meanwhile, Mrs. Sprague and Merry had returned to Acredale, and the lawyer sent letters to Richmond setting forth
the case to Jack—letters which, by some mysterious jug-
glery, never reached their address, as we have seen. Nothing could be done until Jack was either exchanged or until
his advocate had made out a documentary case that could
be presented to the military authorities. As he surmised,
every one in authority had been prejudiced against Jack.
The Congressman from Warchester dared not work against
Boone, who was potent as a Cabinet minister in the councils
of the Government. One of Senator Sprague's old friends,
still in the Senate, advised Brodie to let Jack remain at
Richmond till the peace came, "for," said he, "no Democrat
nor any one identified with that party can hope for impartial justice here."

"But what am I to do? I can get no assistance here.
Every bureau containing documents bearing on the poor
boy's case is either closed to me, or the officials so hostile that
I can not work with or through them."

"You must go about the affair as if it were a State matter. You must go to McClellan. He is a young man of the
most spotless honor, the most generous sympathies. He is
as rigid as a Prussian in discipline, but his methods are enlightened and above board. He is the only man in authority
that has any real conception of the magnitude of the struggle the North has entered upon. He is, however, miserably
hampered. The new rulers have come down to Washington very much in the spirit of the Goths when they captured Rome. Every one is on the make. The contract system is something beyond the wildest excesses I ever read of

in pillage and chicanery. Shoes by the million have been accepted that melt as soon as they are wet; garments are stacked mountain-high in the storehouses that blow into rags so soon as the air goes through them. Food, moldy, filthy, is accumulated on the wharves of Washington, Baltimore, and Alexandria that would be forbidden as infectious in any carefully guarded port in the world. Contracts for vessels have been signed where steamships are called for, and the contractor sends canal-boats. Lines of ships are paid for to run to ports not known in navigation; and the chief men in the great departments share the money with the rings—"

"But why don't you expose it?"

"Expose it? A word in the Senate against these villainies is set down as disloyalty. All that a rascal needs to gain any scope he pleases, is to say 'rebel sympathizer,' and Fort Warren or Lafayette is held up as a menace."

Among the confidential aides of McClellan Brodie knew intimately a young officer, the son of a distinguished lady, whose writings delighted cultivated people fifty years ago. This young man, Captain Churchland, had often been a guest at the Spragues, and to him Brodie went for advice. Inheriting a great deal of his mother's intellect, with a droll sense of humor, not then so well understood as the lighter school of writers have since made it, Churchland was the delight of the headquarters. He listened to the melancholy story of Jack's compromising plight.

"It's a bad fix—no mistake," he said, gravely; "but I suggest that your fiery young friend come home and shoot the father, marry the daughter, and, as a wife can't testify against the husband, your client is secure."

"Ah, captain, it's not a matter for joking. Think of his wretched mother."

"That's just what I do think of—murder's no joke, though it's more of a fine art than it was when De Quincey wrote. I'm perfectly serious. I would shoot the scoundrel Boone. Why, do you know the man has cleared a million dollars on rotten blankets since he came here? McClellan ordered a report made out showing his rascalities a few weeks ago.

It was disapproved at the War Office, and the condemned blankets have gone to Halleck's army. Doesn't that deserve shooting? Napoleon directed all the army contractors to be hanged. I say shoot them. For every one put out of the way a thousand soldiers' lives will be saved."

"Well, well, let Boone go. It's Sprague I'm interested in."

"So am I. It is Sprague that Boone seems to be interested in, too, for he has filled the new Secretary with, what he himself would call, righteous wrath against the poor boy and his friends. But make your mind easy. The exchange of prisoners will soon begin. Sprague's turn will come among the first, and then I will keep track of the affair. Beyond that I can promise nothing. You may be sure, so far as purely military men have to do with the business, there will be impartial justice. When the politicians take hold, I can give no assurance."

And with this cold comfort the disheartened lawyer betook himself to Acredale, where his report, guardedly given, brought no very strong hope to the anxious mother.

CHAPTER XXVIII.

THE WORLD WENT VERY ILL THEN.

ACREDALE was not the sleepy, sylvan scene we first saw it, when Mrs. Sprague and Merry drove through the wide main street from the station, four months after they had quitted it in search of their soldier boys. The stately elms still arched the highway to Warchester, but here and there rough gaps were seen in the trim hedge-rows. Staring new edifices jutted through these breaks upon the grassy walks, and building material lay heaped in confusion all along the graveled walks. Merry railed at these evidences of commercial invasion, wondering who had come to the vil-

lage to transform it into city hideousness. Mrs. Sprague did
not give much heed to her companion's speculations. Her
mind was far away on the James, wondering where her
boy was. It was very hard to settle down to the common-
places of home life; but, even in all her distraction, Mrs.
Sprague saw that a change had come upon the people as well
as the place. With the war and its desolating sights fresh
in her memory, she saw, with sorrow and aversion, that social
life was gayer than it had ever been, that the rush for wealth
had become a fever, and that the simple ways and homely
joys of the past were now remitted to the very elde.·ly. The
story of Dick's mad pursuit of Jack and the Caribees, after
the disaster at Bull Run, was soon known in every home in
the county. Friends came from far and near to hear the
exciting adventure; and the younger boys, who had been the
lad's classmates in the academy, at once made up a company
of youngsters, adorned by the name of the "Perley Rangers,"
to be in readiness for the hero's command when he should
return.

The feud between the adherents of the houses of Sprague
and Boone had become acrimoniously embittered by the point
of view from which each side saw the conduct of Jack.
Among the Boone feudatories he was set down as a traitor,
a spy, a murderer. The first malignant rumors that reached
the village after the battle were still maintained stoutly by
the Boone lictors. Jack had ingloriously shirked his part in
the battle with the Caribees; he had skulked in the bushes
until the issue was decided, and then had followed the sympathies of his secession family; he had gone to the Atterburys, well known for their hatred to the North. It was to
prove his sincerity in the Southern cause that he had wormed
himself into the confidence of Wesley Boone's comrades, and
in order that he might be chief agent in the frustration of
the plan of escape.

He had won high regard in the Confederacy by saving
Davis from capture. He had, with his own hand, shot Wesley Boone when the plan of capture was on the verge of success. Could anything be clearer than his odious treason?

Hadn't he, of all the unfortunates of the battle, found favor
and luxurious quarters in Richmond ? Hadn't he cunningly
cajoled the Boones into the visit to the rebel household, in
order to wrest the secrets of the Union rescue from them ?
It was in vain that the Perleys and others set forth the real
case. " Very likely, indeed," the Boone side cried, " that
rebels like the Atterburys would receive true Unionists into
their house, and treat them as friends! A real Unionist
would have refused hospitality from the enemies of his
country." There was talk among the more zealous patriots
of having the Sprague family expelled from Acredale. Loyal
zealots looked up the law on expatriation and attainder, and
complained bitterly that no applicable provisions were found
in the statutes. Stirring addresses were sent to the member
from Warchester, imploring him to have laws enacted that
would enable the patriots to deal summarily with covert
treason. It was true that the Spragues had contributed
many thousand dollars toward the equipment of the Caribees, had endowed twenty beds in one of the city hospitals
for the wounded—but this was when Jack expected high
command in the regiment. Failing in that ignoble self-
seeking, he had gone where his heart was, while the family,
to retain their property, remained among the loyal, to insult
their woe and gloat over their misfortunes.

At a great "war meeting" in the town-hall, over which
Boone presided, one thrilling orator hinted that fire, if not
the law, could "relieve a loyal community of the Copperhead's nest!" "It was an insult, as well as a menace, to have
the patrician palace of disloyalty flaunting its grandeurs
among a people loyal and devoted, whose sons and brothers
were battling for the Union. Every rebel sympathizer driven
from the North would strengthen the Union cause; ashes
and salt sowed on the ground their insolent homes had dese-
crated, would be a holy reminder to the loyal, a warning to
the secret foes of the Union."

There were loud expressions of approval, and a solemn
" Amen " to this intrepid plan of campaign. Lawyer Brodie,
who was present, arose under a thunder of discordant notes

—" Copperhead!" " Traitor!" " Dough-face!" " We don't
want to hear from rebel sympathizers! Out with him!" and
other more opprobrious taunts. Now, Brodie was Boone's
counsel, and had been identified with him in some very difficult litigation. It would not do to have him discredited.
The chairman rapped loudly for order.

"I can vouch, my friends, for Mr. Brodie's patriotism.
He is a Democrat, it is true; but he loves the Union. I know
that to be a fact. You can do the Union no better service
than listening to what he has to say."

Brodie, who had held his place, calmly smiled as Boone
sat down, and, surveying the audience from side to side,
began:

" Free speech was one of the cries that aroused the North
in the late campaign. I believe in free speech. I have done
my share toward securing it, but I never was refused it before. I look among the men here and see among you neighbors whom I have known since boyhood, neighbors who have
known me since boyhood, and when I arise here to take a
citizen's part, in a meeting called to aid and comfort the
cause of the Union, I am permitted to speak only by the
personal request of one man. If that is your idea of free
speech, if that is your notion of aiding the Union cause, and
strengthening the hands of the Administration, I don't need
to be in the confidence of the rebel authorities to tell you
that they could ask no more powerful allies than you!
[Sensation.]

" There are three hundred men in this hall. The light is
good, and my eyesight is not impaired; but I can not see
a man among you who was not a Democrat a year or two
ago. There are not fifty men among you that voted for
Abraham Lincoln. [Murmurs.] Are the two hundred and
fifty, then, traitors ? Are they rebel sympathizers ? Are they
Copperheads ? One thousand men marched under the Caribee flag; not a man of them voted for Lincoln. Are they
Copperheads ? This township, by its vote at the last election,
was five to one Democratic. Is this a Copperhead community ? Nearly a half-million dollars have been subscribed

for bounties and war measures; the tax-payers, almost to a man, are Democrats. Is it possible, then, that the Copperheads are supplying the money to carry on the war ? You propose to burn the mansion of my old partner, Senator Sprague! Why ? Because his estate has given more to the Union cause than any other family in the township ? "

"The son has gone over to the rebels," a voice cried.

"Thank you. There—I'm glad you have given me the chance to crush that cowardly calumny—the invention of some envious malefactor. Jack Sprague has gone over to the rebels, just as Anderson and his men went over at Sumter; just as fifteen hundred of his comrades went over at Bull Run; just as some of our sons and brothers here in Acredale went over; just as my friend, Boone's son, went over—because he was surrounded and wounded."

"Stop a moment, if you please, friend Brodie; I protest against your making anything in common between my son and this young man. The matter is to be investigated, and then we can tell better."

Boone spoke in great excitement, and the audience, now feverishly wrought up, urged the lawyer to say his say out. He continued in the trained, impassive tones of the advocate:

"Every one in this room knows the two young men. It would be waste of time for me to strive to make anything in common between John Sprague and Wesley Boone. Here, where they both grew up, that is quite unnecessary."

"I—I—referred to their conduct as soldiers," Boone cried, hoarsely. "My son lost his life in the service of his country. I can't have his name coupled with a—murderer's—with a traitor's."

"Ah, my friend, when hate draws your portrait it is bound to be black. When prejudice holds the pen, your virtues stand in the shade of vice. I will tell John Sprague's story from the day he quit Acredale to the unhappy hour his comrade was killed in the dark, in the sleeping-room of the mother and daughter who had nursed him from the very jaws of death. He was in that house by his father's urgent

request, though it would have needed none to open its doors
to any one in want of succor. Nor," he added, significantly,
" can it be told who killed Wesley Boone until all the shots
fired in Mrs. Atterbury's chamber are accounted for."

Then he narrated rapidly, but tellingly, the substance of
what has been already set down in this history—the facts
taken from Jack's letters and attested by the corroboration
of Barney, Dick, and the company's officers. There was a
visible revulsion in the larger part of the audience as the tale
went on; and when the lawyer wound up with the story of
Mrs. Sprague's baffled efforts in Washington to have her boy
brought North, there was an outburst of applause and a faint
cheer from the younger men for " glorious old Jack."

The factions shifted a good deal after this official render-
ing of the affair. There was no longer any talk of burning
the Sprague property, and opinion was about evenly divided
as to Jack's conduct. December had come, and the township
was busy packing boxes to send to the army. No news
had come North from Richmond. Active movements were
looked for every day, and in the momentous expectation
such lesser incidents as exchange were forgotten or ignored.
The daily journals were filled with details of contemplated
expeditions, and one morning Mrs. Sprague read with beating heart this paragraph in the *Herald :*

" A score or more of the men who escaped from the Richmond prison a few weeks ago, arrived at Washington to-day
from Fort Monroe. The party endured untold privations in
the swamps between Williamsburg and our line on the Warwick, but all came in safely, except two men who died from
the results of their wounds. The expedition was planned
and carried out by an agent of General Butler, who has been
in Virginia since the unfortunate attempt to rescue Captain
Boone of the 'Caribee' regiment. At the moment the
party reached the Union outpost, one of the most daring of
the Union men, Sergeant Jacques of the Caribees, was, it is
thought, mortally wounded."

Merry, too, had seen the story, and came over to show it
to Mrs. Sprague.

"I have seen it, I have seen it. Who of the Caribees can these be? Who is Jacques? I never heard that name here."

"Ah! he must be one of the town recruits. It's a French name."

"Yes, it is part of a rather famous French name," Mrs. Sprague replied, half smiling at Merry's innocence. "Something must be done to get into communication with these escaped men. Some of them must have seen Jack. If there are Caribees among them, you may be sure they have messages from our boys. I think I shall set out for Washington, or ask Mr. Brodie to go."

"That's better. Mr. Brodie can get at the men and you couldn't. I shall be in a fever until we have heard from them."

Brodie agreed with the ladies when, later, they discussed the matter with him, and that evening he set out for Washington. Mrs. Sprague at the tea-table with Merry, who made it a point to give the lonely mother as much of her time as she could spare, was still pondering the paragraph when the sound of carriage-wheels came in through the closed curtains. Then the front door opened without knocking, and there was a rustle in the hallway, and then, with a simultaneous scream, three agitated females, to wit, Mrs. Sprague, Merry, and Olympia, in a confused mass.

"O my child! my child!"

"Mamma!"

"Dearest, dearest Olympia," Merry splutters, wildly embracing both.

"Oh, how delightful to be here, to see you, mamma as peaceful and serene as in the old days! I thought I should never get home. I left Richmond three weeks ago. I was held at Fredericksburg for ten days. Then I had to turn back when we got to Manassas, through some red tape lacking there. But here I am. Here I am at home—ugh!—I shall never quit it again—never."

"But, my child. Tell us—Jack!"

"Jack? Haven't you heard from him? He escaped

22

three weeks ago. It was he who got the men out of the prison. Dick was with him. Surely you have heard of that ?" and Olympia sank into the nearest chair, all the gayety gone from her face, her eyes questioning the two wretched women. Neither could for the moment control her agitation; neither was capable of thinking. All that was in their minds was this dire specter of a month's silence. Alive, Jack or Dick would have found means to relieve their anxiety.

"Surely you heard that a party had escaped from Libby and made their way to Fort Monroe ?" Olympia cried, desperately.

"Fort Monroe ?" Mrs. Sprague echoed mechanically. "Yes, ah, yes. Merry, where's the paper ?"

Olympia devoured the meager scrap and then dropped the journal on her knees. Her mind was in a whirl. In Richmond the escape had been announced, then the news that the party had been surrounded in the swamp, then day by day details of the taking of straggling negroes and one or two soldiers, but no name that even resembled Jack's. The Atterburys, after the first painful sensation, had given their approval of Jack's going, and used all means in their power to get such facts as would comfort Olympia. They assured her that Jack had reached the Union lines, and then she had set out northward, expecting to find him at home or in communication with his family. No word from Dick ? No word from Jack ? They were dead, and she—she had urged them to the mad adventure ! She had given Jack no peace, had fired Dick to the fatal enterprise. She dared not look in the tearless eyes of her mother. She dared not face the ghastly questioning in Merry's meek eye. Brodie had gone down to see the escaped men. Perhaps he would discover something. This was the small comfort left the three when, near midnight, they ended the woful conference.

The next day Olympia was visited by a representative of the *Crossbow*, the chief journal of Warchester, and urged to write a narrative of her adventures in the rebel capital.

Until her friends made her see how much effect it would have in clearing Jack's reputation she shrank from the publicity, but with that end in view—Jack's honor—she wrote, and wrote with strength and clearness, the moving incidents of her brother's capture, captivity, and escape—or his bold effort to escape. This she told so simply, so directly, so vividly, that the truth of it at once struck the most prejudiced reader, who had no cause to continue in his prepossession. After the publication in the Warchester paper scores who had sided with the Boone faction either called or wrote to confess their error. Even the Acredale *Monitor*, a weekly sheet notoriously in the interest of Boone, felt constrained to copy parts of the account and publish with it a shambling retraction of previous criticism, based on imperfect knowledge, that it had printed concerning Sergeant Sprague. "Death," it declared, "has obliterated all feeling that existed against our young townsman, whose conduct, though open to grievous doubt in the early part of his military career, has been amply atoned for in the intrepid enterprise in which he seems to have lost his life."

CHAPTER XXIX.

A WOMAN'S REASON.

THE still, small voice that makes itself a force in the heart, which the poets call our mentor and the moralists conscience, had been painfully garrulous in Kate Boone's breast since the angry parting with Jack at Rosedale. At first, in the wild grief of Wesley's death, she had hugged hatred of Jack to her heart as a sublime revenge for the murder. But with the hot partisanship allayed in the long weeks of reflection preceding the rumor of Jack's own death, she began dimly to admit of palliation in her lover's fatal act. Her father, the Boone faction, all who had access to her, held the shooting to be a craftily planned murder, calculated to bring advantage to the assassin. To check the sacrilegious love she felt in her heart, she too had been forced to believe, to admit the worst. But when the image of Jack came to her mind, as it did day and night, it was as the gay, frank, chivalrous Hotspur, as unlike a murderer as Golgotha to Hesperides. She had never dared to confide to her father that vows had been exchanged between them—that they were, in fact, affianced lovers. He, never suspecting, talked with her day after day of the signal vengeance in store for the miscreant; how he had enlisted the aid of the most powerful in Washington ; how he had instructed the emissaries sent to Richmond to effect Wesley's release, to direct all their energies to entrapping the murderer into the ranks of the escaping prisoners.

She had often been startled by her father's far-seeing, malignantly planned vengeances, and, now that the rumor of Jack's death began to settle into belief, she was appalled by a sudden sense of complicity in a murderous plot. Not that she believed her father capable of murder or its procuration, but, knowing his potency with the authorities, she saw that there were many ways in which Jack might be sacrificed in the natural course of military duties. She had heard things of the sort discussed—how inconvenient men had been sent into pitfalls and never heard of again.

She began dimly to see that, at worst, Jack's act was not the calculated murder her father held it to be. In her own tortured mind there had been at first but one clear process of reasoning. That process, whenever she began to gather the shreds, had led her mind straight to the conviction that Jack's shot had been premeditated, that the chance had been prearranged with the enemies of her brother. At first her only distinct thought was that the hapless Wesley had been lured to his death. The hand of the man she loved had sent the fatal shot into the poor boy's body. Had it been in self-defense—even in the heat of uncontrollable anger—she could have found mitigation for Jack; but there was nei-

ther the justification of self-defense nor the plausible pretext
of anger. One word of warning, which Jack could have
spoken, would have saved Wesley from the rash, the dastardly attempt upon the Rosedale household. The plot, in
all its details, must have been known to Jack or Dick, else
how explain their presence in the chamber, armed and ready
for the murder ?

It had been a conspiracy of delusive kindness from the
day Wesley entered Rosedale. The frankness and kindliness
of the Atterburys had been assumed to lure him to his fatal
adventure. Boone himself believed that Jack's ignoble ambition and envy had been the main motives in the murder.
To this Kate, from the first, opposed a resolute incredulity.

" You don't know the fellow, I tell you," Boone doggedly
argued. "He's as like his father as two snakes in a hole.
Old man Sprague never let a man stand in his way. Jack's
the same. He thought Wes' kept him from the shoulder-
straps, and he got him out of the way. Wasn't he always
snooping 'round in the regiment trying to undermine your
brother ? Wasn't he always trying to be popular ? Ah, I
know the Spragues. But I'll give them a wrench that'll
twist their damned pride out of them. I'll have that cold-
blooded young villain shot in a hollow square, and I'll have
it done in this very district, that the whole county may
know the disgrace of the high and mighty Spragues."

"No, father." Kate had heard all this before, but she,
for the first time, resolved upon setting her father right.
"No, Jack hasn't a particle of the feeling you ascribe to him.
I don't think he liked poor Wesley. They were totally unlike in nature, and I think that Jack felt deeply that he had
been wronged by Wesley's appointment. But it was not in
his nature to seek revenge. He would have fought Wesley
openly, but he would never be one of a gang of murderers.
I think I can see how Jack was led into the part he played.
It does not lessen the guilt, but it relieves him of the odious
suspicions I first felt."

Then Boone, in irritable impatience, reminded her of
her own earlier utterances ; how from his first coming

Wesley had been treated with studied distrust ; how he had
been denied the boyish intimacy that existed between Jack
and Dick ; how he was insensibly made to feel that he was
in the house under a different cartel from that of Jack and
Dick ; that he was a prisoner on parole, and his word was
doubted.   Nothing could make him believe, he declared,
getting up moodily, but that the whole lot of them had set
out to drive Wesley into a corner and then kill him, as they
had done.

Kate sighed wearily as her father left the room.   If she
could only be as well assured as her strong words implied !
Ah ! if she could fetch back her lover by getting at the
truth, how willingly she would fly to Rosedale and learn all !
But she dared not question, lest questioning should confirm,
where she now at least had the miserable solace of doubt.
Could it be true ?   Could Jack be the base schemer her father
depicted him ?   Then her mind ran back to Rosedale.   She
lived again all the enchanting days of that earthly paradise.
She saw Wesley's furtive starts, his strange disappearances,
his growing melancholy, his moody reticence when she
questioned him.   Ah ! if he had but confided to her !   If
she had but dreamed of the desperate purpose born of the
loneliness he lived in !   If Jack had been loyal to him, loyal
to her, Wesley would have been warned that eager eyes
were upon him, ready wits reading his purposes, and revengeful hatred ready to slaughter him.

When the news came that Jack had lost his life in the
very enterprise Wesley had contemplated, Kate collapsed
under the shock.   Now, when it was too late, she convinced
herself that he was innocent.   If she could have recalled
him to life, she cried in self-reproach, she would not ask
whether he was all her first impulse had painted him.   She
had borne up with something like composure when Wesley's
death came upon her ; but now, tortured by a sense of responsibility in Jack's fate, she gave way to the grief she had
so long repressed.   If she had not upbraided him, if she had
not accused him, in so many words, of murder, he would
never have embarked on the mad plot of escape.

She had driven him to his death. She had sat silent
while Acredale rang with calumnies against him. It was
not too late yet to make reparation. She would proclaim
publicly that her brother had rashly courted his own death;
that Jack had unknowingly shot him down, as many a man
does, in battle, shoot his best friend. She resolved on the
instant to go to the stricken family and make such expiation
there as was in her power. But was there any certainty
that the report of Jack's death was true ? Grievous mistakes
of the same sort had been made repeatedly in the public
journals. She was not able to formulate any plan at first.
Her father was more morose than ever. He seemed in his
way to deplore the young man's death, but not in pity, as
she soon learned. Death had robbed him of a cruelly meditated revenge. She wisely made no comment when this
brutal feeling betrayed itself ; but for the first time in her
life the girl shuddered at the sight of her father. The vague
rumors of years, that had been whispered about him—rumors which of old had fired her soul with hot indignation,
came back insidiously. She shuddered. Was she to lose
all—brother, lover, father—in this unnatural strife ? She had
been so loyal to her father. She had been so proud of him
when others reviled. She had felt so serenely confident of
the nobleness of his heart, the generosity of his impulses.
She had always been able to mold him, as she thought.
Could it be possible that he was human to her, inhuman to
the rest of the world ? Then her mind, tortured by newly
awakened doubts, ran back over the events leading to the
rupture with the Spragues. She groaned at the retrospect.
It was injustice that had displaced Jack in the command of
the company. It was injustice that had marked her father's
conduct in the Perley feud.

Grief is a logician of very direct methods. Its clari-
fying processes work like light in darkness. Kate saw the
past in her father's conduct with terrifying vividness. She
realized that it was her father's harsh purpose that had
arrayed Acredale against him. It was his pride and arrogant obstinacy that had brought about the loss of all she

loved. The fates had immolated the helpless; were the fates preparing a still bitterer expiation? Life had very little left for her now, but she resolved that she would no longer be isolated by her father's enmities. The great house had been gloomy enough for father and daughter during the last miserable months, but he still fled to her for comfort. It was one evening when he came in, apparently in better spirits than he had shown since Wesley's death, that she told him what had been filling her mind since Jack's death.

"O father, I think I see that our lives have been unworthy, if not altogether wrong. Surely such neighbors as ours could not all take sides against you, if you were in the right in all the feuds that have divided us as a family from the people of Acredale."

Then, in an almost imploring tone of reproach, she retraced the harsh episodes in the father's dealings with the Perleys, with the community, and, finally, the quarrel with the Spragues, involving in it the lives of Wesley and Jack. Her voice softened into tremulousness. She arose, and in her old pleading way pulled the shaggy head down on her breast, pressing her lips on the high, bare forehead.

"Dear father, all this is unchristian; you have in reality been waging war against women and children. Jack was a mere boy. Richard is a boy. I don't go into other enmities, where you have used the enormous power of wealth to crush the helpless. If you had not alienated the Spragues and encouraged Wesley in overbearing Jack, my brother would be alive to-day. My sweetheart—yes, Jack was dearer than all the world to me—he would not be dead to-day. Ah! father, father, what good comes of anger—what joy of revenge? You have brought about the death of these two boys. Is it not time to look at life with a new heart—with clear-seeing eyes?"

Elisha Boone sat quite still. He had listened at first with a flush of anger, which deepened as the girl pleaded, until it died away and left his face very pale. He pushed himself away from the clinging figure, as if the better to see her face. Then his head drooped. He sighed heavily, rose and without a word left the room. Kate heard him ascending the stairs, then the sound of his room door softly closing. Had the hateful fires of vengeance been quenched? It was her father's way, when resolutely opposed, to quit the scene and without confessing himself in the wrong, do as Kate urged. The next morning he was gone before she reached the breakfast-table. There was a note on her plate in his handwriting. She read with a sinking heart:

"MY DAUGHTER: If what you said last night is true, you can not be the daughter to me that you have been. I am going to Washington, and when I come back you will know that your brother was deliberately murdered, and that his murderer, even in the grave, is held guilty before all men of the crime."

The servant confirmed the tidings. Her father had arisen early and departed on the first train. What could it mean? Had he some evidence that she had not heard? Had Jack left papers incriminating him? Ah! why carry the hideous feud further? Why blast the melancholy repose of the living, by fastening this stain upon the dead? But they could not. She knew it. She could herself refute any proof brought forward. She would tell all. She would reveal their tender relationship, and surely then any one, knowing the young man's nature, would scout the assertion of his willfully shooting Wesley. But surely Olympia and Mrs. Sprague must be able to tell, and tell decisively, the circumstances in the tragedy. She would go to them. She owed this to the living; she owed it still more imperatively to the dead. She had not seen Olympia since her return. Mrs. Sprague had been too infirm to see her when she called. But she would not heed rebuffs now. In such a cause, on such a mission, she would have stood at the Sprague door a suppliant until even the obstinacy of her father would have relented. On her way across the square she saw Merry coming from the post. She turned out of her way, and hurrying to the near-sighted spinster held out her hand, saying, softly:

"Ah, Miss Merry, I'm so glad to see you! I have been meaning to call on you ever since I heard of your return, but, what with sorrow and illness, I have put it off, and now I want you to take me home with you. Will you not?"

The pleading tone, the caressing clasp of the hand, the sadly changed face, the somber black weeds, made the voice and figure so much unlike the old Kate, that Merry stood for an instant confused and blushing as she stammered:

"Bless me, Miss Kate, I—I—shouldn't have known you. Ah, I am very glad to see you; sisters will be very glad to see you, too. Do, do come right along with me. I'm afraid the parlor won't be very sightly, but you won't mind, will you?"

Kate squeezed the hand still resting in her own, and drawing the long veil back over face, she walked silently with the puzzled spinster, unable to broach the theme she had at heart. Merry spared her the torture of going at it obliquely.

"I have just been at the Spragues. Poor dears, they are in dreadful distress. Mrs. Sprague is preparing to go in search of the body, but Olympia won't give in that Jack is killed. She says that if he had been she certainly would have known it in Richmond, for there are couriers twice a day from the rebel outposts to the capital; that the Atterburys had taken special measures to learn the fate of the escaped prisoners; that, besides this, several young men in Richmond, who knew Jack well, had been sent down the peninsula with the prisoners, to befriend him in case he were retaken."

"And Olympia believes that Jack is alive?"

"Yes, firmly."

"Where does she think he is?"

"She believes that he is among a squad separated from the rest of the prisoners, near the Union lines. It was asserted in Richmond that many had crossed the James River, and were making for the Dismal Swamp, or into Burnside's lines in North Carolina."

"Dear Miss Merry, I—I—think I won't go in now," Kate

said, tremblingly. "I must see Olympia. Perhaps I can help them in the search for Jack, and you know there is no time to lose. I shall come and see you all soon."

She squeezed the astonished Merry's hand convulsively, and shot off, leaving the bewildered lady quite speechless, so speechless that, when she reached the stately presence of Aunt Pliny, she forgot the commissions she had been sent to execute, and was at once reviled by the parrot as "a no-account dawdler."

Meanwhile, Kate, with wild, throbbing hope in her heart that kindled color in her pale cheeks and light in her weary eyes, sped away to the Spragues. There was no tremor in the hand that raised the dragon-headed knocker, nor hesitancy in the voice that bade the servant say that "Miss Boone requested a few moments' conversation with Miss Sprague."

Olympia came presently into the reception-room, and the girls met with a warm embrace.

"Ah, Olympia, I have been made so—so—glad by what Merry tells me! You—do—not believe that your brother is dead?" Her voice faltered, and Olympia, gazing at her fixedly, said:

"No, I shall not believe Jack is dead until I see his body. Poor mother, who believes the worst whenever we are out of her sight, has given up all but the faintest hope. I shall not. I know Jack so well. I know that it would take a good deal to kill him, young and strong as he is. Besides that, I know that the Atterburys would find means to let us know, if there were any certainty as to his fate. Poor Jack! It would be an unendurable calamity if he were to die before the monstrous calumnies that have been published about him are proved lies."

"Dear Olympia, that is one reason of my coming. In my horror at Rosedale, I, too, believed that John had been in a plot to entrap Wesley; but I—I—know better now, and I have come to tell you that it is no less my duty than my right to see that your brother's memory is made as spotless as his life."

"I knew it; I knew you would do it; I told Jack so in Richmond, almost the last words I said before he set out on this miserable adventure. I told him you were not the girl I took you for if you could believe him to be such a dastard, when you had time to get over the shock of poor Wesley's death. You never heard the whole story of that dreadful night. I must tell it to you—as he would if he were here, and I know you would believe him." The two girls sat down, hand in hand, and Olympia told the tale as it has been set down in these pages.

Kate was sobbing when the story ended. She flung her arms about Olympia's neck, and for a time the two sat silent, tearful.

"Oh, why didn't he tell me this at the time? It was not Jack's bullet that entered poor Wesley's body. Jack was at his right, at the side of the bed. Wesley's wound was on the left side, and the shot must have come from Jones's pistol!"

"I remember that; but Jack's remorse put all thought of everything else out of my head. I recall, perfectly, that the wound was in Wesley's left side. Oh, if I could only get that word to Jack! If—"

"I'll get it to him if he's alive. I, or mine, have been his undoing! I shall make amends. Ah, Olympia, I—I am ashamed to feel so full of joy—forgive me."

"It isn't your fault, dear, that you didn't know Jack as we do," Olympia said, tenderly.

"What are your plans?" Kate asked, presently.

"Mother insists upon going to the peninsula and examining the ground, questioning all who took part in the pursuit, and seeing with her own eyes every wounded man in the neighborhood. I don't know whether we can get passes, but we shall set out at once and do our best."

"O Olympia, I must—I must go with you! I shall die if I remain here doing nothing—helpless! Let me go. I can aid you much. I can surely get all the passports required. I can do many things that you couldn't do, for my father—"

She stopped and colored. Her father! What was she

rashly promising for him? Dead, he was bent on Jack's dishonor; living, he would never rest until Jack's life was condemned.

"Ah, yes—that's true. Your father is potent at headquarters. I can answer for mamma. We shall be delighted and comforted to have you. I shall need you as much as mamma needs me. We are only waiting for Mr. Brodie's report. I don't expect much from his researches. It is only a woman's heart that upholds one in such trials as this search means."

The plans were agreed upon at once and the two girls separated, knit together by the same bond in more senses than one, for, while Olympia set out to rescue her brother, she secretly hoped that the search would bring her near some one else; and so, as soon as Kate had gone, she sat down and wrote Vincent of Jack's disappearance, asking his aid in finding such traces as might be in the rebel lines. She merely alluded to their projected plan, adding, in a postscript, that she would write him as soon as the party approached the outposts. Kate wrote at once to her father, at his Washington address, narrating her visit to the Spragues, telling him of the new hope that had come to her, and beseeching him to lend his whole heart to the distressed mother and sister. He should see her in Washington within a few days, and she counted on his sympathy with her to help to restore the lost son and brother if alive, to co-operate in giving the body honorable burial if he were dead. These letters dispatched, the party waited only to hear from Brodie. He came a day or two later, but he could give them no hope. He had been repelled from all sources of information, insulted in the War Office, and denied access to the President. He was convinced that there were secret influences at work to obscure the true facts in the case of the escaped prisoners, but what the agencies were he could not guess. When Olympia told this to Kate, she was surprised at her look and response.

"I know the influences, I think, and I can discover the agencies. Take comfort. I believe Jack is alive. I promise you that I shall never rest until he is found, alive or dead."

"O Kate, what an impulsive ally we have gained! I wish Jack could have heard that speech; it would have put power in his arm, as poor Barney used to say."

Twenty-four hours later the three women were in Washington, Kate remaining with her friends, instead of joining her father at Willard's.

CHAPTER XXX.

A GAME OF CHANCE.

IT was the end of January, 1862, when Olympia and her mother found themselves in Washington for the second time in quest of the missing soldier. They took lodgings in the same quiet house, not far from Lafayette Square—Kate with them. Kate counted upon her father's aid, active or passive; but when her messenger returned from Willard's with word that Mr. Boone had gone from the hotel several days before, she was numb with a dreadful foreboding. He was avoiding her deliberately. She drove at once to the hotel. The clerk summoned to her aid could only inform her that her father had given up his room and had left the hotel late at night. She could get no further clew. She telegraphed at once to Acredale and returned to the Spragues, not daring to breathe her apprehensions. Yes, her father was plainly keeping away from her. He meant to persist in his savage vengeance. What had he learned? Was Jack indeed dead, and was his good name the object of her father's hatred? Whither should she turn? Why had she not thought of this—her father's passivity or even opposition? How could she reveal her terrors to the mother and sister? How make known to them the unworthy side of her father's character? If in the morning no telegram came from Acredale, it would be proof that her father was bent, implacably in his purpose to undo Jack, living or dead. When she reached the lodging, Olympia was dressed for the street.

"You are just in time. I have matured my plans. First, . we must find out at the proper quarter the names of all the wounded brought here from Fort Monroe. Then we must trace the report in the *Herald* down to its origin. Then we must visit every hospital in and near Washington to find out from actual sight of each man whether Jack or Dick, or any one we know, is in the city. As we go on, we shall learn a good deal which may modify this plan, or perhaps make the search less difficult."

Olympia said this with composure and a certain confidence in herself that struck Kate with admiration. She felt ashamed of herself. Here was Olympia, unconscious of Jack's real peril if living, the menace to his reputation if dead, planning as composedly as if it were an every-day thing to have a brother lost in the appalling mazes of war; and she had been weakly depending upon her father, Jack's most persevering enemy! She recoiled from herself in a shiver of self-reproach as she said:

"Olympia, you have the good sense of a man in an emergency. I am ashamed of myself. I, who ought to do the thinking for you, am as helpless as a kitchen-maid set to playing lady in the parlor. I can at least help you; I can make my body follow you, if I haven't sense enough to suggest."

"Dear Kate, it isn't sense, or insight, or any fine quality of mind that is needed here. All I ask is, that you won't get dispirited, or, if you do, don't let mamma see you are. Poor mamma! She is as easily influenced as a baby. Jack is her darling, remember. All the world is a small affair to her compared with our poor boy. I fancy, if we were as much wrapped up in him as she is, we should make poor pioneers in the wilderness before us."

But Kate could stand no more of this. With a choking sob she turned and fled up the stairway, crying as she disappeared : " Wait — wait a moment ; I must get my purse."

When she reappeared, the heavy mourning-veil was drawn down, and Olympia, with a reassured glance, opened the door.

"You must affect confidence, if you have it not—even gayety. I warn you not to be shocked at my conduct. I must keep up mamma's spirits, and to do it I must play indifference or confidence, and you must be careful to say nothing, to do nothing, to excite her suspicions."

Kate's cab had driven off, and the two girls walked through Lafayette Square into Pennsylvania Avenue to get another. The wide streets were filled, as of old, with skurrying orderlies, groups of lounging officers, and lumbering army wagons. But even the untrained eyes of Olympia soon took account of the better discipline, the more business-like celerity of the men on duty as well as the flying couriers. The White House was gay with bunting, and salutes from the distant forts were signalizing the news that had just come of Union successes at Mill Spring and Roanoke Island. The girls, procuring a hack, were driven to the provost-general's office. Here, after an interminable delay they were admitted to the presence of a complacent young coxcomb in spotless regimentals, who, so soon as he saw Olympia's face and bearing, threw off the listlessness of routine, and, rising deferentially, asked her pleasure. She told her story simply, and asked his advice as to the course to be followed. When the extract from the *Herald* was shown to him, he examined an enormous folio, and then rang a bell.

"It is more than likely that these names are wrong. This happens constantly. The operators are raw and some of them can barely read. The names are given hurriedly, and if not written plainly they make wretched work of them. The newspapers make many a fool famous, while neglecting many a hero who deserves fame, simply through the blundering or carelessness of the writers or operators. Here is an orderly who will take you to the surgeon-gen-

eral. You will find in his books the names of all the wounded in hospital in the Eastern armies. But if your brother
was wounded or brought in wounded at Fort Monroe, his
name will be on the books of the Army of the Potomac or
the Department of Eastern Virginia."

They were treated with the same deferential gallantry at
the surgeon-general's office; the young doctors, indeed, became almost obtrusive in their eagerness to spare the young
women the drudgery of scrutinizing the long lists of invalids. But, after two days' careful search, no names resembling Sprague or Perley could be found.

"I wonder who this can be?" Kate said, returning to an
entry made a month before: "Jones, Warchester; Caribee
Regiment."

"I know no one of that name," Olympia said, "but perhaps he might know something of Jack. Let us go to him.
It will do no harm to find out who he is."

The surgeon's clerk readily gave them Jones's address,
reminding them that the hospital was in Georgetown, and
that they would be too late to obtain entrance to the patient
that day. Next morning Mrs. Sprague was too ill to rise
from her bed, and Olympia could not leave her alone. Kate
undertook the investigation into the Jones affair alone.
When she reached the hospital there was some delay before
she could see the personage intrusted with the admission of
guests. She was shown into an office on the ground-floor
and given a seat. As she sat, distraught and eager, she
heard her own name in the next room, the door of which
stood open:

"It's at Boone's risk. He would have him moved, and
the surgeon-general gave him *carte blanche* with the patient."

"Well, it will cost the man his life. I'll stake my diplo-
ma on that. Why, the journey to Warchester alone is
enough to down the most vigorous convalescent."

Kate trembled. What did this mean? What was she
hearing? Boone—Warchester? Whom had her father been
taking from the hospital—Jack? Her heart gave a wild

23

leap. Yes—Jack. Who else did her father know in the army? She arose trembling, fainting, but resolute. She reached the open door, but tried for a moment in vain to ask:

"If you please, tell me, tell me—" But she could say no more. The occupants of the room, in undress uniform, turned upon her at first in hostile surprise, but, as she threw her veil farther back in alarm, the elder of the two said:

"Pray, madam, what is it; are you ill?"

"No; may I sit down, please? Thank you. I am come to, to—" What should she say? How expose the doubt of her father? How find out for certain who had been removed to Warchester—abducted was the word her agitated thoughts shaped. Oh, if Olympia, intrepid, self-possessed, were only with her!—but no, not Olympia; no one must ever know the unutterable crime she suspected her father of. She must be brave. She must be resolute. Oh, where were her arts now, when she most needed them? She tried to speak. A hoarse gasping came in her throat and died there.

"Ah—ah—some water!—I—I am faint."

In an instant a goblet of cool water was at her lips. She drank slowly, deliberating all the time to recover her senses; the surgeons—both young men, mere lads—waiting respectfully, inferring much from the melancholy robes. The water cooled her head, and she began to be able to think coherently.

"I have the surgeon-general's permit to visit a patient in your fever ward—Jones, the name is. Can I see him?"

"Pray, let me see the permit, madam?" He glanced at it, looked significantly at his comrade, and said:

"This man was removed three days ago."

"Where to?"

"Warchester."

"Ah!" Kate's veil, by an imperceptible gesture, fell over part of her face. A great trembling came upon her again. The young surgeons exchanged glances.

"Who—who—did—who asked for his removal?"

"A Mr. Boone, also of Warchester."

"Thank you—I am too late—I wanted to—to ask this Mr. Jones some questions concerning a dear friend in his regiment. But I can write, if you will kindly give me the address."

"I am very sorry—beyond Warchester we have no record here of his whereabouts. If he had been officially transferred to another government hospital, we should have all the facts. But the removal was a personal favor to Mr. Boone. He is well known both here and in Warchester, and you can have no difficulty in communicating with him."

"Ah, true; I had forgotten that."

"If we can be of any service to you, Miss Sprague," the young man said, handing Kate back the permit, made out in Olympia's name, which Kate had never thought of, "you can always reach us through the surgeon-general's office." He handed her a card with his own and his comrade's name in pencil.

Thanking the young man with as much self-possession as she could summon, Kate reached the carriage in a whirl of wild imaginings, more terrifying as she strove to reduce them to definite shape. Who was this Jones? Why remove him to Warchester? If it were not Jack, what interest could her father have in his removal? But, first, what could she say to Olympia? She could say she did not know Jones, but Olympia would surely ask what questions she had put to him. What should she say? That he had been taken away from the hospital? She knew Olympia well enough to know that this vague story would only incite her to further inquiry. She would find out the father's handiwork in the affair, and she, too, would be set on the rack of suspicion.

When the carriage reached the door, Kate dared not enter. She dismissed the man and set out toward the green fields below the rounded slope of Meridian Hill. Here she could breathe freely. "I can think clearly now," she panted, with a gush of warm tears. If she could only remain calm,

she could look into the black abyss with the eye of reason,
rather than terror. Calmness came soothingly as she walked,
and she began at the beginning, weighing probabilities. All
seemed dark and hopeless, until she came back to the record
in the surgeon-general's office. Jones, sent from Hampton
Hospital, December 13th. This was about the time Jack had
reached the Union lines. He had left Richmond late in
November. All Brodie's inquiries at Fort Monroe had been
fruitless in finding the whereabouts of the fugitives that
came through the lines at that time. Dick had been one of
them. If Jones were not Jack himself, he must have been
one of the group that escaped with Jack. It all led back to
the first frightful conjecture. Her father was abducting a
witness who could divulge Jack's whereabouts, or he was
secreting Jack until he could work him harm. The walk
began to revive Kate's courage as well as her faculties. She
must act with energy. The hardest part of the problem was
to get clear of Olympia, for Kate at once made up her mind
to quit Washington that very night for home. She must
evade Olympia's inquiries as best she could, and make some
excuse for journeying thither.

When she reached home, fortune had intervened to save
her conscience from the falsehoods she feared she would
have to employ. The landlady met her in the hallway with
a white face.

"O Miss Boone, Mrs. Sprague is taken very bad. The
doctor's with her now. I think it is typhoid fever."

Up-stairs misfortune gave her a further release. Olympia
came into Kate's room, agitated and in tears.

"Ah, Kate, mamma is suffering pitiably. The doctor
thinks it is typhoid, and he ordered me to remain away
from her. You must leave the house. It won't do for all
of us to be ill together. I may not be able to see you for
days, until the crisis is past. But you must continue the
search, and you must let me know, from day to day, what
you learn. There are letters for you— I hear mamma. I
will be back in a moment."

Kate fairly hated herself for the passing thrill of relief

over the timely illness that had intervened to expedite her mission. She glanced over the letters. There was one in her father's hand, postmarked Acredale. It contained no clew to his purposes, but she read tremblingly:

"MY DAUGHTER: You are doing a foolish thing. The search you propose can lead to nothing. All that can be done has been done by his friends. They have found no trace of him. Women can not hope to succeed where so keen a man as Brodie has failed. I have every confidence that in good time the matter will be cleared up, but you must remember that the Government and its agents have all they can do to manage and keep track of the millions of soldiers in the field, and they can not be expected to take much interest in the fate of the wounded or dead. Always affectionately,
"YOUR FATHER."

All doubt of her father's sinister intervention in Jack's disappearance now took the form of certainty in the girl's mind. When Olympia came back, a few moments later, Kate said, tenderly:

"I have news from home. I must go back at once. It is less of a grief to me, since I should be banished from you if I were here. I shall not be gone long. I shall certainly be back as soon as you can receive me. In the mean while, don't despair. I have been put on a new trail that I can not explain to you now. But I can say this much, when you see me again you shall know whether Jack is alive or dead."

Olympia, who had been so strong, cheery, and masterful when it had been a question of reassuring her mother, was now the stricken spirit. She looked at Kate through swimming eyes, and her voice was lost in sobs as she tried to speak. The girls held each other in a tearful silence, neither able to say what was in the minds of both. Even the uncertainty had a sort of solace compared with the dreadful possibility of the worst.

"Remember, dear, you have your mother. What is our

poor grief to hers ; what is our loss to hers ? It ought to comfort you to know that whatever human thought, courage, love can do to recover Jack, I shall do, just as you would in my place. I am very strong and resolute now, and I am filled with hope—so filled that I can not talk to you. I dare not let you see how much I hope, lest if it be not fulfilled you will hate me for inspiring you with it."

"I will hope. I do believe you will do better than I should. The loving are the daring—you will find Jack. I know it."

"Ah, God bless you, Olympia! That removes a curse from me—I—I mean that fills me with a courage that is not my own. I have learned yours or stolen it. But you will forgive me, for I mean to use it all in your behalf."

Olympia smiled sadly, and the two parted. By the night express Kate left the city, and, the next afternoon, reached Acredale. As she anticipated, her father was not at home. He had only been an hour or two in the house since his return. The servants had no idea where he was. His letters were forwarded to him under cover of his lawyers in Warchester. If, as she fearfully surmised, her father were engaged in some cruel scheme to the hurt of Jack, her best way with him would be perfect frankness. She had never yet failed in swerving him from his most headstrong impulses when she could talk with him. She must have him now to herself. Her best plan, therefore, would be to write. Yet she hardly knew how to frame the note, reflecting bitterly, as she sat twirling her pen, on the monstrous state of things that made writing to her own father almost a duplicity. At length she wrote :

"Dearest Papa: I am come all the way from Washington, leaving poor Mrs. Sprague very low with fever, and her daughter tormented and ill with anxiety. I feel, I know, that you can relieve the distress of this miserable mother and devoted sister. I must see you. I felt sure of seeing you in Washington, and you can imagine my surprise and grief when they told me at the hotel that you had gone. Do

come to me, or let me come to you. Your daughter's place
is with you or near you now. We have only each other
in this world; pray, dear father, let nothing come between
us; let nothing make you doubt the constant love of your
daughter.   KATE."

The note dispatched, she went immediately to the Perleys. Perhaps they had news that might be of help. No.
The three ladies met her with agitated volubility. Had she
heard from their nephew? Had Dick escaped with Jack?
Olympia had assured them that he had quitted Richmond
with her brother. They had written to the Caribee regiment, and received word that no trace of him could be
found. The regiment, or what was left of it, was home re-
filling its ranks. The officers, indeed, knew nothing of such
a person as Richard Perley. McGoyle, who was now colonel,
did vaguely recall the lad at Washington, but had no idea
what became of him. Kate found a new grief in the misery
of the helpless ladies. But she could give them no comfort,
and returned home to to await her father's coming. In the
evening a messenger brought her a note. It was in the
straight, emphatic hand of her father. He wrote:

"DEAR DAUGHTER: I am just now engaged in very important matters that require me to move about considerably. I shall not be home for some days. I am glad you
have come home. That's the place for you. You had better let the matter you speak of alone. The mother and sister are enough in the business. I don't see how it concerns
you or me. If the man is dead it will be known as soon as
the commissioners of exchange hand in their lists. If he is
not dead, it is certainly no business of yours or mine to bring
him home. I will write you soon again. Love your father.
Keep the house well till I come."

That was all. More than evasive. Subtly calculated to
make her believe that he had dismissed all thought of Jack
and was immersed in his own affairs. She sat staring and

helpless, a cold horror creeping into her heart and a nameless terror taking outline in her senses. Hideous alternative. To be coherent she must suspect, nay, accuse, her
father of a dreadful duplicity. He was deceiving her; else
why no mention of his mission to Washington—his abduction of Jones? Jones! Who was he? Oh, blind and sense-
less that she had been! Why had she not asked the young
men at Georgetown to describe Jones? That would have
revealed all she needed to know. Was it too late to write
them? Yes; but could she throw suspicion upon her
father by writing to strangers, and of necessity exposing
the sinister secrecy of her father's action. But she could
hurry back to Washington, and, without letting the young
men know, get a descriptive list. This she resolved to do.
Twenty-four hours later she was in Washington. The
journey was thrown away. The descriptive list had been
sent by the hospital steward with the invalid. He could be
found in the military hospital in Warchester. His name
was Leander Elkins. This was something gained. Two
days later she was at the hospital in Warchester. The steward, Elkins, came to her in the waiting-room. He was a
young giant in stature, with light flaxen hair, a merry blue
eye, and so bashful in the presence of a woman that he colored rosily as Kate asked him if he was the person she had
sent for.

"Yes'm, I'm Lee Elkins," he stammered, very much perplexed to find ease for his large hands and ample feet.

"Are you—is Mr. Jones, who came from the Georgetown
Hospital, in your care?" Kate had thought out her course
in advance, and had decided that the direct way was the
best. Unless the man had been charged to conceal facts,
an apparent knowledge of Jones's movements would be the
surest way of eliciting his whereabouts.

"Oh no, miss, Jones wa'nt brought here; he was took to
a private place. I don't rightly know where, but I calculate I ken find eout of ye want to know."

"Yes, I should like very much to know. I am deeply interested in him. Did you have charge of him?"

"I can't say I did. I was sent from Washington in the same train, but the old chap that got Jones removed did all the nussing. I only got a sight of him as he was lifted into the carriage."

"Should you know him again if you saw him?"

"Think I should. Yes'm, think I should. His head was about as big as a pumpkin."

"He had been wounded?"

"Well, I should say so."

"Have you seen the gentleman that brought him on from Washington lately?"

"Not here, mum; I did see him in the street the other day. He was in a wagon—leastwise, it looked mighty like him."

Kate began to breathe more freely. Her father had, at least, avoided any collusion with inferiors. His handiwork had been natural, involving no conspiracy or bribing of menials.

"Do you think you could find out for me where Mr. Jones is?"

"Wall, I reckon it could be done. It may take some days, as I must trust to the luck of running upon old Dofunny again."

Kate started. "Old Dofunny"—the unsuspecting humorist meant her father by this jocular *nom de guerre*, and she dared not resent it. How should she gain her end and yet save herself from the humiliation of seeming to spy upon her father? It wouldn't do for Elkins to go to him, for he would at once suspect, inquire, and learn that she had come upon his tracks. If she could only see him face to face, she would be spared all this odious complotting. But she dared not reject the means Providence had put in her hands. And yet, how use them, and avoid throwing suspicion upon her father in cautioning Elkins not to approach him? She was not equal to the invention of a plan on the moment, and said in a doubting, reflective way:

"Never mind. I may be able to learn from some of his friends where he is. The gentleman you speak of does not

live in this city, and you would hardly be able to find him.
If I could find him I could find Mr. Jones."

"Ah, yes ; jes' so. Wall, I think I can find him in
another way. I remember the carriage that took him from
the station. I can find out from the driver. 'T'wan't no
mystery, I reckon."

Kate looked into the innocent blue eyes as the young fellow scratched his tow head, wondering whether he was as
simple-minded as he seemed. He stood the scrutiny with
blushing restiveness, in which there was nothing of the
malign, and she resolved that he was to be trusted.

"Very well," she said, indifferently, "that does seem the
shortest way to find out the poor fellow's whereabouts. Get
the facts, and you shall be well paid for your trouble."

"'Tain't no trouble, miss, if it's a service to you. It would
make me powerful glad to do anything for a comrade or his
sister."

Kate smiled at the astute mingling of sly fun and questioning implied in the gently rising inflection in this query.

"Yes," she said, "you will be relieving the anxious heart
of a sister if you find what I am seeking."

"Nuff said, miss. Just as soon as I get my relief I'm off
like a shot. Where shall you be ? "

"Ah, yes; you can come to me at the Alburn House.
Here is my card, and you will doubtless be at some expense.
Here is money to pay—spare no expense."

The big eyes opened in wonder as Kate handed him three
new ten-dollar greenbacks, just then something of a novelty
to soldiers especially, who got their pay infrequently. It
was a bold stroke to intrust her name to this unconscious
agent of her father, for, if he were really playing a part, his
first act would be to reveal her visit and thus set her father
on his guard. But she trusted him implicitly. His wide-
open blue eyes, the artless admiration mingling with his
bashful diffidence, all were proof that he could not be deceiving her. She took rooms at the Alburn House, which
was not the chief hotel, as being better adapted for her purpose of seclusion. At the big hotel she was known, and if

her father were in town she would be under his espionage without the solace of writing him. Late in the evening her agent came in radiant. He had found the man.

"Easy as rolling off a log." The hackman had taken him to the house where Jones was lying. It was on the outskirts of the city toward Acredale. He described the house. Kate knew it very well. It was the property of her father.

"Did you see the patient ?"

"No, indeed. You didn't tell me to, and I had nothing to see him for. Ef you had told me that you wanted I should see him, I'd have seen him as easy as greased lightning."

"Thank you. I am relieved of a great burden through your kindness. You must permit me to give you something to show my gratitude. Here, use this money for some one who needs it, if you do not need it yourself."

"But I don't need it. Here is what you gave me this morning, 'cept a half-dollar I spent in treating John. I couldn't think of taking so much money. I'ts more'n Uncle Sam allows me for five months' pay."

"No, I shall feel distressed if you do not accept it. You can find use for it. It will bring you luck, for it is the reward of a very important service. Perhaps some time we may meet again, and then you shall know how important."

The tow hair stood up in wild dismay, and the blue eyes were perfect saucepans, as Kate gently forced the money into the big palm.

"Wall, I vum, miss, I feel like I was a-robbing you, but ef yeou den want I should take it, why I will, and send it to my old mother, who will find plenty o' use for it. Good-by, miss. Ef you should want me again, I'm at the hospital. I shall be mitey tickled to do anything for yeou or your brother."

CHAPTER XXXI.

TWO BLADES OF THE SAME STEEL.

It was too late to follow up the discovery that night. Kate, after a feverish rest, set out early in the morning. She went first to Acredale, where she could get her own equipage and driver. The tenants of the house did not know her. She rang boldly at the door, and when a maid answered, quite taken aback by the girlish figure in deep black, Kate asked, confidently:

"I want to see the sick man, Mr. Jones."

"Yes'm. Come right in. This way, please, ma'am." The girl led the way up a flight of stairs, but if she had been part of the balustrade Kate could not have been more immovable. Whom was she about to see? Jack, wan, emaciated, on the verge of the grave? They had said in Washington that the journey would kill him; was it to that end her relentless father had persisted in the removal? Was she about to see the dying brought to death's door by her own flesh and blood? She reeled against the stair-post and brought her veil over her face. The girl had turned above and was waiting in wonder. With a desperate gathering together of her relaxed forces, she mounted the stairway. In the corridor the girl turned to a closed doorway and knocked lightly. There was no sound within; but the door swung open, and Elisha Boone stood on the threshold. He did not in the dim light observe the figure in black, but, looking at the maid, said, softly:

"What's wanted, Sarah?"

"A young lady to see Mr. Jones, sir," and, stepping slightly aside for Kate to enter, the father recognized the visitor.

"You here, Kate? What does this mean?"

With a great throb of joy she flung herself into his arms; too happy, too relieved to take into consideration the defeat of her purpose involved in the meeting. For an instant she lost all thought of anything but that her estranged parent was in her arms, that she would not let him quit her sight again, that her pleading would keep him from any act that could cause her or any one else unhappiness.

"Ah, father, I'm so relieved, so glad! I was miserable, and did not know where you were. I—I will not let you leave me again."

"But my child, you must not be here; this is a house of sickness; there is dangerous illness here."

"It's no more dangerous for me than for you. I know who is here." She looked archly at him, as he started in surprise. "I will help nurse Mr. Jones." She said this with immense knowingness in her manner as she squeezed the astonished man to her heart. The maid meanwhile had retreated to a safe distance, where she lurked in covert to make report of the extraordinary goings on.

"Impossible, Kate ; you must not be here. I will not have it; you must go." His voice grew stern. "You must go, I say, Kate ; you must go down-stairs this instant."

"Come, Boone, I say, this isn't fair; let the lady come in if she wants to see valor laid low." Boone, who had been insensibly moving Kate from the open doorway, caught her eye fixed on the room, and looking over his shoulder at these jocular words he saw Jones leaning against the post, a wan smile on his face. Boone turned, almost flinging Kate from him, and, fairly lifting the invalid, carried him back into the room.

"This is madness; you are in no condition to rise. I won't be responsible for your life if you persist in this course."

"So much trouble off your hands, old man. I'll be more use to you dead than living. Better let me blow my own flame out. It won't burn long at best or worst."

In the overwhelming revulsion of feeling brought about by the actual sight of Jones, Kate stood, interdicted, in the corridor, uncertain what to do. She heard the man's words and shuddered at the bantering levity with which he spoke of his own death. Who could it be ? It was not Jack, as she had feared and hoped. But he must know something of Jack. She must speak with him. How ? It would not do to irritate her father. She caught Boone's almost whispered words:

"I tell you, Jones, you shall be brought about, but you know the danger of seeing any Acredale people. My daughter knows you—knows the Perleys. I should think that would be reason enough why you should not be seen by her."

"Oh, I don't mind; the sight of a pretty girl is the best medicine I know of. I'd risk all Acredale for that."

Kate turned softly and waited at the foot of the stairs for her father. He came presently, looking worried and embarrassed.

"Now don't go to imagining mysteries here. This is a man who has been on my hands a good many years. He is an irreclaimable spendthrift. He was in other days a man of repute and station. I am interested in him, through old ties, since the days we were boys."

"The carriage is here, papa; won't you come home with me ?"

"Yes; you get into the carriage."

He reappeared presently, the face of a strange woman, that Kate had not seen, peering over his shoulder into the carriage as he came down the steps. Kate instantly divined that he had been warning the landlady against admitting strangers to the sick man's room. During the drive home Kate strove to reassert her old dominion over the moody figure at her side. It was useless. As the carriage stopped at the door he turned toward her and said, not unkindly:

"Daughter, there are some things I know better how to manage than you do. You have been spying on your father. This is another count in the long score of grudges I owe the Sprague tribe and their scoundrel son. Understand me clearly, my child; you must not speak of this matter again. The whole business will soon be at an end: that end is in my hands, and no power this side the grave can alter a fact in the outcome. You are very dear to me; you are all I have left in the world; you must trust me, and you must believe that I am doing everything for the best. Try to think that the world is not coming to an end because I insist on having my own way for once."

Nothing but the sense of having giving hostages to good behavior rather than honor upheld Kate in the line she had marked out for herself. She was not, in the modern sense of the word, a strong-minded young woman, this sorely beset champion of the overborne. She hadn't even the perversity of the sex in love. Chivalrously as she loved the lost soldier, she loved her father with that old-fashioned veneration which made her see all that he did with the moral indistinctness, without which there could not be the perfect filial devotion that makes the family a union in good report and evil. She had not even that, by no means repellent, secondary egoism which upholds us in doing ungrateful things that abstract good may follow. Opposition, which becomes delightful when we can call it persecution, had no charm for her. If her father had suddenly adopted the *rôle* of the stern parent in novels and ordered her to her chamber, Kate would have regarded it as a joke, and felt rather relieved that she could thus escape the pledge given to the Spragues. But, as it was, she felt morally bound by her promise to Olympia; and, though she realized dimly that her instrumentality was slowly involving her father in a coil of unloveliness, she resolutely braced herself for the worst. In spite of herself she had believed in conquering her father's severity and changing his mind. She had rescued him from revenges quite as dear to him as this, at least so far as she understood it, forgetting that her father believed himself to be pursuing the deliberate murderer of his son. When we have achieved a victory over our own less noble impulses and put the sophistries that misled us behind us, it is impossible to realize that others have not the same vision, the same mind as our own. Kate had accused Jack of cold-blooded murder. She had reasoned herself out of that hateful spirit, and, forgetting that her father had not the vital force of love to act as a fulcrum, she could not quite comprehend how difficult it was to shift the wrathful burden in his mind. She had gone too far to recede now with honor. Olympia had trusted her, had indeed given over into her hands the active work of finding the strangely lost clew of Jack's whereabouts. Perhaps for her father's sake it was better that she should be the instrument. She might be able to dissemble his intervention, shield him from obloquy—if, as she feared, he was responsible for anything doubtful.

She knew her father too well to suppose that he would flinch from any measure he had proposed to himself. She knew that she need not count any further upon her accustomed powers of persuasion. His own words were final on that score. If she could only learn his intentions! If she could be sure that he was ulteriorly shaping events against Jack—was acquainted with his whereabouts—she would have known exactly what to do. But, pilloried in doubt, shackled by the dread of exposing him in some hateful malevolence which would forever disgrace him in the community, she hardly dared stir, though she felt that every hour's delay was a new peril to Jack in some way. The more she thought of the scene of the morning, the surer she felt that Jones—or Mr. Dick, as her father sometimes called him—was in some way an instrument in the paternal scheme. If she could but see Jones ten minutes! Her father, she well knew, had guarded against that. Whom could she send in her place? Ah! there was the double check. She couldn't expose her father to a stranger; yet if her apprehensions were grounded on anything more substantial than fear, strangers must in time know all. Could Merry be made use of? No—that would not do. The libertine tone of the invalid, his impudent allusion to herself, convinced Kate that a man must be her agent, if any one were to be. But what man did she know? If she sent any of the servants, her father would recognize them, and the attempt fail. She had trusted Elkins. He seemed an honest, incurious lad, just the one to be trusted in the business. She could invent a fable which would satisfy his ready credulity without compromising her father. It was plain that he was the only resource. She dressed at once and returned to the Alburn.

Thence she dispatched a note to Elkins, begging him to call at his earliest leisure. While waiting his return, she wrote a letter to be handed to Jones. This was a work of no little ingenuity, forced as she was to avoid all allusion to her father and the scene of the morning. When completed, this stroke ' of the conspiracy ran:

"DEAR SIR: A mother and sister who have exhausted all official sources in vain to get trace of a lost son and brother, John Sprague of the Caribees, have reason to believe that you can give them a clew to his whereabouts. Will you therefore kindly confide in the bearer of this letter, giving him by word of mouth such facts as will enable John Sprague's relatives to work intelligently in the search for him, living or dead?

"Very truly yours,

KATHERINE BOONE."

It was hardly written when Elkins himself appeared, radiant with satisfaction and blushing like a peony under lamplight.

"Yeour note came just in th' nick o' time. I have leave of absence for twenty-four hours, and was just goin' inter teown."

"If you can spare me the day, I have a very important matter I think you can attend to for me. I want you to go to the sick man Jones. You must see before entering whether he is alone or not. I don't know how you can find out, but you can invent some way. If you see the man who brought him from Washington, you are not to enter. But if you find that he is not in the house, ask boldly for Jones, and when you reach him hand him this note. He will give you an answer, and you must be careful not to lose a word, for life depends on the accuracy of your report. I fancy that your regimentals and hospital badge can gain you admission, if, as I have reason to believe, there are orders to refuse strangers admission. I depend on you to overcome any difficulty you may meet. If you knew how much de-

24

pends upon it, I'm sure you would not be baffled by anything less than force."

The big blue eyes were fairly bulging, like two monster
morning-glories, as Elkins, putting the note carefully in his
jacket pocket, said, softly:

"Ef I don't get thet 'ere letter into Jones's hands, you
may have me drummed out o' camp by the mule-drivers."

"I believe you, and trust you. I shall be here to-morrow
morning early, and shall hope to hear something from you.
Good-by."

"Good-by, miss. Just you make up your mind I am
goin' to do what you command."

When she reached home she found her father in the
library. He looked at her inquiringly as she came over and
kissed him.

"I have been in town all day, and am run out."

"Still plotting ?"

"Yes, still plotting."

"You're wasting your time, my dear. You'll know all
you care to soon enough, if you'll just keep quiet."

"Yes; but I can't. I want to know all you know, and I
want to know it now."

"All I know wouldn't be much, according to the
Spragues, who gave me my status in this town, long ago, as
an ignoramus."

"Perhaps you were then, papa."

"Yes; I hadn't been schooled fifteen years by my accomplished daughter."

"A lie is truth to those who only tell the truth."

"What does that mean ?"

"It's simple enough — a home-made epigram. People
who tell nothing but the truth are easiest made to believe
a lie. The Spragues had heard of you as ignorant, and believed it. You can't blame them for that."

"I don't blame them because it was a lie. I blame them
because it was the truth. I don't care a straw how many
lies are told about me — it's the ill-natured truth I object to."

"I'm afraid that you will have a hard time in life if you like lies better than the truth."

"I didn't say that."

"Then I don't understand English."

"You don't understand me."

"Ah, yes I do, papa. I do understand you. I know that at this moment you are doing something that you are ashamed of—something that later you will bitterly repent. You are carrying on now through pride what you began in wrath. Stop where you are. The dead can not be avenged. That's a barbarous code. Remember, in all the petty irritations of the past, when you have been hurt by your neighbors, you were never so triumphant as when you surprised those who injured you by a magnanimous return—"

"There, I made an agreement with you that we should not speak of these things. I mean it. I find that you take advantage of me. I shall be banished from the house if you do not keep to your bargain."

Kate sighed. She had hoped that the early banter was paving the way for a reconciliation. She took up some work and tried to busy her hands.

"Suppose you read me something? You haven't read in an age."

"What shall it be?"

"Oh, something from Dickens—anything you like."

"Very well, I shall show you a counterfeit presentment of yourself," and, with an arch-smile, she began to read from The Chimes.

He listened soberly until the last page was turned. and then, rising, said abstractedly:

"I sha'n't see you for a few days. I wish you would remain at home as much as possible. Get some of the neighbors' girls to keep you company, if you're lonesome."

"Oh, I shall not be lonesome. I shall have too much to do—too much to think about."

He laughed. "You are enough like your father, my girl, to pass for him. Very well, you'll be penitent enough when I come back."

He was gone in the morning, as he had said, and she was free to keep her appointment with Elkins. He was waiting for her when she reached the hotel.

"Well?" she cried, breathlessly.

"I saw him."

She seized the blushing lad's two hands. "Ah, you splendid fellow! And then?—"

"He wrote this note for you," and he handed her an envelope with her own name written on it in an uneven, uncertain scrawl. She tore it open and read:

"DEAR MADAM: I can not understand why there should be any difficulty in finding what became of Sprague and his party. We all reached the lines together, but, as I was hit by a bullet in the head at the moment of rescue, I knew nothing of their movements after reaching the Union lines. I, too, am interested in the young man. I should like to see you or some of his friends at once, as I suspect foul play of some sort.　　　　Obediently yours,　　　　JONES."

"Did you get to him without trouble?" Kate asked, keenly, disappointed by the result of all this strategy.

"I made them believe I was on hospital business. I showed them a large official envelope, and they let me go up. Jones told me to tell you that he would see you there in the parlor if you would come; that he is unable to leave the house, or he would come to see you."

"Can you take me there now?"

"I have four hours of my leave still. It does not expire until two o'clock."

"Then we will go at once. Will you call a carriage?"

While he was gone, Kate read the note again. She was more puzzled than ever. The man wrote as if he had no idea that Jack was not easily traceable, yet all the Spragues' money and influence had been spent in vain. He expected her. Where could her father be? He wrote as though he had no idea that he had been virtually a prisoner. When she reached the house, the servant made no difficulty in admitting her. Elkins remained outside in the vehicle, with an admonition from Kate to remain unseen unless she called him. Jones, the shadow of the burly soldier we saw in the famous escape, was seated in a deep, reclining chair, and, as Kate entered, rose feebly.

"Pray, don't rise, don't disturb yourself in the least. I will sit here near you, and we can talk, if it won't make you ill."

"No. It isn't talking that troubles me—but never mind that. Your note has pulled me down a good deal. I was given to understand that the boys were home and all right."

"The boys?"

"Jack and young Perley."

"Who gave you—who told you that?"

"Your father. He is the only person I have talked with since I got my wits back."

Kate drew back with a shuddering horror.

"Are you quite sure, Mr.—Mr. Jones that my father told you that?"

"Perfectly certain. Do you suppose that I would not have taken measures to find out where my own—I mean where friends were? These boys saved me from prison once and from a death nearly as dreadful as Libby. Could I be indifferent to them?"

"But why should papa tell you they were safe, when—when our hearts have been tortured? Ah! I see. He wanted to spare you the anxiety. Ah! yes. He knew that you would fret and worry, and that you could not recover under the strain." Kate's heart swelled with a triumphant revulsion. She had vilely suspected without cause. She must now do justice. Jones eyed her pensively, holding his head with both his hands.

"Nothing has been heard of the boys since when?"

"Nothing directly since the escape from Richmond. Miss Sprague brought that news, and about the same time a paragraph in the *Herald* announced that prisoners from Richmond had reached the Union lines on the Warrick."

"When was that?"

" Late in November."

" Yes, I was one of them. I escaped from Richmond.
Jack and young Perley got me out of the tobacco warehouse.
We reached the Warrick after a hard week of marching and
hiding, and the boys were alive and well when we reached the
Union outpost. I was last to cross the bridge, and as I plunged
into the thick bushes a bullet struck me. I knew no more
until I found myself here. I had agents at Fort Monroe
waiting for me. They probably forwarded me at once. But
I don't understand how there can be any difficulty in tracing the two boys. Haven't they written ?"

" Not a line, not a word concerning them has been heard.
Mrs. Sprague sent agents so soon as the *Herald* paragraph
was shown to Olympia. They are in Washington now on
the quest. It was there we got track of you—before you
were sent here."

" Why was I sent here ?"

Kate was about to speak. Again the shadow of her first
fear—again the dread of some malevolent purpose on her
father's part—choked her speech.

" I—I—don't know," she faltered.

" Who came with me ?"

" My father."

" Ah!" Jones's eyes were penetrating her now. She felt
the questioning in them, and turned her face to the clinging
folds of the veil.

" Miss Boone, you seem to be deeply interested in these
boys. Are you really their friend ?"

" Ah, believe me, I am heart and soul their friend!"

" Does your father know it ?"

" Yes; he knows that I am seeking them."

" Does he approve your search ?"

" No, he does not."

" Good. Now listen. We have short time to work in.
You have a carriage outside. Your father will be here any
moment. I could never keep from him my indignation and
even distrust. I shall get into that carriage with you, and
you must conceal me somewhere and give me time to set the

proper machinery in motion to find these boys. There is no other way. Your father has some reason for keeping their whereabouts concealed. I may know the purpose and I may not. The boys may have been killed in the volley that struck me. It will require a mere telegram to find out. I know whom to address, but I must be where I can use trusted agents. I have no money. You can, I hope, provide me with that, or the Spragues if you can't."

He spoke with a flush deepening on his face, and arose with something like vigor.

"Ample means—you shall have any sum you need," Kate said, handing him a well-filled purse.

"Good—I have one or two articles in my room. I will fetch them and follow you to the carriage."

Ten minutes later the carriage was whirling over the broad road to Warchester. By Jones's advice it was stopped at the hospital. Here he proposed remaining for the night, to mislead suspicion if any one had taken the precaution to follow.

"I will remain with our friend Elkins to-night, as you suggest," Jones said; "to-morrow I will send you word of my whereabouts, and you may expect to have news of the boys within the week."

"My address will be in Washington," Kate said. "I shall go at once to the Spragues. They have been there, as I told you, to seek every possible source of information. I left them to follow you, hoping that through you I should find the missing."

"You made no mistake. I shall find them. You can tell your friends that," and he added, with a gleam of savage malice, "God help the man that has raised the weight of a feather against them, for he has put a heavy hurt on me if he has harmed them!"

Kate shuddered. Was she never to emerge from this hideous circle of vengeful hatred—this condition of passionate vendetta—where men were seeking each other's harm? On reaching home she addressed a note to her father explaining frankly that she had entered into communication with Jones; that she had been pained by all that she had heard; that the inquiry had now passed out of her hands and was in that of the authorities, and begging him to drop any participation he might have meditated. In a late letter Olympia had given good news of her mother, saying that Kate could return with safety, and, informing her father of this, Kate bade him good-by for a time.

When Kate reached Washington she found Mrs. Sprague convalescent, but painfully feeble. The poor mother reproached herself for the interruption of the search, and implored the two girls to begin again without a moment's delay. Kate gave her as much hope as she dared. She hinted something of the outlines of what she had done and the new agent in the field. With this Mrs. Sprague was greatly comforted, but begged them to remit no efforts of their own. It was after three days' fruitless searching among the records of the department and among the men of the Caribee regiment, now returned to Washington *en route* to the front, that Kate bethought herself of her father's probable presence in the city. She got out of the carriage and entered the long reception-room of Willard's to make inquiry. The boy who came at her call said, as soon as she asked for Mr. Boone :

"Why, I just saw him at the desk, paying his bill. He is probably there still. Wait here until I see."

But Kate, fearing that he might be gone before she could reach him, followed the boy. There was no sign of her father at the desk, and, turning hastily out of the main corridor, filled with officers and the clank of swords almost stunning her, she reached the porch just as a cab set out toward the station. She caught aglimpse of her father's face in it. He was leaving the city. She must see him. The inspiration of the instant suggested by a cabman was followed. She hastily entered the vehicle and bade the driver keep in sight of the one her father was in until it came to a stop. The driver whipped up his horses, but there wasn't much speed in them. Kate dared not look out of the window, and sat in feverish anxiety while she was whirled along Pennsylvania Avenue, almost to the Baltimore Station, then the only one in the city connecting with the North. To her surprise, the driver stopped near the curb a block or more short of the railway. She looked out, and as she did so the driver pointed to her father's carriage halted just ahead. She took out her purse, but was delayed a moment in getting the fare, keeping her eye, however, on her father as he hurried from the cab to a building before which a sentry was lazily pacing. She was not two minutes in reaching the doorway, but he had disappeared.

The soldier asked her no questions, and of course she could ask none, as probably her father was unknown to the military filling the place. She must follow on until she overtook him. There were clerks busy at long desks, military officials moving about with files of documents. The presence of a few women in widow's weeds reassured Kate, and as no one molested her she persisted in her design. He was not on the lower floor, and, coming back, she ascended a broad stairway. The hall was wide, and filled with people all in uniform. She could hear a monotonous voice reading in front, where the crowd clustered thickest. She looked about helplessly, and tried to push forward. Suddenly she heard the words : "Guilty of taking the life of the same Wesley Boone. Specification third : And that the said John Sprague is guilty of the crime of spying inside the lines of the armies of the United States." For a moment Kate stood stupefied—rooted to the floor. Jack was undergoing an ignominious trial for murder—for desertion! All fear, all timidity, all sense of the unfitness of feminine evidence in such a place fled from her. She pushed her way through the astonished throng which fell aside as they saw her black dress and flowing drapery. She reached the last range of benches, where men were seated, some writing, some consulting documents, while the clerk read the charges. Her eye fell upon her father seated near the place of the presiding officer. She grew confident and confirmed by the sight: it was a signal to the daring that fired her. "Stop!" she said, in a clear voice. "I don't know what this place is; I don't know what meaning these proceedings have. I heard a charge that is not true. It is false that John Sprague murdered Wesley Boone. Wesley Boone was my brother, and he was killed in the dark by one of several shots fired at the same instant. Furthermore, my brother was armed and in the sleeping-room of the mistress of the house at the dead of night. If John Sprague's bullet killed him it was shot in self-defense and in the safeguarding of two terrified women. He had no more idea of whom he was struggling with than—than the soldier who fires in battle. Furthermore, he is no spy. He risked his life to rescue prisoners. He saved the life of one of them who can be brought here to testify. He—"

But here Kate broke down. She had spoken with a passionate, resentful vehemence, her mind all the time seething with the fear and shame of her father's responsibility for this hideous attack upon the absent. She stretched out her hand exhaustedly for support. A young officer near her pushed up a chair and helped her into it. Boone had turned in speechless amazement as the first words of the voice sounded in his ears. His back was toward the door, and he had not seen Kate. He turned as she broke into this fervid apostrophe. Whether from surprise, prudence, or anger he sat silent, uninterrupting till she tottered into the seat placed for her by a stranger. Then he arose and went to her side, in nowise angry or discomposed so far as his outward demeanor betrayed him. The presiding officer of the court-martial had attempted to silence Kate by a gesture, but with eyes fixed steadily upon him she had disregarded his command. Now, however, he spoke:

"Madame, you must know this is highly disorderly and indecorous. The court can take no cognizance of this sort of testimony. Do you desire to be heard by counsel? If you do, the judge-advocate will give you all lawful assistance."

"If the court please, this lady is my daughter. She is somewhat excited. I will take the necessary measures in the matter," Boone began.

Kate pushed her father from before her and again addressed the president.

"I refuse my father's aid in this case. I don't know what is necessary, but I ask this court, if it has anything to do with John Sprague, to give his friends an opportunity to present his story truthfully and without prejudice."

"The judge-advocate will give you all necessary information. Meanwhile, the case will be adjourned until to-morrow."

Elisha Boone stood beside his daughter, a figure of perplexity and chagrin. He dared not remonstrate openly. He was forced to hear the judge-advocate question this extraordinary witness, and instruct her on the steps necessary to be taken; worse than all, hear him inform Kate that the citations to John Sprague had been regularly issued, and that the evidence of his desertion rested wholly on the fact that he had put in no answer to the charges promulgated against him by his commanding officer; that the trial was proceeding on the ground that Sprague had deserted to the enemy, and refused to answer within the time allowed by law.

"But he has never heard of the charges," Kate cried, indignantly. "He has not been heard of since he escaped from Richmond."

"As we understand it, he reached the Union lines merely to ambuscade our outposts, and then returned to Richmond."

"His sister left Richmond ten days after his flight, and he had then passed into our lines, as she had the surest means of knowing."

"There is some extraordinary error in all this. If Sprague can be produced before the term fixed by the regulations, he can vindicate himself by establishing the facts you have told me. If not, we have no alternative but to condemn him to death as a spy and deserter. The testimony on these specifications is uncontradicted. The murder we may not be able to establish, though we have witnesses of the shooting."

It was arranged that Sprague's counsel should see the judge-advocate at once, Kate giving him the address in case

by any accident she should be prevented from seeing the
Spragues. As she left the room, under a fusillade of admiring glances, she leaned on her father's arm, trembling but
resolute. She now knew the worst, and she had no further
terror. As they reached the door, her father asked:

"Where are you going? I suppose I need not tell you
that I was on my way home when I came here, for I suppose you have been spying on my movements."

"Never. I feared you were acting unwisely, but I never
dreamed of watching you. Providence has put your plans
in my hands at nearly every step, but I was so ignorant that,
of myself, the information would have done but little service
to poor Jack. I came into the court by the merest chance.
I saw you get into the cab at Willard's, and as I had only
reached Washington, I wanted to see you before you went
away. I drove after you—followed without the slightest
suspicion of the place or your purpose in it."

"Well, all your running about is useless. He will be
sentenced to death and the family disgraced. Nothing can
now prevent that."

"Yes, Jack can prevent it! I can prevent it!"

"How?"

"Jack will be found. Surely they dare not commit such
a monstrous crime against the absent, the undefended!"

"Well, we won't talk of it. I suppose you are with the
Spragues?"

"Yes; I shall remain with them until this is ended."

"What if I should tell you to come home with me?"

"I should, of course, obey you if you commanded me.
But before doing so I should have to put my statement in
legal shape—that is, swear to it, and give my address to the
court that I might be regularly summoned."

"You know something of law, too, I see. I sha'n't ask
you to go home, nor shall I go myself. I shall remain to
see how this affair turns out."

They were driving down Pennsylvania Avenue now.
Kate, recalling her departure, asked, "You did not get the
letter I left for you at home?"

"No, I did not know you were gone."

"I left a few lines to tell you that I had seen Jones." She watched him as she said this. He did not start, as she expected. His lips were suddenly compressed and his eye grew dark; then he smiled grimly.

"I hope you felt repaid for your trouble."

"Yes. I felt amply repaid. Jones has undertaken to find out what became of Jack after his arrival at the Union outposts."

"Did you discuss the whole affair with him ?"

"Yes. I was greatly relieved by what I learned. I was afraid you had some sinister purpose in secreting him as the only link between Jack and his friends. It gave me new life to find that you had been so tender and thoughtful to Jones, for, as the event proved, he no sooner learned that there were apprehensions as to Jack's safety, than he set about his discovery."

"Did Jones share your grateful sentiment ?"

"I think he did. To spare you agitation, he set out at once alone, in order that you might be relieved of all responsibility."

"Ah !" And Elisha Boone sank far back in the cushion. The carriage stopped in front of Willard's; then he said: "I shall remain here now. I will order the driver to take you home. Come to me as often as you can." He kissed her in the old friendly way and hurried into the hotel.

"On reaching her lodgings she found a telegram waiting her. It read: "Jones gone South. He will advise you of his movements.   ELKINS."

CHAPTER XXXII.

THE LOST CARIBEES.

MEANWHILE war, in one of its grim humors, had prepared a comedy when the stage was set in tragic trappings. In the withdrawal of Johnston's army from Manassas—signalized in history as the Quaker campaign, because our army found wooden guns in the deserted works—that ardent young Hotspur, Vincent Atterbury, ran upon a disagreeable end to a very charming adventure. In chivalric bravado, to emphasize the fact that the withdrawal of the Confederates was merely strategic, not forced, the young man, with a lively company of horsemen, hungering for excitement, formed themselves into a defiant rear-guard. The Union outposts, never suspecting that Johnston's army was not behind the enterprising cavalry, withdrew prudently to the main forces.

Then, when they were convinced that the little band was merely on an audacious lark, forces were sent out on either flank, while the main body feigned the disorder of retreat. The result was, that Vincent's squadron was handsomely entrapped, and in the savage contest that ensued the intrepid major was hustled from his horse with a dislocated shoulder and broken wrist. He was brought, with a half-dozen more of his dare-devil comrades, into the Union lines, and in the course of time found himself in the hideous shambles allotted rebel prisoners at Point Lookout, Maryland. Too weak at first, or too confused, to bethink himself of his Northern friends, Vincent shared the hard usage of his companions and resigned himself patiently to the slow procedure of exchange, which was now going on regularly, since the Union victories in the West and South had given the Northern authorities ten prisoners to the Southerners' one. The prospect of his own release was, under these circumstances, rather distant, as without special intervention he would have to await his turn, the rule being that those first captured were first exchanged. He knew that his family's influence and his own intimacy with General Johnston would probably hasten the release, but he could not count upon an immediate return to his duties, and in view of this he was not very reluctant to undergo convalescence in the North.

Jack's influence, he counted, would soon relieve him from the hardships of confinement, and then he should see Olympia—that, at least, was recompense for his misfortune. His mother and Rosa would immediately learn of his capture, and he might count upon hearing from them, as very generous latitude was allowed in such cases by the authorities on both sides. He caused a letter to be written to Jack, addressing it to his regiment, in care of the War Department, and waited patiently the response. His disappointment and anxiety, as days passed and he got no answer, began to tell on his health, already weakened by his wounds. Thus, one day, when a young lady was shown to his bedside—who fell upon him with a glad cry, and held his head to her breast—he was too far gone in delirium to distinguish his sister.

"My darling ! O Olympia, I knew you would come," he murmured, and Rosa, terrified, but composed, soothed the fevered lover as best she might. He grew worse in spite of all her devotion. The physicians, burdened with patients far in excess of their powers, assured her that her brother would require the most patient care and enlightened nursing ; that medicine would do him but slight good, and that she must make up her mind to a prolonged illness. Rosa was alone in the vast hospital, save for the presence of her maid Linda, who had come through the lines with her and was, of course, under the Northern laws, free. Worse than all, she was poorly provided with money, and this need, rather than Vincent's love-lorn babbling about Olympia, reminded Rosa to call upon the Spragues for help. She wrote at once to Olympia, telling the distressing story, and then set about bettering Vincent's surroundings.

Point Lookout had been selected for its natural prison-like safeguards. A rank bog surrounded the place on three sides, and thus but few troops were needed to guard the great mass of rebel prisoners lodged in wooden barracks and long lines of tents. Vincent's case seemed to have grown stationary after her coming. He slept a fitful, troubled sleep half the day. At night he grew delirious and restless. Rosa and Linda divided the hours into watches, and administered the draughts prepared by the stewards. Through the humanity of the physician in charge, the invalid had been transferred to an A tent, where Rosa could remain day and night unmolested with her maid. Vincent thus cared for, Rosa began to think of the other poor fellows in her brother's squadron, and set about a systematic search for them. Many of them she found in the general wards of the hospital. It was on this kindly mission one day that she heard her brother's name mentioned by a civilian, who was talking with an official in uniform.

"Major Atterbury? Oh, yes; he was removed to division D. You will find him in a separate tent. He has a woman nurse. I will send an orderly with you."

Rosa did not recognize the civilian at first, but as he turned to accompany the soldier she remembered where she had seen him before. He was the prisoner Jack had spoken with in Richmond the day the party visited the tobacco warehouse. She hastened her step, and, as she came up with the men, she said, tremulously:

"I am Major Atterbury's sister. My brother is unconscious. Can I attend to the business you have with him?"

Jones turned and stopped, glancing in surprise at the girl.

"I'm sorry to learn that your brother's so low. But you can do all that I hoped from him. Here is a letter addressed to John Sprague. It was received at his regiment three days ago. I happened to be there making inquiries for him, and the colonel handed it to me. Under the circumstances I felt justified in reading it, and it turns out that I did well."

"John Sprague is missing?" Rosa cried, her mind instantly at work in alarm for some one else.

Jones, dismissing the orderly, told her the facts as we have already followed them. Leaving out all mention of

Kate, he told her how he had hurried down to Newport News, and thence to the outposts on the Warrick.

There he had learned that Jack and Dick had been wounded, fatally the story went, in the final volley fired by the pursuers. They had been carried to the hospital at Hampton. But there all trace had been lost. The steward who received them and the surgeon who had taken their descriptive list had been transferred to St. Louis. There was, however, no record of their deaths, and upon that he based the hope that they were either in hospital, or had been, through some strange confusion, assigned among rebel wounded, a thing that had frequently happened in the hurry of transporting large numbers of wounded men.

"And does Mrs. Sprague know all this?" Rosa cried, understanding now why Vincent's letter and her own had not brought a response.

"Partly, I think. Mrs. Sprague and her daughter are in Washington, in the state of mind you may imagine, and exhausting bales of red tape to reach the lost boys."

Poor Rosa! She had thought her grief and terror too much to endure before. Now how trivial Vincent's fever in comparison with this appalling disappearance of Dick and Jack! She walked on over the sparse herbage, over her shoes in the soft sand, when Linda came running from the tent in joyous excitement.

"De good Lord, Miss Rosa, she's here; she's done come!"

"Who is here—who is come?" Rosa cried, impatiently; "not mamma?"

"'Deed no, Miss Rosa; Miss Limpy."

"What?"

"Yes, indeed; and, oh, bress de Lord, Massa Vint knows her, and is talkin' like a sweet dove!"

It was true. Miss "Limpy," blushing very red, was surprised by Rosa in a very motherly attitude by the patient's cot. The two girls melted in a delirious hug, mingled with spasmodic smacks of the lips and a soft, gurgling *crescendo* of exclamation, not very intelligible to Jones and Linda, who discreetly remained near the door on the outside.

25

Vincent's eyes were fixed on Olympia. For the first time in ten days they shone with the light of reason. He smiled softly at the scene and murmured lightly to himself. Warned not to tax the feeble powers of the invalid, Rosa and Jones withdrew, leaving Olympia to recover from the fatigues of her journey in the tent with Vincent.

"Now, you're not to talk, you know," Olympia said, with matronly decision. "I shall remain here to mesmerize you into repose. You know I am a magnetic person. Be perfectly quiet, and keep your eyes off me. They make me nervous."

"I can only keep my eyes away on condition you put your hand in mine. Then the magnetic current can have full play."

"My impression is that you have not been ill at all. I believe you have been shamming, to escape the harder lines of the prison. Very well, you needn't answer. I'll take that shake of the head as denial and proof for want of better. Now, I will give you the history of our doings since I saw you at Fairfax Court-House in January. I got home safe. I found mamma in painful excitement."

He moved impatiently, and said, beseechingly:

"But tell me how you got here so soon. How did you learn I was here? Jack told you when he got my letter?"

"O Vincent, that was what I was coming to! Jack has never been seen or heard from since he escaped from your troops near the Warrick. I did not know you had written. I got a letter from Rosa yesterday morning and went at once to the War Department, where we have a good friend—"

"I can't understand it. All these things are done with system in an army like yours. Men can't disappear like this, leaving no record. I'll stake my head there's foul play, if the boys can't be found. Have you made inquiry in the company on duty where Jack and his companions got into your lines?"

She explained all the efforts that had been made—how Brodie had been baffled, and how letters had been sent to the commanding officer at Fort Monroe.

"We had begun to think that Jack had been recaptured; but surely, if he were, you would have known of it."

"Of course I should."

"Then that confines the search to our own lines. I can not make myself believe that Jack is dead, though mamma has nearly made up her mind to it. The mysterious part of the affair is, that we can not find one of the men who escaped with Jack, though it was announced in the papers weeks ago that a party of them had arrived at Fort Monroe."

"And young 'Perley'?"

"He, too, we can get no trace of."

"Good heavens! I'm glad Rosa doesn't know that; she'd be in every camp and hospital in the North until she had found her sweetheart."

"That sounds something like a reflection on us—mamma and me."

"Ah! never. What I mean is, that Rosa is such an impulsive, silly child, she would do all sorts of imprudent things. How could you do such a thing? Preposterous!"

"Well, I began it yesterday morning. As I said, so soon as I read Rosa's letter, I went to headquarters, where we have a good friend, and gave my word for your safe keeping. You are to be our prisoner; but if you escape you will get us into trouble, for we are none too well considered by the folks in power."

"God forgive me, Olympia! escape is the last thing I think of now, when I am near you. I was going to say I should never care to go back, but I know you wouldn't think the better of me for that."

"I don't know. Why should you go back? The South is sure to be beaten. We are conquering territory every day, from the armies at Donelson to the forts at New Orleans. We shall beat you in Virginia so soon as General McClellan gives the word."

"Even if that were the case, my duty and my honor would point to but one course—to return to the natural course of exchange."

"Honor? Vincent, it is a vague term under such circumstances—"

"I could not love you, dear, so much, loved I not honor more. You know you gave me that for a motto."

"Poetic rubbish, Mr. Soldier; but I must leave you now. You will insist on talking, and, as I shall be held responsible to your mother and Rosa, I must be firm—not another syllable! Besides, the imprudence will keep you here longer, and if you are to be carried away you must get well at once. I can't leave mamma alone in Washington with such grief preying upon her."

He answered with a glance of pitying pleading. He looked so helpless—so woe-begone—that she bent over near his face to smooth his disordered bandages. When she withdrew she was blushing very prettily, and Vincent was smiling in triumph. "On these terms," the smile seemed to say, "I will be mute for an age."

What an adroit ally war is to love! Here was the self-contained Olympia—so confident of herself—fond and yielding as Rosa; when war rushed in, infirmity came to the rescue of Vincent's despairing passion.

Meanwhile, Jones began a systematic search among the prisoners for the missing Caribees. Rosa joined with impatient ardor. There were three thousand inmates of the improvised city, but no one resembling Jack or Dick could be found. Linda, ministering to some of Vincent's comrades, was piteously besought to ask her mistress's good offices for an orderly in the small-pox ward. This was a tent far off from the main barracks on the beach, attended only by a single surgeon and a corps of rather indifferent nurses. Two of Vincent's men were in this lazar, shut off from the world, for the soldier, reckless in battle, has a shuddering horror of this loathsome disease. Rosa instantly resolved that she would herself nurse the plague-smitten rebels. She had no fear of the disease, the truth being that she had only the vaguest idea of what it was. With great difficulty she obtained permission to visit the outcast colony. She was forced to enter the noisome purlieu alone, even the maid's devotion rebelling against the nameless horror small-pox has for the African.

Once within the long marqueé, however, Rosa was relieved to find that the casual spectacle was not different from that of the other seriously sick-wards. A melancholy silence seemed to signalize the despair of the twoscore patients, each occupying a cot screened from the rest by thin canvas curtains. Double lines of sentries guarded each opening of the marqueé, so that no one could pass in or out without the rigidly *viséd* order of the surgeon-in-chief. Braziers of charcoal burned at the foot of each bed, while the atmosphere was heavy with a strong solution of carbolic acid, then just beginning to be recognized as a sovereign preventive of malarious vapors, and an antiseptic against the germs of disease. Rosa inquired for the *protégés* she was seeking. They were pointed out, on one side of the tent, the steward accompanying her to each cot.

"All have the small-pox?" she inquired, shuddering, as she glanced at the white screens, behind which an occasional plaintive groan could be heard.

"Oh, no! there are some here that have no more small-pox than I have."

"Then why do you keep them here?" Rosa asked, indignantly.

"Oh, red tape, miss. There's two men that were brought here three months ago. They'd no more small-pox than you have, miss; but they were assigned here, and I have given up trying to get them taken to the convalescent camp. The truth, is the surgeon in charge is afraid to show up here. The others make by the number they have in charge, for we are allowed extra pay and an extra ration for every case on hand."

"Why, this is infamous!" Rosa cried. "It is murder. Why don't you write to the—the—head man?"

"And get myself in the guard-house for my trouble? No, thank you, miss. I wouldn't have spoken to you if it hadn't been for the sympathy you showed coming in, and to sort o' show you that you are not running so much danger as folks try to make you believe."

Rosa had a basket on her arm filled with such comforting delicacies as the surgeon had advised. She set about administering them to her brother's orderly, when a feeble voice in a cot a few feet away fell upon her ear. She started. Though almost a whisper, there was a strange familiarity in the low tone. She turned to the steward—

"Who is in the third cot from here ?"

"Let me see. Oh, yes, number seven; that's a man named Paling.

"And the next ?"

"Number eight; that's a man named Jake, or Jakes, I'm blessed if I am certain. They've been out of their head since they come. They're the two I spoke of who ain't no more small-pox than I have."

"May I see them ?"

"Certainly. I'll see that they're in shape for inspection, and call you."

He disappeared behind the curtain and could be heard in a kindly, jovial tone:

"There, sonny, keep kivered; the lady is coming to bring you something better than the doctor's gruel, so lie still."

Beckoning to Rosa, he made way for her to enter the narrow aisle of number seven, but he nearly fell over the man across the bed, when Rosa, with a shriek, fell upon the body of number seven, crying:

"O, my darling, my darling, I have found you!"

It would have required the eyes of maternal love of Rosa's to recognize our jaunty Dick in the emaciated, fleshless face that lay imbedded in the disarray of the cot. Dick's blue eyes were sunken and dim, his lips chalky and parched. He made no sign of recognition when Rosa drew back with her arm under his head to scrutinize the disease-worn face.

"Sometimes, miss, he is in his right mind—but he goes off again like this. Is the other man his brother ? They seem to understand each other when they are at the worst. Once when we separated them they fought like maniacs un- til we were forced to let them be near again."

"Oh, yes—the other." Rosa started and hastened to the

next cot. Yes, it was Jack—or a piteous ghost of him. He was sleeping, and she withdrew gently.

"Please distribute the contents of the basket to the men I named. I will be back presently."

With this she darted out, running at the top of her speed, heedless even of the peremptory challenge of the sentries, who thought her mad or stricken with the plague, and made no attempt to molest her. She ran straight to Jones's quarters. He was writing, and started in surprise as she entered panting and breathless.

"Ah! I have found them; I have found them!" She could say no more. Jones helped her to a seat and held a glass of water to her lips. Then she regained breath.

"They are in the small-pox ward, but they haven't the disease. Ah! they are there, they are there. Come at once and take them away. Ah! take them away this minute."

"By 'they' do you mean Perley and Sprague?" Jones asked, breathlessly.

"Yes, ah, yes. Thank God! thank God! Ah! I could say prayers from now until my dying day. But, oh, Mr. Jones, do, do hurry; because they may die if we do not get them away from that dreadful pest-house."

"It will take some time to get the order for the removal. Meanwhile, they will need good nursing. If you hope to help them you must be calm; you must keep well. Now go to your brother. It is just as well that Miss Sprague went away this morning. Before she comes back, her brother will be in a place she can visit with safety. You can not go back there. You must remain patient now until I get them away from that dangerous place."

It was not until the next day that the red tape of the establishment was so far cut as to warrant the surgeon in charge in making a personal inspection of the two invalids. He at once, and in indignant astonishment, pronounced the two untouched by the disease set against their names in their papers of admission. Early in the afternoon they were carried on a stretcher to a clean, fresh tent on the sandy beach, where the laurel bushes almost ran into the water. Letters had been dispatched to Olympia informing her that Jack was found, and urging her to come on at once. The next evening the three ladies arrived—Mrs. Sprague, Olympia, and Kate. With them they brought a renowned physician who had been uniformly successful in treating maladies of the sort the lads were described as suffering.

Days of painful anxiety followed. Once, all hope of Dick was abandoned, and his aunts were telegraphed for. But, in the end, he opened his big blue eyes, sane and convalescent. There was rapid mending after this, you may be sure. Kate had, through Olympia's unobtrusive manœuvring, been forced to bear the burden of Jack's nursing, and, somehow, when that impatient warrior mingled amorous pleadings with his early consciousness, she forgot upon which side the burden of repentance and forgiving lay. She listened with gentle serenity to his protestations, checking him only by the threat to quit the place and return to her father.

During all this, Rosa was divided in her mind. She resented the assiduity of Jones in the recovery of Dick. That reticent person had installed himself in Dick's tent and never quitted the lad, day or night, unless to relinquish him to Rosa's arbitrary hand. When, one day, Pliny and Merry Perley entered the tent, Jones changed color. The two ladies, not heeding the stranger, fell upon the convalescent on the cot, and Jones slipped away. Thereafter Rosa had her invalid to herself, Jones only reappearing at night, to keep the vigils of the dark. A month later, the invalids were strong enough to be removed. An inquiry had been set on foot to account for the presence of the two Union soldiers among the rebel prisoners. The result was confusing, however. The facts seemed to point out design in the original entry of the young men's names at Hampton, where they had been taken when brought in by the outposts.

The dispersion of the rest of their companions from Richmond was accounted for by furloughs granted them so soon as they reached the provost-marshal's office. Just before leaving Point Lookout Jack received a much-directed letter that gave signs of having been in every mail-bag in the

Army of the Potomac. It was from Barney Moore, bristling with wonder and turgid with woful lamentation at Jack's coldness in not writing him. He had been sent by mistake to Ship Island, near New Orleans, to join his regiment, and had only at the writing of the letter reached Washington, where the Caribees were expected every day to move to the Peninsula in McClellan's new campaign.

So soon as he was sufficiently recovered to write, Jack reported by letter to the regiment. He had received no reply. The explanation was awaiting him so soon as he reached Washington. While seated with his mother in Willard's, a heavy knock came on the door. It was thrown open before the maid could reach it. A provost corporal stood on the threshold, a file of men behind him:

"I have an order for the arrest of Sergeant John Sprague."

"I am John Sprague. Of what am I accused?"

"I have no orders to tell you. My orders are to deliver you at the provost prison. You will hear the charges there."

"But I am still under the doctor's charge. I am on the hospital list."

"I don't know what condition you are in. My orders are to arrest you, and you know I have no option. All can be remedied at the provost's office."

"I will go with you, my son," Mrs. Sprague said, trying to look untroubled. "It is some error which can be explained."

"No, mamma, you can't come. Send word to the counsel you engaged in the search. I fancy it is some mistake; but I wish it hadn't occurred just now. I wouldn't write Olympia about it." Olympia had gone on to Acredale with Kate, to set the house in order for a season of festivity. Jack, Vincent, Dick, and the rest, were to join them so soon as the invalid had taken rest in Washington.

The guard indulged Jack in a carriage to headquarters. Here he was handed over to a lieutenant in charge, and conducted to a prison-like apartment in the rear.

"What is the charge against me?" Jack asked, as the officer touched a bell.

" I am not acquainted with the papers in your case. My instructions are to hold you until called for.—Sergeant," he added, as a soldier in uniform entered, " the prisoner is to be confined in close quarters, and is not to be lost sight of night or day."

The soldier saluted and motioned Jack to follow him, two other soldiers closing in behind him as he set out. At the end of a short hallway the sergeant stopped, took a key from a bunch at his belt, unlocked a heavily-barred door and motioned Jack to enter. It was useless to protest, useless to parley. He knew military procedure too well to think of it, but his heart swelled with bitter rage. This was the reward of an almost idolatrous patriotism—this was the *patrie's* way of cherishing her defenders. He flung himself on the cot in a wild passion of tears and rebellious scorn. But his humiliation was not yet ended; while he sat with his face covered by his hands, he felt hands upon his legs, and the sharp click of a lock. He moved his left leg. Great God ! it was chained to an enormous iron bolt. He started to rise; the sharp links of the chain cut his ankle as the great ball rolled away from him. With a cry of madness he flung himself on the harsh pine pallet, groaning his heart out in bitter anguish and maledictions. In time food was brought him, but he sat supine, staring ghastly at the dull-eyed orderly, silent, unquestioning. Dim banners of light fell across the corridor. They were broken at regular intervals by the passing figure of a sentry. The night wore on. There was a lull in the monotonous tramp. Steps came toward Jack's cell—stopped; the key grated in the lock; some one touched him on the shoulder. He never stirred.

" Cheer up, Sprague; it's all a mistake." It was the voice of the lawyer.

At this Jack started, his eyes gleaming wildly. " Ah, I thought so. I knew I could never have been disgraced like this in earnest. They have discovered the wrong done me ? "

" No, no; not exactly that, Jack, but we shall show them the mistake, I make no doubt."

"Why am I dishonored? Of what am I accused? Why am I here?" Jack cried, shivering under the revulsion from despair to hope, and from hope back to horror.

"You are dishonored, my poor young friend, because a court-martial has found you guilty of murder, desertion, and treason against the articles of war, and you are here because you are sentenced to be shot one week from Friday, in the center of a hollow square, seated on your own coffin."

CHAPTER XXXIII.

FATHER ABRAHAM'S JOKE.

IN her own mind, as the train rolled toward Acredale from Washington, Kate was enjoying in anticipation the victory she had to announce to her father. He had written her regularly from Warchester, where he was engaged in an important suit. She had written more frequently than he, but she had made no allusion to the happy ending of her troubles. It was partly dread that the knowledge of Jack's restoration might bring on more active hostility, as well as a whimsical feminine caprice to spring the great event upon him when all danger was over. She watched Dick and Rosa in the seat near her, for they, too, were of the advance guard to Acredale, where, when Olympia had arranged the house, Vincent and Jack were to come for final restoration · to health. When the party arrived at the little Acredale Station there was a great crowd gathered.

A company of the Caribees was just setting out for the front. Some of the old members recognized Dick, and then straightway went up a cheer that brought all the corner loiterers to the spot to learn the goings on. It was in consequence rather a triumphal procession that followed the carriage to the Sprague gateway, and even followed up the sanded road to the broad piazza. Rosa remained with Olympia, while Kate carried Dick off to commit him to the aunts waiting on the porch to welcome the prodigal. Kate had telegraphed her coming, and her father was at the door to meet her. He was plainly relieved and delighted to have her with him again, for he held her long and close in his arms. "Then all's forgiven ; we're friends again," she said, laughing and crying together.

"There is nothing to forgive. It may be a matter of regret that you are a Boone in blood rather than an Ovid, and that you imitate the Boones in obstinacy. But justice has been done, and there's no need to quarrel about strangers."

She didn't understand in the least what he meant about justice being done. Remembering that all was well, she smiled as they entered the library, and when she had removed her wraps, said, in repressed triumph: "You need never attempt the role of Shylock again. I play Portia better than you play the Jew. You have lost your pound of flesh."

"Well, be magnanimous. Don't abuse your victory. I shouldn't, in your place; but women are never merciful to the fallen."

"I am to you. For, see, I kiss you as gayly as when I believed you all heart and goodness."

"Now you believe me no heart and badness ? "

"I didn't say that. I say you are given over to sinful hates, and I must correct you."

"Well, I'm willing now to be corrected."

"But the correction will be a severe one; you must prepare for a very grievous penance."

"Knowing you, I can foresee that you won't spare the rod. Very well, I'll try to get used to it."

At this moment a servant came to the door.

"A note for Miss Kate," she said. Kate tore it open and read:

"Come to me at once. I have frightful news from Washington. As it concerns Jack you ought to know it.

"OLYMPIA."

She read the lines twice before she could seize the meaning. Frightful news concerning Jack! Had he suffered a relapse? Had he been accidentally hurt? No; if it had been news of that sort, Olympia would have come herself. A gleam of prescience shot through her brain. The court —the charges against Jack! That was it. That was the secret of her father's equanimity under her raillery. She turned with a rush into the library. The bad blood of the Boones was all up in her soul now. She walked straight at, not to her father, and, holding Olympia's note before him, said in bitter scorn:

"Tell me what this means. I know that you know."

He took the paper with leisurely unconcern, affecting not to remark Kate's flashing wrath: he read the lines, handed the paper back, or held it toward Kate, who put her hands behind her.

"Since it concerns you, my child, suppose you go over and ask Miss Sprague. How should I know the affairs of such superior people?"

"Could nothing soften you?—humanize you, I was going to say. Could nothing satisfy you but the death of this injured family?—for this blow will kill them. Kill them? Why should they care to live when that noble fellow has been dishonored by your cruel acts? Ah, I know what you have done! You have brought the court to disgrace Jack— to make him appear a deserter. You it was who, in some mysterious way, caused him to be abducted into the small-pox ward among the rebel prisoners. But it shall all be made known. I shall myself go on the stand and testify to your handiwork. Yes, I am a Boone in this. I will follow the lesson you have set me. I will avenge the innocent and save him by exposing the guilty."

"On second thought, daughter, you are not in a frame of mind to see strangers to-night. You will remain home this evening. To-morrow you can see your friend and advise her in her sorrow, whatever it is." He went to the door and called the servant. "Go to Miss Sprague with my compliments, and tell her my daughter is not able to leave the house this evening." As the man closed the outer door, Kate made a step forward, crying:

"You never mean to say that I am a prisoner in my own father's house?"

"Certainly not. We're not play-actors. I think it best that you should not go to the neighbors to-night, and you, as a dutiful daughter, obey without murmur, because I have always been an indulgent parent and gratified every whim of yours, even to letting you consort with my bitterest enemies for months." As he spoke, there was a ring at the door-bell. Presently the servant entered the room and announced "Mr. Jones." Before Boone could direct him to be shown into another room Jones entered the library, fairly pushing the astonished menial aside. Boone held up his hand with a warning gesture, and nodded toward Kate; but, without halting, Jones advanced to Boone's chair, and, seizing him by the shoulder, held up a copy of the afternoon paper.

"Read that? What does it mean?"

Boone's eyes rested a moment on the paragraphs pointed out. Then, throwing the paper aside, he asked, coldly:

"Why should you ask me what it means? If you are interested in the affair, you might find out by writing to the court."

At this, Jones, looking around the room, marked the two doors, one leading to the hall, the other to the drawing-room. He deliberately went to each, and, locking it, slipped the key in his pocket. He glanced reassuringly at Kate, as she sat dumfounded waiting the issue of this singular scene. He confronted Boone, leaning against the mantel.

"It's just as well that we have a witness to this final settlement, Elisha Boone.—Twenty years ago, Miss Boone, I was a citizen of this town. I was the owner of these acres. I am Richard Perley. In those days I was a wild fellow—I thought then, a wicked one; but I have learned since that I was not, for folly is not crime. In those days—I was barely twenty-five—your father had a hard ground to till in his way of life. I became his patron, and from that I became his slave. I never exactly knew how it came about, but

within a few years most of my property was mortgaged to
Elisha Boone. I won't accuse him, as the world does, of
inciting me to drink and gambling. God knows he has
enough to answer for without that! In the end I was driven
to a deed that imperiled my liberty, and Elisha Boone put the
temptation and the means to do it within my reach. Detection followed, and the detection came about through Elisha
Boone. All my property in his hands, my name a scorn,
and my person subject to the law, Elisha Boone had no further fear of me, and thenceforth doled me out an income
sufficient to supply my modest wants. I strove to turn the
new leaf that recommends itself to men who have exhausted
the so-called pleasures of life. I was living in honesty and
seclusion in Richmond, when Boone, who had never lost
sight of me, came with a mission for me to perform. I was
engaged as an agent of the detective force of the United
States, with the special duty of rescuing Wesley Boone from
captivity.

"I was further commissioned to get evidence against John
Sprague, fixing upon him the crime of betraying his colors
and aiding the Confederacy. In the attempt to rescue Captain Boone at Rosedale circumstances pointed to the guilt of
young Sprague, but that was all dissipated a few weeks after,
when, at the peril of his own life, not once, but a score of
times, he rashly liberated a score or two of prisoners, and
personally led them through an entire rebel army to the
Union lines. I, who would have been abandoned by a less
noble nature, for I was weakened by captivity and bad fare,
broke down, but Sprague and—and—young Dick—my son,
clung to me with such devotion as few sons would exhibit under such trials, and brought me safe to the outposts. Here,
by some mysterious means, we were all dispersed. When I
found my senses I was under Elisha Boone's Samaritan care
in the house where you saw me at first. The two boys,
Sprague and Perley, spirited away from the hospital at
Hampton, where they had been entered under assumed
names, Jacques and Paling, were by some curious instrumentality hidden in the small-pox ward of the rebel prison

at Point Lookout. While they lay there, and while some one in Washington knew that they were there, a court-martial in that city hurriedly convened, found John Sprague guilty of murder, desertion, and treason, and the evening dispatches from Washington state that John Sprague is to be shot a week from Friday in a hollow square, in which a company of the Caribees is to do the shooting.

"Miss Boone, you worked faithfully to rescue the life of this young man, but your father has brought that work to ruin. Worse, the death you dreaded when you gave heart and soul to the rescue of the lost was a mercy compared to that in store for him. He is to be shot by a file of his own company, seated upon a rough board coffin, ready to receive his mangled remains. You will—"

But Kate, at this hideous detail, fell with a low, wailing cry to the floor, happily dead to the woful consciousness of the scene and its meaning. Jones ran to the door, and, unlocking it, shouted for the servants. When they came, she was carried to her room and the physician summoned. Almost at the same time Olympia, in her traveling-dress, drove up. She was informed by the servants of Kate's state, and, without stopping to ask permission, ran up to the sick-room. Kate was now conscious, but at sight of Olympia she covered her face, shuddering.

"Ah, Kate! Kate! what is it? Have you learned the dreadful news? I am going to take the train back this evening."

"I, too, will go with you. Stay with me; don't leave me!"

She stopped, put out her hand, as if to make sure of Olympia, then broke into low but convulsive sobs. Her father, with the doctor, entered the room; but at the sight Kate turned her head to the wall, crying, piteously:

"No, no—not here, not here! I can't see him now! Oh, spare me! I—I—"

"Do your duty, doctor," Boone said, in a quick, gasping tone, and with an uncertain step quit the chamber. Olympia explained to the physician that Kate had heard painful news from an unexpected quarter, and that her illness was more nervous than physical.

"I don't know about that," the doctor said, decisively. He felt her pulse, then with a quick start of surprise raised her head and examined the tongue and lining of the palate. A still graver look settled on his face as he tested the breath and action of the heart. When he had apparently satisfied himself he turned to Olympia with a perturbed air, and, beckoning her into the dressing-room, said:

"Miss Sprague, this is no place for you. Miss Boone has every symptom of typhoid fever. She has evidently been exposed to a malarial air. Her complaint may be even worse than typhoid—I can't quite make out certain whitish blotches on her skin. I should suspect small-pox or varioloid, but that there has not been a case reported here for years. Where has she been of late?"

Olympia turned ghastly white with horror.

"O doctor, she has been nursing Jack, who was for weeks in the small-pox ward at Point Lookout!"

"Good God! Fly, fly the house at once! I wondered if I could be deceived in the symptoms. I must insist on your leaving at once."

"But the poor girl must have some one of her own sex with her. Whom can she get if not a friend?"

"She can get a professional nurse, and that is worth a dozen friends. Indeed, friends will be only a drawback for the next ten days."

He took her gently by the shoulders and pushed her out of the room. He was an old friend of the family, and she was accustomed to his tyrannical ways. He held her sternly under way until the front door closed and shut her out. Then, turning into the library, he saw that the host was alone. Closing the door, he said:

"Mr. Boone, your daughter has been exposed to a great danger. We may be able to save her, but it will require great patience."

"Danger, doctor! What do you mean?"

26

"Your daughter has caught the most hideous of all diseases—small-pox!"

Elisha Boone started to his feet. "Great God! where could she catch small-pox?"

"She caught it nursing young Sprague. I thought you knew of that;" and the doctor regarded the incredulous, terror-stricken face of the father with bewildered fixity. Well he might. The first rod of the moral law had just struck him. The vengeance he had so subtly planned had turned into retributive justice. He had refused Kate's prayer; he had driven her to this mad search and the contagion now periling her life, or, if it were spared, leaving her a hideous specter of herself. This passed through his shattered mind as the doctor stood regarding him.

"What do you propose doing?" he finally asked, to get his thoughts from the torturing grip of conscience.

"I propose to install two trained nurses in the house. You are not to let a soul know what your daughter is suffering from. I hope to be able to check the evil in the blood, but I must be secure against any form of meddling. You must avoid your daughter's chamber—indeed, it would be better if you could quit Acredale for a few days. You would be less embarrassed by intrusive neighbors and keep your conscience clear of evasions."

So it was settled that Boone should take up his quarters in Warchester, coming out late every night for news.

Meanwhile, Acredale had read with amazement, first, of the finding of Jack Sprague among the rebels at Point Lookout, then, the extraordinary story of the court-martial and death-sentence. Every one called at the Sprague mansion, but it was in the hands of the servants, Olympia and her guest having returned to Washington so soon as the story of her brother's peril reached her. Dick, too, had flown to his adored Jack, and Acredale, confounded by the swift alternations in the young soldier's fortunes, settled down to wait the outcome with a tender sorrow for the bright young life eclipsed in disgrace so awful, death so ignominious.

We have looked on while most of the people in this history worked through night to light in the moral perplexities besetting them. We have seen warriors in love and danger gallantly extricating themselves and plucking the bloom of safety from the dragon path of danger. We have seen a moral combat in the minds of most of the people who have had to do with our luckless Jack. But all herein set down has been the merest November melancholy compared to the charnel-house of dead hopes and baffled purposes that tortured Elisha Boone. Unlovely as Boone has seemed to us, he had one of the prime conditions of human goodness—he loved. He had loved very fondly his son Wesley. He loved very tenderly his daughter Kate.

With this love came the sanctification that must abide where love is. I don't think he had much of what may be called the second condition of human goodness—reverence. If he had, we should never have seen him push revenge to the verge of crime. Richard Perley, it is true, accuses him of a turpitude that makes a man shudder and abhor; but allowances must be made for the exaggeration of a careless spendthrift—a "good fellow," than whom I can conceive of nothing so useless and mischievous in the human economy. For my part, I think I could endure the frank heartlessness of a man like Boone more philosophically than the false good-nature of the creature men call a good fellow.

Obviously, Boone did not take Dick Perley's estimate of him very seriously. He, too, could have told a tale not without its strong features of a shiftless set, constantly borrowing, constantly squandering, constantly provoking the thrifty to accumulate unguarded properties. All this, however, had faded from the old man's mind now. He had avenged himself upon the life-long scorners of his name and fame; but the blow that shattered their pride had sent a dart to his own heart. His beautiful Kate, his big-hearted, high-spirited, man-witted girl!—she would bear a leper-taint for life, and his hand had put the virus on her perfect flesh!

In a few days the black in his hair withered to an ashen white. His flesh fell away. He could neither eat nor sleep. He shambled through the obscure streets of Warchester, or lingered wistfully in the beech woods behind his own palatial home in Acredale, staring at the window of his daughter's chamber. The week passed in such mental torture as tries the strong when confronted by the major force of conscience. Then the doctor told him that he had balked the plague; that Kate was recovering from varioloid; that beyond a transparency of skin, which would add to her beauty rather than impair it, there would be no sign of the attack.

Elisha Boone slept in his own home that night, and, for the first time in forty years, he fell upon his knees—upon his knees! Indeed, the doctor found him so at midnight, when he came with a request from his daughter to come to her room. The doctor, with a word of warning against agitating the sufferer, wisely retired from the solemn reconciliation which, without knowing the circumstances, he knew was to take place between father and child. She was propped up upon pillows whose texture her flesh rivaled in whiteness. She opened her arms as the specter of what had been her father flew to her with a stifled cry.

"O father, we have both been wicked! we have both been punished! Help me to do my part; help me to bear my burden."

It was hope, mercy, and peace the meeting brought. The next day Elisha Boone bade Kate a tender farewell. She did not ask him where he was going. She knew, and the light in her eye shone brighter as he rode in the darkness over the bare fields and through the sleeping towns to the capital, where Jack's fate was hanging in the balance. With Boone's influence to aid them, Jack's friends found a surprising change in the demeanor of the officials, hitherto captious and indifferent. Boone himself laid the case before the President, omitting certain details not essential to the showing of the monstrous injustice done a brave soldier. The President listened attentively, and with the expression, half sad and half droll, with which he softened the asperities of official life, said, humorously:

"I wish by such simple means as courts-martial we could find out more such soldiers as this; we need all of that sort we can get." He touched a bell, and, when a clerk appeared in response, he said, "Ask General McClellan to come in for a moment before he leaves."

What need to go into the details? The court reconvened, and traversed the charges, which were disproved or withdrawn. John Sprague was pronounced guiltless on every specification, and, on General McClellan's recommendation, was promoted to a captaincy and assigned to the headquarters staff. I might go on and tell of Jack's daring on the Peninsula and his immeasurable usefulness to McClellan in the Williamsburg contest and the final wondrous change of base from the Chickahominy to the James; how his services were recognized by promotion to a colonelcy on the battle-field of Malvern; and how, when McClellan was wronged by Stanton, and removed from the army, Jack broke his sword and swore that he would never serve again. But, thinking better of it, he applied for a place in Hancock's corps, and was by his side from Fredericksburg to Gettysburg. You have seen from the very first what was going to happen. The marriages all took place, just as you have guessed from the beginning. Young Dick was too impatient and too skeptical to wait until the end of the war, and, to the amazement of his aunts and the amusement of Acredale, he carried Rosa off, one day, and was secretly married in the rector's study at Warchester, so that his first son was born under the Stars and Bars in Richmond, while Dick was beleaguering the walls at Fort Walthall, four miles away. The other young people waited rationally until a month or two after the peace, and while they were still entitled to wear the blue, and then they were wedded. It was said that Kate made the most beautiful bride ever seen in Warchester, for it was there they were married.

THE END.

A WASHINGTON BIBLE-CLASS. By Gail Hamilton. Large 12mo. Cloth, $1.50.

"The author of this book needs no introduction to American readers. But we will venture to say that she has never before shown greater brilliancy, intellectual grasp, and critical acumen than in this collection of papers, which were originally read in Washington last winter, before a Bible-class composed of prominent women of that city. As we have already intimated, this book will be sternly criticised by many; but in freshness of analysis it takes its place as one of the most important of the more recent contributions to Biblical literature."—*From the New York Tribune.*

"That these lectures are interesting, even entertaining, that, more than that, they are stimulating and suggestive, need hardly be said. They are by Gail Hamilton, that is enough. It is a book of fragments, interesting, entertaining, stimulating, suggestive, and useful, but still of fragments."—*From the Christian Union.*

"She has at least one merit—she is never dull. Whether her readers agree with her or not they are interested. The volume gives the reader a very clear idea of the religious discussion of the day, and marks the wide divergence from the older teachings of theology."—*From the Chicago Inter-Ocean.*

"The whole book is overflowing with fresh, often original thought, and with deep, devout feeling, and style is crisp, pungent, occasionally caustic, but always firm, confident, and compelling attention if not convictions."—*From the Chicago Times.*

"That the volume is fresh, bright, and sparkling, goes without saying, and it will be enjoyed by those who have kept abreast of the result of modern biblical criticism, and will be found deeply suggestive and profitable by those who have not."—*From the Boston Traveller.*

THE PRIVATE JOURNAL OF WILLIAM MACLAY, United States Senator from Pennsylvania, 1789–1791. With Portrait from Original Miniature. Edited by Edgar S. Maclay, A. M. Large 8vo. Cloth, $2.25.

"In Mr. Maclay's time sessions of the Senate were held with closed doors, and the authentic records we have of its proceedings are meager. As Mr. Maclay's journal is concerned almost wholly with the proceedings of this body, its value as a record becomes very great. Students of the period must henceforth include it among their valuable sources of original information. The circumstances in which it was written give it peculiar value. Mr. Maclay wrote while his knowledge was still fresh and clear."—*From the New York Times.*

"So meager are the official reports of the doings of the first Congress after the adoption of the Constitution, that Mr. Maclay's journal must always be of great historical value. While Senator he recorded in his journal each evening the proceedings of the day, and these records, many of them voluminous, give the book its value."—*From the New York Herald.*

"The descendants of William Maclay, who was United States Senator from Pennsylvania from 1789 to 1791, have brought all the people of this country under obligations a to them by publishing, just as it was written, a 'Journal' of their illustrious ancestor, kept by him while in the public service."—*From the Journal of Commerce.*

"No elaborate book on the political and social status of a hundred years ago can begin to equal in interest the present one, with its daily fresh pictures—plainly projected upon the writer's journal for his own mental relief—of the bad manners and bad political and other morals of his fellow-legislators, such as leave to politicians of our day quite a balance often of propriety in any comparison that may be made. It is a mine as well of political faith and proposed practice in plain democratic methods, antedating nearly all the political doctrine that Jefferson is celebrated for as the founder of Jeffersonian, Madisonian, and Jacksonian Democracy."—*From the Brooklyn Eagle.*

New York: D. APPLETON & CO., 1, 3, & 5 Bond Street.

A CHARMING AUTOBIOGRAPHY.

*T*HE LIFE OF AN ARTIST. By Jules Breton. With Portrait. Translated by Mrs. Mary J. Serrano. 12mo. Bound in cloth, $1.50.

". . . One of those books the success of which is assured from the first because of its perfect naturalness. . . . The reader of Jules Breton's memoir . . . will close the book without having experienced one misgiving as to its entire truthfulress. From the first page to the last his memoir will be found not merely readable, but fascinating, and the translator has very well reproduced his charms of style, his beautiful simplicity, and that perfume of the love of Natuie which breathes through the book and ennobles it."—*New York Tribune.*

"The method and spirit . . . are most delicate and delightful. . . . Filled with the poet's glow and the philosopher's peace."—*New York Sun.*

"One understands modern France the better for this autobiography of her highly gifted son."—*Boston Pilot.*

"Jules Breton, by writing his autobiography, has conferred a lasting favor on the lovers of this class of literature."—*Detroit Journal.*

*W*IDOW GUTHRIE. A Novel. By Richard Malcolm Johnston. Illustrated by E. W. Kemble. 12mo. Bound in cloth, $1.50.

"*It is understood that Colonel Johnston regards 'Widow Guthrie' as his strongest work.*"

"One of the happiest, sweetest, quaintest novels that have come from the press in a long time is 'Widow Guthrie,' a vigorous, breezy, and faithful picture of life in the South in the days before the war. There is no lack of virility, but there is also a refinement which is exquisite because it is genuine, and a humor which is mellow and sweet because it springs from a clean imagination."—*Brooklyn Standard-Union.*

"It is full of strong descriptions and curious and forcible character delineations. There is remarkable freshness in the figures of the story. The duel and the slaying of Duncan Guthrie are descriptive masterpieces."—*New York Sun.*

"The Widow Guthrie stands out more boldly than any other figure we know—a figure curiously compounded of cynical hardness, blind love, and broken-hearted pathos. . . . A strong and interesting study of Georgia characteristics without depending upon dialect. There is just sufficient mannerism and change of speech to give piquancy to the whole."—*Baltimore Sun.*

". . . Some remarkably vivid portraitures of character. . . . The book is one that will please men as well as women."—*Boston Evening Gazette.*

New York: D. APPLETON & CO., 1, 3, & 5 Bond Street.

RECOLLECTIONS OF THE COURT OF THE
TUILERIES. By MADAME CARETTE, Lady-of-Honor to the
Empress Eugénie. Translated from the French by ELIZABETH
PHIPPS TRAIN. 12mo. Cloth, $1.00; paper cover, 50 cents.

The inside view which these Recollections give of the Court of Louis
Napoleon is fresh and of great interest.

"We advise every one who admires good work to buy and read it."—*London
Morning Post.*

MEMOIRS OF MADAME DE RÉMUSAT.
1802–1808. Edited by her Grandson, PAUL DE RÉMUSAT,
Senator. 3 volumes, crown 8vo. Half bound, $2.25.

"Notwithstanding the enormous library of works relating to Napoleon, we know
of none which cover precisely the ground of these Memoirs. Madame de Rémusat
was not only lady-in-waiting to Josephine during the eventful years 1802–1808, but
was her intimate friend and trusted confidante. Thus we get a view of the daily life
of Bonaparte and his wife, and the terms on which they lived, not elsewhere to be
found."—*N. Y. Mail.*

"These Memoirs are not only a repository of anecdotes and of portraits sketched
from life by a keen-eyed, quick-witted woman ; some of the author's reflections on social
and political questions are remarkable for weight and penetration."—*New York Sun.*

A SELECTION FROM THE LETTERS OF
MADAME DE RÉMUSAT. 1804–1814. Edited by her
Grandson, PAUL DE RÉMUSAT, Senator. 12mo. Cloth, $1.25.

MEMOIRS OF NAPOLEON, his Court and Family.
By the Duchess D'ABRANTES. In 2 volumes, 12mo. Cloth,
$3.00.

The interest excited in the first Napoleon and his Court by the "Memoirs
of Madame de Rémusat" has induced the publishers to issue the famous
"Memoirs of the Duchess d'Abrantes," which have hitherto appeared in a
costly octavo edition, in a much cheaper form, and in a style to correspond
with De Rémusat. This work will be likely now to be read with awakened
interest, especially as it presents a much more favorable portrait of the great
Corsican than that limned by Madame de Rémusat, and supplies many valuable and interesting details respecting the Court and Family of Napoleon,
which are found in no other work.